THE
HUMAN
COUNTER
MOVE

LOGAN SIDWELL

The Human Countermove
Copyright © 2025 by Logan Sidwell

Paperback ISBN: 979-8-9995461-0-4
E-book ISBN: 979-8-9995461-1-1

This is a work of fiction. Names, characters, places, and incidents are either products of the author's imagination or used fictitiously. Any resemblance to actual events or persons, living or dead, is purely coincidental.

Cover design by Katarina Naskovski

First Edition

FOR MOM

TURN ORDER

PART
ONE

1 - JUST A GAME

RANK: 83

A space opened in the queue. I closed the gap, steel panels flexing under my step. A stream of LINE players stretched off into the distance. Security was never like this at a LINE event. A rush-job hall of steel tossed in front of the hotel's front doors—what were the Minds thinking? Probably had something to do with that new directive.

No one spoke in the metal tunnel, every noise was echoed back and amplified into incoherence. I glanced behind me. Two bodies back, a hand waved in my direction. Jamie. I mouthed hello back. She was a strong player, better than I was these days. She had on a dark-green dress I had never seen, and her brown hair curled with the precision of a recent salon visit. A big change from her regular loose shirts, capris, and ponytails. Her eyes gleamed with life. Maybe she was finally over that insomnia, I'd have to ask her.

A new gap formed, I hurried to close it. In the wait, my mind began to wander. I used to relish moments like this, every idle second was a chance to review and revise my game plan. Not these days, let one of the players with a chance to win do that. I was well on my way out of the top one hundred, may as well have been retired. Thirty might seem young for retirement, but when all you've done is lose for over a year, it's best to be honest with yourself.

The queue rounded a corner and the Greater Charters Hotel entrance came into view—an extravagant place with a penchant for gold trim. A full-body scanner in front of the lobby doors ruined the luxury aesthetic, which was well enough, considering I was wearing jeans. A guard's voice echoed down the tunnel. "Step inside, arms out, legs shoulder-width apart."

He was the same guy the Greater Charters Hotel always used, but the uniform was different. Bulletproof vest, at least three weapons, a wire running to his ear. It was a whole lot of security for a board game. At last, I reached the front. "Step inside, arms out, legs shoulder-width apart."

His voice was tired and he didn't even glance at me, his eyes locked on a screen. I followed his instructions. The booth was quiet and compact. My jeans kept my legs from reaching shoulder-width apart, but the guard said nothing. He pressed something in the corner of his screen. There was a momentary compression, the air felt oddly still. No more than a second. A 3D scan of my face appeared on-screen. Almost perfect. He had the same short black hair, receded hairline, and beginnings of a beard in need of a shave. He even had my smile, though the eyes looked a little dead, a little darker brown than I remembered. Maybe that was just what being thirty was like. A sweet, automated voice pumped through the speakers. "Welcome. Zouk Solinsen."

"You're good."

I nodded my thanks and proceeded through the double doors. The lobby opened to an enormous conference hall. I always wondered how many rooms a hotel had to sacrifice to get ceilings to go that high. The room went on and on, filled with row after row of sleek black tables, like a great hall for gaming. Figures they'd spare no expense for The Global Playoffs. It was one of the biggest tournaments there was. Players flew in from all over to represent their countries. Best of the best, all here. These days, I'd be lucky to land in the middle of the pack.

The venue was still empty, mostly walked by arbiters. You could always spot an arbiter, the best-dressed people at the tournament. Maybe it's easier to tell someone they lost when you're wearing a suit. The pre-event instructions had emphasized the importance of good grooming and formal dress. Hopefully the polo would make up for the jeans.

"Zouk Solinsen?"

A woman in a black pantsuit approached, touchscreen in hand. Definitely an arbiter.

"That's me."

The arbiter scrolled through some list. After a moment, she glanced up. "Follow me."

Her feet carried her at an incredible speed. I jogged just to keep up. Every couple steps, we passed another dozen seats. In front of each, a folded white square listed a player's name. A few popped out to me: Alexandria, Oliver, the world champion Bergamaschi. My foot caught on the carpet. The arbiter barely glanced back. These were the best in the world, here to represent their province. Here I was, hoping to go home with a single win and a free lunch. Maybe coming at all was a mistake.

The arbiter stopped three-quarters of the way down the hall. A little further down, at the end of the hall, the hotel had set up a big platform overlooking the tables. We were close enough I could see a few of the empty seats, they looked a lot more cushioned than the ones for players. VIPs. It might explain the security. The arbiter turned sharply and led me between the rows of tables to my seat. Row six, position five. She came to a stop and pointed at a straight-back black chair.

"This is your seat, Mr. Solinsen. If you need anything before the game, please feel free to reach out to one of the arbiters." I looked past the arbiter. No one was within a hundred feet. "We're around. If you have a pressing issue during a game, pause the timer and raise your hand. Bathrooms are in the corner. Any questions?" She spoke at a breakneck pace, but I was pretty sure I had gotten it.

"None. Thank you."

I took my seat and the arbiter hurried away. Like every other seat, there was a little folded note bearing my name: Zouk Solinsen, Sulmar Province. My eyes narrowed. There was something off about the label. I grabbed a name card one seat to my left. The color was different. Mine had a subtle yellow hue. I grabbed the name card to my right. All the others matched. Another sign I wasn't supposed to be here.

"Zouk!" I turned quickly at the sound of my name. "You didn't tell me you were playing!"

Jamie approached quickly, in a rush to keep up with her arbiter. I knew there was a reason I had been thinking about her. I spun the name card opposite mine around. Jamie Mendez, Reanrum Province. This was gonna be a tough first match.

"I didn't even know I was playing until last week." I returned each name card to its original position. "Pretty sure I'm a replacement."

Jamie sat down. "Don't do that. You were a good player."

I leaned back in my chair and stared at her. We both knew I was past my prime. Her eyes narrowed. "How can you be sure?"

I slid my name card across the table. "Look. Different paper. I wasn't in the original batch." Jamie lifted the name card to her glasses and scrutinized it carefully. She had always been big on details.

"Different font too—they could have lost the original." She slid my name card back to me.

"There's more. My invitation came directly from the coach." Jamie's lips pressed into a thin line. She was getting convinced. "You know the lineup for the tournament? Released six hours after I accepted my offer. Come on, I'm a replacement."

Jamie raised her hands in surrender. "So you're a replacement."

"You're convinced?"

A smirk crept onto her lips. "I am, and that means you haven't strategized with your team."

Always looking for the advantage, Jamie. It's what made us good rivals. I shook my head. "We all play our own games, what's there to strategize? It's not like they expect much of me."

She leaned slightly forward. "Maybe you should throw the game, teach 'em a lesson."

I chuckled. She was probing for advantages, but she'd never forgive me for a free win. One more and she'd have a winning record against me. Then again, the team captain probably wouldn't even notice. Even one win today would probably be categorized as an 'over-performance'.

We chatted for a while about nothing. Showing up to all the same tournaments means either a lifelong hatred, or a lifelong friendship, and neither of us were good enough to waste time hating each other. That didn't stop her from making every effort to wipe the floor with me, but it was nice to see a familiar face.

The hall went from empty to filled in no time. I did a sweep of the hundreds of faces for anyone else I recognized, then noticed Jamie's eyes were locked on the front of the room. A crowd of well-dressed visitors were taking their seats on the platform. As one entered, Jamie sat up a little straighter.

"Maya's here," she whispered.

"Who?" I squinted into the crowd on the platform. In all the movement, one stood still, shaking hands and smiling at every person passing by. She was a beacon of positive energy in a short body. Her hair was somewhere between blonde and grey, and she wore a mauve pantsuit.

"Human Autonomy Activist. She convinced the Minds to pass the new directive." The new directive. The "special" tournament.

I had read it once, but knew I'd never qualify. It explained the extra security—the elite were here to watch our games live. To pick out potential champions.

"People are taking that seriously?" I asked. Jamie looked back at me with a raised eyebrow.

"The opportunity for a LINE player to join The Three? The chance to be the voice for humanity on the council? We're all taking it seriously." She leaned in close. "Zouk, you and I are among the one hundred players good enough to win this thing."

I adjusted in my chair and picked at a piece of loose thread. "We're not the best in the world, Jamie. We're not even in the top ten." Jamie said nothing, but her furrowed brow was enough to tell me her feelings.

The lights dimmed. My teammates finally arrived, all at once taking their seats. Table by table, soft blue LEDs flicked on, illuminating a thousand LINE players' faces. A glass wall rose up between Jamie and I, and a message appeared in the virtual space, "CONNECTED".

"Good luck, Zouk" I could barely make out Jamie's face through the holographic separator, but whispered my thanks. All at once, the screens updated. A 12x12 grid of blue squares appeared on the table in front of me and in the image on the glass.

Back when I was teaching full time, students always told me their biggest fear in a game of LINE wasn't playing poorly, it was the moment the game started. An empty board. An infinite garden of choices, from which players pruned a single game. But those were novices. I didn't see the infinite anymore, I saw my plan, and I saw my opponent.

Another figure rushed past me to a seat at the end of the table. Someone was always late. Two little clocks appeared in the corner of the screen. One for me, one for Jamie. Each read 60:00. Looked like the tournament was starting on time. A gong played through the room, and the timers started ticking down.

The objective in a game of LINE (Leadership in Near-Range Emulation) was simple: use troops to attack your opponent, build walls to slow them down. Each squadron was represented by a set of six little blue dots. With some good strategy, a smart player could build a base, capture the board, and take their opponent's command post. A dumb player could charge in and win in a few moves, but that was rarer. The graphics were simple—red dots, blue dots, a few lines representing the walls—but the complexity was near infinite.

I ordered a wall be placed near the bottom of the screen, near my command post, then pressed 'Submit'. My clock stopped ticking. Jamie's continued to count down, she was still deciding. After a few seconds, Jamie's clock stopped too, and our moves were revealed.

A blue wall appeared where I had ordered it, the beginnings of a base. Jamie had brought out her first squadron, six dots with the power to tear my base apart. This would be an aggressive game. I had hoped for that. Jamie was the stronger player these days, let her lead the attack.

Her squadron could only move one square at a time, so even with her extra initiative, I had time to get my side of the board organized before she hit me.

At move four, I deployed my first squadron. They took cover behind the walls and waited for the red troops to reach them. Jamie called her first squadron back to her base, not much point in attacking a well-defended position. But then again, she had already forced me into defense.

By move seven, the basic footprint of the Lost Star formation had taken shape in my base. It kind of looked like a spiky porcupine centered around my command post. Over the years, I had leaned on it more than a few times. Lots of cover, lots of mobility for squadrons, it tended to get the job done.

On move twelve, Jamie's squadron count climbed to five. I continued the development of my base, waiting for the attack.

Six moves later, I glanced at the clock. I had burned fifteen minutes, Jamie had spent twenty-one.

I input another move and thought on Jamie's comments about the new directive. Did the other pros really believe it? Win a few games of LINE and get put in charge of the government? It was ridiculous. Add in all the amateurs that thought they had a chance and the whole thing was a circus. Even if the offer was good, it wasn't meant for middling players like me. The directive tournament was meant for the best, for players like Bergamaschi.

I pulled back from the board. As much as I respected Jamie, my head really wasn't in it. I was thinking about the next match. Not much had been able to distract me from it the last few days. A gust of cold wind blew my way, an air conditioner had just turned on. Jamie had already input her next move. Time was ticking down, I needed to focus.

Her first squadron poked its head out from behind cover. A fight was just what I needed. I stretched my fingers, then input the attack orders. On the left, my little blue dots moved up through one of the Lost Star's points and took firing positions. On the right, troops waited patiently.

Nine squadrons emerged from Jamie's base. A proper army. The moment they came within three tiles of my walls, I gave the order for my troops to open fire. Gold-yellow flashes flew out from both sides. With every hit, a dot faded off the board. At the end of the first turn, I had lost five troops, Jamie had dropped considerably more.

Still, she pressed on. A steady stream of weapons fire down the left side tore through the Lost Star. My troops were sitting ducks. She closed in, lurching ever closer to the center of the base, and more importantly, abandoning her own. I ordered the counter offensive, three squadrons pushed out of my base and charged across the map.

Through the holographic separator, I could see Jamie's eyes widen. Both sides were attacking. Both sides were defending. It was a precarious position. A single misplaced piece could end the game. Just as I had hoped, a chance to put skill against skill.

The next move rolled in. Jamie's squadrons ceased fire and turned away from the mangled remains of my base. I blinked repeatedly. That wasn't right. They were retreating. No. I craned my neck closer to the screen. Not a retreat, a pivot. She was coming for my counteroffensive.

I realized my mistake in an instant. I had forgotten to wall up the center of the board. Instead of a two-pronged skirmish, we were two armies facing each other in no-man's-land. I counted out Jamie's troops. Six more troops. No way out. My heart sank. In an open field there was no room for clever tactics, just flat numbers.

Weapons fire lit up the screen. In a single turn, three of my squadrons were wiped from the board. In exchange, Jamie had only lost four tiny red dots.

I put my head in my hands. Every little sound in the hall bothered me. A hundred players tapping at their screens, coughs and sneezes that made the whole place feel like a hospital, whispers from the politicians in the viewing gallery. The game was over, but I needed to see it through.

I ordered a retreat, but it was already too late. A flurry of golden light erased what was left of the blue army. I took in the rest of the board. My base could hold up for a few more turns, maybe even rebuff the attack. But against a pro like Jamie, defeat was inevitable.

My hand shook as I pressed 'Resign'. The board vanished and the separator lowered. Jamie had a quizzical look on her face, as if she was surprised it was over. We shook hands over a final image of the board, projected onto the flat of the table.

"That was a dangerous plan, going for a flank on my army like that."

I paused a moment, confused at her words. "It was supposed to be a counter-attack."

Jamie held a thoughtful look, her eyes jumping back and forth, the sign of a player calculating moves. "You were missing a few walls."

"Yeah."

My chest felt heavy. It was an amateur mistake. But for me, mistakes like that were becoming the rule rather than the exception.

Jamie grabbed her bag off the floor. "Who are you facing next?"

I let out a nervous cough and reached into my pocket, pulling out a copy of my schedule. Jamie glanced at it and let out a laugh. "Bergamaschi?"

I nodded.

"How did you get him?"

I shrugged. "The coach wanted one of his lower-tiered players to face the champion. Manage the balance of wins and losses."

She gave me a pitying look. "Cannon fodder, eh? Sorry, Zouk."

That looked to be the story of the tournament for me, a last-second replacement set up to lose. "Hey, maybe that's why the last guy dropped out."

Directive 2149-M-13-A

"On Reintegrating Human Voice in Government" - Readable title appended by The Mind of Communications and Influence.

The following directive was presented and voted upon unanimously during session 1034 of the year 2149. Deliberations extended for eleven minutes and nineteen seconds. Transcripts have been sealed.

OBJECTIVES (ordered by anticipated impact):

Improve perception of human representation in government (Code: O-HP)

Reduce domestic counter-governmental actions (Code: O-CG)

Reduce foreign counter-state actions (Code: O-WR)

Produce live entertainment (Code: O-EN)

BEGIN

Upon ratification of this directive, a voluntary L.I.N.E. (Leadership In Near-Range Emulation) tournament will be made available to all citizens. The details of the tournament are as follows:

1. The rules of the game will follow the 2088 L.I.N.E. Rulebook.

2. Opponents for this activity will be chosen from a list composed of

A. The Mind of Communications and Influence

B. The Mind of Manufacturing and Distribution

C. The Mind of Strategy and Warfare

3. Should a citizen achieve three victories without suffering a defeat, said citizen will be awarded membership on the Nation's Legislative Council.

4. At least one match will be conducted in a non-simulated environment.

5. This directive will be terminated after one player claims victory.

Competitors may join the tournament by filing a Voluntary Activity Admittance Form and entering activity code J199LI.

END

A Note from the Mind of Communications and Influence:

Hey folks! I know there's a whole lot of directives coming down these days. I just wanted to take a moment and really highlight this one. For the last few months, the other Minds and I have been having some coffee and chat sessions with Human Autonomy Activist Maya Torrez. In case you don't know her, first off, you are missing out, she is a blast and has made me spit out my coffee laughing on more than one occasion. But secondly, she is one of several leaders of the Human Autonomy Movement. And after a whole lotta chattin', we ended up putting this thing together.

Here's the rundown, we want a living, breathing, human being on the council. But we also need to stay true to the virtues that define our nation. We don't want to be just another country plagued with corrupt politicians driving unrest and fear. So we're being a little picky.

I know what you're thinking, LINE? How can a game be the right tool to choose a fourth Mind? Well, let me tell you about the candidate we're looking for. We want someone who isn't just a speaking head, and isn't just a vote. The person that joins this council has got to be a deep thinker, someone who can go head to head with any one of us and come out on top, someone ready to make a difference.

Here's the thing, if you challenge us, we won't hold back. Even the best in the world are gonna have a pretty tough time (looking at you Bergamaschi!). Our models project the only people who have any chance of winning this thing are professional LINE players (I know, shocker), but anyone is free to throw their hat in the ring, we love a good surprise.

So there ya go, take us out to lunch, challenge us to a game of LINE, and maybe start running the government. Good luck to everyone, and if you have the skill, we've got a chair waiting for you.

P.S. No, there is not a punishment for losing. It's just a game people!

Mind of Communications and Influence

2 - ZOUK V BERGAMASCHI

RANK: 87 ▼ 4

Looks like you have a few minutes, want to use the Unified Activity Manager to analyze your last ga—I pressed hard on the dismiss button. Jamie was heads down in her analysis, but I needed to clear my head before the next game. I stood to leave and the team coach grabbed my arm and dragged me over to meet the rest of the team.

I shook hands with each of the young upstarts, every one of them had taken a big tournament win in the last year, but none of their names stuck. I was too distracted by the wrinkled old man at the end of the line. His bald head craned in front of his body, his brownish-red suit was nice but worn down by thirty years of use. I smiled, happy to see another familiar face.

"I forgot you were coming to this thing, Yolniv."

He put on his signature scowl. "I've been twelve feet from you for the last hour."

Yolniv was my mentor, and a living legend. Playing for decades and still in the top fifty. We met regularly to host community events, maybe teach a few classes. Of course every time he talked about a historical player, he'd sneak a couple of his own games into the list. Even when he grumbled, there was always a twinkle in his eye.

"We've got some time before the next game." I gestured behind us. The hall lights had raised, and players all the way down were analyzing games, running drills, even recording videos. The Unified Activity Manager never stopped recommending activities. He nodded. We shut off our screens and started a walk along the perimeter.

Neither of us said much, we were content to watch the wallpaper. The pattern repeated every twelve or fifteen steps. I kept thinking about my next game, wondering how many moves I'd get before Bergamaschi trounced me.

"Lost against Jamie, huh?"

The old man was staring right at me. I hated when he did that. "Jamie's a strong player, I made a mistake. If I had been more careful I could have won." It came out a little defensive.

"Don't underestimate your opponent, Zouk. A good player's instinct is fierce. Twenty years ago I faced The Sleeping Dragon, back when he was good—" I rolled my head from side to side, this was far from the first time Yolniv had told this story.

"There was this one move, I put a squadron on a square. No idea what I was doing, I just didn't want to keep burning time. But a couple turns later—bam! That perfect squadron in the perfect place. The best defense and the ultimate support for an attack. After the game, The Dragon told me he's never seen anything like it. An accident? Maybe. But I think my head knew what it was doing."

We reached the hotel's double doors and slowed. Normally Yolniv ended his stories with a moral. Not this time. He probably worried about upsetting me. The mistake against Jamie was far from the first.

A pit formed in my stomach. How could I win against the world champion if I couldn't even make the right moves? "I was asleep at the wheel. We'll figure it out."

We turned and started down the width of the hall. Yolniv's mouth shifted from side to side, clearly trying to think of something to say that could help. As we passed the bathrooms, he patted my shoulder. "Nothing like a good loss to wake you up, eh? You have anything for the next guy?"

I exhaled sharply. The funny thing about facing someone like Bergamaschi is that even if you don't have a plan, you're still prepared. No one gets to the pros without studying the world champion's games.

"I've been practicing the style you suggested. Perfect games and perfect moves." I paused. "But last night, I noticed something in Bergmaschi's style, something I could exploit."

"Oh yeah?"

"It's not a full fledged strategy, but—"

Yolniv stopped at the corner of the hall. There was an open door leading to a pitch-black room. Through it, we could make out the echoes of voices and tools. I turned to keep walking, then saw the thrill in Yolniv's eye. "Keep an eye out," he said.

The old man vanished into the dark before I had a chance to answer. I leaned against the doorframe, he'd be fine. Yolniv always had a way of slipping out of trouble. My eyes scanned the room. Most players were still in their seats, doing whatever practice the Unified Activity Manager recommended. I hated the thing. It never ran out of recommendations, and none of those recommendations included things like "Take a nap" or "Go for a walk". A fast track to burning yourself out.

A figure sped past me. Looked like an arbiter. Another followed close behind, then another. It was a long line of them, all carrying hefty shapes in black canvas bags. Probably something for the well-to-do in the viewing gallery. I squinted towards the far end of the hall. Waiters had rolled out trolleys of dishes. That woman in mauve, Maya, was perusing the selection.

Yolniv's voice pulled my attention back to the door.

"I see-I see. I'm just so sorry. Looking for the restroom, that's right. Yes I understand . . ."

Yolniv stumbled back into the playing hall, followed by a man dressed in black pants and a shirt bearing the INN logo. He pointed behind us, gave me an annoyed look, and passed back through the doorway. As soon as the man was gone, a sly smirk crept onto Yolniv's face.

"What did you find?"

"They've got quite a setup in there. I'd say it's the big day."

"What big day?"

Yolniv started back down the long end of the hall. He waited until we were far from the door before speaking in a hushed tone. "The big day where the whole world's watching. It's been a while since LINE's had one." I leaned close, Yolniv had never spoken like this. "—You never know when it'll happen, but it only happens once every decade or so. And I think today is it. Probably that new directive."

I wished I had followed the old man inside. "What was in there?"

"Three news stations, at least. They had those long walls filled with logos. Must have been at least eight cameras. Did you see that techie who escorted me out?"

"Iom National News," I whispered. Government coverage. That was as big as big got.

We passed a large column marking the great hall's halfway mark. Our next game was about twenty feet away. Yolniv grabbed my shoulder, stopping me in my tracks. His eyebrows were sunk and his jaw set, it unsettled me. "Zouk, you said you spotted something in Bergamaschi's play last night, a weakness?"

I swallowed. "It'd be a gamble. But we don't do gambles anymore, right? Perfect moves, perfect games?"

Yolniv smacked his teeth. "Use it anyway. Play like you used to."

"I thought I was trying to break those habits?"

"It's just one game. You're going to lose anyway, right?" He put on a smile, but his eyes stayed serious.

"Probably," I answered. More like definitely.

"Then for today, show me the player that once hit the top ten."

I took a step back, trying to distance myself from Yolniv's unrelenting stare. We had been practicing 'proper LINE' day in, day out for half a year. After I slipped, we had agreed it was the only way to get better. The idea of throwing that all away . . . "You think it has a better chance of winning?"

Yolniv sighed, his eyes dropped to the floor. "I think," he spoke slowly, "I think the habits we are training will create a player that could one day be the best there is. But today, that player doesn't stand a chance against Bergamaschi." He looked back at me with a mischievous glint in his eye. "The old you might be able to steal a win."

A musical tone played through the hall. Five minutes to the game. Without a word, I started towards our table. After all that practice, all those arguments, the old man still had more faith in who I was than in who I am.

When we arrived, someone was already in our seats. "Mr. Zouk, Mr. Yolniv." A young woman in a suit approached us holding a screen. "We've had a few changes to the table layouts. Would you follow me, please?"

The arbiter led us down the hall. Yolniv kept trying to catch my eye, but I kept my gaze fixed straight ahead. We passed row after row, only stopping at the last seat at the end of the line. Table 1, row 1. I could hear the hushed whispers from the onlookers on the platform.

Yolniv tapped my arm. "This is a game that matters, Zouk, make it count."

I gave him a curt nod, then sat at the row's end. On the other side of the holographic separators, Bergamaschi looked relaxed. His arms were draped over the chair, his blond hair hung loose. Even in a T-shirt, he still looked stylish. He raised a hand in acknowledgment, I shakily returned it.

A red light blinked on in the corner of my vision. Someone had installed a camera, fixed on my face. The arbiter's hand pointed past me to the camera. "If one of the streams ever switches to your game, this light will turn green. Understand?"

I gave no response. My thoughts were a mess. Yolniv had just told me to abandon everything we had worked for in the last six months. A board projected onto the glass. My screen on the table lit up. The clocks started their countdown.

I spent nine minutes on the first move. Every second was a panic, a mad dash to remember my analysis from the previous night. Even as I input the move, even as I hit 'Submit', I couldn't believe what my hands were doing. Yolniv had talked me into playing some half-baked gambit against the world champion.

By move five, it was clear Bergamaschi was playing the Shattered Spoke System. It was a strategy designed to guide me into a lost position without firing a single weapon. I wouldn't let that happen. On the ninth move, I ordered two squadrons to the right edge of the board, just a little past the midway point. Once they were in position, I built walls around them. An outpost.

Professional LINE strategy states you should strive to make the optimal move on every turn. That means you don't take risks. You calculate. You anticipate your opponent's moves and choose the maneuver that will give you the best long-term position. My meager outpost did none of that, and by all definitions, it was a bad move. But Bergamaschi wasn't perfect, and as I had discovered last night, he hated outposts.

On move sixteen, the world champion ordered his troops forward, opening fire on the outpost. The walls crumbled to nothing, my squadrons vanished, and the outpost became a ruin.

The attack was beautifully executed. I barely even got a shot off. On the bright side, his army was vulnerable. On orders, my army charged down the middle of the board. Bergamaschi's exposed troops rushed for cover. A smile crept up the sides of my lips, he had missed the essence of my plan.

Rather than attacking the undefended squadrons, I ordered my army to continue their charge. Through the separator, Bergamaschi's eyebrows raised. The champion was catching on. Before he could do anything, my forces had wedged themselves between two of the shattered spokes. I dropped a few walls, and secured the position. The vast majority of my army was now huddled in cover halfway into Bergamaschi's base.

A green light blinked on at the edge of my vision. Someone controlling the cameras realized I had the advantage.

The world champion burned eleven minutes on his next move. Probably the right call. My position was the kind that could morph from advantage to victory in a single mistake.

Bergamaschi kept his cool. His squadrons formed a perimeter inside his own base, but held their fire. There was only a single, thin wall separating his troops from mine. Simple to collapse, but whoever did lost the advantage. For the next four turns, no weapons were fired. We were both coming to terms with the new position. The wedge had turned into a beachhead, the game into a battle of attrition.

At the edges of the beachhead, we skirmished. Fighting over one square at a time. My troops would tear down a wall, Bergamaschi would answer with a flurry of laser fire. I'd rotate the damaged squadrons out for fresh ones, he'd merge his together. For the whole battle, the green light never flickered.

We hit move fifty before I knew it. My troops had dragged themselves three tiles further forward. I wiped the sweat from my forehead and glanced to my left at the spectator's platform. They were all watching. The woman in purple, Maya, leaned so far forward she was nearly falling off the platform. Yolniv had been right.

I blinked the dryness from my eyes and turned to the board. On orders, my squadrons inched forward another tile, ready for a fight. But this time, there wasn't a hail of laser fire. The world champion's forces had retreated. I pushed forward again and Bergamaschi's troops abandoned their posts, all clustering around the command post. I was winning.

Through the board, I caught sight of the champion's expression. He was nervous. Nervous was good, but he should have been sadder. I dropped my hands to my sides to keep them from inputting orders. There was something wrong. Bergamaschi wasn't the type to drag out a lost game. If he was still playing, there were still chances. One mistake was all it would take to lose the game. I needed to understand his plan. The clock read 07:23. Not much time, but enough to think.

Why would Bergamaschi retreat his units? To consolidate. What threats does a consolidated army pose? Just one, a massive attack. I scanned Bergamaschi's base. There were two layers of walls between me and him, how could he attack me?

Five minutes.

I thought back to the last few moves. Bergamaschi had made several uncharacteristic mistakes. His squadrons fired on distant targets, hitting the walls more than troops. He had allowed me to push in, take squares, tear down defenses, almost for free. I bit my lip. There was something here, he had done it all on purpose.

Four minutes.

It hit me. My squadrons were standing in his base, the base we had both been peppering with weapons fire for the last forty turns. Every wall still standing was close to collapse. Bergamaschi's troops weren't missing, they were weakening the structure. Our two armies appeared to be divided by two layers of red wall, but it was just a facade, a curtain waiting to drop.

Three minutes left. I rubbed the tips of my fingers, then input the order. Full retreat. My troops emptied the base I had fought tooth and nail to capture. Bergamaschi sprung the trap. Red troops opened fire, the walls vanished, but there was nothing to hit. I had escaped, my squadrons were intact, and Bergamaschi's position was in tatters.

The screen went black. I raised my hands, worried I had broken something. Then the holographic separator lowered and everything became clear. Bergamaschi had resigned.

A chorus of applause thundered down from the platform. I stared out, slack-jawed. The only thing I could see was the world champion extending his hand. I took it in a rushed, jerky motion. Had I really beaten him? The handshake lasted barely a second. Bergamaschi pulled his hand back and rubbed at his neck. "I shouldn't have let that work. Damn outpost." His accent was heavy and his words were rushed.

"Oh yeah?" My voice shook as I answered.

"If I had used my forces at columns 3, 4, and 6 instead of 4, 6, and 7 I think your wedge would have failed." At the highest level of play, there was an expectation for players to discuss the game afterward. It felt surreal to hear the world champion explain why I had beaten him. I strung together a few words, and Bergamaschi rambled on about my strategy. It was clear his calculations were deeper than mine. Still, I had beaten him.

An arbiter approached the table, and politely waited for Bergamaschi to trail off. "Mr. Zouk?"

I tore myself away from the world champion's comments. "Yes?"

"Follow me, please."

I stood uncertainly. Had I done something wrong? Was I being kicked from the tournament? As I passed Yolniv, he gave a quick thumbs up from the other end of the table. I made a mental note to thank him later. The arbiter palmed my shoulder blade and gently pressed me in the right direction.

We speed-walked down the great hall and towards the front doors. Players whispered and pointed as I passed by. All the other games had finished, and even the Unified Activity Manager couldn't keep them from watching the 87th best player that had toppled the king.

The arbiter nudged me to take a sharp left, right in line with an open black door. He pushed me through into the news room without pause. I slipped on a cable in the darkness, but the arbiter caught me and kept me moving. After a few blind steps, light struck my eyes and the arbiter's hand lifted away.

I was surrounded by a cacophony of sound and light. Flashes came in from every direction. Behind me was a massive Iom News Network backdrop, just as Yolniv described. Massive lights pointed my way from every direction. Cameras too, operated by figures standing out in the dark. Someone shouted for me to look into a camera, I tried to turn, but another voice demanded I turn towards them. My mouth hung open as I looked this way and that. The voices got louder and angrier.

A shadow blocked out the light. "Let the poor guy catch his breath! First the interview, then the photos. Zouk, this way."

The voice was deep and pointed. I turned to see the speaker, but he was already on his way elsewhere. I followed. The man was tall and slim and wore a steel-blue suit. His hair was a delicately styled jet-black. I couldn't pinpoint it, but something about it all struck me as familiar.

We came to a stop in a small room. Two cameras pointed at another Iom National News backdrop. The man turned towards me, and I immediately recognized him. The face of every news report from my childhood, the voice of journalistic specials every weekend. There was no way to mistake the strong chin and flawlessly sculpted cheekbones of The Mind of Communications and Influence. Someone started counting down, and Influence raised a handheld microphone between us.

"Hey folks, welcome back! I'm speaking to Zouk Solinsen, the 87th best LINE player in the world and, as of a few minutes ago, the first player to beat Bergamaschi in five months. So tell us Zouk, how did you pull it off?"

I coughed once, then twice. My mouth was as dry as it had ever been. It wasn't that I was uncomfortable speaking, but this was different. This was national news being reported by one of the three most important people in Iom. Influence waited patiently, watching through the camera lenses in his eyes. They were so close I could see the apertures making micro adjustments second by second.

It had been too long, I forced myself to speak. "Uhh—Bergamaschi is a very strong player and I consider myself lucky to have been able to play him." The Mind of Communications smiled and nodded with every word. I felt my mind start to catch up with my mouth. "He—uh, he overextended near the beginning . . . And I guess I was able to take advantage of it."

"Wow." Influence straightened his back, highlighting our six-inch height difference. "This isn't entirely unprecedented, is it? You used to be ranked eighth best in the world! Do you think this is the start of a big comeback?" I found myself staring at the pores on Influence's face, they looked real. He looked real.

"Maybe. We'll see."

"I, for one, can't wait to see what's in your future." Influence's voice lowered as he changed topics. "Now as you know, there's a new directive that's all about finding the best LINE players in the nation." I nodded. He had written it.

"You were once one of the best, today you beat the world champion. I only have one question left. When are you gonna challenge me?"

Influence held an expectant smile, ever the showman. My voice quivered as I spoke. "Uhh . . . Soon?"

Influence shook my hand and laughed politely. "I sure hope so! It's been great talking to you, Zouk. Back to you, Ezra."

"And clear!"

As soon as the cameras stopped, Influence put down his mike and brought his second hand to shake mine. It was overwhelming, the complete attention of one of Iom's Three Minds. "I hope to see you again, Mr. Solinsen."

I said nothing, afraid if I said anything more I'd make a fool of myself. Influence pointed behind me. "The exit's that way."

I turned and strode through the lineup of cameras and lights again. They were much more patient and polite this time. After a minute, they got whatever pictures they needed and I walked back into the dark of the set.

Near the door out, a figure blocked my path. A man, probably. Looked like he had a beard. He spoke quickly. "You're Zouk, right? One time top-ten player, lives in Sulmar Province, just beat Bergamaschi?"

I took a step back, he stepped forward in response. "That's right."

"Great! That is great! You're my guy. Eighth best. Number Eight!" The guy's teeth shined in the dark. "I'm Derek. I'm a recruiter for an organization that's trying to find the best LINE players in the nation. We want to work with you and train you to challenge the three Minds, is that something you'd be interested in?" Before I could respond, Derek interrupted, "—And we do pay. We pay well. What do you think?"

He sounded nice enough, but today had already been overwhelming without a sales pitch. "I'll think about it," I mumbled and pushed past him.

"Totally understand, if you change your mind, call me here." A piece of paper was jammed into my hand. I hurried the rest of the way back to the great hall.

In the light, it was clearer what Derek had given me. A business card. A phone number. Not a lot of people used those these days. Easier to register yourself in the UAM and reach out to clients through there, more trustworthy too. Either this dude was out of touch, or he was avoiding the spotlight. I wished I had seen his face.

On my way to the next game, every eye in the hall followed me. They hadn't seen the news segment, but in here, they didn't need to. For today, I was more famous than the world champion.

3 - 10 MONTHS LATER

RANK: 103 ▼ 16

The faint smell of disinfectant hung in the air of the transportation terminal. A line of brightly-colored Individual Transit Vehicles idled on the sidewalk, each bearing the face of their next passenger. I never liked the place, and I really didn't like the cutout of my face they always used—too much teeth. My bag dug hard into my shoulder, I shuffled it to the other arm, eight LINE boards was probably overkill. Overhead, the terminal screen displayed my ETA. Twenty-four minutes to the community center. There wouldn't be much time to set up.

Hundreds of us were waiting our turn. Most had their gaze fixed squarely on screens in their palms. A chime played through the terminal and a dozen passengers headed for their vehicles. When the last Individual Transit Vehicle (ITV) shut, the whole line of cars buzzed to life, gliding into a tunnel and off to who knows where and the next line of ITVs took their place.

The screen in my pocket buzzed. I made my way to a lime-green vehicle with my overly-toothy face projected over an open door. The seat was hard plastic and I had to hold my thirty-pound bag in my lap, but at least it was cheap. As soon as every open ITV was filled, our doors slid shut and we accelerated away in perfect synchronicity. Concrete walls flew past, the view widening from tunnel to multilane highway as we got up to speed. There was something comforting in the almost choreographed way the ITVs danced their way down the highway, like you were a part of a flock of birds in migration, instead of one guy on his way to nowhere. Before I could settle in, an image of my route filled the windscreen.

"Close map."

"Closing map. Would you like to view your upcoming events?" I gripped the car handle as the map was replaced with a calendar.

"Close calendar."

"Closing calendar. Here are your recommended activities." A new set of options replaced the old. At the top was the Unified Activity Manager's number-one recommendation. "Based on your history, you should try teaching more LINE classes—"

Amazing, years of data on my behaviors and the UAM was still giving me the same advice. "Close recommendations." No chance I'd waste my time going down that road again. Teaching wasn't the problem here, it was the fact that the UAM's idea of 'teaching' was forty hours of lectures and twenty hours of grading, week after week. Not a lot of room for anything else. The screen faded into the windshield. We were still hurtling down the underground. I spotted another passenger with a transparent windshield, a rare sight these days. She flashed a smile, I responded in kind. Those of us that liked the drive without the distractions were few and far between.

"Incoming call." I rapped my hand against the car's window, never a moment's peace.

"Answer."

Video of my wife's face was projected onto the windscreen. Right, 3 PM. A few strands of raven hair had fallen out of her bun, her frown pulled a little low, her green eyes slightly dilated. There were bins and bins of storage screens behind her. Looked like hour fifteen or twenty of one of Kira's work binges.

"Hey sweetie, is everything okay?" I asked.

"Are you teaching today?"

"That's right! It's Noah's turn. He won a junior tournament last week and I'm thinking about getting his parents to sign him up for something bigger. You know, get him competing for real."

"He's a little old, isn't he? I ran the stats last week, he's down to only a 14 percent chance of making the pros." I tried to smile, but it felt like a grimace. Kira had a real passion for numbers, but sometimes she got a little lost in them.

"He's excited about the game, there's no reason to write him off," I said.

"Okay." Kira blinked a couple times. She disagreed, but wasn't saying it.

"I think I'm gonna start drilling him on openers today, we can't have him face a pro and lose in the first five turns." Kira grabbed for a tool behind the camera and started tinkering with something. I didn't want to interrupt her. Last week, she had told me the quiet moments were the ones that reminded her of why we were together.

After a minute, she broke the silence. "I'm sure Noah will do great." Her gaze broke from the camera, probably monitoring some equipment off-screen.

"We'll see. I'll be back tonight, after the community event."

Kira's attention returned, her eyebrows raised a little. "You only had three people last time, right?" I took a breath. She hadn't meant it, but the comment cut deep.

"Yep. Yolniv, me, and a new kid. Seemed to be pretty interested, he had lots of questions." For a couple months after my game against Bergamaschi, the community had been great. We had gotten forty-six players at one point. But they rarely stayed. That's what happened when you weren't registered with the UAM, and when you didn't charge. The app always had new tournaments, a new coaching opportunity, and a new drill to keep people from coming out. And bit by bit, it worked.

"Maybe you're not targeting the right demographics. If you compare LINE players across location and age distributions—" Kira stopped herself mid-sentence.

"We've tried a lot," I said.

She put on a weak smile. "Okay, see you tonight"

"Love you."

"Love you too."

The call ended. My whole chest was tense. This was easier back in college, we'd spend a whole afternoon running LINE simulations, talking through research, sharing. These days, it was like we were out of rhythm.

Light streamed in through the windshield. Finally free of the tunnels. The ITV glided past hundreds of two- and three-story buildings. Mostly apartments, a few businesses, Sulmar province got a little bigger every year. As the ITV continued down the highway, the buildings got shorter, older, smaller, and cheaper, at last coming to a stop outside a decrepit, dark-brown brick building.

As soon as I was clear of the door, the ITV shut and sped off. I waved it farewell and walked up the steps and through the heavy wood doors of the community center. I paused at the top of the basement stairs. The carpet had come loose, so every step needed its proper footing before taking the next. At the bottom, I flipped on the lights.

The basement was vast and empty. Just old carpeting and a ceiling that was about two inches lower than it should have been. We had been thrilled when Yolniv found the place. It had hosted hundreds of tournaments and classes. Novices, pros, students, everyone came to visit. A place to talk, a place to play, a place to think. These days everyone was on the UAM, and the basement felt a little damp, and very empty.

I leaned my duffel bag against the wall and grabbed a folding table from the corner. As I plugged in the first board, a child's voice called out from behind me. "Hi, Mr. Zouk! Do you need any help?"

Noah was eight years old, stood barely taller than my stomach, and was dressed in a polo and khakis. The kid was clever and respectful. Not to pick favorites, but among the three I still taught, his sessions were the best. "Oh, that's very kind of you, Noah, but I think I have it covered." I plugged in the board and heard a thump on the stairs. A man in a suit was gripping the handrail like his life depended on it. He wasn't familiar, but he had the same bright blond hair as Noah. "That's not your mom, who did you bring with you, Noah?"

"Oh, her hours changed. This is my dad!"

Once he reached the bottom of the stairs, Noah's father stood up, craned his neck forward to avoid touching the ceiling, and offered his hand. "Howard Chewes, so you're teaching my son how to play games?"

I shook Mr. Chewes' hand uncertainly. It was unclear, as of yet, if he was being deliberately condescending. Some folks couldn't help it. I pushed past and put on a smile. "That's right, we're playing LINE. Noah and I have a lot to cover today, is it alright if we get started?"

Mr. Chewes nodded and stepped back, leaning against the faded tan wallpaper. Once the board was activated, class ran just like it always did. I'd throw drills at Noah, he'd work through them. I'd discuss positional theory, he'd catch on quickly. Every day we met, he was more excited than the last.

A dozen feet away, Mr. Chewes watched everything. He looked a little confused, maybe intrigued, but he never turned his attention away from the lesson.

Half an hour in, I asked Noah to analyze his own play and walked off to the water fountain. As I bent down to drink, a shadow fell over the stream. "Noah's pretty good, huh?"

Mr. Chewes's sudden approach left me sputtering. As soon as my voice was clear, I answered, "Yes, your son is very talented."

"So . . . What's the money like in LINE?" I straightened up, aiming to stand as tall as I could. Already, Mr. Chewes was confirming my suspicions of him. Noah's mom loved being here to see her son passionately learning. It seemed his father supported his son for different reasons.

"It's not great unless you're at the peak."

Mr. Chewes scrunched his face, perhaps in thought, maybe frustration. "You used to be—" He started again, "You played professionally, right?"

I looked past Mr. Chewes at Noah. The kid was diligently taking notes on a game, oblivious to our conversation. "I compete when I can. Teaching can take a lot of my focus. Students like Noah are too smart for me to give them anything but 100 percent."

Mr. Chewes eyed me up and down, sizing me up. I had a feeling if I kept talking to the man we would never get back to the lesson. "Your son is really starting to master The Invitation structure. I can show you a few games if you'd like."

Mr. Chewes hesitated, looking uncertainly at the board. After a moment, he nodded. "All right, let's see what the kid did."

On our way back to Noah, I pulled a second LINE board from my bag, placing it next to Noah's. At my insistence, Mr. Chewes sat down in front of it. As soon as the power was on, I pulled up one of Noah's best games. "This is a good one, your son is mastering some very advanced concepts. I think you'll be impressed."

As much as I was happy to share Noah's successes, I mostly wanted Mr. Chewes occupied with something other than questioning me. I hit play, and the first squadrons marched onto the screen, a full replay of Noah's battle from beginning to end. As it continued, I found myself giddy thinking about the upcoming moves, and the clever ways Noah had outsmarted his opponent. Move eighteen, that was the big one. The enemy opened fire on Noah's front line. As they did, flanks crawled up the side of the board, cutting off the enemy's escape. A big moment. Mr. Chewes tugged at his ear. "So Noah just lost that squadron of soldiers, huh?"

I realized my mistake. Noah's father had probably never seen a LINE board, so all he saw was the shooting. "Noah is the player going up the screen—" I pointed at the lower half of the board. "All the blue pieces are your son's. He just wiped out that unit." Mr. Chewes grunted in understanding. I played out a few more turns. "You see that? He's playing very well."

The man's eyes started to glaze as the squadrons moved back and forth to take better and better positions. A couple feet away, Noah had finished his analysis and watched for his father's reaction. At move thirty-six, the big engagement started and Mr. Chewes perked up. "Oh I see now. He's really making a mess of that guy, huh?"

At least the man was trying. "It's closer than it looks, but your son does have a strong position over his opponent. Keep your eye on the left side."

This was the best part, a victory through skill. Something Noah could be proud of. Mr. Chewes cleared his throat.

"You ever apply for that big tournament thing?" Even with a wall of weapons fire in front of his face, the man had pivoted to face me. The fight wasn't over, but the audience was gone.

Noah turned back to his own board, clearly disappointed. I let the game finish before answering. "I've read the directive."

"Pretty wild, huh? Doesn't seem to make much sense to me." I turned off Mr. Chewes' board. This is what LINE had become for the last year. Everyone wanted to hear about the game, but only if you were talking about the tournament. And it was always the same questions too. What's so hard about it? Who could do it? What would it be like to win? Drove me crazy. Was it so wrong to enjoy the game for what it was?

I thought briefly of a certain business card jammed into my bag. Ten months later and I had never called Derek. The Minds and their UAM had ruined the game for me once already, I wouldn't let them do it again. Plus, after the top ten players failed, there wasn't much point in someone like me giving it a go.

"The directive is certainly surprising. You know, there are some valuable life lessons you can pull from LINE. I wouldn't be surprised if your son excels in his classes in school too."

"You think Noah could do it?" Mr. Chewes turned to his son. Noah stayed focused on his board.

"Do what?"

"You know. Do the thing. Noah's already winning tournaments. With the right help and the right luck—I bet he could win it all." Mr. Chewes lit up as he spoke. It was amazing the star power that directive had. Like buried treasure, it took normal people and filled their heads with dreams of power.

"The best in the world have already tried, Mr. Chewes. The world champion only won a single game." Mr. Chewes crossed his arms and eyed me again.

"Sure other players have failed. But you said Noah was good, right? Maybe he's more than good. You keep teaching him and me and my kid could be running the country in a year or two!" He grinned at the thought. "Bet you'd give Noah free lessons after that. Although maybe if he wins he should be teaching you!" Mr. Chewes bellowed at his own joke. I grimaced and waited for Mr. Chewes to be finished. Behind him, halfway up the stairwell, I could make out the worn, brown loafers of Yolniv. After a few seconds of laughing at his own fantasies, I gave Howard Chewes my most diplomatic answer.

"Reaching that level of success will take a lot of hard work. But when Noah makes it, I'll be right there cheering him on—Noah, that's our time for today."

"Thanks, Mr. Zouk." Noah stood and headed for the stairs. Mr. Chewes got up slowly, rubbing his chin and staring off into the distance. I went to the closet and grabbed another table. When I returned, Mr. Chewes was still standing there. "Did you ever try?"

"I'm not one for statecraft," I said flatly.

"You should give it a go. Treat it like a lottery ticket, maybe it'll pay out." Mr. Chewes' eyes widened. "We gotta get Noah on the UAM. I heard that's the real fast-track to making a pro." Before I could stop him, Mr. Chewes jogged past Yolniv and up the stairs to catch up with his son.

Yolniv shuffled to Noah's table. The doors to the community center slammed shut one floor up. The old man had a smirk. "Tough guy. Never seen him before. You okay?"

"He's Noah's dad."

"Sounds like if his plans work out he'll be king soon." Yolniv shook his head as he sat down. "Find anyone to join us this week?"

I placed my palms on the table. "If it isn't in the Unified Activity Manager, people don't want to hear about it."

Yolniv pursed his lips. "We can always stick around and see who shows up."

Twenty minutes in—no one showed. Not even that kid from last week. In a year we had gone from twenty-three simultaneous games and a prize for the winner, to an empty room. We played a couple games between ourselves, but without anyone to share it with, the games felt hollow.

Yolniv let out a throaty sound of disgust. "Can't believe it. Not one person." The old man glanced at me and took a deep breath. "Zouk, you're not gonna wanna hear this, but I've been going to those Unified Activity Manager sponsored events the last couple weeks."

My shoulders fell. One more defeat at the hands of the UAM. I wanted to feel betrayed, but I understood. It was easier to give in, to work within the system, for all its flaws. Sometimes I walked past those events, just to see inside.

"Those Minds run a tight ship. Wanna know how much time they gave me, as the featured speaker for the tournament?" I shut off the board we had been playing on.

"One hundred twenty seconds. Two minutes to inspire. They put up a timer on the screen behind me. Everyone was waiting for the number to hit zero!"

Yolniv's arms flapped around as he spoke. I smiled a little at the story.

"At least people are still playing the game," I mumbled. Yolniv rocked to his feet.

"Don't get me started on the games! Do you know the UAM only gives players sixty-second breaks? That's almost enough time to make it to your next table. No wonder kids these days keep quitting. They don't even shake hands anymore—too inefficient. It's ridiculous. You can't learn if all you do is play. You need to let the game breathe a little." Sounded like the UAM was as bad as ever.

"Those Minds don't have a clue what they're doing." My arms hung limply at my sides. "They don't even know how to let people enjoy a game."

Yolniv turned the table over and started packing it up. "It's all about productivity and gains to them. You can't just have fun, you need to be efficient in your fun."

Yolniv calmed down after a minute or two. We had had these chats before—always concerns, always complaints, always the same problems. But without a single attendee, it felt different.

"Zouk," Yolniv spoke softly, "We can't do any worse at this community event thing than we are now." I tapped the ceiling with my fingers, it was hard to disagree.

"And since our coaching arrangement is over, I'm taking a few weeks off. You may want to do the same."

We walked up the stairs in silence. Community events had been our project for years, decades in Yolniv's case. I wanted to keep fighting, to burn down the UAM. But if the old man said it was over, there wasn't much hope left. Out on the sidewalk, Yolniv's ITV rolled in first. Before getting in, he looked at me with wide eyes.

"I know you don't want to hear it, but people are still playing the game, they're just doing it somewhere else in some other way. We need to get with the times. The UAM has its problems, but at least you can talk with other players again. Consider it."

Yolniv's vehicle sped off, leaving me lost in my thoughts. We had failed. Maybe I hadn't tried hard enough, maybe we had chased the players away. I thought about the UAM, it was supposed to be just an organizational app. But since its release, everything had changed. You didn't stumble across a fun event, you scheduled your attendance in the app. You didn't pick a little teaching on the side, you got forty students and a full-time job.

I thought back to that terrible summer a year and half ago. The UAM had determined that forty hours was the right number for a good teacher and anything less meant I wasn't productive enough. Kira hadn't gotten her new job yet, and I was at the peak of my game, no better time to cash in. A few months down the road and I was exhausted, angry, and a pro past their prime.

They didn't even let me quit. The system said it needed at least six weeks to reassign my students. By the end, I had started to hate the students too.

Even on Yolniv's recommendation, I couldn't do it. Just thinking about re-enabling the UAM left me shaking. Even if the community and the game I loved were waiting for me, I wouldn't attend.

A light-red vehicle with my face on the side pulled up to the curb and opened its doors.

As the ITV rumbled back to the highway, I got to thinking. No community, three students, a dead career. I reached into my bag and felt for the small piece of paper near the bottom. It was a little beaten up after ten months, but the number was still legible. In the world of the Unified Activity Manager, a business card was archaic. But so was I, these days. Maybe someone else who didn't trust the system was the perfect fit.

I dialed the number onto my screen. It warned me that the number wasn't officially registered with the UAM. Good. My finger hovered over the call button, these people would expect me to take on the Minds. Would they still want me a year later, all washed up? Then again, all the best players had already lost. Bergasmaschi only took a single game, would it be so bad to fail alongside everyone else? Before I lost my nerve, I made the call.

4 - AN EXPERIMENTAL PLAY SESSION

RANK: 99 ▲ 4

The ITV twisted around the hairpin, shoving me against the wall. Whoever programmed the things never figured out navigating university sidewalks. Every turn on the way up the main hill jostled me left and right. Then, there were the walkers. There weren't many these days, most had given in to the 'efficiency' of the ITV. But the few still out here sneered as I glided past, like I was an intrusion on their space. Then again, Levin University's campus always had that effect on me. I played here about once a year, usually in some dingy geology building ill-equipped for the hundreds of players that showed up. But this time my pod glided right past the stone columns of the geology building, I was headed straight to the top.

Despite a seventy-three-minute conversation with Derek, he shared very few details: a destination, Torrez Learning Center, and a recommendation to study up beforehand. The pod crested the hill, and even without a map, I knew it on sight. The Torrez Center was a tower of glass and concrete that rose high above the rest of the campus. Brand new, without a doubt. It looked like it belonged in the middle of the city, a modern spectacle planted in the university's garden of stone.

The ITV dropped me off before the center's double doors. It was covered in glass, but nothing was visible inside. I had pestered a few players for info on the place, but no one was willing to break their NDA. It probably wasn't dangerous. And Derek had made it clear I could leave at any time. Still my knees wobbled the same way they used to when I played tournaments as a kid. I stretched my arms. It didn't help. I approached the glass door and pushed it open.

"I knew you'd make it!" Derek stood at the center of an enormous lobby, at last in the light. The guy looked pretty benign, light-blue button-up shirt, darker blue tie, grey pants, pushed-back dirty-blond hair. It was clear he worked out in his spare time. And the forceful way he gripped my hand in our handshake told me he'd rather be competing than doing any of this LINE stuff. "How are ya, Number Eight?" I withered at the nickname. He intended it as a celebration of my skill, but all it did was remind me how far I had fallen.

"Hey, Derek."

He gestured broadly. "So what do you think?"

I gave a cursory glance around, everything was concrete, there were three floors to the nearest ceiling, the stairs ran back and forth in the open air, and there was hardly a single furnishing in the whole place. It was strange, I could feel heaters running, but the air felt cold. "It's nice. Is it yours?"

Derek puffed out his chest. "Wouldn't that be something? It's all Maya's, she commissioned the place. Follow me." Maya, that was the woman who watched my game against Bergamaschi. Derek led me down a hall and continued speaking. "We only got in six months ago, been trying our best to fill out the space, but we kinda have more room than people right now."

We passed lecture halls, conference rooms, even an auditorium. But most were classrooms. I paused at one, there were people inside. They were playing LINE.

"Oh yeah, hope you don't mind, those are some of our students. Don't worry, you won't be able to hear them from the testing zone. Be careful, those kids are smart, pretty sure a few of 'em are already smarter than me."

I gave a half-hearted laugh and kept looking inside. I hadn't seen a class like this in years. "Reminds me of the camps I used to work at," I said.

"Oh yeah? Well, maybe we can bring you in for a guest lecture sometime. They really pick things up quick. Between you and me, one of those kids is gonna be World Champion someday. I'm sure of it. You ready?"

I looked through the glass as long as I could. Seeing all those students analyzing games, running drills, I wished I could put together an event half as successful as all this. Eventually Derek pulled me away, dragging me down a long hall to a heavy, metal door at the end.

Derek rapped on its face and turned to me. "Sorry to cut this short, but I gotta man the front. Our director is gonna take care of you from here. Just do what she says and you'll be fine." He gave me a quick slap on the back and started down the hall. "Good luck, dude, you can do it. You've got that top ten spirit!"

Staring down the large, heavy door, I regretted letting Derek go so quickly. When I had called him from the community event, he had chatted with me my whole trip home. Most of the talk had come from him, how excited he was to see me, payment options, and a weird amount of discussion about how 'sleek' the Torrez Center was. Now, with hardly a few words spoken, he was gone and I was left to whoever was behind the door.

There was a shuffle of feet. The metal knob rattled, and the door swung open to a brunette woman dressed in a lab coat, eyes locked on a screen in her hand. My head jerked back and my voice caught when I saw her face. It had been almost a year, she had vanished off the face of the planet. "Jamie?"

"Come in! You're the last one." Jamie spoke with an authority I had never heard from her. I stepped through the door and followed her down a dim passage. My concerns about the institute vanished, but new questions popped up by the second. "You should have told me Derek reached out to you, I could have gotten you in here ages ago!"

Jamie led me into a sort of half classroom, half lab with a linoleum floor. Four rows of desks faced the front, each equipped with a top quality LINE board. But I was still shocked at Jamie's appearance. "You're a director?" I asked.

"Sit here. Sorry, Zouk. Everyone else is here, and we really don't have a lot of time." I obeyed, dropping into a desk on the second row.

"Was I late?" I asked.

"No. I just start early," Jamie answered as she moved to the front.

I swallowed and faced forward. For the last ten months, I had been losing games, but Jamie had straight-up disappeared. I figured she was experiencing her own career struggles, just like me. Instead she was here, running some LINE research operation. If my paycheck for the day was anything to go by, she was also probably well compensated.

There was a quiet as Jamie tapped away at her screen. She looked comfortable in her role, practiced. With what time I had, I scanned over the other participants. No one in the back stood out. A few faces closer up looked familiar, but there were only two I recognized. First was Oliver, a fourteen-year-old wunderkind from the Eastern Province—rank somewhere between seventy and eighty in the world. He was dressed in a nice suit that was terribly wrinkled. Kids like him were sharper than anyone alive, but tended to act rash and talk big.

The other player was unmistakable. I couldn't believe Jamie had gotten her. Rank twelve in the world and in her mid-thirties. Alexandria

Ruhoy. Her hair was frazzled, her clothes a little worn, but she sat back in her chair with an ease the rest of us lacked. We shared a look, she gave me a nod. We had played each other before.

Jamie tapped her screen and the lights dimmed. An image of the university rendered itself on the front wall. *Welcome to the Torrez Research Institute.*

"Thank you everyone for coming out." Jamie paused a moment and looked over the room. She stood tall and owned the space. I wasn't sure when or how she got it, but this new job suited her.

"We have a wide range of players here today. New faces, some returning, even a few amateurs."

Amateurs? I took another glance around the room. That's why I hadn't recognized the back row. I pursed my lips together. It didn't make sense to bring in amateurs. Could they not afford the big players? Another thought came to mind. Maybe the best had already failed.

"We only have the day, so I'm going to get to it."

Jamie tapped her screen again, and the welcome sign was replaced with a bullet point list. "We are looking for players with the LINE skills necessary to defeat cognitively superior opponents." The room was silent.

"You already know why," Jamie continued. "Someone's going to beat the Minds and I'm here to find that person." The air felt thick. No one had gotten past the second round against the Minds. After a year of failure, pros stopped talking about the directive. They acted like it was sacred, a mythical quest or something. I didn't care for all that, but the others did. Alexandria's eyes were laser-focused on the board.

"All of you have skill in the game, we wouldn't have invited you otherwise. But regular skill isn't enough. The best players have tried their hand against the Minds and failed. I'm not wasting my time coaching fifteen players to fifteen defeats." Amidst Jamie's speech, a little green light on the ceiling drew my eye. A camera. Jamie mentioned a team, but she was the only one here. How big was this operation? Was Maya up there? What did she want from all this? Jamie spoke again.

"We're looking for one player with the right skill set. To that end, we will be testing all of you. If you are selected, my team and I will personally coach you through your games on the national stage."

"What if I already have a coach?" A young voice in the back drew the room's attention. One of the amateurs. Alexandria raised an eyebrow. This guy didn't have a clue.

"Jonas Thurnbell, is it?" Jamie didn't move from her spot. "The directive permits players to challenge the Minds freely, no third party required. If you think you can win, you are free to file an application. Should be no more than five weeks before you're onstage playing against The Mind of Communications and Influence."

"Is there a downside?" An older man next to the kid spoke in a hoarse voice. The pair leaned in their chairs to the left in the same way. They looked like father and son.

"You'll lose," Jamie said flatly.

"How can you be so sure?" Jonas asked loudly. "Haven't two players made it to the second round?" He had a cocky smile. Jamie exhaled through her nose. It sounded like she had been through all this before.

"Nine hundred thirty-six players lost their first game. Nearly every pro in Iom that's ever played LINE has already failed. But you're right, two players did manage to get a win on the board."

"So we could get one of them to train us," Jonas's father piped in. Jamie put down her screen and walked between the desks, approaching the back.

"Two players made it to the second round, know who they are?" I shook at the forceful tone in Jamie's voice.

"Bergamaschi." Jonas wiped at his mouth and grinned, he looked proud of his answer.

"That's right, the world champion. Good job. And the other one?" Jonas and his father shrugged.

"You don't know?" Sarcasm crept into Jamie's voice. "The other one, Otso, trained in my program." My eyes went wide. I had always wondered how the 35th best in the world stole a game from Influence.

"There are a lot of coaches out there, but every one of them specializes in facing human players. We are the only team in the world with the research and training to help you beat a Mind. So unless you think you're better than the best, this is your only route to challenging the Minds without humiliating yourself." As Jamie passed me, I saw her face. Her eyes were set, her mouth a scowl. This job had hardened her.

At the front, Jamie took a moment to flick a hair away from her face before picking her screen back up. "So for those of you who haven't done your research, let's talk about your opponent. What makes the Minds such dangerous players?" We were all silent. I just wanted to see more of this new Jamie.

"Imagine the strongest LINE player in the world."

"Bergamaschi." The young voice came from just behind me, Oliver the wunderkind.

Jamie tapped her screen, switching the wall's display to a blueprint. It looked like a mess of electronics and numbers.

"Yes, Bergamaschi. A player that always makes great moves, sometimes he even makes a brilliant move. The kind of move that has to be studied and broken down for years to be fully understood." I nodded along. I had seen moves like that firsthand, sometimes even the player couldn't explain it—there was just something in our gut that told us the move was right.

"Now imagine Bergamaschi is incapable of error. Imagine that instead of making one brilliant move every few tournaments, he makes two or three in every game. This is what the Minds are capable of. They have studied every game ever played. Each of them has personally played more games than any of us could in our entire lifetimes. Their brains literally process the world forty-four times faster than we do."

Throughout her speech, Jamie pointed at various parts of her blueprint, but I found myself focused on one stat. Forty-four times smarter. I could see myself on the stage already. Sitting in one of Influence's strange cupped chairs. He's looking back at me with a charming grin. I'd spend sixty seconds coming up with a pretty good move. Two seconds later, he'd find something better.

"Without help. None of us stand a chance. Which is why we're here."

Jamie tapped her screen and a calendar replaced the blueprint on the wall. "This is our schedule for the day, as you can see other than lunch, all we're doing is testing. Please power on your boards."

I hit the power button. Even after Jamie's explanation, one question kept coming up in my mind. This wasn't a charity, what did Maya and Jamie stand to gain?

The board lit up with a blue glow. I had been itching to see what kind of tests were waiting for us. The devices were top of the line, there had to be some kind of custom programming, maybe specialized puzzles waiting in a hidden screen.

"Now that you have your screens up, please open the 'Learn with a Trainer' program." I followed Jamie's directions, and watched for any sign of custom scripts. Nothing came, it was just a LINE board. In the corner, a friendly cartoon general stood under a speech bubble reading 'Upload a game or make your first move!'.

"To determine your fitness as a player, we will be conducting a single challenge. Pass and we begin coaching immediately. Fail and you go home."

My breath caught. A single challenge? Normally LINE tests involved a series of drills and puzzles designed to identify a player's strengths and weaknesses, the results of which were then tallied to determine a player's skill level. If Jamie wasn't looking for a quantifiable measure of our skill, what was she looking for?

"The 'Learn with a Trainer' tool is used to analyze games and recommend better moves." Jamie spoke primarily to the back of the room, the rest of us were well acquainted with the trainer. It was the tool you used to figure out what you did wrong after a tough loss.

"We have locked the trainer to its highest setting. It will always make the best moves at a depth of twenty turns. Your objective today is to go against the trainer and win." I narrowed my eyes. The task was too simple. There was nothing custom at all. I could have run this test at the community center. Clearly, Jamie was testing for something unique.

"Each of you is free to view the trainer's advice, rewind moves, whatever you want really. Just find a way to beat the trainer opponent. You have six hours, excluding lunch. Any questions?"

None of us said anything. The challenge left no room for ambiguity. Jamie exited, leaving us all alone with our boards.

5 - QUALIFICATION

My mind was reeling. I had stayed up half the night running drills and studying puzzles. For this? Just to beat the computer? I frowned. Maybe that was the point. I was approaching my training all wrong. I was preparing to face a human opponent, I should have been preparing to face a computer.

The board sat blank in front of me. People didn't beat the trainer, they used it to analyze games, to discover the 'perfect move' in a given position. How do you beat a perfect player? Hundreds of players had already been here, maybe thousands. I needed to find a way to separate myself. There were only six hours. I needed to avoid time wasters and find ideas that set me apart.

My first 'move' was to look around and see what everyone else was doing. A row ahead, two amateurs were a few turns in and already losing. To my left, Oliver was pretty far into his first game. He input orders at lightning speed. There was hardly time to think between moves. The game had gone on for thirty turns. Thing was, he was losing. Moves were coming in by the second, but they seemed so pointless. Didn't he hear what the trainer was capable of? A single mistake guaranteed defeat, and every good move only stalled the inevitable.

I tapped the corner of my board to open a text editor. Using the touch pad, I keyed in a few words, "Rule one: *Don't fight a losing battle.*" Jamie had told us we were allowed to rewind and restart all we wanted. If I made a mistake, I couldn't waste time on a lost cause.

To my right, Alexandria had barely begun. It looked like move seven or eight. Her head stayed perfectly still, a single finger on her right hand was pointed at the board. It moved almost imperceptibly, back and forth. Already deep in calculation, I couldn't believe it. Was she trying to invent the perfect game from nothing? Did she really believe she could outthink the computer for forty-plus moves?

There was no way she could keep up that level of focus. At my best, I could enter deep calculation for maybe ninety minutes in a day. It wasn't an issue of intelligence, it was endurance. Deep thought was like any other physical activity, it came at a cost, and Alexandria was thinking at a full sprint.

I returned to my notes. "Rule two: *For the little decisions, let the trainer do the thinking.*" The trainer was my opponent, but it was also my ally. If I didn't have something to contribute on a turn, there was no reason to reinvent the wheel.

With my new rules, I began my first game. My hand shook a little as I input the commands. I could see why everyone was so focused. Loss was all but guaranteed, but it still felt like every move mattered. Like Jamie's team would judge me for misplacing a wall or losing a squadron.

I went with the Lost Star formation. May as well start familiar. Whenever the little general on the side of the screen suggested a move, I listened. The trainer's side of the board was a mess. Scattered walls, exposed squadrons, thin pathways. It looked like a surrealist art piece, a base devoid of good fundamentals and even thinner on military forces.

Then I launched my attack.

One by one, my squadrons marched out from the left point of the fallen star. The enemy's forces weaved through its forest of walls, emerging only to fire and retreat back into its base. Guerrilla warfare. The kind of strategy that worked great until you made a mistake and lost everything.

The enemy's outer wall collapsed and my squadrons pressed towards the center. My leg was bouncing a little under the table. This was going surprisingly well. The trainer kept up its hit-and-run tactics as my forces bore down on its command post. I was down to my last three squadrons and five tiles from victory. I crept forward, the enemy fired, and a few more of my troops fell away. Forward again, another squadron lost. Two tiles from victory, my army was gone. The attack was over and so were my chances of winning. I hadn't done anything wrong, the enemy's defenses had been barely enough.

I was tempted to keep going, to see what I could salvage from such a scrappy fight. My eye caught sight of Rule one: *Don't fight a losing battle*. I tapped the rewind button to start again.

Losing the first game was nothing to be ashamed of. Everyone in the room had already lost except Alexandria. She looked to be on move nineteen. Still, it was disappointing. As the board rewound through the turns, I thought about the little adjustments I could make to turn things in my favor.

My second attempt was broadly the same as the first. I made a few adjustments, but in the end, my last squadron fell four tiles from the opponent's command post. Attempts three through six were all variations on the second, and all ended the same way, a few tiles short of victory.

For the sake of testing, I ran one game without the trainer's assistance. One of my moves took ten minutes and the trainer congratulated me on finding the third best move. That attempt was abandoned.

No matter what I did, that cartoon general's defense was perfect. Every defeat came by the slimmest of margins: a tile from the command post, two too many enemy troops. Maybe that was the art of these calculating machines. They could see a billion possibilities and find the one move that guaranteed victory in all of them.

I kept up my general strategy, making adjustments and retrying after every failure. Attempt nineteen was interrupted by a shout at the back of the room. How long had I been playing? I glanced at the clock—noon already.

"I did it!"

Jonas's dad's fists were in the air as he spoke. "I beat the trainer—it's over! I can't believe it."

I jerked my head around to see father and son hugging one another. It didn't make sense. Half my head was still calculating my next move, still, I couldn't imagine a world where an amateur could beat Jamie's challenge. But the dancing cartoon general on Jonas's dad's screen told another story.

The room was speechless. After a few seconds, Jamie's voice piped into the room.

"That seems like as good a time as any for lunch. Thanks for your hard work everyone, we've got food in the hall." Jamie's voice sounded disinterested. As if she found the victory boring, or insignificant. Jonas got out of his chair and stared directly into the camera, arms wide. "That's it? My dad just made your dreams come true! Come on, I thought this is why you brought us here!"

"Let's discuss it outside," Jamie responded over the speaker.

Now that I wasn't playing a game, I realized how exhausted I felt. My head ached and buzzed and spun all at once. Most of us shambled together towards the door, but Jonas stood firm. He glared up at the camera, hand on his father's shoulder. As I passed his father's desk, my eyes flicked to the screen. The trainer's base was in tatters and the command post was captured. Total victory. The kind you'd never see in a professional game. I followed the crowd into the hall, wondering if they'd only pay me half for a half day of work.

Tables lined both sides of the hall with more food than any of us could hope to eat. The institute seemed eager to impress. Each of us took a place and queued up, all except the Thurnbells, who strode out of the lab and waited near the door with angry looks.

I reached for a sandwich, only to find another hand already there, caressing the sourdough. Alexandria's arm was motionless, her eyes were drooping, her body swayed back and forth. Mental burnout. "You all right?" I asked.

Alexandria's eyes flicked up and she stared at me for quite a while before speaking. "Just thinking about the game." Her voice was hardly a mumble.

I reached over and moved the turkey sandwich into her hand. "I can see that. You should get something to eat, take a break."

She nodded and swayed past the buffet to a bench on the side of the hall, across from the other players. Her eyes stared out at nothing as her hand slowly delivered a bite to her mouth. I had come home from a tournament or two in her state, but never by lunch.

Past the buffet line, Jamie had met with the Thurnbells. She looked to be explaining something, but it was too far to hear. I turned to Alexandria.

"You really think that guy beat the trainer?"

Alexandria didn't even look. "I don't think any of us can. It is an impossible task."

Jonas's shouts echoed down the hall. I stood, ready for action, only to see a door fly open and two burly security guards line up at Jamie's side. We really were under constant observation. Jonas took a step back, but his father moved closer. Security put their hands on the man's chest. In the whole exchange, Jamie didn't flinch. This was a version of her I had never seen before. The guards said something, and a moment later, Jonas and his father were on their way down the hall and out of the building. Jamie disappeared back into the security office. I slowly sat back down and returned my mind to our conversation.

"You say it's impossible for us to win," I started. "What about Bergamaschi? He did it, didn't he?"

Alexandria gave me a scowl and bit down on her sandwich. When she finished swallowing, she spoke, "Our enemy can think twenty turns ahead. You've seen it. It doesn't matter what formation you make, what tactics you create, it will always see them, and it will always play better." Alexandria took another bite. The players on the other side of the hall slowed their eating, clearly hanging on every word.

"It isn't a test of our LINE skills. You see that, yes?" Alexandria asked. I thought for a moment about the question and nodded.

"What do you mean?" Oliver's voice rang across the hall. Alexandria shot me a side-look, then spoke loudly enough for all the listening players to hear.

"Anyone who tries to beat the trainer with skill is a fool. The machine will always beat you. Our job is that of the artisan. We must not play the game, we must craft a single beautiful turn. The machine will always play itself to standstill. We must find a way to tip that perfect balance in our favor. Then, we allow the machine to defeat itself."

The other players were dead silent. Most had put down their food. Alexandria took a deep breath. I could see she was starting to get her energy back. "How is that not a measure of our skills?" Oliver asked.

"Because it is only a measure of a single ability. We are being evaluated on our ability to find brilliance."

It suddenly made sense why Alexandria had invested so much of her thought into every move. She was poking at the game, testing every move one at a time for an opportunity for 'brilliance'. It explained her pessimism too.

"I've had a few brilliant moves," Oliver responded. I glanced at Alexandria, she was back to her sandwich, a million miles away. So I answered.

"Oliver, right?" He nodded. "Do you know how many brilliant

moves you've had in your career?

"Maybe three or four," Oliver answered. I set my plate down and leaned forward. It was funny, I had lectured students about every aspect of the game, but I had never had the chance to teach someone about 'brilliant' moves before.

"I have eight brilliances to my name and there is exactly one common factor between them." All the players in the hall were listening now, I wondered briefly if I should be telling them all this, but maybe collaboration would give us a better chance. "Dumb luck. All my brilliant moves came out of nowhere. Most of the time I didn't even recognize them as such until the game was over." I could sense a certain resignation in my own words, maybe I had let Alexandria's pessimism get to me. I spoke again.

"Still—there's a chance. Playing a brilliance is like winning the lottery. It could happen, it could be any of us—It could have even been the Thurnbells." I indicated down the hall, all signs of Jonas and his father were gone. "The problem is the time limit. Give me three years and a brilliance is guaranteed, give me six hours and I won't stand a chance."

For a few minutes, we all ate in silence. Alexandria had figured it out. I chastised myself for not realizing sooner. Now half the day was gone and I only now understood what I needed to do. Without a brilliance, all the attacks in the world would fail. I should have spent more time thinking and less time playing.

The bench rocked as Alexandria got to her feet. She still looked dead tired, but there was fire in her eyes, the kind of fire that made champions.

"What are you doing?" Oliver asked. "I thought you said it couldn't be done."

Alexandria blinked her eyes a few times before looking at Oliver. "I'm seeing if I can make lightning strike. I see no reason to quit before the deadline, nor to delay."

She was right. There was still so much I could try in the next few hours. No reason to sit around and chitchat while we were on the clock. I stood and followed her to the classroom. The others followed suit.

Jamie was waiting in the lab, she wore a stern expression. "Welcome back," she muttered.

I reached my seat but didn't sit down. "Are we still going?"

"We are," Jamie said.

"What happened?"

Jamie remained silent until the room was full.

"As you are all aware, one of our players claimed they had defeated the trainer earlier today. After a brief review, it was determined that the player had forced their opponent to make suboptimal moves to secure their win. We did not consider this a valid victory."

I smiled to myself. The 'supposed' winner must have realized they were allowed to input moves for the trainer, then thought they had somehow outsmarted the system by placing the trainer in a no-win situation. A part of me was relieved, an amateur hadn't pulled off the impossible. On the other hand, the trainer was once again 'unbeatable'.

A voice in the back spoke up, "Are they gone?"

Jamie nodded. "Yes. Our conversation raised some security concerns." She paused, there were no follow-ups, we had all heard the shouting.

"To be clear, those two were not escorted out for claiming they had won. If you think you've beaten the bot, please let us know." Jamie moved a stray hair out of her eyes. "If there are no more questions, you're free to continue. Good luck."

I opened my game in progress, still sitting at move thirty-five. One brilliant move. That's all I needed. Easier said than done. The real trick about brilliant moves is that they were boring. Never 'shock and awe', never squadrons in battle. A brilliance was a wall at the side of the board, a retreating squadron, a decision to wait. They were quiet, they spoke in a whisper that echoed through the whole game.

I burned thirty minutes searching for the unfindable brilliance. Alexandria was still at it, head in hands, deep focus. Was I even good enough anymore to recognize a brilliance? It had been four months since the LINE Association had reclassified me to 'semi-pro'.

The little cartoon general waggled his finger at me from the corner, taunting me with his smug smile. It was starting to piss me off. He reminded me of my final session training with Yolniv: 'You found the fifth best move! Try harder!'.

This whole thing felt like one of Yolniv's drills. An exercise in playing smart, conservative LINE. It was all about being 'right', being 'brilliant'. To me, it's always been more interesting to play my opponent, to uncover their weaknesses. In a game like that, even bad moves could be brilliant.

I glanced behind me. Oliver's hair was a mess. He tussled it every time a move turned out not to be a brilliance. The wunderkind was having as much luck as the rest of us.

It had already been an hour, and trial and error wasn't getting me any closer to a solution. Alexandria was the best thinker among us. If anyone in here had a chance of stumbling into a brilliance, it was her.

I took my hand off the mouse. There were two and a half hours left in the day and I was tired of trying to be brilliant. It wasn't like it was working very well. No. I needed to change my approach. Leave the brilliant moves to Alexandria or Oliver. It was time to treat the trainer like a human opponent. I expanded my notepad, moved the cursor to the bottom, and started asking questions.

Question one, was my opponent perfect? Only at a depth of twenty moves.

How many games has this player played? Millions. Not useful.

When does it make errors? Never. It seemed my methodology didn't adapt to machines very well.

So what do I know? The machine was unorthodox, it built base structures that make no sense. It calculates defenses down to the slimmest margins. I thought back on Jamie's rundown of the trainer.

The machine will never make a mistake and it will never miss a tactic. Why? Because it would perfectly calculate twenty turns into the future before making a move.

This was all information I already knew, if I could make one move that saw further than twenty moves into the future, I'd win. The brilliance. I paused, but why just one move? What if I led an attack that took more than twenty moves? Would the trainer spot it? Or would it be like building an outpost against Bergamaschi?

I devised a slow, grinding attack. It started with the Fallen Star formation, as always. When it was time to strike, I kept things slow. Instead of moving every squadron, I moved a few of them. The dots slid slowly across the screen. They fired weapons, but only when they needed to.

It failed. As did my next attempt. And the next.

After an hour, I had made five attacks and by the end of each my squadrons were gone and the little cartoon general was eager to help me learn from my defeat.

Predictability. That was the problem. Even though I was moving slower and attacks took longer, the attack was basically the same as one I would have led in a faster game. The general could see what was coming and spring to the defense.

Ninety minutes left in the day. My body was thrumming with excitement and anxiety. My solution had failed. But I was closer. There was an idea out there that could work, I could feel it tickling at the edge of my thoughts. My head dropped into my hands, I needed to think. A chair squeaked behind me. Oliver let out a quiet humph. Someone pounded a desk. Every time thoughts started to form, some sound would whisk them away.

I jumped to my feet and left the room. The food was long gone. Derek was leaning against the opposite wall with his phone out. I dropped to the ground, crossed my legs, and shut my eyes. "Giving up already? I really thought you had it, man."

My eyes popped open, another thought gone. "No—Uh. No, I

think I'm closing in on an answer."

"No kidding? That would be awesome news. We haven't had someone pass the test, in like, six months. You think you've got enough time?"

His voice grated on my ears. "Maybe, I just need to think for a minute." I brought my palms up to my eyes.

"Cool. Yeah, you do your thing. Sometimes I need a few minutes to get things done too, so I totally get it." Derek returned to his phone. At last, quiet. Thoughts were reforming, joining and coalescing.

In my last attack, I had moved slowly to prevent the trainer from building defenses. But the trainer could still see the elements of the attack even if I didn't execute it in twenty turns, so the strategy failed.

Derek tap-tapped on his phone. I pushed past it. What I needed was to create an attack that couldn't be seen by the trainer. Something that wasn't clearly dangerous, didn't demand an answer, and was only advantageous from a perspective of twenty turns or more. An invisible threat.

I sat up suddenly, my head bumped the plaster wall. Maybe instead of a single attack, my moves needed to be a part of a broader strategy. If every move I made was focused on the distant future, the trainer would fight for the short term and overlook my long-term advantage.

All I needed was a slow, crawling strategy. My hands dropped to the floor. My breath was shallow and quick. I knew what I needed. "You figure it out?" Derek asked.

I nodded. "The Elephant's Tail." I scrambled back into the lab. For the first time since starting Jamie's test, it felt possible. I could be the one in a thousand. Maybe I didn't win at tournaments anymore, but beating Influence? That was a career defining victory.

My feet slipped slightly on the linoleum as I hurried to my desk. Seventy minutes. Not a lot of time to put a plan into place, and the Elephant's Tail needed time.

It wasn't a common strategy. The Elephant's Tail was a base

structure that took fifty or sixty moves to build up. It emphasized extreme defense and a slow conquering of the map, like an elephant backing onto the board. In practice, the pros could tear the structure to pieces. There were too many walls, too much space, not enough squadrons. Unless you could play perfectly, the Elephant's Tail was nothing but a novelty. Lucky for me, I had a trainer to give me all the help I needed.

As soon as the board turned on, I started inputting moves. Every turn I dropped a new wall, creeping across the map with my base. The trainer was convinced I was making the wrong moves. I pumped my fist, that was proof of concept. It couldn't see my idea.

My half of the board quickly became a winding line of walls that stretched up the sides and through the middle. With each turn, the trainer would throw more squadrons my way, and I would take the trainer's advice to defend them. The analysis reported again and again that I was losing, but fifty turns in, the bulky elephantine structure dominated the map. The trainer had no room to maneuver, and each assault from my opponent was weaker than the last. At turn eighty-three, I controlled two-thirds of the board.

My teeth chattered and my hands shook as I tapped the 'Request Analysis' button in the corner of the screen. Every second put me closer to running out of time. My computer played a quiet chime, it has completed its analysis. Due to my overwhelming control of the board, I officially had the advantage.

I suppressed a yelp. For the whole day, that little cartoon general had been taunting me, dancing around a button I could never use. Now it was time. My fingers pressed slowly on the yellow square labelled 'Try the Best Move'.

Turn by turn, the trainer made moves against itself. Squadrons marched forward, weapons fired, and walls collapsed. Eight minutes left in the day. I pressed 'Try the Best Move' again and glanced around the room. Half the players were gone, some must have given up. Oliver was still going, but his face drooped and his finger was inputting slow, lazy orders. Alexandria's head was buried in her arms, asleep maybe, possibly just disappointed. No one else had a chance.

The last few red troops vanished under an unstoppable wall of weapons fire. Fifty blue dots surrounded the command post. Victory was assured. I wasn't sure what would come after all this, or what the Torrez Institute would ask of me, but at least I still had a little skill. I input the last order manually. Three troops charged onto the command post, and the colors flipped from red to blue. The cartoon general appeared at the center of the screen. He danced under a banner that read 'Good game! Care to play another?'.

6 - EVALUATION

Jamie returned to the lab at exactly five o'clock. I was buzzing with energy as she read through her goodbye script. Oliver and the semi-pros walked out one by one. I didn't sense any disappointment in Jamie at their failures, just indifference. Once they were gone, Jamie gave me a questioning look. I grinned back at her. "I won my game."

She snorted.

"I'm serious, wanna see it?"

I slid my chair out of the way and gestured to the board. Jamie approached my desk apprehensively, then started the replay. Fifteen turns in, her head had tilted to the side. She paused and nabbed a chair. I watched the whole game with her. My hands wouldn't stop shaking. Excitement was pumping through my veins.

A snore sounded. I jumped. To my right, a bleary-eyed Alexandria lifted her head out of her arms in a daze.

"Is it over?" Her voice was weak.

"Everyone else is gone." My smile wouldn't seem to drop. "Hey, I beat the trainer."

A little life crept back into her eyes. She glanced past me at the board. "Really? Can I see it?"

Jamie's ears perked up. Her hand shot out and powered off the screen. In seconds, Jamie was on her feet and projecting professionalism. "That won't be possible, Zouk's game and its replay are the property of the Torrez Institute. Zouk, would you please wait here while I lead Alexandria to the exit?"

Alexandria gave the board a final, longing stare, then left with Jamie. I felt a tinge of regret at not sharing the game. Fifteen minutes passed without a word from anyone. I needed to talk to someone, to tell them what had happened. I pulled out my screen and called my wife.

Kira answered fast, the call showed the cabin of an ITV. Looked like she was on a long drive back from a twenty-four-hour binge. I told her everything that happened. She seemed captivated, except for those times when I caught her blinking away the fatigue. It was just like old times.

"Next time you could probably cut the discovery time in half. In fact, if they told you the challenge an hour before giving you the board, you could—"

"Kira"—I stopped her—"I did it." Her mouth hung open as she realized she had gotten carried away.

"Right—" Kira put on a smile. "Yay! You did it! Congratulations! Woo!" Her celebrations sounded stilted, but she was trying, so I joined in. "Yipee! Hooray! Victories!"

The half-baked cheers boiled into real laughter. As things settled down, Kira's eyebrows furrowed. "Sorry."

"Don't be—" A cool wind rushed into the lab, followed by footsteps. "I have to go, see you tonight!"

"Okay. Good job again!"

"Thanks!" I ended the call. From the passageway, one of Jamie's lab assistants emerged. He looked to be at least forty and wore a white coat over a tweed jacket.

"We're ready for you."

I followed him out of the lab. Down the hall, Derek caught my eye and gave a double thumbs up. We stopped two doors down at an unlabelled room. When the door opened, a wave of hot dry air rolled over me.

Jamie stood at the center of a wide octagon room. All around, towering black servers whirred and hummed. Scientists in lab coats manipulated massive screens rendered onto the walls. I didn't know where to look. My game against the trainer was everywhere. Jamie's resources were vast. She was pouring an entire team's energy into the sole task of analyzing my game. Who would fund something like this?

"Normally we have more time to review the game before meeting the player."

"How often has this happened?"

"Just the two now. You and Otso." Two players, that was it? Otso, a middling player that beat Influence without breaking a sweat. There were plenty of players better than him, but that didn't stop his name from coming up in every conversation about the LINE directive. If he was the only other player to pass her test, maybe she wasn't exaggerating about getting me a victory against Influence. That could change the trajectory of my career, my life.

"The Elephant's Tail. Who would have guessed?"

I nodded quickly. "Once I understood what I needed, there was no better tool."

Jamie led me to a screen at the back. "We're still in the process of understanding your strategy. But from what I've seen, you treated the trainer like a grease fire. Rather than fighting it directly, you slowly put a lid on it and let the trainer fizzle itself out."

I raised my chin as I spoke. "Slow and steady."

Jamie let the game keep playing. She couldn't seem to drag herself away. "Sometimes the trainer's moves are so insightful, it feels like it's thinking. But it really is just a bunch of circuits and wires." Her voice faded off as she spoke. "It didn't even realize it was losing until it had already lost."

Jamie looked like she could watch my game for hours, but after a very long day, I was eager to get home. I hit pause on the wall. "What happens now? What's the coaching strategy?"

Jamie took one last appreciative look at the board and turned to me. There was an impish look in her eyes. "There is none. You're ready."

It had taken me eight hours to win one game against a trainer. As good as the Elephant's Tail was, there was no way I could improvise another one on the fly against Influence. "Could we at least practice some more?"

"You don't need to, the game you just played will do fine."

"Jamie." I gave her a serious look. "I have been boiling my brain all day just to beat a computer, please don't talk in riddles."

Jamie's smirk vanished. "You're right. You've done enough. Bear with me a moment." Jamie slid her hand across the wall-screen. "I can only show this to you in here. Our opponent has extensive surveillance capabilities."

Six LINE boards rendered onto the wall in a 3x2 pattern. 'Influence' was written along the top, 'Trainer' was written along the bottom. "You already know your first opponent. The Mind of Communications and Influence. We have reviewed all nine hundred eighty-four games—"

"Eighty-seven," one of the lab assistants interjected.

"Every game Influence has ever played. We scraped a lot of sources."

I looked back at the lab assistant that had spoken. Who were they, PhDs? Was their thesis on winning LINE games? It seemed like an awful lot of investment and continuing expense.

"Watch the boards, there's a pattern."

Jamie hit play, and the boards sprung to life. I spotted the pattern immediately. Every one of Influence's moves on the top was perfectly reflected on the bottom. It was so simple, I couldn't believe it. Incredulity seeped through my voice. "He plays identically to the trainer."

Jamie nodded. "They both use the same algorithm."

The same algorithm? I stepped back from the wall-screen. Influence was a complex, thinking Mind. Using an algorithm meant he was predictable, it meant he was beatable. Why would he do that? "How confident are you?"

Jamie looked around at the rest of her team, some of them nodded. "Completely."

"Why haven't you used this tactic before?"

"We used it once, with Otso. After he lost against War, I kept the strategy under wraps."

"Show me more."

We spent an hour going through the evidence. Jamie pulled footage from the directive tournament and input player's moves against the trainer. Time after time, Influence would make a move, and the trainer would do the same. At some point, I found myself laughing. It was so simple. I could walk into the studio and win the game without calculating a single move. "How can the Minds have such an obvious blind spot?"

"You give them too much credit. They're just machines." Just machines. I thought back to that interview with Influence. If he was just a machine, he was the most convincing machine I had ever seen.

We loaded a few more games, but we didn't need to. She had proven it. Jamie had found the fast track to beating Influence, to the biggest win of any LINE player's career. And all this was being given to me for what—for passing Jamie's test? It didn't make sense. I shut off the wall screen. "Why is the Torrez Institute doing all this?"

Jamie shrugged. "That's Maya's territory. She'll talk to you after you beat Influence. Don't worry, I'll put in a good word." She gave me a wink. "You are with us, right?"

In a day, my world had changed. Possibility was in full bloom. If I won against Influence, folks would come from all over to hear what

I had to say. Maybe I could get a sponsor, or a partnership with a university. I probably wouldn't even need to keep playing LINE. Then again, if she was wrong, my TV-broadcasted failure would probably be the last professional LINE game I would ever play.

But there was confidence in Jamie's eyes. She knew what she was doing, she had done it before, all I had to do was play my part. "I'll do it."

Jamie shook my hand. "We'll submit your application for the directive tournament today. You need to start memorizing moves."

7 - ZOUK V THE MIND OF COMMUNICATIONS AND INFLUENCE

RANK: 96 ▲ 3

Standing before the Iom National News building's flat, grey exterior, I was oddly calm. Tournaments gave me the jitters, but this didn't feel like a tournament, it was more like a dance. I knew all the moves and after weeks of rehearsal, all I had to do was perform them. But even one slip, one misplaced piece, and the music would change under me.

The sliding doors opened in welcome. As I waited for security, my hand kept going to the outside of my jacket pocket. Through the fabric, my finger traced the creased edge of the invitation. I probably didn't need it. Influence's media team had already put me through a ninety-minute interview and shot every conceivable angle of my home for pre-roll. The guard waved me through and I patted the invitation one last time.

At the end of the lobby, a familiar figure was tapping away on a screen next to the elevators. "Hey, Derek."

Derek slid the device into his pocket and threw his arms out. "There he is! Number Eight! Hey man, you know we really don't need to get here this early. Thirty minutes is fine. Two hours is overkill." I shrugged, we had discussed the arrival time at length the other day, I wanted to be ready. Derek pointed me towards the elevators. "This way. Feeling good?"

I nodded. Derek leaned in close, it was probably hard to imagine a player being calm at a time like this. "Come on Zouk, let me in. What's going through that head?"

I pressed the button for the elevator and took a moment to formulate my answer. The doors opened and we stepped inside. It was one of those strange glass elevators that overlooked the whole city. Derek hit forty-one. "As long as I make the right moves, there are only two outcomes to today's game. Either Influence does his part and I win. Or he doesn't, and I lose."

My body felt a brief pull and the box began its slow ascent of the news building. We quickly rose above the twisted concrete jungle that joined all the buildings in downtown. To my right, Derek cleared his throat. "So you could lose. That's gotta make you nervous, right?"

I exhaled through my nose. Was he concerned, or just trying to get a rise out of me? The elevator overlooked the roofs of downtown's high-rises. It was the first time I had ever seen the full scale of Sulmar City's sprawl. It went on and on, merging into smaller towns, falling away only by the horizon. There had been a time when patches of farmland split up the city, now there was nowhere to catch your breath, just businesses and homes and roads as far as the eye could see. Derek's hand touched my shoulder. I turned to him and spoke sharply, "When I lose a game of LINE, it's because I made a mistake. Either

I overlooked an attack, or I didn't spend long enough calculating, or maybe I underestimated my opponent. In all those cases, my failure is my own. There's room for improvement. Not today. I can play perfectly today and still lose. And that's a bit freeing. As long as I don't make a mistake, I can go home proud of my efforts." I tilted my head toward Derek. "So no, I'm not nervous."

Derek pulled out his screen and stayed quiet for the rest of the way up. Maybe he really was just trying to connect with me. The elevator stopped on floor forty-one. Its doors opened to a mundane hallway with yellowing walls. We stepped out onto the faded carpet, worn by decades of use. A young man in a dark-blue shirt and pants labelled 'page' approached us from down the hall.

"Mr. Solinsen?"

"Just Zouk is fine."

"Zouk, your room is ready, please follow me."

The page led us down the hall and deeper into the building. Every so often, I'd trip on a prop left from another show or catch a famous face in a dressing room, but the page stayed focused on getting me and Derek to our destination. "This is the green room."

He pointed us into a small white room. There was barely room for the three-person couch and a coffee table. I took a seat on the too-smooth blue couch and Derek made for the remote on the table. The page stayed near the doorway. "I'll pick you up when it's time. Our cameras stream straight to the wall screen. Let me know if you need anything."

Derek fumbled with the remote until the wall lit up with the view of the tournament set. The layout was a bit like a big multi-tier metal cake, with a LINE board and two backless seats at the top. They hadn't changed a thing since the tournament began a little over a year ago. Nine hundred some-odd players had sat up there, stuck in those red half-sphere stools that served form more than function. Influence had sent all but two of them.

"Where's the audience?" I asked.

Derek dropped the remote on the coffee table. "No one watches the first round of the tournament anymore, man. It's all screens now."

A little disappointment settled into my shoulders. If I had known there wouldn't be an audience two weeks ago, I would have been thrilled. But I had been prepping for it and now it felt like a bit of a let down. Just a curved black screen surrounding the set.

Derek patted my shoulder. "They're still broadcasting it, and if you start winning, they might upgrade you to primetime. And if you get lonely, me and a few members of the research team are gonna be downstairs watching the whole game. Usually they superimpose guests of the player into the audience, so keep an eye out!" Derek turned to the door.

"You're going?" I half stood as I spoke.

"I have a few people up here I want to catch up with, plus I gotta pee. Number Eight, it's been a pleasure." Derek headed down the hall in the wrong direction. He'd figure it out.

I spent a few minutes scrounging the green room for a LINE board, none turned up. Probably for the best, I wasn't supposed to practice unless it was on one of Jamie's 'encrypted' boards anyway, she'd kill me if Influence got a hold of my moves before the game. On the wall, footage of the set was replaced by the smiling, charismatic face of the Mind of Communications and Influence. His hair was slicked back and styled perfectly as always. Today he was wearing athletic gear, as if he'd need to run a marathon in the middle of the game. The camera zoomed out and revealed he was walking somewhere, down some ash-wood hall I had never seen.

"Nearly one thousand players have thrown down the gauntlet. Among the many, two have risen above the crowd. Today I will be facing a pro-turned-teacher with over a decade of experience and we'll find out if he has the talent to take the win."

I folded my legs up onto the couch. Influence was talking about me, but he made me sound so much more impressive than I was. Influence stopped next to a picture of a younger me holding a trophy high above my head. That was the one they always used, my eyes were a little too open and I looked kind of crazy.

"This is Zouk Solinsen. Almost a year ago, this underrated fighter defeated Bergamaschi and ended the world champion's latest winning streak." The portrait was replaced with an image of Bergmaschi's head in his hands, sitting across from me. "We haven't heard much of Zouk since. Was it a fluke, or evidence of future potential?" My mouth couldn't seem to close. Here was my career, shown in stark detail to the world. And by Influence, no less. The guy used to dominate the airwaves, but these days he only showed up for investigative segments, specials, and LINE games.

Influence continued his walk, and the comfortable library was replaced by the eggshell-white interior of a museum. All along the way were 'art pieces'. First was twelve-year-old me holding a trophy as big as I was, *Zouk Solinsen Wins the National Open*. My big break. Next came a video, *Prodigy Qualifies for the World Finals*. I was an older teen, standing in a line with fifteen of the best players in the world. If you looked close, you could see my hands shaking so much I could barely hold the sheet with my player number on it. I did pretty well for a teen.

Influence paused at a set of news clippings, *Young Upstart Breaks the Top Ten*. Yolniv was with me this time, twenty-three felt like half a lifetime ago.

"Three years ago, Zouk was crushing the best players in the world left and right. Climbing the ranks all the way to number eight." I winced a little at Derek's nickname.

"His standout achievement? The Premier Open. He fell to the loser's basket in the third round. A single loss would drop him from the tournament. Zouk had no room for error. He pushed through thirteen rounds of brutal play, eliminating the best in the world in relentless pursuit of victory."

I rubbed at my arm. They made it sound so heroic. It helped when the other players kept throwing away their chances. Down the hall, I could hear murmurs and footsteps, but nothing would distract me from this once-in-a-lifetime program. On-screen, the gallery hall ended in a final exhibit. A rotating 3D hologram of me poised to make a move against Bergamaschi.

"So who is Zouk Solinsen? Is he a washout, wringing out the last few drops of genius? Or has he just been unlucky, and today's the day we witness his resurgence?" The walls of the museum fell away. I should have realized sooner it was all computer generated. A chair floated in from nowhere and Influence took a seat. "If he wins, that would put Zouk in an exclusive club of the best of the best. I had a chance to speak to Zouk earlier today, let's take a look."

The footage cut to a shot of me and Influence in my living room. "Huh?" My brow furrowed and I leaned in to look closer. Influence hadn't been there. It had just been a camera crew and a woman with a clipboard asking questions. He looked so real.

A shadow blocked the light from the hall. "May I join you?"

His voice sounded almost like an echo. The same man as on the TV stood at the entrance to the green room. Influence looked just like he did on TV. Perfectly styled hair, black athletic shirt and briefs, and his face still carried that signature smile.

"—Of course." It took me a second to find the words. Influence plopped himself down on the couch next to me. I sat still and quiet, hands in my lap. Were we supposed to be talking about something? On-screen, I answered a question about my career and the footage cut to Influence nodding thoughtfully.

"Normally we don't fake it like this, but you did such a good job keeping your eyeline steady the team realized it wouldn't be hard to drop me in there."

Even in person, his voice had that deep newsman timber. I gave no response, I wasn't sure what to say and didn't want to embarrass myself before the game. The man was an icon figure, more than that, he was powerful. He—it, whatever a Mind was—left me starstruck. I couldn't even bring myself to adjust my seat in fear of offending him.

The on-screen Zouk answered some questions about his upbringing. "Good answers too. You gave us a lot to work with, but kept it brief."

I gave him a weak smile and he turned his body towards me. "Sometimes with these LINE players, they mumble their way through it or they go on and on and on and we have to cut it up to make them look good in post. Smart cookies. But man they could use a little speech training–Ah! This is my favorite part."

Influence leaned in towards the screen. His on-screen doppelgänger looked at the ceiling thoughtfully, then asked, "Now Zouk, no one's ever made it to the end of the tournament, but you and I know what's waiting if you win. So tell me, why do you want to be on the council?"

The me on-screen was quiet for a moment, thinking of an answer. I couldn't help but cringe a little hearing myself speak. "You know, if I can be honest, I'm not sure how driven I am to be part of the government. All that legislation and budget control just sounds like a headache."

On-screen, I laughed a little, and the camera cut to Influence nodding. Then I continued, "I want to bring my community back. When the Unified Activity Manager came out, we all got so busy. I teach these days. And let me tell you, even the eight-year-olds are working full-time jobs now. Maybe it's a small reason to take on the Minds, but really I just want to enjoy the game again. When I was young, I used to love exploring dumb strategies with my friends, messing around even if it meant I wasn't getting any better. We've lost that."

I closed my eyes to the interview. It was a naively optimistic answer.

"Exceptional. Really exceptional." To my left, Influence was enraptured.

"I think it was too much," I muttered.

Influence frowned, then put his hands on the couch and leaned in towards me. His eye apertures were like oceans in the night, deep and pitch black. "You know, most players say they dream of remaking our nation. Building it back from the ground up. But you chose something personal, a change that meant something to you and your life." There was a long pause. Influence's gaze was weighty, like a hundred pounds pressing in on my body. After a time, he exhaled and his eyes seemed to soften. "It was a good answer, sincerity is in short supply these days."

Finally, Influence broke away and got to his feet. As he took a step towards the door, a question jumped into my mind, one just for Influence that I had thought about for years. "Didn't you use to look older?"

Influence stopped and looked back at me. "I did."

There was something almost forlorn about the way he answered. "Your hair used to be grey, right?"

He touched his hair, gelled to near immobility. "Salt and pepper."

I knew it, when I was a kid I remembered it being almost grey. He looked distinguished, and wizened, not like the sharp young newsman of today. "I think I preferred it that way."

He nodded. "So did I. But a younger me got better numbers, so my team 'refreshed' the look."

Influence swayed out the door. Past the doorframe, he leaned back to speak again. This time with a deeper, sadder voice. ""Good luck kid, hope you don't disappoint—I really do."

A couple minutes later, the live interview faded out. A swell of brass instruments boomed through the wall-screen. The live stream of the arena began. This time the stage was lit up by hundreds of moving blue and gold lights, all coordinated to give the place a cinematic feel. Behind it, the long, curved screen now projected a cheering audience.

"Mr. Solinsen, it's time."

I took a deep breath, stood up, and followed the page down the hall towards the sound of applause and music. Influence stood halfway up the multi-tier stage and gave his standard introduction. I was really here, I was really gonna play. There was a tingling in my fingers.

"Go! Onstage!"

I started walking. Influence shook my hand from the third stair, then walked to the top. I took my time on every step. All my confidence had vanished, I wasn't even sure I could climb the platform without tripping. At the top, I shook out my arms and scanned the audience. Up close, the smiles were a little too wide, and the applause a little too uniform, and the curved screen warped their faces at odd angles. All calibrated for the cameras. Down on the front row, a real Derek was clapping along with the rest of them.

"Have a seat."

Influence directed me towards my half-shell chair. It was surreal being here, the same place a thousand other LINE players had already failed. I had watched at least a hundred of them. Influence looked so different from the man in the green room. Charm, excitement, and sharp intellect was all that was visible.

"Zouk, are you ready to begin?" A music behind me thrummed, keeping a heavy tension.

"I am."

There was a big show of light and sound. The faux audience cheered. A holographic separator rose up between us, and the LINE board lit up on-screen. A timer appeared in the corner and started counting down. The piped-in sounds of music and audience slowly faded to silence. To the world, this was a match in front of a thousand excited viewers, but to me and Influence, it was one-on-one.

Ninety-three turns, six hundred forty-eight moves. That's all I needed.

Move one, wall on E4. In the warped image of a crowd, Derek cupped his hands and shouted something. I don't think he knew he was muted.

There were a near-infinite number of ways for your opponent to start their game, but we were betting on Influence doing exactly what he was supposed to—starting with a wall. Any change, any variation, meant the whole game was a wash and I'd be sent home in less than forty turns. The timer counted down thirty seconds, and Influence made his first move.

A wall on E10. I let out a sigh of relief. We were on track. Six-hundred forty-six moves to go.

The early game was easy to remember, troops were too far away to fight, so all I had to do was build my base. Each time I made a move, Influence would take precisely thirty seconds. He never deviated from the moves in training. It was just like we had practiced.

Like a slow tide, the Elephant's Tail crept across the board. Right on time, Influence lined his pieces up for an attack. I rubbed my thumb and forefinger together. We were out of the intro. From now on, most units would move on every single turn. Precision would be essential, one misplaced squadron and the game changes under my feet.

Influence's forces charged as one, bashing against my base's right flank. The front walls crumbled and he pressed further inside. With each move, my squadrons would fire, then withdraw, delving deeper and deeper into my defenses as Influence pursued. The attack dissolved six tiles from my command post. It felt good to be on the other side of that kind of failed attack.

Twenty-five moves complete. I leaned back in my chair and stretched my arms. This was the end of the dance's first movement. Every piece, every wall, every enemy squadron was still precisely where they needed to be.

Most of the audience appeared to be fully engaged with the game, but down on the front row, Derek and a few faces I recognized from Jamie's team were chatting to one another, browsing their screens, and generally looking disinterested. That seemed more authentic to watching a ninety-minute game of LINE.

The game descended into the interlude, a long quiet of thirty-three tranquil turns. During practice, I tended to get a little fuzzy here. I needed to bring my troops forward, but not too forward. Stop at E6 and F8, far enough to pressure, but not so much as to draw Influence into another engagement.

The Elephant's Tail inched across the halfway mark.

At move fifty-seven, I paused. My head was suddenly blank. Twelve squadrons needed to be moved, I remembered that much. Eight of them moved forward, that was easy. But the other four . . . My thumb rubbed at my temple. The movements were weird, neither attack nor defense. A purely psychological lateral move that dissuaded Influence from building more squadrons.

The clock read 40:21. Plenty of time. My head craned forward to scrutinize the position. I tried moving all four squadrons to the left, but that didn't look right. Moving to the right didn't work either. Fifty-fifty looked even worse. Each time I tried to imagine the moves, they never quite ended up in the same place.

A question started to creep into my psyche. What if I got it wrong? I controlled just over half the board, but Influence's position was far from hopeless. One slip up and he could easily wrest back control of the game.

On instinct, my body rocked back and forth in that half-sphere egg chair. It was just four moves out of hundreds. When I got things wrong in practice, Jamie had had me play them out until I was either defeated, or victorious. Victory was rare.

A pounding started in my ears. 25:33 left. My memory had failed. There was no other choice. It was time to rediscover the moves from scratch. I started with my most forward squad, Charlie. If they moved forward, Influence would feel threatened. What about left? There's a wall there. To the right? Possibly.

Twenty-five minutes burned down to twelve in no time. All I had was a best guess. Charlie moved to the right, Hotel retreated, Tango forward, and Delta made no move at all. I had my doubts on Delta, but there were still thirty more turns to get through. My fingers input the move and I held my breath.

No attack came in. I blinked away the dryness in my eyes. Was I safe? The next ten moves came in with no drama. The Elephant's Tail crossed the two-third boundary and pressed down on Influence. Everything seemed to be on track. Move seventy-five was Influence's biggest attack. A final lash out in a losing position.

My troops deflected it with ease.

The game was officially in my favor. I took quick, shallow breaths. In the audience, new faces joined Derek and the research team. I didn't recognize them, but they had that halfway-engaged look of a real person. Maybe I had been moved to primetime. Through the holographic separator, Influence stared directly ahead. His expression was the same as it had been when we started, a performative kind of thoughtfulness. Did he know he was losing? How had he taken his other losses? As I watched, Influence's eyes shifted a degree. I sat up straighter in my chair. He wasn't watching the board anymore, he was looking at me.

A couple turns later, the Elephant's Tail reached the top-left corner. All that calmness and tranquility I had arrived with was long gone. I was winning, and there was nothing quite as exciting as winning.

Influence was sequestered to a quarter of the board. My troops lined up at the edges of the base walls and shelled what was left of his base. Each turn, another layer of walls were shedded and Influence's troops retreated another tile. One last engagement, and the game would be over. At this point, even if I got the moves wrong, winning was a certainty.

All at once, the sounds of music and audience flooded back onto the set. The stage lights spun around and the LINE board went black. On the other side of the separator, Influence had swiveled his chair out towards the cameras. I glanced around at the techs and waved my arms in confusion. We still had another eleven turns to go.

The cameras panned from me to Influence. He climbed out of his chair and walked to the platform edge. "Ladies and Gentlemen, you may be somewhat confused. The board is gone, but neither myself nor Mister Solinsen has captured the other's base. As it turns out, very few professional LINE games actually end when they're supposed to. Once a player believes they no longer have a reasonable path to victory, good etiquette dictates that that player resign." Influence took a dramatic breath. I waited with baited breath. "My base is collapsing.

My squadrons are gone, and my opponent controls the board. As such, in the tradition of professional LINE players the world over, I cannot in good conscience drag this game out. Zouk"— turned to me—"I resign."

Cheers filled the studio. My mouth hung open. Had it really been this easy? A historical victory with barely a month of planning. Influence extended his hand. His face shifted in color as lights spun all around us. I leapt out of my chair and rushed to shake it. My chair clattered down the steps behind me. I turned to fix it, but Influence kept his grip tight. He had a thoughtful expression. We couldn't hear each other, but through the rapidly changing color scheme, I could see him mouth the words, "Well done".

Someone yelled cut, and everything dropped to silence. Influence dropped the handshake and a page led me down the steps, past the fallen chair, out of the studio, and down the hall. The air was electric, all along the way back voices shouted their compliments and congratulations.

I needed to thank Jamie. Her plan had worked perfectly, and I hadn't even needed the last eleven turns.

My body was energized in a way I had never felt after a LINE game. Maybe it's because I hadn't had to spend most of it calculating moves, but for once my head didn't feel like it had been run over, and my legs were ready for a jog.

The page turned and led me into a line of cameras. Ezra, the short blonde fireball and face of the National News, approached with a microphone. "Zouk Solinsen, you just became the third-ever player to win a game in the directive tournament. How are you feeling?"

I stared off into space for a moment. My head was going in a hundred different directions. Did Influence know my strategy? Had I somehow cheated? How would I win the next one? Would the crowds hate me if I lost? Surely, performing as well as the world champion was enough.

At some point my mouth start moving. "I'm sorry, Ezra, I'm still trying to get my thoughts together. Uhhh—I am feeling very good right now, the game was extremely difficult, and I'm just glad things worked out in my favor." Bad answer. I knew it even before I stopped talking.

"A lot of experts were surprised with your strategy today. Can you tell us a bit about it?"

Experts. How many people had watched my game? I talked a little about the Elephant's Tail but kept things vague. It was a bad idea to give too much away. LINE pros loved watching interviews to learn their opponent's mindset. Ezra pivoted to asking me about my prep process, my coaching team, and why I had chosen to play now. My answers were all bland, I didn't dare give too much detail. Plus, half my head was still processing the victory.

"Do you have plans for your next game?" Ezra asked.

"No—uhhhh, I wasn't sure I was gonna win this one."

"I see. Congratulations again on the win." Ezra turned to address the camera and the page led me out and down to the first floor, where Derek and a small crowd were waiting. They must have rushed out when they realized I was on course to win my game. Before I could address them, Derek gripped my shoulders and guided me past the gathering to the front doors. "Sorry man, there's way more people outside. We've gotta get you out of here before you get stuck taking photos for the next six hours."

Derek wasn't exaggerating. There must have been two to three hundred people waiting outside. When they saw me, they exploded into cheers and applause. I ignored the screen in my pocket that was buzzing incessantly, no telling how many notifications were waiting for me.

The size and passion of the crowd was overwhelming. I shook a hand here or there, said a few hellos to folks I had never seen before, but Derek kept me moving. When we reached the Individual Transit Vehicle, he pushed me in, shut the door, then took a moment to wave to the crowd before closing his. As soon as we were both on the road, we started a video call.

"Holy crap. Number eight and then some! How's it feel, man?" I rubbed my face and looked out the window at the folks walking next to the ITV and waving. This was crazy. "Feels good," I answered curtly.

"Good? You have a fan club—I wish I had a fan club!" I half chuckled and stared out the window. Some guy in yellow blocked one of the ITV's wheels until he got a photo. I didn't mind the idea of fans, but fans like these may take some practice to get used to.

"That was a close call in the game. Why did you change the move order without telling Jamie?"

My eyebrows scrunched and I turned to Derek. "What do you mean?"

"Move sixty-three, why'd you change it?"

I thought back to that terrible turn, the one that I had spent half the game reinventing. "That wasn't the right move?"

Derek grabbed for a screen on the console. "No. You changed it, look."

I watched the recorded game play out. Move sixty-three played, and my stomach lurched. Of the four units, I had only gotten two right. At least I had been right about Delta not moving at all.

"I couldn't remember the moves, so I just made my own." The more I thought on it, the stranger it seemed. I had gotten it wrong. How had I made it to the end of that game? I felt like I had just had a near-death experience. I got the move wrong, but Influence had still reacted the right way. I shut my eyes and sighed. Now I had something to regret. My skill had failed, and I had gotten lucky.

Derek closed the replay when he saw my expression. "You won though! That's the important thing. This is big. You did it, man! And when you couldn't do it, you improvised your way through it like a champ! Come on, no one becomes the best without a little luck, right?"

"I guess." Our ITVs had reached the highway, far from the news building. I only half listened to what Derek had to say. Most of my mind was orbiting a single thought, I shouldn't have won.

"Remember man, we're not done. You've still got two more games." Two more games. I couldn't even imagine it. Wasn't this enough? Derek and the Torrez Institute seemed to be under the impression I was about to rewrite history.

"And then what?" I stared at Derek with suspicious eyes. He folded his arms and leaned back in the ITV seat, he looked oddly pensive. "That's up to you. Maya's gonna want to have a talk before you get much further—You'll like her, she's not a big fan of how the Minds operate either." He took a second to look out at the speeding highway. "My thoughts, though. If you win those games, the world will be yours to shape."

We rode the rest of the way to my apartment in silence. Derek sounded almost wistful about the idea of changing the world. To me, the idea of all that power, of all those eyes on me, it was terrifying.

PART
TWO

8 - MISCOMMUNICATION

RANK: 80 ▲16

I paced back and forth. Around the oversized couch, past the mismatched chairs, across the door, and back to the curtain. My hand lifted the fabric slightly so I could glance outside. We had to keep the curtains closed ever since the cameras started making the rounds. No reporters today, just an empty sidewalk. How could Jamie do this? Five days from my game against The Mind of Strategy and Warfare— and no plan. My head was clouded, filled to the brim with frustration and anger. There was a creak behind me, Kira was on the bottom step of the stairs.

"She's still not here?"

I shook my head. Already an hour late and no message. Who did she think she was? I spent three weeks speaking at podcasts, news shows, any interview Jamie could find and she couldn't even be bothered to show up to a single appointment on time. I paced another lap.

"Can I listen in?" Kira asked.

I gestured to the couch. It was a good idea, Kira could probably sense the storm I was brewing. I paced another couple laps, then sat down next to her. We held hands for twenty minutes before the front door chimed.

"Your guest has arrived."

I put on the best smile I could manage and threw open the door. Jamie marched straight inside carrying a thick laptop. She stopped next to the red, high-back chair and paused. "Does she need to be here for this?" Kira pulled her legs up under her body. I gave Jamie a scalding look, she was already on my nerves.

"—She works for the government, Zouk. Do you really want to risk letting her hear this?"

I walked slowly around the coffee table and sat down on the couch. My hand went to Kira's knee. With all the hostility, she probably wouldn't say much tonight.

"Kira helped me memorize the moves for the first game. You have your team, I have mine. Did you bring a game for me?"

Jamie gave a final glance at Kira, then lowered herself into the red chair. "Before we get to that, Maya wanted me to forward her regrets on being unable to meet with you. She's been traveling for the last month. But she's seen what you have to say and how you conduct yourself. So far she's very happy with it all. She's looking forward to meeting with you next week."

Maya, my silent benefactor. Regardless of my frustrations with Jamie, I did owe Maya a lot. But a week from now seemed odd. "After the game?"

"That's right."

I shrugged. That seemed the way of things with Jamie. No heads up, no warning, just one sentence informing me I was scheduled for three interviews tomorrow morning. I didn't mind talking about my game against Influence, but all it was doing was driving hype. More hype wouldn't help me win the game, the interviews were increasingly feeling like essential time thrown in the trash.

"You haven't given me much time to practice."

"You don't need more time than that."

I straightened my back, and considered telling Jamie exactly what kind of time I needed. Kira put her hand on mine and squeezed. I leaned back into the couch. It could wait until I knew the plan.

"We aren't prepping for some regional tournament, it's the Mind of Strategy and Warfare," I spat.

"I know. It doesn't matter." Jamie opened her laptop and turned the screen towards me. The dim-blue LINE grid was waiting. Even now, with all my frustrations, I was eager to see the game. My eyes flicked to Jamie's. She beamed with excitement.

"Hit play. All you need to do is memorize it, just like last time." I hesitated. Another memorization game? I tapped the screen. Kira gripped my hand a little tighter as walls and squadrons slid out onto the board.

Her strategy had my troops pushing along the left side, and leaving space for War to push along the right. The Dueling Spires. Not a common strategy. I watched for the moment of collapse, the turn when both spires stopped their forward charge and struck out at one another. But it never came. Jamie's squadrons passed the three-quarters mark on the board, and still didn't stop. It was a relentless, reckless charge all the way to the other side. War's pieces stayed focused, firing at stray squadrons and securing their position. One of 'my' squadrons touched the top of the board, and the game suddenly stopped. I tapped the screen, but that was it, no more moves. Jamie watched me expectantly. My eyes swept across the position again. I was losing on every front, an unequivocal defeat. "I don't get it."

Jamie cupped her chin in her hands. Her eyes darted left and right, as if she was worried someone was listening. "We found a blindspot," she whispered.

"What?" I asked.

"A blindspot, a part of the board War doesn't see, or at least doesn't evaluate properly."

I shook my head. "War's the best player there is. How— Why— It's not possible."

Jamie grinned an impish grin. "Maybe War's too good at attacking for their own good. Can't see a piece that's right in front of them—" She saw my incredulous look. "I didn't believe it at first either. We spent a long time looking. War has played more games than anyone, all publicly available. Turns out War never reacts to pieces placed at the top of the board between columns D and H."

I looked over at Kira, her eyes were wide. She wanted evidence. "Do you have the data?" I asked.

Jamie switched the screen over to a series of historical games. "Not many games. It's pretty rare for a player to reach the top row of the board." As soon as Jamie turned the screen back, Kira was knee-deep in analysis. But even if War's fatal flaw was real, I still had questions.

"You mentioned memorizing the game. War doesn't play like Influence. How can we be sure the moves will work?"

Jamie brought her hands up behind her head and leaned back in her chair. "Because the moves are bad."

Kira paused her typing, we shared a look. Jamie began again, "Look, in a complex game between two good players, the 'best' move is often up for debate. If we played like that, there would be no way of knowing War's next move. But in a noncompetitive game, a game where one person is losing decisively, there's only one 'best' move. Exploit your opponent's weakness. I'm giving you bad moves so we can rely on War to make the good ones."

Jamie looked pleased with herself. She was probably right, but making bad moves was risky. "If War figures out what I'm doing, those moves are gonna make me look like an amateur."

Jamie waved her hand dismissively. "You're already on hallowed ground from beating Influence. No one expects you to win again."

Easy for her, she wouldn't be making bad moves in front of all her peers. I crossed my arms. "So imagine your plan works, what happens next? What happens when I reach the blindspot?"

"You take the advantage I've given you and win the game."

I gave Jamie a long, hard stare. Improvise. She was asking me to improvise against the best LINE player ever.

"Come on, Zouk, we both saw how Influence fell apart. They're just machines, we can beat them."

I stood, shuffled past the coffee table, walked to the window and pushed open the curtain. My fingers touched the cold glass. Did Jamie really think I could memorize the moves and prepare some improvised victory in five days? Was it ego, or overconfidence? Could I do it in the first place? I turned back to the living room. Boards flashed across Kira's glasses—still caught up in her research. She'd be like that half the night.

"Okay, I'll make it work. Should we talk about the fact that this game is being played on a field?"

Jamie shrugged. "Board. Field. It's all the same. There might be a tiny difference, but the troops on the field are professional soldiers. You just play the game I gave you."

I grabbed the string that controlled the blinds and ran my fingers over the knot. Again with the dismissal. She was acting like all this was par for the course rather than the third-ever game of its kind. I thought back to the two live LINE games. There was weather, crowds, time for soldiers to walk off the field—a hundred factors I had never dealt with in my career. "It's not that easy, Jamie. Bergamaschi failed here. So did Otso. I thought he was your guy, what happened there?"

Jamie stood from her chair and sighed. "It was a disaster. I gave him a hundred tools to fight War. Nothing like this, but a workable strategy for a champion-tier player. Once real human beings were involved, he stopped thinking like a LINE player. He ignored every bit of good sense in his head and played 'according to his heart'." Jamie gripped the top of her chair and looked me in the eye. "Learn the plan and stick to it. There's a lot of research behind those moves."

We stood in silence for a moment, then Jamie headed for the door. I turned the knob numbly and pushed it open. From the frame, Jamie cast a final appraising eye on my living room. "We need to upgrade your setup. Once you win, I'll have a team over here to remodel the whole place."

Kira looked my way with worried eyes. If we left it up to Jamie, a dozen contractors would rip the place to pieces. "No thanks, Jamie, we value our peace too much for that."

Before Jamie could turn away, Kira's voice sputtered from the couch. "Don't forget the lecture."

I looked back at Jamie, she looked eager to leave. "That's right. I've done your interviews, made appearances, played in a tournament—"

"Fourth place, not a great performance. Did Yolniv help you?"

"He doesn't coach me anymore." There was a pause. "—So what about the lecture? When can I give it?"

Jamie pursed her lips. "Let's go with next week—same day you meet Maya."

"Good enough." Jamie headed for the ITV idling next to the curb. Once it was gone, I shut the door and turned to Kira. She was hunched forward, face lit up by the laptop screen, scrolling through game after game. "Is it real? Is Jamie right?"

Kira didn't even look away from the screen. "It's a weakness."

I leaned against the door and took a deep breath. A weakness was just the start, I still needed to figure out how to win.

9 - ZOUK V THE MIND OF STRATEGY AND WARFARE

RANK: 76 ▲ 4

Derek and I met at the steps to Fenner Stadium. Apartment buildings and skyscrapers boxed it in on all sides. My hands were ice as we passed through security. I tried pumping them, but each squeeze was limp and weak. We walked straight to the basement. Derek raved about the locker room. I missed most of it, apparently it was used by some top-notch athletes. Sounds and thoughts came in slowly, like they were piercing a wall of molasses.

The locker room was impressive. The fountains looked inviting, the showers were luxurious, every corner was spotless, and it was all sized for a team of thirty.

"When do I get to meet my squadrons?" I asked.

"Once you're playing. Let's get a preview of the field," Derek said.

I didn't have the strength to voice my disagreement, so we walked down to the tunnel's edge and surveyed the expanse. It was all just as it had been for Bergamaschi and Otso. The commander's platforms were a pair of forty-foot lumber mammoths, lined by soldiers. The grid was a square of light projected down onto the field. A pile of white-grey metal panels were stacked up on the north and south side. Once they were placed, a wall of styrofoamy material would spring up from the mechanisms, weak enough to collapse after a few shots.

I leaned against the tunnel's concrete edge as numbness crept up my arms. The bleachers were extensive. Thirty-thousand seats circled the field. Row upon row of plastic chairs climbed hundreds of feet into the air. Derek was still going on about the place, but I couldn't stand it another second.

"I'm taking a shower."

***

The tile sent a cold chill across my back. The shower had shut off ages ago, but I still sat against the wall, knees pulled to my chest. Each breath was a labor, my head a hurricane. A mess of LINE moves mixed with images of the tens of thousands waiting in the stadium. A door slammed open and I heard a pair of footsteps.

"Number Eight, you ready? We got ten minutes, man."

Unmistakably Derek. I gave no response, focusing instead on the gentle sway of the thin white curtain. After a few seconds of silence, someone else shouted.

"Zouk?" The voice was much older, sounded like Yolniv. How long had I been in here?

"I'm here!"

Shoes slapped on the tile, headed in my direction. I made no move, my head was still swimming. Yolniv threw open the curtain, but Derek was close behind. I realized that at some point I had taken off my clothes.

"Woah—Hey! You relaxing in here?"

Yolniv threw Derek a side-eye. "Get him some pants, some water, and something he can chew." Yolniv was almost commanding. He had seen me like this before.

Derek gripped the curtain. "What about the game?"

"Tell them he'll be a few minutes late." Derek sped off, Yolniv stepped into the shower and leaned against the wall. I was hit by a gentle, freezing breeze. His large hand touched my shoulder.

"It's been a while since we did this." I blinked a few times to clear my head.

"I can't stand up."

"Mmm-hmm. How's the noggin?" Yolniv asked.

"Not great."

He stayed quiet after that, listening to Derek's scuttling footsteps. The muggy feeling in my head was starting to fade. Derek showed up with snacks, pants, towels, and six different sugar-water varieties. Yolniv took the pair of corduroy pants and handed them to me. They were as wide as my shoulders, I wondered which locker Derek had stolen them from.

Yolniv gave me some privacy as I pulled the pair over my legs. Derek helped me to a bench in the main locker room. As soon as I was seated, Derek dumped a handful of snacks next to me and ran out the door to buy us time. I opened a packet of crackers, feeling was starting to come back to my hands.

"So . . . How are you feeling about the game?" Yolniv asked.

"I'm gonna play it."

His brow furrowed. "That's not what I asked. How are you feeling about the game?" I thought back on the last five days. Every waking moment had been dedicated to prep. Memorizing moves, prepping contingencies, analyzing positions. A nonstop rush, trying to make the best of what Jamie had given me.

"The moves are bad, the strategy is crazy, and there's a lot of guesswork going on behind the scenes. But I can handle all that, it's the crowds. It all hit me at once, I didn't think about how many—and if I fail . . ." Yolniv nodded slowly, and walked to one of the lockers across from me.

"Failure never stopped you before. And I seriously doubt you could do worse than Otso."

I laughed weakly, that had been a disappointing day. "Depends on how bad my moves are."

"Maybe— Lately I've started to wonder about good moves and bad moves." Yolniv rubbed his ear. "But enough of that, so you say you're going to disappoint everyone?"

I looked at him with a curious expression. "It's a distinct possibility."

"Then get up there and get it over with! I have to cast this game and I'd like to go home early. Don't drag it out, the only thing worse than a disappointed crowd is a bored and disappointed crowd."

Yolniv looked completely serious, but I knew him too well. My lips grinned a little as I spoke. "Maybe I should go out there as-is, topless and commando."

"Good idea! The chill will keep you making fast moves!"

I chuckled and Yolniv's stone-faced expression started to crack. My head was finally clear, not a hundred percent, but clear. I finished my cracker, and pulled myself up. My legs shook, but they held. I swapped out the corduroys for dress pants, a button-up shirt, and a light-blue jacket that hung next to the shower. As I buttoned the final buttons, Derek charged in and grabbed my arms.

"Please tell me you can play." His eyes were wide and his chest rose and fell rapidly. He had probably circled the whole stadium buying us time.

"I'm playing." Derek fell back onto the bench and covered his face with his hands. Behind him, Yolniv headed for the exit.

"Good luck! I'll be in the livestream room telling the whole world what a disappointment you are." He paused at the threshold. "Ah, and Bergamaschi sends you his best." Before I could respond, the old man was gone and Derek was pushing me towards the tunnel.

The size and sounds of the audience were staggering. Every seat was filled. There were so many faces my eyes couldn't focus on any single one. Yolniv's advice popped into my head, the quicker the disappointment, the better the experience. We walked to the foot of the commander's platform, Derek was waved away and a soldier led me up a spiraling ramp.

Another soldier, a man with sharp eyes, short blond hair, and a blue stripe down his arm, met me at the top.

"This is yours, Mr. Solinsen." He handed me a screen that showed the field from a top-down position. There were controls to input moves and end turn, everything I needed. "Did Derek explain how things work here?" I shook my head.

"I met Derek and a few members of his organization the last time they got this far—that was a short night." The soldier cracked a grin. "I'm Lieutenant Denvers. After you input your commands in your screen, I relay the orders down to the squadrons on the field. Same is true of the other side. Follow me."

We walked to the platform's edge. Across the field was the second commander's platform, identical to mine except for the massive industrial cube occupying the top. War. The words 'Di-Cerebral Enterprises' were molded into the side. A myriad of thick cables ran in every direction. Armed soldiers were stationed at each of the platform's corners.

To War's left, a single pair of hardened eyes met mine. I swallowed. He was the only unarmed man on the platform, and his flashy uniform was unmistakable.

"Why is the secretary general here?" I asked.

"It's in the Constitution. 'Man will not fight man, except under the orders of other men'. Even in a game."

I knew the amendment Denvers was quoting, at least as well as I remembered it in history class. The first invasion Iom faced under War's leadership. Turned out orders from Minds had a negative effect on morale when compared to orders from people. The constitution was changed in less than a week and the position of secretary general was created.

"There's not really a concern for morale here, is there?" I asked.

Denvers let out chuckle. "Morale issues. That's a funny way of saying soldiers weren't following orders. Think for a second, Zouk. If you were handed a tiny note telling you to 'kill everyone on the other side of that river', and you knew it came from some unfeeling hunk of metal, would you follow it?" I stayed silent. If it meant defending my country—

"You wouldn't. Most folks wouldn't. So be happy the general is here. It means the Minds know we don't take orders from them."

There was an intensity to Lieutenant Denvers' voice that unsettled me. An absolute kind of confidence I was unfamiliar with.

A cough echoed through the stadium. On the other platform, the secretary general was holding a microphone. He waited as a hush washed over the crowd.

Thirty thousand eyes were focused entirely on us. An ocean of humanity, and so many more watching from home. Most wouldn't understand the game, some wouldn't even know the rules. But I needed to play my best.

I remembered back when I had been in that audience, watching Bergamaschi. The clouds were drizzling and most folks were zipped up with jackets and personal heaters. The champion made his fatal slipup. He realized it instantly, you could see it on the footage. It took three turns for the best of us to realize what had happened, and another half hour for his failure to be truly comprehended by the crowd. Now it was my turn, and I had just as many people watching.

"Squadrons! Into position!" The secretary general's voice was scratchy, but carried the unmistakable martial edge. From the tunnels, hundreds of feet marched in perfect synchronization. Men and women flooded the field, all dressed in red and blue uniforms. A pit formed in my stomach. These were the people executing my orders. My bad orders. The columns divided, and troops lined up along the top and bottom of the board.

"Ladies and Gentlemen!" the general began.

"I and The Mind of Strategy and War thank you for your attendance to this exhibition match. Per Directive Two-One-Four-Nine, officers selected from our country's armed services will be engaging in a battle simulation defined by the LINE Assemblage Rulebook. We welcome the challenger, Zouk Solinsen, who has already taken one victory against The Mind of Communications and Influence." There was a scattering of applause in the stands. The general turned, and marched to a monitor installed at the corner. The pit in my stomach quietly churned.

A pair of timers appeared on the stadium scoreboard. "For the benefit of the players and participating squadrons, we ask all members of the audience to remain quiet throughout the game's proceedings. Mind of Strategy and Warfare, are you ready?"

"Yes." War's voice came through heavy and metallic.

"Zouk Solinson, are you ready?"

I looked briefly for a microphone, but there didn't seem to be one. My back straightened and I shouted, "Ready."

"Then we begin."

On my screen and on the jumbotron above the field, the timer started ticking. I scrambled to input my first move. It took a second to get a grasp of dragging on the handheld screen. As soon as the move was ready, I hit 'Submit'. My time stopped and Lieutenant Denvers put a finger to his ear. "Construction Unit A, wall at G5:G6."

The secretary general did the same for War's order. When both stopped speaking, a loud echoing gong played through the stadium. Two blue soldiers grabbed a white-grey panel and carried it out to the G5:G6 line. They placed it quickly, tapped a small button on the panel's side, and stepped back. A half-inch thick wall expanded into place. The walls weren't much stronger than drywall and tended to crumble under pressure, as close an emulation as there could be for the game. As soon as they were confident it was standing, the builders evacuated the field. A second gong played, and the timers resumed.

A brand new wall sat right where War always put it, G9:G10. I shook out the tension in my hand and played on. The early game was just as Jamie had planned. Make terrible moves and ensure War exploits them. I could already hear what Yolniv was saying in the caster's room. "An unconventional start for Mr. Solinsen." Code for a bad move.

By move twenty-three, both sides had deployed nine squadrons to the board. Their uniforms were heavily padded and every one carried a large, launcher-type weapon in their hands. I wasn't looking forward to seeing them used.

The Dueling Spires stretched slowly up and down the board. I controlled the left, War the right. It was strange how much slower a game of LINE was when everything had to be done manually, it gave the game a heaviness I wasn't used to.

The sun began its evening descent and the wind started to pick up. At move twenty-eight, I paused to zip up my jacket. Mine and War's armies stood four tiles from another, maybe forty feet apart. There was no going back after this. I took a deep breath and input the order. Denvers glanced at it and pressed a finger to his ear. "Blue troops, prepare for combat."

The blue soldiers clicked off the safeties on their weapons and started eyeing targets based on Denvers' direction. War's troops hurried to do the same, even before they had gotten their orders. No one wanted to be the one caught off guard. I pressed my hair back against my head. Every soldier in the field was within range of the enemy. At last, the secretary general finished relaying his orders. People were about to be removed from the field.

The gong played and the field exploded into action. Soldiers took aim and fired across the blue-red dividing line. With every trigger pulled, dark black balls shot through the air. They struck bodies with audible thuds and embedded themselves into the game's soft walls. Troops on the sidelines took cover from the missed shots peppering the stadium. Then it stopped. The turn only lasted ten seconds and each soldier fired twice, but it had felt like forever.

Red and blue troops limped off the field, clutching their sides, catching their breath. The blood drained from my face. Clearly those black rubber balls hurt. I saw now why Derek hadn't introduced me to the team. If things went according to plan, everyone would be hit sooner or later.

When the field was clear, the timer resumed and I assessed the damages. It wasn't quite how things had gone in the simulation. Some squadrons had taken more hits, some less. Hopefully it'd be close enough and we could stay on track. That was the real advantage of terrible moves, it ensured even the chaos of reality couldn't change the plan.

I drew my finger up to order the next attack, and hesitated. Was I really about to order three squadrons into an impenetrable position? Sure it would slow War's momentum and buy us a few more turns, but was it justified? Twelve blue soldiers stood near the center line, waiting for orders. If the plan failed, they'd be injured for nothing. I suddenly understood why Otso had made so many mistakes.

Three minutes passed in a game where every second counted. I swallowed down the disgust in my throat and submitted the order.

"Squadrons Echo, Foxtrot, and Hotel. Proceed right and fire on the enemy."

The three sacrificial squadrons glanced between one another. A line of walls and weapons stared them down. Their fate was obvious. I held my breath, clenched my jaw, and waited.

The gong played. My squadrons charged, firing hopelessly at any target in sight. War's troops leaned out from behind cover and took aim at the mob. Squadron Echo's front man was struck in the shoulder and thrown to the ground. Two seconds later, a projectile struck one of Foxtrot's boys. The kid leaned forward to try to catch his breath. Another shot nailed his knee and dropped him into the grass. The rest of the troops caught on quick. If you were hit, get on the ground, then feel the pain.

When the turn was up, ten walked off the field, and two were carried. All they had to show for it was a couple holes in a wall and some broken plaster.

My hands trembled, there was a pulsing in my ears. This was just the beginning. The next move was another charge, this time to pull War's forces from the front line. There was still an imprint on the field where a soldier's face had been. Could I really keep doing this? I dropped my arms to my side. To my right, footsteps approached.

"Hey, don't worry about them. They've been through worse." Lieutenant Denvers looked out at the field with a smirk.

"I can't do this," I muttered.

"Sure you can. They knew what they were signing up for. Most of our simulations use electric pulses to take you down, hurts for days. All these folks get are a few bruises."

Off field, a few troops limped their way into the stadium tunnel, I suspected Denvers was downplaying things. Denvers shook my shoulder. "Don't hold back. War won't. Someone's gotta tear the circuits outta these oversized calculators, right?"

"Yeah." I wasn't convinced, but the pulsing in my ears was fading. After a moment, Denvers let go and walked back to his position on the corner of the platform.

My stomach was still tight. The man was more right than wrong. The clock read 43:18, I had wasted a quarter of my time on conscience. This was the strategy. It would be worse to change things now. Slowly, I raised the screen back to my chest and ordered another charge.

The audience applauded the next display of violence, as if that was the point of the game. I doubted more than a handful even knew what was happening. Somewhere in the stadium's basement, Yolniv was explaining to the audience back home that I was already at a disadvantage. But even the pros didn't know about the blind spot.

Seven moves later, squadrons Alpha, Golf, Delta, and Charlie reached War's edge of the board. A few voices in the crowd cheered very loudly when this happened, probably thinking the game was over. I sat down on the cold wood of the platform to input my next move. This was it, the blind attack. My right flank was crumbling, most of my squadrons were depleted and fatigued. If the blind spot didn't work, War's assault would tear my base to shreds. I'd resign before that happened. I triple-checked my work, then submitted the order.

"Alpha, Golf, Delta, Charlie. Proceed towards center, fire on supporting walls."

Fourteen seconds after my moves were submitted, War submitted theirs. On the other platform, the secretary general brought a finger to his ear, looked out at the field, and stopped. His finger slowly lowered from his ear as he stared down at War's base. Did he see it? Could he interfere? After a moment, the general's finger returned to his ear and began relaying orders.

When the gong played, every inch of the board became a battlefield. War began their attack on my right flank. At the same time, forces in the center fought a losing battle for control. But none of it interested me as much as the four forces marching from the top-left corner of the board towards War's command post.

Twenty-three soldiers left the field that turn. Mostly mine. None of that mattered. War hadn't moved a single troop to defend against my army along the topside. Five tiles to War's command post. The blind spot had worked. I jumped to my feet. This wasn't over yet, War's attack on my right flank was making steady progress. If War detected their mistake and fixed the bug, things would get very messy. I submitted the next order and Denvers' voice echoed my commands. "Alpha, Golf, Delta, Charlie. Press the attack, provide an opening, and eliminate defending reds."

War submitted their orders twenty seconds later. The churning in my stomach had moved from dread to excitement. Across the way, the secretary general hadn't raised a finger to his ear. In fact, for the first time since the game's start, he was moving away from his position. He paced from corner to corner, scanning the field. Eventually his gaze stopped on my infiltration squadron. He might not know LINE, but he knew those squadrons were a threat. The general's eyes jumped briefly to mine, then he brought his finger to his ear.

The gong played. On my right flank, War closed in, collapsing wall after wall in a relentless push towards my base. At the far side, my squadrons tore through War's outer walls. I couldn't believe it, War had done nothing to stop them. Four tiles from the command post. Only a few more turns to victory.

Cheers rose up from the audience. From my perch, I could see people waking each other up, leaning forward, pointing at my northern troops. The crowd was charged. Folks didn't know the game, but everyone could see something was happening. I tapped the back of my screen nervously, Kira and I had prepped about ten contingency plans. But this was the ideal scenario. I had the advantage, I just needed to close it out. My next order was easy, carve through War's base and don't stop moving.

When the gong played, the field was a blur of motion. The tip of War's dueling spire halted their assault and turned towards their base. Everything had. The entire board had turned to face my four squadrons at the top. War had finally realized their error—too late.

Long-range shots were lobbed at the infiltration unit. Delta was eliminated, Charlie barely managed to take cover in War's base, and Alpha and Golf crashed through another wall. Three tiles to the command post.

"You got it, Blue!"

The shout from the stands shook me from my focus. People were on their feet, applauding and cheering and pointing at the hero squadrons. I forced myself back to my screen. Victory was close at hand, but now wasn't the time to get complacent.

With so many of War's troops on the retreat, the defense was easy. Shooting fish in a barrel. It was the infiltration squads that needed my focus. Alpha, Golf, Charlie—eleven soldiers remaining between them. Two tiles, a wall, and eight soldiers were all that was left between them and the heart of War's base.

"Alpha and Golf, fire on the wall dead ahead, use all available shots." I side-eyed Denvers. He was signaling them with his orders, prepping them for the enemy on the other side.

The gong played and Squadron Golf was the first to fire. The wall fell in a cloud of dust. As soon as Golf was out of ammo, they kneeled and Squadron Alpha fired over their heads. The projectiles flew through the dust like raindrops. Two of mine were hit, but everything else was clouded. The turn ended, I leaned out over the edge of the platform, waiting with the rest of the stadium for the cloud to clear.

Three blues limped out of the cloud, half of Squadron Golf. Then came a red, then another. Four more walked out together. The dust floated away with the wind and confirmed my counting. Two reds, seven blues.

I covered my mouth with my hand, and a tear welled up in my eye. The crowd was going mad. War had a better position, more troops, and a stronger strategy, but none of that could fix raw numbers. I tapped in the next round of orders, but my troops really didn't need them.

"Alpha, Charlie, proceed towards enemy command. Eliminate all hostiles." The last two reds barely got a shot off before they were on the ground. War's troops had started firing on their own base, desperate to get to the command post. I didn't even bother giving orders to my defenses.

When the gong played, the last member of the Golf squadron was the one to seize the flag. As soon as it was taken, the crowd began its celebration. Their cheers and applause dwarfed anything I had ever heard. A tension I hadn't realized I was holding drained from my body, and I was awash in emotion. Denvers walked over and slapped me on the back.

From the tunnel, a crowd of blue troops stormed back onto the field. Many of them were limping and clutching their side as they joined with the reserves to mob the Golf squadron. The soldier that had taken the flag was raised onto their shoulders and waved the bold blue as high in the air as she could reach.

A man on the front row hopped the railing and ran in towards the mob. Three more followed, then nine, then a tidal wave. Thousands of people swarmed onto the grass. It was a chaos I had never seen before. Denvers shouted orders into his earpiece and the few armed soldiers on the field moved to block the ramp to the commander's platform. Everywhere I looked, bodies were pressed tight and cheering my name. I should have been flattered, honored by the crowd's passion, but this was scary.

Soldiers and police officers ran out of the tunnels onto the field with weapons drawn. It took nearly twenty minutes to get the crowd off the field. They wouldn't stop cheering my name. Tens of thousands of voices. I waved and applauded and cheered back at them, but inside I was terrified.

At last the crowds were back on the bleachers, and the volume sunk to a dull roar. The secretary general's voice boomed across the field. The man stood front and center on the platform with a stone face.

"Zouk Solinsen's third and final game will be held in ten weeks. Please make your way outside in an orderly manner." As soon as he was done speaking, the general took several steps backward. Both he and War's cube were lowered out of sight. A retreat, not that I could blame them.

Lieutenant Denvers tapped my shoulder and led me off the field. Thousands of hands reached out from the stands. Someone shouted my name, but I didn't look back.

From the tunnels, the muffled sounds of chants and cheers slowly died away. Denvers stopped at the metal door leading to the locker room.

"Holy crap," he said.

I gave an exasperated laugh. "That crowd was wild."

"More than wild. I've worked this stadium dozens of times and I've never seen 'em like that."

I stood a little straighter. "No one's ever beat War before. It's a once-in-LINE-history event."

He chuckled. "That's not it—I mean yeah, you beat the unbeatable. But that's not why things went crazy back there. It's you."

"Me?"

Denvers' dead stare unsettled me. I grasped at the handle to the locker room.

"You're well on your way to having the power to change things, Zouk. That means hope. And God do people get riled up about hope. You're the first politician these people have seen in a generation. Like it or not, you just had your first rally."

A rally. I didn't even want to think about it. I was here to play LINE and build a career. Those crowds just needed time to get used to me, that's all. I threw open the door to the locker room and stepped inside.

"Zouk!" I turned back to Denvers.

"Your voice has power. Ignore me if you want—but figure out what you stand for."

10 - ZOUK SOLINSEN PRESENTS: LINE'S TIMELESS GAMES

RANK: 48 ▲28

The Torrez Institute lecture hall did not disappoint. Fifteen hundred desks fanned out in rising half rings, all turned to face my little desk and the big screen on the wall. I sat at the edge of my swivel chair and swiped through my notes for what must have been the hundredth time. Every move had a page of comments, several annotations. For this presentation to be the kickstart of a career as a LINE instructor, I needed to be the expert.

The instructor's door opened behind me. An old, gruff voice shouted, "Zouk! Ten minutes till doors open."

I swiped back to the start of the presentation. *LINE's Timeless*

Games, Presented by Zouk Solinsen displayed on the back wall. Yolniv's footsteps closed in behind me.

"Is that Grimes v. Herriman?" The old man was leaning over my shoulder now trying to get a good look.

"That's right." Yolniv's face soured. "You don't like it?"

Yolniv hemmed and hawed as he wandered to a seat on the front row. "It's a good game. I just don't think it's suitable."

I tossed the handheld screen onto my desk. This was why I hadn't asked for his help on this in the first place. "Not suitable? This is the game that laid the foundation of modern LINE."

Yolniv raised his hands weakly. "It's a great game, perhaps the greatest. But the folks lining up outside—I don't recognize them. If you're not careful, you may find yourself teaching calculus to kindergarteners." I tilted my head up towards the doorways at the top of the lecture hall. I was hoping for a full room, but novices? I hadn't prepared for those.

Yolniv leaned back and gave a sort of half shrug. I hated when he did that. It meant he knew the right answer, but was perfectly happy to let me get it wrong. I glanced at my handheld and the wall of notes I had prepared. The old man had a strong instinct for these things. "What would you suggest?"

"The Highway Game."

I popped out of my seat. "So you want me to turn this into an intro-level course?"

"Come on! It's fun, it's easy to follow, it's got a nice story." He talked as if pivoting was the easiest thing in the world.

"This series is my new beginning, Yolniv. I don't want to just be the guy that won two games against the Minds, you know? I want to be the expert, the teacher, the guide for future players."

Yolniv eyebrows pulled together. He didn't speak, he just stared. I couldn't tell what was going on in that head. Did he think I couldn't succeed or something? Maybe he was just waiting for me to change my mind.

A clang echoed down from the top ring. Yolniv and I both craned our necks towards the source. Derek's dirty-blond cut emerged over the top row of chairs.

"It's time, can I open the doors?" He paused between words, winded.

"How close are we to full?" I asked.

Derek blinked. "Uh—Full. Well, more than full. We've been turning people away for the last fifteen minutes."

My breath caught. There weren't that many folks that came out to LINE lectures, and the few that did usually only showed up for Bergamaschi. I glanced at Yolniv, he gave me another half shrug. The message was loud and clear. This was no normal lecture. I snatched my screen off the desk. Yolniv hopped up and ran to my side.

"The Highway Game is ID 15092." The game popped right up. Yolniv had a subtle smile, he knew it'd turn out like this. I went to work loading The Highway Game into the presentation.

"He'll need another minute!" Yolniv shouted.

Every seat was taken, and a hundred more people were sitting on the stairs. They were dead silent, giving their absolute attention. It was unlike any lecture hall I had ever seen. From the front row, Yolniv gave me a subtle nod. I stood, grabbed my screen, and stepped out from behind the desk. "I'm Zouk Solinsen, and today we will be discussing LINE's timeless games."

The audience applauded. Odd. "How many of you have played LINE in the last twelve months?"

A quarter of the audience raised their hands. I silently cursed Yolniv for being right, then swiped to the next screen. "Then this is a good introduction! Let's talk about The Highway Game."

I could have given the lecture in my sleep. The Highway Game was a rite of passage for LINE teachers. Grandmaster Sylvan is resting in a park, a wealthy inventor cajoles him into one of the first-ever Individual

Transit Vehicles. Half an hour into what had turned into a very scenic tour, the grandmaster cuts a deal. One game of LINE. If Sylvan wins, he gets to leave early, if not, he's stuck for the rest of the tour.

The story was fun. I spent the first fifteen minutes reminding everyone of the rules. The audience laughed at the photos of the boxy ITV prototypes Yolniv found. It was hard to say if this would do anything for my career, but at least the lecture was going well. Eventually, I arrived at the good bit. The board analysis.

"—So this is the big moment! You're Grandmaster Sylvan, desperate to escape this unexpected roadtrip, but the inventor of the ITV is throwing everything he has at you. How do you save the game?"

The audience was quiet. I glanced at my handheld. Sylvan's muli-layered base and the inventor's attack were being projected to the whole room. Before I could start making up fake answers, there was movement at the back of the room. High above the other players' heads, a young boy stood atop his desk and waved his hand frantically. Next to him, a serious man in a suit sat uncomfortably. I grinned at the sight of my old student.

"Noah! What do we need to do?"

The boy scrambled to his seat and pulled up his board. His high voice bouncing around the room as he shouted. "Nothing!"

"Nothing? What about the attack?"

"It won't work! We've already drawn the enemy's forces onto one side of the board and cut off reinforcements. By the time they attack, they'll be too weak to breach our defenses."

I was pleased, pleased to see Noah and pleased to see that he was still studying. I had stopped our lessons when I was preparing to face Influence. It had been two months and the kid was outthinking all the adults in the room. "Correct! The attack looks terrifying, but Sylvan has total control of the game and more than enough defenses to survive. When the devious inventor makes his attack—" I hit play and let the squadrons run through their animations. Four turns of constant laser fire, until at last the red troops were eliminated. "Our grandmaster takes his win and returns to a peaceful afternoon in the park."

Another round of applause. It lasted exactly as long as the first. I wasn't sure what they were applauding or why, the faces in the crowd looked so serious. The clock showed six minutes left in the lecture. Time to close it. "We're just about out of time, and for many of you, this was probably your first ever LINE class. So before I leave, consider this: it's exciting when armies collide, but rarely is that when the game is decided. A good player thinks ahead. They don't just react to threats, they guide the board, build their own ideas, and choke off their opponent's options. If you're only ever playing to survive, you'll be stuck playing your opponent's game. Thank you."

The crowd stood as one and applauded emphatically. It was the longest applause I had ever heard at a lecture, but most still had somber expressions. After a long sixty seconds, the applause died down and the audience retook their seats. I turned towards my desk, but a woman's voice stopped me.

"Is that how you beat The Mind of Strategy and Warfare?" I spotted her on the third row. She wore a blue beret and held a screen in her hands.

"Partially," I answered. "But there was a lot more going on in that game than meets the eye."

"How are you going to beat The Mind of Manufacturing and Distribution?" She spoke with the speed and sharpness of a reporter. The audience had drifted during the lecture, now we had their undivided attention.

"I can't answer that, not until I've won."

I directed my voice to the whole room. "Were there any other questions?"

On the front row, Yolniv was subtly shaking his head. A gruff voice shouted down from the row behind the reporter. "What are you going to do once you're on the council?"

I took a step back towards the instructor's table. Since the game, I had spent all my time prepping for this lecture. Politics was supposed to be next week. The eyes of the room were unyielding, my voice caught a little as I spoke. "I-I I'm not yet ready to announce my plans."

"What are you going to do about the Minds?" the reporter asked. There was a quiet tension in the air, I just needed to calm things down.

"Do we need to do anything?" Those words never should have left my mouth. As soon as I had said them, shouts filled the room. It reminded me of the chaos in the stadium, only this time I didn't have armed guards. On the stairs on the right side of the hall, a man's shrill voice pierced the jeers. "Why should some board game player be put in charge of my life? You don't even have a plan!"

There were murmurs of agreement. I knew I had to say something, my arms waved helplessly as I searched for a response. "If I were to really answe—"

Yolniv was out of his seat and in front of me in seconds. "No more questions today, thank you all for coming."

The shouts continued from the audience, the reporter was writing furiously on her screen. I whispered in Yolniv's ear, "I can answer, it's fine."

He spun me around and pushed me towards the exit. "Not now." Before I knew it, we were out the door and next to the second floor elevators. Yolniv slapped my hand away from the buttons and dragged me to the stairs. It all seemed a bit melodramatic.

In the lobby, Derek was lounging on a bench, tapping his screen lazily. "Hey guys, how did things—"

"Where can we hide?" Yolniv barked.

"Hide?" The sound of doors slamming open four floors up forced Derek to his feet. Footsteps thundered down the stairwell.

"Anywhere with a door and very few windows." I was at a loss, Yolniv had never moved so fast or spoken with such intensity.

Derek thought for a few agonizing seconds. Eventually, he turned and led us down the hall that led to Jamie's lab. As soon as we reached the door, Yolniv yanked it open and dragged me and Derek inside. All the towering computers hummed quietly, but Jamie and her researchers were absent. As soon as Derek understood what had happened, he left to find security.

I leaned against one of the server towers. "You didn't have to drag me out of there like that."

"Yes I did. There are dangerous times when it's best to make a retreat." Yolniv put a hand to his chest and breathed slowly.

"The crowd wasn't dangerous."

Yolniv scowled. "Not yet. But it would have been. You were pouring gasoline on a fire, Zouk."

Couldn't even give a lecture without causing a riot. I turned away. One of the servers was calculating some variation of the game I had played against War. The game that had changed everything. These days I couldn't go for a walk without journalists snapping photos. Kira didn't answer the door anymore, not that I could blame her. Yolniv was acting like the world had changed. That man on the stairs had been so angry, maybe I was the one with my head buried in the sand.

"Today's been a disaster."

Yolniv grunted in agreement.

"I didn't sign up to become a politician."

The muffled sounds of footsteps faded away. Yolniv's breathing slowed and he lowered his hand from his chest. He looked at me with sharp eyes. "Then you shouldn't have won that second game. Or done all those interviews."

"That was the institute's idea."

Yolniv gave me a side-eye. "And why do you think they want you to do all that?"

I pushed off from the server. "I thought we could make a trade. I give the institute a few wins against the Minds, it helps fund their research, and they help me build the next steps of my career." Even saying it out loud, I could hear my own naivete. The truth was I accepted their deal because I had no other prospects.

"There's a lot of cash here, Zouk, far more than belongs in LINE.

They aren't giving you the spotlight so you can make them look good. They're giving you all this because your success translates to actual, real, power. The kind people kill for."

I hung my head. The warnings had been there. Even Derek had told me what was coming. But I wanted to be a household name. Now I was, and I wasn't ready for it. "I never thought I'd make it this far." I glanced at my ex-coach. "I should have asked you for help with all this."

Yolniv's eyes softened. "Don't blame yourself. I've given you a lot of bad advice over the past couple years."

Derek re-entered the lab. Yolniv and I both sat up. "Are we okay?" I asked.

He nodded. "Yeah. Security got everyone out of the building. Some folks did a little damage, but nothing worth stressing over."

Yolniv and I started for the door. Derek stopped me. "Hey—I know today's been crazy, but she's still expecting you."

My muscles stiffened. Maya. We still hadn't met. "Can we do this another time?"

"Not if you want the institute's help with your last game." His words had the undercurrent of a threat.

"Everything okay?" Yolniv asked.

I nodded. "It's fine, I just need to meet someone."

11 - A MEETING WITH THE SPONSORS

The elevator stopped on floor eighteen. It opened to a small, dark-wood room next to a set of big double doors. Maya's secretary pointed me to a padded seat and told me to wait. My whole body was on edge. Derek had called this a 'get to know you' chat, but didn't go into any details. I kept thinking about what Yolniv said. By winning games, I was accumulating real power, and these were the people I was indebted to. The best thing was to figure out what I owed them, pay it off, and get off the fast-track to politics.

After ten minutes, a ding sounded from the secretary's screen. "She's ready for you."

I pushed open one of the doors and stepped onto the thick, cyan carpeting. It was warm, a little humid. The office took up the whole top floor. Bookshelves lined every wall, separated by huge portraits of historic figures from Iom's history.

"This way, honey!" On the far side of the room behind a heavy wood desk, sat Maya. I recognized the done-up grey-blonde hair and the mauve pantsuit from The World Open. Up close, little gold earrings and a thin necklace glimmered in the light. She was writing something on a pad of paper. "Are you Maya Torrez?"

She continued writing for a moment, then put down her pen. Maya looked at me with a bright, friendly expression. Her eyes were wide and blue. Nothing like the shrewd financier I had come in expecting. She hopped out of her chair. "Of course I am! And you must be Zouk." She came around the desk, flying forward on high heels and wrapped her arms around me. A heavy scent of tulips washed over everything.

"Today must have been so frightenin' for you."

She pulled away and walked back around to her seat. I stood there uncertainly.

"At least you made it out in one piece. Have a seat, hon'."

Her voice carried a certain natural authority, but laced in courtesy. I circled around a little lilac chair and sat down. She stared into my eyes with a welcoming curiosity.

"Jamie has told me quite a bit about you, Zouk. I was getting worried you'd sweep the whole tournament before we got a chance to talk." As she spoke, Maya turned around and returned holding a plum tea tray. She poured two cups and slid one to me.

"Seems like just yesterday I was watching you all wide-eyed on the tv talking about your win against that Bergamaschi fella. Things have changed a lot since then. You've changed a lot since then. How have you been enjoying' the high life?"

I took a sip from my cup. The tea had heavy undertones of orange and pear. I settled further into my chair. "Well Miss Torrez—"

"Maya, please."

"Maya, sorry. It's been tough. I want to build a community, teach people, become a face of LINE. Having the whole nation's ear wasn't a part of the plan." Maya's eyebrows raised in concern. She was really listening. "I'm incredibly thankful for everything your institute has done, I just don't think I'm cut out for this whole politician thing. Especially after what happened downstairs."

It was cathartic, admitting my weakness. I rubbed my hand across the soft fuzz of the chair and took another sip. The steam filled my lungs and warmed my chest.

"Some folks are born itchin' for a fight. The second they learn to speak, all they wanna know is 'when do we burn this place down?'" Maya opened a drawer and put away her notepad. "Honey, I think we can be honest with each other here. You are no politician. You don't have a lick of training talking to people, but that can be taught. That's why I have a team, they make sure I only say the things I'm supposed to say."

I gave Maya a weak smile. Sounded like she still wanted me talking to the public. Maybe with some training it wouldn't be so bad. "I just wish I didn't have to deal with all this."

"Yeah, for a guy looking to build a small community you sure overshot your target." She paused and took a sip of tea. "Hey, how about we make things easier for you? Get you a handler, someone to be with you whenever you have to deal with the public. They can handle your schedule, keep people off your back, protect you in case something goes wrong."

"What, like Derek?" I asked.

"No, that sweetheart already has enough on his plate. Someone a little more capable. If that Lieutenant Denvers wasn't in the army, he'd be a great choice. We'll find someone though."

It sounded like a dream. Yolniv had looked out for me today, but he wasn't exactly a silver tongue. A handler might be exactly what I needed. "That would be great! When Jamie was scheduling me I was more overrun than when I was using the Unified Activity Manager." At the mention, Maya got up and moved to sit on the corner of her desk.

"You had a bad experience with the ole' UAM?"

I must have ranted for ten minutes straight. I told Maya everything. From being in the top eight to making a little extra money on the side, and eventually my burnout and drop out of the pro scene. She listened through all of it, asking the occasional question, but mostly just letting me talk.

"Now that just irks me. A fine young man, one of the best in his field, run ragged to teach some brats." She paused a second, then leaned in. "You know, you are far from the first person to tell me a story like that."

"Really?" I asked.

She nodded. "It seems to me there is a real problem these days just letting people live their lives."

"Yes." I hung on her every word.

"We're all stuck taking orders from the top, and those Minds don't even tell us how they write the rules."

"Absolutely! That would be the first thing I'd change. Release the transcripts of all meetings." My arms were out in front of me and I was just barely sitting on my seat now. Maya tapped her fingers on her desk.

"Now you're thinking! There's no telling what they're up to behind those closed doors."

My head was rushing. I got up out of my chair and walked to the window. It was nearly black out, but I could still see the roads across the valley to the city. The council seat had never meant that much to me, but now real ideas were sprouting in my head. If I won this third game, I could make real change, fix things before they got worse. I turned back to Maya, still sitting on her desk. "Once I'm on the council, I'll talk to the Minds. We can make the world better."

Maya's eyebrows lowered. "People have been trying to do that for a long time. Will they listen?"

I was quiet for a while. It was clear Maya had a strong grip on the issues regular people were facing. If she thought the Minds wouldn't listen, maybe they wouldn't. I thought back to my little talk with Influence before our game. He had listened to me then, but it could have been an act. "I don't know."

"Ya know, Zouk. I was a part of the committee that convinced the Minds to add a person to their council. We talked for months. No progress. Then one day, out of the blue, they announced the tournament. It was a far flung thing from what we had discussed, an idea all their own. I've always been a little afraid . . ." Her voice trailed off.

"What?" I asked.

"It's just— One measly vote on a four-person council doesn't do much. Have you ever heard of a directive that wasn't approved unanimously?" I shook my head. One vote out of four was only good for making ties, but if they always voted together, it meant nothing. "That's what I thought. I've always been afraid that whoever did end up on the council would be less like a peer, and more like a . . . show piece. Does that make sense?"

I stepped back from the window. My dream of fixing the nation was dead before it had even begun. What was the point in winning these games in the first place if I couldn't do anything with the power? Maya's arm wrapped around my shoulder.

"Oh hun, I'm so sorry for saying this to you."

I let her lead me back to my chair. "No it's good. We need to be honest. And the honest truth is that even if I win a seat, I won't be able to do anything with it."

"I wouldn't say that. You still have your voice." Maya handed me back my tea.

"My voice?" I asked.

"People listen to you, Zouk. And once you win, once you become the sole witness to the Mind's secretive legislative process, they will be dying to hear what you think of things."

My ears perked up, Maya was talking a little different now, a little quieter. She had danced around the issue, but I could feel The Ask coming. "So?"

"So imagine what you might hear. What you might see." Maya looked left and right. Her voice was almost a whisper. "Being humanity's eyes and ears is no small task. You could walk out of that first legislative session and tell the world you've never seen a fairer system of government. Or—" My jaw clenched. This was no hypothetical. "You could walk out a changed man, a man who had seen injustice and horror on a scale no one thought possible."

This was it, this was the ask. "Like what?"

She waved one of her hands thoughtfully. "Like— What if the Minds had ambitions beyond our borders? What if, heaven forbid, they saw no value in human life? That a soldier was nothing but a piece on a board, sacrificed to serve their aims."

She wanted me to lie. One carefully cultivated lie, the kind that could burn down a nation. "That would mean war," I answered.

Maya stayed close, watching for my expression. "—And, if we're lucky, a change of administration. A chance to make right what the machines did wrong."

I put down my tea. This is what Yolniv had been warning me about. A power people were willing to kill over. The power to tear down the Minds. "If it were true—if the Minds were monsters, I'd shout it to the whole world. But what if—" I hesitated. "What if they aren't so bad?"

"I thought you wanted to fix things. That's the Zouk Solinsen that Jamie told me about, the Zouk I see in interviews." Maya took the tea cup from my hand and placed it on the desk without looking away. The kindness in her eyes was gone.

"I do. But what you're proposing is to tear the nation apart and start again." Maya's head seemed to crane in towards me.

"Small price for freedom." Her words were sharp, there was a menace behind them. I wanted to say yes, to give her what she wanted. To some degree, I owed her. And she might be right about the Minds and the council seat. Nothing but a puppet. But if it did it, how would that make me any different? I couldn't close my eyes to the Torrez Institute twice. Saying yes today would mean belonging to Maya for life.

"I can't. I'm sorry. Is there any other way I could repay you?"

Maya's look softened, her eyes regained their kindness. She

slowly walked back to her seat behind the desk. "That won't be necessary, hon'. Please let me know if you change your mind. The door's thataway."

Maya retrieved her pad from the desk and resumed writing. I stood and walked to the elevator. The secretary was very busy typing away at her screen. I was relieved when I was finally inside the elevator. There was no way I could support a plan like the one Maya had proposed, but as I descended, one question came back again and again. Will the Minds listen?

Derek and two large security guards were waiting at the lobby. "Hey, Zouk, I'm really sorry about this, but these guys are gonna be escorting you off the property."

This must have been what the secretary was so busy typing. "I can walk out fine on my own."

Derek looked at me with a regretful expression. "Not my call, man, sorry. I'm also supposed to inform you that the institute's resources are no longer open to you."

I stepped out of the elevator and followed the guards out the front doors. From the moment I told Maya no, this was the only outcome. A great ally gone. The next eight weeks of prep were gonna be a nightmare. Then again, with the way people were losing their minds, defeat might be the best outcome.

Little drops of rain pelted me as I stepped outside. It'd be a cold night getting home. I stuffed my hands in my pockets and started for the closest ITV station. "Hey, Zouk!" Derek shouted over the wind. "Maya left a message. She's open to have another talk whenever you'd like."

There was nothing more to say. I gave Derek a quick wave, he gave me a longer one. After a moment, I turned my back to the institute.

12 - OBSERVER

RANK 26 ▲ 22

Eighty-three players showed up for the community event. I wanted to be out there, to play the game alongside them. But I couldn't. There were seven weeks until my game against Maker and I needed a strategy.

Yolniv was the one to propose the back office. We never expected to use it. Now that I was in here and my nose was itching from the musty air, I could say confidently it was crap. The carpet was frayed, the ceiling was stained, the desk was short, and the fabric panel walls shook if I so much as breathed on them.

I adjusted my back against the plastic of the chair and looked again at the monitors hanging above my desk in a 3x3 grid. They were supposed to be helping me research, but my head wasn't in it. Maker had very few public games. I wouldn't be able to find a weakness, or even properly prepare for my opponent. As things stood, my current plan was to lose. It was a lot less stressful to spend the night watching the community event through a camera, anyways.

On the feed, Yolniv walked from game to game, checking on players. He eventually found his way to the door at the back corner of the basement. Behind me, a knob jiggled and the old man's wrinkled face popped in. "You okay in here?"

My hands raised uncertainly. "Do I even want a seat on the council?"

Yolniv shuffled into the office and shut the door. "So not great. I suppose it comes down to your politics, have you figured that part out?"

"Making progress. I keep thinking about those people at the lecture. They were so angry. I looked up the stats on some of their concerns: crime, homelessness, debt, it's all getting better. I don't know how I could improve any of it."

"Maybe any change at all is a good start." Yolniv rubbed his chin. "You've had a terrible influence on the novices by the way, never in my life have I seen so many Dueling Spires and Elephant Tails. I don't think they realize how strange your strategies are."

I chuckled.

"Your protege, Noah, is here. Have you seen how he's doing?"

I leaned towards the cameras, my chair squeaked in complaint. It didn't take long to spot the ten-year-old in the freshly ironed suit. His chin was in his hand, and his arm limply input the moves. "Looks like he's losing."

Yolniv nodded. "Definitely struggling, spends a lot of turns staring off into space."

This didn't look like the Noah I had been training for a year. I scooted my chair away from the desk and stood up. "I'll talk to him."

Yolniv raised a palm. "It'll be a distraction for the players. Besides, you have bigger things to worry about."

I shuffled past him, the idea of spending another minute stuck in my own head was intolerable. "Sorry, I need to get out."

Yolniv pulled the door open. Every player was heads down in their games. I jogged to the edge of the fourth row. When I caught up to Noah, his eyelids were drooping. "Hey, Noah! How are you doing?"

He blinked slowly as he looked at me, then frowned. "Hi, Mister Zouk. I'm fine."

Noah's voice was low and quiet. He looked exhausted, bored, and ready for a week-long rest. Nothing like the life-loving kid I knew. I kneeled next to his LINE board, the timer was ticking, but it didn't seem to matter to him. "Is everything okay?" I asked.

His eyes drifted to the LINE board. "Things are good." He input a move, a rudimentary attack, far below his skill level.

"I'm sorry I didn't say hi to you after my lecture—" I paused, the lecture. That must have been terrifying for the kid. "Did someone scare you at the lecture, Noah?"

"No, we left when the people started shouting." Noah stopped tapping his screen and met my eyes. "Mister Zouk, is it okay if I don't want to play LINE anymore?"

My stomach dropped. I had been coaching Noah for over a year. This was such a sudden turn, he had seemed so happy the last time I saw him. "You're really good at LINE, do you know that?"

He nodded. "Yeah. My dad takes me to a tournament every weekend, I win a lot. But it's just not fun anymore."

"Every weekend?" Noah's timer ticked away the minutes. I thought about reaching over and resigning for him.

"Well, I'm not allowed to compete unless I go to a tournament every week."

"What? Who told you that?"

"The app. It says that unless I go to a tournament in seven of every eight weeks, I'm not allowed to sign up for any of its big events."

My blood ran cold. The Unified Activity Manager ruined lives again. I thought it only targeted adults, but clearly the Minds had set up some junior LINE league too. Even the semi-pros didn't play tournaments every week. And with Noah's dad the way he was, the poor kid was probably being worked to the bone.

"Noah, it's perfectly okay for you to stop playing LINE if you're not having fun. Don't hold it against your dad, okay?"

Noah exhaled slowly, I could see a little life coming back into his eyes. "I know. Dad's just trying to help me be the best I can be."

His game timer hit zero. The guy on the other side stood up and walked away. "That's right, Noah. And it's okay to like doing something without being the best at it."

I paused. There was something to all this. An over-eager app trying to help everyone 'reach their potential'. Instead, it was a helicopter parent, hovering over everyone's shoulder to make sure they work hard enough to hit their goals.

"Is it okay if I go home early? My dad's upstairs." I gave Noah a nod and a hug before he toddled off for the stairs. When I stood, the eyes of the room were on me. Yolniv was right, I was a distraction.

I hurried back into my office, the UAM on the forefront of my mind. If it was bad enough to affect me and Noah, how many more had suffered the same fate? What was the UAM like outside of LINE? It wasn't hard to imagine a person picking up a part-time delivery job and ending up working sixty or seventy hours a week. Or a hiker being signed up for marathons. It needed to be fixed. But if I were to fix it, first I needed to beat Maker.

The monitors flicked on one by one. I reached to switch to the LINE analysis board, but a blinking notification stopped me. Jamie had sent me a message. We hadn't spoken since my game against War. Partly because I had been fired, but mostly because of the way she had treated me. I still got worked up whenever I thought of that last conversation in my living room. All it read was, Got time for a chat?

My hands rested on the table. I couldn't imagine the topic. There was always the chance she could hand me a secret weapon to defeating Maker. I rubbed the chill from my arms, stretched my neck, and hit call.

The Jamie that appeared on my screen wasn't the insurmountable juggernaut I had worked with over the last couple months. Her eyes were sunken in, her hair jutted out in several directions, and she was dressed in a ratty T-shirt. If I didn't know better, I would have assumed she was back to playing tournaments.

"Hey, Jamie."

"Hi, Zouk. I—" She hesitated. "Before we begin, I'm supposed to ask you if you've changed your mind."

I responded instantly. "No change. You know what Maya asked me to do, right?"

Jamie clenched her jaw. "She told me. Seems like a pretty small favor to ask for changing your life. You know they're just machines, right?"

Her voice spoke bitter and hard. There she was. The Jamie of the institute. "I'm not going to lie to the nation because Maya doesn't like the fact that the Minds are writing the laws. And you shouldn't be working for her either."

"This is a once-in-a-generation moment, Zouk," she retorted. "Don't you see that? If you don't step up, you're consigning all of us to another century under electronic tyrants." A bit of spittle hit Jamie's lens. No chance I'd be changing her mind today, but maybe I could soften it.

"The Minds don't seem like tyrants to me. From what I've seen, they haven't done anything particularly self-serving. It's more like they're tending to the nation, helping us grow. Maybe arbiter is a better word."

Jamie grimaced. "Arbiter? They're circuitry and wires!" Her shouts peaked the audio. "How long until one of them crashes? Or glitches and decides to go to war with all our neighbors? I—" Jamie's voice trailed off. She closed her eyes, covered her face with her hands, and took a deep breath.

"I'm sorry, Zouk, this isn't why I called." She lowered her hands, and I could see she had a much softer expression. "I've been thinking about how we left things, about how I treated you—It wasn't right, I'm sorry." Jamie sunk into her chair. A deep regret seemed to pull her body down. I stayed quiet and let her speak.

"Things have gotten a lot harder since you left. Maya asked me to—it doesn't matter. There's been a lot going on, and I at least wanted to say goodbye—sorry I let it end so badly."

She was clearly allied to Maya, but the old Jamie was still there. The one that loved LINE and cared about other people. It was hard to forget the stress she had put me through the past couple months, but she was reaching out, I owed her the same. "Thank you, Jamie. I hope we play against each other soon. Got any hints for beating Maker?"

She gave a weak smile and shook her head. "Maya would kill me." I got the feeling her joke wasn't entirely a joke. "Get a team. You can't win on your own."

The call ended. I moved my hands behind my head. Get a team. Easier said than done. There were plenty of pros and coaches in the world, but the good ones cost a fortune, and very few would be available with so little notice. Even if I got the best, there was only one real expert at facing the Minds, and she had just told me to find someone else.

I looked up at the cameras. The place was cleared out. My heart fell, I had even missed the little trophy giveaway at the end. With my game against Maker and my rising prominence as a politician, maybe I'd have to drop the community events. The monitors flickered off and I ran outside to help with the cleanup.

"Twenty-five tables going, good turnout." Yolniv spoke as he carried a pair of chairs to storage. I followed him with a table.

"At least we had players this time. I saw you managed to sneak in a quick lecture. One of your games?"

He smirked. "It's been so long. How could I resist showing the new players a game from one of the best?" Yolniv hung up a pair of chairs and stepped out of the way. "Were you aware Noah left early?"

I put down the table before answering. "He quit LINE today."

Yolniv crossed his arms and leaned against the chair rack. "Don't give up on him. People need breaks from time to time."

I gave a dejected nod, and we walked out to fold another set of chairs. Even if I didn't completely believe him, Yolniv always brought a wizened confidence to things. We had worked together a long time, he had become a master of keeping me focused on the task at hand.

"Yolniv?" He grunted as he lifted a chair. "I need a coach for my game against Maker. Should it be you?"

The old man lowered his chairs to the ground and rolled a shoulder. He looked like he had been expecting this. "Things didn't work out so well last time."

I was quiet, we had never talked about what happened. After my win against Bergamaschi, the next half year was one long line of defeats. One day I stopped scheduling sessions and Yolniv got the picture. "It's only one game."

"The biggest game of your career. I took you from top ten all the way down to 'barely a professional.'" Yolniv's voice shook as he spoke.

"You also got me there in the first place."

"What keeps me from making the same mistakes again? This is your renaissance, I can't be the man that kills your career twice in one lifetime." There was a strained look on his face. For the past half year, I have blamed myself for my failures. It was clear he had taken on the same burden.

"You won't. I know where we went wrong last time." His eyes raised to meet mine. "Perfect play."

He frowned. "I'm well aware 'perfect play' was a bad method. But knowing 'what' went wrong does not tell us 'why' it went wrong. Do you have the answer to that?"

I leaned my chairs against the wall. His question had been running around in the back of my mind for months. "I figured it out when I was training to beat Influence. Our problem was that we didn't know what kind of player I was."

Yolniv set his chairs aside and crossed his arms. "What kind of player are you?"

I took a breath. "The kind of player that plays LINE to defeat my opponent."

Yolniv's head tilted in thought. He started muttering to himself, as if he was deep in calculation. After a moment, he looked back at me, a slight smirk on his lips. "Of course you are—you always have been, haven't you? I should have seen it the day you beat Bergamaschi. You aren't one of these intellectuals who dreams of being unbeatable. You're a fighter."

"There's no one I can trust with this but you, Yolniv. Can you coach me?"

His jaw slid from side to side. After a moment, he looked up at me and gave a thumbs up. "So long as we play to your strengths, we can remake that conniving and dangerous player you used to be." He and I laughed together. "But first, we need the public to trust you. We need to get you speaking again. There's an event coming up next week. You should be there."

"My game against Maker is in seven weeks. Is there really time to play in some tournament—"

"Analyze, not play. They want you at the caster's table."

My breath caught, a casting opportunity, dumped into my lap. "What if they ask about my politics?"

"They will, and they should. We'll make sure you're ready. Ready enough that the public doesn't tear you limb-from-limb anyway." Already I felt good about my new, old coach. In a couple minutes, he had taken my lost, directionless self and gotten me back on track. Yolniv picked up his chairs with renewed vigor. "Let's talk about your strategy. Catch me up, how did you beat War?"

13 - JAMIE V INFLUENCE

RANK: 21 ▲ 5

The caster's green room was far better than the one for players. It was on the third floor of the news building, down where everything important happened. There was a minifridge, four bowls of snacks, and the walls were covered in epic athletic scenes. I had the four-man couch and Yolniv was in the massage chair. For once, the weight of the world was off my shoulders. All I had to do was be engaging on TV. Sure, it'd be strange to cast the person who had given me my first two wins, but not that strange. This was my big debut and a chance for people to see me for who I am.

Thirty minutes before the stream, the door to the green room slid open. Influence's smiling face looked down on us. "Hey guys, sorry I don't have long! Congrats on the big win, War's been fuming for a week. Good luck!"

The door shut a second later. Influence seemed like a nice guy.

When I looked back at Yolniv, he was wide-eyed and holding the sides of his chair in death grip. He spoke, "Does this happen to you frequently?"

I shrugged. "Two for two. Maybe Influence just likes me."

Yolniv slowly released his grip and relaxed back into the massage chair, but his eyes stayed locked on the door.

With fifteen minutes to go, an intern led us into the sports set. I was sat on a low-back stool at the main table in front of a large, animated screen. Yolniv was shuffled to the side with a big ready-for-camera LINE board. Most of the lights and cameras were pointed at me. As the minutes rolled by, I began to wonder. Had they made me the host without warning? That wouldn't make much sense. I fidgeted, my eyes jumped from the camera to the bored cameraman behind it, all my normal behaviors suddenly felt wrong.

Five minutes to air, Ezra Hart walked on set. No one had to introduce her, there were hundreds of posters of the anchor throughout the building. She sat down next to me and adjusted her blonde pixie cut. My mouth went dry. Ezra looked out at the camera and spoke from the side of her mouth, "Take a deep breath, Zouk, we have a long show ahead of us."

"I-I didn't know you reported on sports."

"I report big news. Today is big news—" She turned to me. "My team sent you some questions, did you get them?"

"Yes. I'm ready for all of them." All five questions were carefully rehearsed.

"Hopefully not too ready. Those are just a starting point, I'll be using them to jump off into some bigger questions during the interview."

I placed my palms on the news desk. "Actually—I'm really only ready for those five questions, could we stay focused on the game today? I might be able to say a few words at the end if that would help."

"Fine." Ezra smoothly returned her focus to the cameras. On a preview screen, Jamie was talking to Influence. "That poor girl," Ezra muttered almost to herself. I looked to her inquisitively. "Just not cut out for TV. Always has that 'deer in the headlights' look."

On the screen, Jamie was dressed in the same green dress she had worn at her last tournament. I watched for a couple of seconds and saw what Ezra meant. Jamie's face twitched as she spoke, her eyes were locked dead ahead, her arms moved in sudden and sporadic ways. It was hard to look at.

Soon the video faded and the camera cut to the big stage. In the corner of my eye, Yolniv gave me a last thumbs up. Jamie shuffled her way up to the top of the tiered set. Even when she was sitting, her feet kept jumping around on the floor and her fingers rubbed together nervously. It explained why she had called me the other day. She must have been terrified. The timer on-screen started, and a voice behind the cameras started counting down.

"On in 5, 4, 3—"

I took a deep breath and a small light lit up on the main camera. Ezra introduced the team. When she turned to me, I was able to respond without flubbing or sounding too nervous.

Jamie and Influence started their game at a sprinter's pace. Eight minutes into the broadcast and I could already see where things were headed.

"Zouk, the game is starting to take shape. What do you think of Jamie's strategy so far?"

I suppressed my desire to be sarcastic. It was the Elephant's Tail. The squadrons and the walls were a little different, but she was using my strategy. "We are seeing Jamie play a very patient game. Her goal isn't to win immediately, but to slowly capture the board and strangle her opponent."

"Would you say this strategy is similar to what we saw you use two months ago?" I hesitated a second after Ezra's question. Was it that obvious?

"Yes, yes I would."

Ezra brought her hands together. "Perfect, there's a question that's bothered me since I saw your game, and since it looks like we're watching a bit of repeat, I want to ask it: Normally we use Yolniv's big board to predict the next move, right?"

I hesitated. There was something pointed in Ezra's question. "That's right."

"Well there was an accuracy problem with the first game you played. Every time you made a move, it wasn't any of the moves predicted by the board. Why is that?"

I pivoted towards Ezra. Her eyes were probing. The question was a dangerous one to answer. My moves never appeared on the board because the board used the same algorithm as the trainer and Influence. Yolniv and I still needed every advantage we could get. I let out a nervous cough and spoke, "I can't read Jamie's mind, but there are certain techniques players can use to—" On the screen, a few squadrons fired on one another. My best chance to change the subject. "Wow! Looks like we have our first combat of the game. Yolniv, we're just entering the mid-game, how are things looking on the analysis board?"

The feed cut away and Ezra turned herself entirely towards me. Yolniv talked and talked about Jamie's position, but all I could see was Ezra's piercing look. She knew something about my strategy to win, and she was pressing for it. Yolniv finished running through Jamie's options and the cameras cut back to us.

"—Thanks for the breakdown, Yolniv. Now Zouk, you and Jamie worked together to get you this far, what was that like?" Finally, a question I could handle.

"Jamie and her team are brilliant. I wouldn't have made it half as far as I have without their help—"

Ezra cut me off. "What happened there? Jamie's now competing on her own, clearly there was some kind of disconnect."

I ran my hand through my hair. Yolniv had trained me plenty on LINE trivia and interesting anecdotes, but Ezra didn't seem content to ask the easy stuff. Her question felt targeted to knock me off balance.

"We had some differences of opinion. I guess once I was gone, Jamie decided she wanted to win the tournament herself."

My co-anchor gave me no hints as to what she thought of my answers, instead she just turned back to camera. "Fascinating. We will return in a few minutes to continue our report on one of the biggest LINE games of the year. See you soon."

As soon as the little light shut off on the camera, I stood from my stool. "What were those questions? Your team didn't send me anything like that. I thought we were here to talk about Jamie's game"

Ezra stood and started towards the hall. "Follow me."

We stepped over heavy cables and past the crew towards the exit. She shut the door quickly behind us, all the polite professionalism dropped from her expression. "Our viewers are not here for this Jamie girl, they're here to see you. I need to keep things interesting throughout the broadcast and you told me 'no politics'. Which leaves me with two options. One, dig into the drama. Or two, I keep peeling back the curtain on how you're winning your games."

I swallowed nervously. Now I understood why Influence had chosen her as his successor for lead anchor. "There's still a third game, I can't answer strategy questions. Can't we cast this thing the normal way?"

A cameraman popped his head into the hall and informed us we had three minutes.

"You're an amateur. This is broadcast TV, if you aren't willing to be interesting, we can bring on someone who is." Ezra started to walk away, then paused and gave me an incredulous look. "I thought you wanted this."

I rubbed at my ear and took a step back. "I do, I just wanted to save the politics for the end of the night."

"Not an option. It's drama with Jamie, the secret to your success, politics, or get replaced. There's plenty of options there." Without another word, Ezra walked back to her seat on set.

Two minutes to air, no time to make a decision. This was far from what Kira and I had practiced for. No way I was talking drama—drama with Jamie was really drama with Maya, and I didn't need that woman any more antagonized than she was. Spoiling my strategies could doom my game against Maker. Was I really considering talking politics? Sure I had come here with plans to dip my toes in the water, but a few platitudes would never be enough for Ezra. And then there was the risk I would start another riot.

One minute to air.

I hurried onto set, speed-walking to Yolniv's side of the stage. "Those were some tough questions, Zouk. Are you alrigh—?"

I cut him off, "The last time we talked politics, we had two big ideas, do you remember them?"

"Do you need them now?"

I nodded. Thirty seconds to air. Yolniv shut his eyes and rubbed them with his hands. "They both started with 'C'." He dropped them away and looked at me apologetically. "That's all I remember. Use your personal story as a driver."

A director shouted for fifteen seconds and I ran to my seat. Ezra spoke quietly, "Did you decide?"

I kept my focus on the camera. "Politics, we can talk politics."

"Thank God."

From a little chair behind the cameras, the director counted us in on his fingers. Two cameras panned close as the stream returned. We discussed the eleven moves we had missed in the break. The Elephant's Tail was starting to take form. The conversation felt a lot easier this time around. Ezra was more amicable, open to letting me talk freely of LINE.

On move forty, the game slowed. Jamie's head was in her hands, deep calculation. When this happened to me, it was because I had forgotten the move. Jamie seemed too smart for that, and her face didn't show frustration, it looked like confusion.

"Zouk, what's causing this delay of game?" Nothing had changed in Ezra's voice, but there was something a little kinder in the questions she asked.

"Jamie's finally in her first big think of the game. What she does next may prove decisive to this game's result." It was the default answer, but I was still piecing things together. The feed cut to Influence, he had made his move, and watched Jamie with unwavering attention. Had he figured out Jamie's game?

"Then we have some time on our hands!" Ezra raised her arms and the background faded to a dark blue animation of waves. "If you're just joining us, we are forty moves into a thrilling LINE game. But I don't think I'm alone in saying I'm ready for a break from all the analysis. Luckily, we are joined today by an awfully interesting guest."

I swallowed uncertainly as Ezra rotated her body in my direction. "For all of today, I've been talking to Zouk Solinsen, the LINE player. But he's so much more than that. Mr. Solinsen is one historic game from joining our nation's council. So for the first time on television, we need to ask the bigger questions. By the end of tonight, we will all know the answer to 'Who is Zouk Solinsen?'."

As Ezra said the words, a title card reading Who is Zouk Solinsen rose out of the waves on the back wall, a crop of my face looking perplexed was slapped right in the middle. The lights dimmed. I adjusted myself in my chair as a stagehand slipped a set of flashcards under Ezra's desk. This was no improvised segment.

"Zouk Solinsen, Iom is the only nation on Earth to be governed by artificial minds. What do you make of their performance as leaders?"

My conversations with Yolniv, Jamie, and Kira popped into my head. This was an easy one. "I think they've given us everything we asked for."

"What do you mean by that?" Ezra leaned towards me as she spoke.

"From what I've seen, the Minds don't seem to put themselves in the way of decisions. They analyze and legislate according to what's best for the country. I don't know a lot about economics, but as far as I understand it, we are one of the most prosperous in the world.

Like I said, they've given us everything we asked for." I looked past the camera at the director for a reaction, he was watching with rapt attention and subtly nodding his head. That probably meant this was good TV, at least.

"So nothing needs changing?"

I rubbed my nose. Yolniv and I had talked about all this in a very high-minded way a few days ago. Now I was preaching a late-night hypothesis like it was truth. "No, things still need changing. The big problem is that we as a society are all complicit in a lie. Every time the Minds ask 'What do you want for our nation?', we answer 'more wealth', 'more jobs', 'a better economy.'"

Ezra slid her flashcards onto the table. "You don't think people want to be more wealthy?"

"I think we trade away a lot for wealth. Time, community, art. It's not always intentional." I knew where to go from here, pivot to the personal story. I took a beat, sipped from a water bottle under the table, then continued, "It happened to me. I used to be one of the best LINE players there was. Then I wanted a little more cash and signed up for the UAM. Over the next few months, I got the cash I wanted, but there was a cost. The joy of the game left me, I wasn't speaking to my colleagues, and my rating tanked. I had traded what I loved for a little more spending money." My throat caught, Ezra waited for me to put myself together. I hated sharing so much of myself on TV.

"To some degree, this is happening to all of us. We convince ourselves that we're perfectly industrious and that we have endless passion. We believe that we can level a mountain one spoonful at a time, if only we worked a little harder. That's the lie. Every time we ask the Minds for more productivity, they 'help us' by throwing away another part of what makes life worth living." In the moments of silence after I finished speaking, all my energy seemed to drain out of me. I was complaining about suffering from the consequences of my own decisions on national TV. There were a lot of thoughtful faces behind the cameras, my words seemed to have had some impact.

Ezra flipped one of the cards on her stack. "With all that in mind, if you end up on the council, how do you fix things?"

"Two changes." As I said it, my head was sweeping through words trying to remember their titles.

"And what are those?"

It was dead quiet in the studio. Yolniv and I had only talked about them for a couple of hours. I rewound back to my conversation with Noah, how tired he was, how his father just kept pushing him. One of the words popped into my head and I blurted it out, "Communication!"

"What about communication?" I shot Ezra a glance. No doubt she could see me struggling up here, but the script was starting to flow back into my head.

"We need to reinvent how we communicate. I've seen very little back and forth between the citizenry and the Minds."

Ezra jumped in, "It took months of protest for the Minds to be willing to add a person to their council."

"Right!" I was pretty sure that comment was her helping. "The Minds can't keep letting the situation get untenable before they do anything. They should be listening better and earlier. Once I reach the council, I can make them listen."

From the secondary set, Yolniv was waving and indicating towards his board. Written across his screen were the words *GAME ABOUT TO END*. The game was pretty far along when we had left it off, either Jamie figured things out or Influence had crushed her. Ezra tapped the table and brought my attention back to the stream at hand.

"And your other proposal?"

"Change." I could see the words in my head now. "We need to change the way laws are created. Maybe that's just more improved communication, but I for one want a better understanding of what's happening behind the scenes. Don't you?"

I realized my question had been directed at the cameramen rather than the lens. He raised his eyebrows and nodded approvingly. It wasn't something I could read into, but the little reactions off-set felt positive.

Behind me, the screen behind us shifted back to its regular, black cityscape. The lights returned to their normal levels, and the cameras pulled away. I glanced around as Ezra matter-of-factly rotated back to face the cameras. I didn't want to celebrate too soon, but it sure seemed like we were done talking politics.

"I'm sorry, but we'll have to resume our interview with Zouk another time. I've just heard that The Mind of Communications and Influence, after sixty-one turns, has resigned. Making Jamie the fourth-ever player to defeat Influence and reach the second round."

On-screen, Jamie stood in front of the false audience, smiling weakly and looking exhausted. Ezra jumped in, "Yolniv, take us through the game."

The cameras switched to Yolniv. It was slow and patient as the Elephant's Tail always was. Something had gone wrong at move forty. Maybe she had made a mistake, maybe Influence had figured her out, but every turn after forty had taken multiple minutes to make. On each one, Jamie's advantage shrunk. She had been down to six minutes at the end. She was definitely winning, but if Influence had dragged it out, he could have forced Jamie to make a blunder. Still, he had resigned and she was off to face War.

A part of me was happy for her. It was great to see a colleague—and the person responsible for giving me back my career—see success. Another part of me was worried, worried what would happen now that I was down to my final game and Maya had found a replacement.

"In just a minute, we'll be talking to the winner. Zouk, thank you so much for joining us today."

I thanked Ezra and walked off the set. A few minutes later, Yolniv joined me in the green room, lounging again in the massage chair.

"Good answers tonight."

I covered my eyes, it felt like I had just improvised my way through one of the biggest games of my career. "I should have prepared more."

Yolniv smacked his lips, but before he could speak, the door to our room slid open. A woman stood in the doorway. She was taller than anyone I had ever seen, over seven feet at least. She was dressed in a black suit and wore sunglasses. The figure bowed slightly and stepped into the green room. Her form blocked the light. Yolniv turned off his massage chair and I stood up slowly. "Can I help you?" I asked.

Through a pair of sunglasses, she stared down at me. I wondered if she was just going to stand there. In a slow, calculated movement, her hand reached into her jacket. "There's been a change in venue."

Her voice was deep but hushed. Almost metallic. She handed me a box, then turned and left the room. A change in venue? What did that mean? I followed her to the doorway and looked down the hall. She walked strangely and at an unnaturally fast pace. A moment later, she was gone.

The box was made from a carbon alloy. Light, but sturdy. I glanced back. Yolniv was leaning forward in his chair, trying to get an eye on the package. "They have good security here, right?" I asked.

Yolniv shrugged and pointed at a metal imprint of conjoining cubes on the top of the box. "That's the seal of the Minds. Touch it."

I lowered the box onto the table and pressed my thumb on the imprint. The box clicked and I pulled it open. It was just a letter. I looked to Yolniv. He stared at the little folded paper. After a moment, I flipped it open.

LOGAN SIDWELL ⎯⎯⎯⎯⎯⎯⎯⎯⎯⎯⎯⎯⎯⎯⎯⎯⎯⎯⎯

14 - HOME

The hill at Green Pine Park was plenty green, but the pines were long gone. Even with nothing but grass, I had spent enough of my childhood there to love the view anyway. My hand caressed the little metal box next to me on the bench. I still wasn't ready to go home.

"Are you gonna make your move?"

Bill's voice pulled me back to the game. The board was one of a dozen built a decade ago. I tapped my move onto the peeling plastic. "Sorry, just looking around."

Bill and I had made our acquaintance about ten minutes prior, a little after I had rerouted my ITV. He wore a heavy coat and thick wool gloves. I could just make out a dour expression behind the beard.

"Eh?" Bill glanced back. "Oh, not too much to see."

I raised an eyebrow and looked over the field at the base of the hill. The goalposts were missing, instead the field's perimeter was traced by a long flat sheet of metal.

"What happened to the soccer field?" I asked as I input my next move.

"Torn down. Someone replaced it with a Game Keeper, same as most parks around here."

"Game Keeper?"

"Choose a game, and those bits of metal open up to set the court for you. More flexible, I guess. Kind of a waste. You can't do anything with 'em without scheduling it in advance on the app. I just think someone out there really likes tracking how people spend their free time."

I murmured in agreement. Another victim of the UAM. We played a while in quiet. Bill was pretty good, but he never stood a chance. He resigned just as the sky began to amber. This was as good a chance as any to quit and head home. To talk with Kira about the letter.

"One more?" I asked.

Bill grumbled and started another game. On the board, faded troops fired on barely visible walls. My mind kept going back to that interview with Ezra. Across the table, Bill was staring down the board with a furrowed brow and a scowl. "Did you see me on the TV today?"

He locked eyes with me and his scowl deepened. "A bit of it— My roommates wouldn't shut up about the whole thing."

I pulled my hands back from the board. "Really, what did they say?"

"I don't know man—they liked it. Every time you gave an answer they argued with each other about what you said until you gave your next answer."

"Anything in particular?"

Bill pressed hard on the plastic. "Ask them, dude. You had an impact and they didn't hate it, is that enough for you?"

For a first appearance, Bill was probably right. Still, he seemed to be dancing around the issue. "What did you think of it?"

"It was fine," Bill mumbled.

I rubbed my forehead. Bill was a hard man to get answers from.

"How about my ideas, do you think they'd work?"

Bill didn't answer for a while, focusing on his turn. When he hit 'Submit', I kept my hands away from the board. My timer burned away, I wanted to hear his thoughts. He waited thirty seconds on the clock before answering. "I dunno, man. You seem nice enough. Maybe."

"Come on, give me more than that."

Bill took a deep breath and leaned away from the board. "Things don't change, man. You say the Minds don't listen enough, cool. Maybe we work too hard—fine. But how does that turn into something that actually improves my life?" He wasn't wrong, every idea I was proposing was modification on what was already there. I sighed and input another turn.

"Fine—the roommates loved it. They really think you've found something. Go make change, give it a try. You can probably do some good." He tapped the table. "We playing a game or what?"

I took it a lot easier on Bill the second time around. I found something. It wouldn't fix everything, but something was a start. The second he lost, Bill was out of his chair and headed down the sidewalk. I waited a few more minutes, a couple birds flew overhead and the shadow of the park's hill grew long. There was no more putting it off, Kira and I had to talk. I pulled out my screen and requested an ITV home.

The streetlamp barely lit up the two floors of our little grey townhouse. A hundred others just like it ran down the street in both directions. I dragged my feet up the concrete steps and turned the knob to the front door.

"Hey." Kira was curled up in her spot on the couch, reading a screen in her hands.

"Hey."

"What's that?"

I looked down, the box was in my hands, maybe so I wouldn't forget to tell her. I wondered if I could have played another game against Bill, delaying things a little longer. "I have a favor to ask." Kira put down her screen. "I need you to come with me to my next game."

Kira's eyes jumped to the box. "Is that what that says?"

I walked to the couch, opened the box, and handed the letter to my wife. Her eyes went wide when she saw the symbol on the back. I closed my eyes as Kira read the contents.

Most of it was a long list of 'security concerns'. The crowds at War's game, the riot at the institute, general protests. The Minds were spooked and rewriting the rules of the tournament before my eyes. There were a lot of wacky security changes, but the big one was a change of venue for my final game. Kira finished reading and placed the letter back in the box. "Facility Five. Your last game is at my work?"

I looked her in the eyes and nodded. Most of the time the government was comfortable letting Kira work from home, but every once in a while she had to make the two-hour drive. From her descriptions, the place was more practical than aesthetic.

"What about Yolniv?" she asked.

"His background threw a flag in the system. An individual wholly unwelcome in the nations' highest security facilities."

Kira's eyebrows scrunched. "And the letter mentions you're going all the way to the bottom. No one gets to go down there."

My head pulled back. "Is it safe?"

"I think so. Sometimes I measure how long it takes for the freight elevator to get back to me to figure out how deep it is. Last I calculated it's at least a couple hundred feet." She reached for her screen, probably to start running the numbers. I took her hand. "So what do you think? Can you be there?"

She looked away. "You don't need me there."

That's what I was expecting. Going to big events was outside Kira's wheelhouse. I wouldn't even pose this request if I didn't know Facility Five was a bunker. She'd need convincing. "I do need you there. You and Yolniv are the only people I can trust. It's the biggest game of my career—probably the biggest moment of my life. If something happens before the game, I'll need you."

"I shouldn't go." A flat no, I wasn't sure what to make of that.

"Please, I need you there."

Kira pulled her hand away and gazed at our closed window. "We still haven't figured things out, Zouk."

I sunk into the couch. We had avoided long conversations with each other for a while, sticking to whatever kept the mood light. It was lucky Kira enjoyed the analytical side of LINE so much. But it was time to stop running. "We're gonna get past this. Things have been getting better, right? We don't go places with big crowds, I don't force you to meet new people, I don't put you in the spotlight—and until you're ready for those things, we don't have to."

She crossed her arms. "It's not a readiness problem, Zouk. It's not something to get past. I am who I am. Getting into the world, talking with crowds, that's who you are, not me."

"With enough practice—" I started.

"I'm not going to get better no matter how much you try to ease me into it." Her voice quivered. "And it's not just me. You may act like things are fine, but you're hurting too."

I wiped my eyes. She was right, even when things were good between us, it felt like work. "We can still figure it out. I'll keep making adjustments and you can too."

"I hope so, Zouk. I really do."

A heavy tension hung in the silence. We had said all this before, but the roots of the problems weren't changing.

"What did you think of my interview?"

Kira looked at me a long time before answering. "I liked . . ." When she spoke, her words were slow and far apart. "I liked that you shared a personal story during the interview."

I stood up from the couch. She was using her 'practiced kindness' voice. "What did you really think?"

"It didn't have a lot of meat—I'm sorry! I've been practicing, I promise."

I walked past the couch and into our tiny kitchen. The energy at the station had been so positive. Maybe that was all just superficial support for the promise of change. Either that or Kira and Bill were in a very select crowd of cynical people.

"If you want me to believe you, you need to fix your voice."

Kira pulled her legs back up onto the couch.

"I'm trying, Zouk. The person you want isn't the person I am. I can't see how you feel, and no amount of practice will fix that."

She looked lost and hurt. I had crossed a line. I shut the kitchen cabinets and circled around the couch. There was nothing in what she had said that was wrong. Kira was basically the same person she had been when we married. Nothing had changed but our expectations of one another. "Sorry, love." I gently touched her arm, then wrapped my arms around her. "I thought we'd be able to reason our way out of this, practice a perfect marriage. But we're totally different people, aren't we?"

Kira raised her hand and caressed my arm. Despite her best efforts, a tear slipped down her face. After a few minutes, she spoke, "I'll keep trying. I really did like what you said about yourself during the interview."

"I'll try harder too. I'd still like you at the game."

"How many people?" After all that arguing, she was considering it. Maybe we needed all that arguing to know that both of us were still committed to making things work.

"Very few in the bunker, I don't know how many on the surface. We'll keep you away from them."

I lowered myself back onto the couch while holding Kira close. She didn't ask any more questions. After all, she knew Facility Five better than I did. I could probably get by alone, but if the Minds kept hitting me with surprises like this one, I'd need Kira there to keep me level.

Ten minutes later, Kira gave her answer. "I'll be there."

My eyes misted over. She was making a real sacrifice to support me. I made a quiet oath to find a way to repay her. But first and foremost, I had an opponent to prepare for.

15 - FACILITY FIVE

RANK: 18 ▲ 3

The ITV rumbled past the chain-link fence, over the sun-bleached asphalt, and to a stop at the coastline. I stepped out onto the road. The lake was quiet and tranquil, an oasis in the desert, a nice break from hours weaving through the mountains. It was a shame there was a concrete bunker to ruin the view. My skin pulsed under the dry heat of the desert. Time to get my head in the game.

One thousand moves. Three weeks of training. Hopefully it would be enough.

Yolniv and Kira's vehicle came to a stop behind mine. Kira joined me at the coast, Yolniv's eyes were on the base perimeter. "Incredible." He wiped a line of sweat from his brow. "Three-hour drive and you still have an audience."

Beyond the edge of the road was a fifty-foot moat of sand, a chain-link fence guarded by soldiers, and a thousand spectators waving and screaming. Kira backed further towards the coast. "Yolniv," I said.

He was quick to catch on. "We'll meet you at the entrance." Without another word, he led Kira towards the base, leaving me with the crowd.

I waved and their excitement mounted. Some raised signs above their head, others shouted incoherent messages into megaphones, and the rest gripped the links in the fence and shook it passionately. They had probably waited half the day in the hot sun just to see me. I didn't want to disappoint. I stepped off the asphalt, my feet sunk deep into the sand. With every foot forward, the volume of the cheers grew.

A soldier stopped me twenty feet from the perimeter. I couldn't repay these people their time, but I owed them more than a wave.

"Folks!" The crowd went quiet. "Your presence— You being here means the world to me."

My audience was motionless, hanging on every word. Already, the sand was stinging my throat. "I might win, I might not. But I promise you this, it's gonna be the best game of LINE you've ever seen!"

The audience cheered again, I was just glad they had heard me. I turned to the base, and a dark, black object hit the sand a few feet to my left. A soldier tackled me to the ground and another was shouting commands to the crowd.

"Get down! Get down!"

A hand pressed my head into the sand. The cheers had stopped. My heart was pumping hard in my chest, I could barely breath. Was it a grenade? A bomb? We waited a while in silence, anticipating the bang. But none came. A dud? After a minute, the soldier helped me up, dusted me off, and pointed to the road.

I hurried as well as I could through the sand, glad Kira hadn't seen any of this. When I turned back, someone was holding the little black ball in their hands. A little holographic cartoon was projected into the air. I let out a chuckle. Just a hologram sphere.

"What does it say?"

The soldier lowered the sphere to his eyeline, rotated it left and right, then yelled back, "Win it for us!"

The crowd applauded, but with a somewhat muted energy. I gave them a final wave and strode towards Facility Five.

It took a good five minutes to reach the bunker doors. Sand rubbed between my clothes and sweat stung my eyes. I couldn't believe Kira got out here twice a month. Outside the entrance, Yolniv was sitting in a camp chair, looking ready for a drink.

"Where's Kira?" I asked.

"Inside. You look worse for wear." He gestured to my sand-crusted suit.

"I took a swim in the dirt. You coming in?"

Yolniv shook his head. "This is as far as I'm allowed. Too much history making trouble."

"What did you do?"

"Something stupid half a century ago, War still holds it against me. I'll tell you another time." He paused. "Remember the plan?"

I nodded, it was hard to forget three weeks of drills. "Good. Don't let Maker get in your head."

I pulled open the bunker doors and enjoyed a blast of cool air. Kira and Influence were waiting on the other side. Kira looked as comfortable as I had ever seen her outside the house, clearly she had missed the bomb scare.

"Zouk Solinsen! Here to make history!"

Influence had on a showman's grin as he escorted me into the belly of Facility Five's manufacturing. We passed quickly through the main production lines. Machines whirred, and electricity arced in the background as we walked. The whole place smelled of industry. I glanced back at Kira and shouted a question, "How do you handle all this?"

She tried to speak but the clanging and cracking was deafening. Eventually she just pointed towards the ground. "She works downstairs! Second sub-basement!" Influence shouted. Just then I noticed a woman following a few feet behind us.

"What's with the camera?" I yelled back.

"Just some B-Roll! We'll add a voice-over later."

Another few minutes of manufacturing lines, and we arrived at the freight elevator. The whole group stepped into the metal box. Influence inserted a key and pressed an unlabeled button near the bottom. The elevator rattled downward and the sounds of industry faded away. "Zouk." Kira grabbed my hand and pointed at the rising rock wall ahead of us. "This is me."

I barely caught a glimpse of the linoleum lab, but it looked like the same place as Kira's videos. A couple more floors passed us by, and then it was nothing but rock. I knew we were going to the bottom, but the elevator didn't seem to stop, piling more and more stone on top of our heads. "How much further from here?" I asked.

"Another thousand feet I think," Influence answered.

Kira eyes widened, seemed like this elevator was deeper than she thought.

"It's gonna be a while." Influence's eyes jumped to the camera. "Thank you, Melanie, you can stop for now."

Melanie lowered the camera from her shoulders and leaned against the elevator's railing, staring out at the rising rock walls with disinterest. Influence's presenter's smile fell away. He looked so different when he wasn't on TV. His eyes were wider, his mouth curved a little down, and his eyebrows arced almost apologetically.

"Zouk, I need to share some complicated news with you. It's not an easy thing to bring up."

Kira's gave my hand a squeeze as I braced myself for the worst.

"Is that why we're playing the last game down here?" Influence shook his head. "That was more of a security thing. This is more—War has requested a review of your previous game. I've looked over the evidence and there is enough to warrant a full investigation." I had never seen Influence fumble over his words before. "You have a lot of zealous supporters out there, many of whom are eager to hear the results of today's game. All of that puts us in a tight spot—we've decided not to broadcast today's game and we'd like a few days to review things before releasing the results."

I pulled my hand away from Kira's and took a step towards Influence, the elevator swayed a little. "This is the biggest game of my career."

"It's a big moment for the nation, Zouk. If everyone hears you won before we've completed our investigation, it could spark riots."

I walked to the elevator wall. They could have told me this earlier, they could have delayed the game. There were plenty of better options. What was this? A mind game? I had a thousand moves stored in my head, a surprise right before the game would be perfect to shake one or two loose.

"Are you trying to keep me off the council?" I asked.

Influence turned away. "Come on, Zouk—this isn't fair, I know that. But we're trying to be fair to everyone. It's only a couple days. Can I trust you to keep the results secret?"

The elevator vibrated slightly against the rock. I gripped one of the metal handles. A little secrecy wasn't so bad, but this was the most anticipated LINE game ever. The moment I walked out after the match, a thousand people would demand to know the result.

"What's this about an investigation?"

"Just some concerns about game integrity, I'm just asking for a few days, a week at most."

Game integrity. Code for cheating. I hadn't, for whatever that was worth. And I was already halfway down an elevator shaft, no reason to put the game off when all the moves were already in my head. I nodded my assent.

"Thank you, Zouk. How about you, Kira?"

Kira had been a trooper to get through things so far, now she was a part of whatever this 'favor' was. "I don't talk to people much anyway," she answered.

Influence rubbed an eye with his pinky. "Good! That was the hard part. Melanie, you can resume filming. For this part Zouk, don't talk, just try to look heroic."

The camera came around the side of my face before I could register Influence's instructions. "Ladies and Gentlemen, I am joining you now hundreds of feet beneath the ground in a classified location." His voice was hushed. "It is here that Zouk Solinsen will play his final game."

As he spoke, I straightened my back and stared out at the dark rock. It felt awkward, hopefully it was heroic enough.

"Mind's Bane. Circuit Cutter. The Enigma. All names for one player. To him, it's a game"—the camera inched in closer—"To the nation, it represents a tectonic shift in the political landscape."

A question entered my mind as Influence spoke. If the investigation was as bad as they said, would they use any of this?

The elevator rattled to a stop and the gates opened. "And cut!" Melanie lowered her camera. Kira grabbed my arm and together we stepped off the lift and into the carved square tunnels.

Kira said nothing, but her eyes took in every detail. Influence passed us by and started down the rightmost tunnel. "Follow me, you don't want to get lost down here."

He kept a fast pace, not like there was much to see. Every branching tunnel looked the same as the first. We continued further and further inside, and I started to hear something. A distant rumble.

"Is that—?" Kira whispered something almost to herself.

I slowed to a stop. "What?"

"The lake, it has no surface rivers. I always thought it poured out somewhere underground. This could be where it flows."

"That it is!" Further down, Influence had turned to face us. "There's a whole lake down here. It meets some of our more demanding thermal needs. Come on, we aren't far."

The rumble grew to a dull roar. Our path led to a stone chamber and the source of the sound. Through a pane of glass, water endlessly tumbled down onto the nearby stone. At the base of the waterfall, liquid pooled and flowed through a hole at the end of the room. On the other wall, a hundred camera feeds were displayed onto a hundred monitors. Most of the footage was dedicated to one section of the facility's fencing. The crowd outside had settled down, relaxing under umbrellas and tents. Without me, they were a lot less hectic.

Influence rolled a pair of chairs away from the long desk and took a seat. "This is my stop." He pointed at Kira. "Yours too. The rest of the journey is Zouk's alone. Maker's waiting."

A dark tunnel lay at the end of the room. I turned to my wife. She looked up at me as if to say something, then simply wrapped her arms around me. Everything we had been through to get here. "Is there no way she can join me?"

Influence tapped the table a second, then shook his head. "I'm sorry, we can't be flexible on this. Down the tunnel and across the bridge. For what it's worth, it's freezing in there."

I didn't respond, choosing instead to hold Kira. She had gone through a lot to support me here. It was so much easier when we didn't have to speak.

"Are you going to be okay back here?" I asked her.

Kira pressed her head into my shoulder and nodded, her nose grinding into my arm. I pulled away and Kira looked back into my eyes. "I am proud of you. Good luck."

My eyes got misty. She had gotten a lot better at the sincere comments. I pressed my lips against hers and Influence politely turned to the cameras. When it was over, Kira leaned close to my ear and whispered, "Yolniv wanted me to tell you something before the game."

My eyes widened. The old man always liked to keep his good advice for the last second, but I never imagined he'd have someone else deliver the message.

"He said don't be afraid to improvise."

Kira stepped back and I wiped the tears from my eyes. Figured, Yolniv spends weeks training me on a single game, then tells me to get ready to improvise. A thousand moves were a lot to get right. I let go of Kira's hand, turned to the dark tunnel and started walking. It was time to face Maker.

16 - MAKER

The tunnel ended at a concrete dock and an underground lake. Its surface was pitch black, lit only by a trail of lights running along the coast. The black water extended off into the darkness of the cavern, a wall of nothing. I grasped back for Kira's hand then realized my mistake. Probably for the best. I didn't want to stay in this place any longer than I had to.

The bridge turned out to be fifty feet to my right. A bit of concrete resting an inch above the lake's surface. As I approached, a glimmer out in the water caught my eye, a subtle metallic reflection. A black dome, almost invisible in the darkness. That had to be The Mind of Manufacturing and Distribution. I straightened my jacket, rubbed the chill from my hands, then hopped a thin gap onto the bridge. My feet moved quick. Being alone sapped the novelty of the adventure.

On the dome, two metal panes slid open with a hiss. A colossal silver cube was waiting on the other side. My opponent. People didn't talk much about Maker. They didn't make public appearances and had never released anything but written statements. Kira had submitted a few reports to Maker in the past, but the responses were exceedingly formal. This was a one-of-a-kind moment. A meeting with a reclusive Mind in its very own home in the depths of the Earth. But it had taken five hours to get here and I was ready to play.

"Come in! Come in!"

Maker's voice was gentle and soft, like the strained voice of an older woman. I entered the dome and the metal panels closed behind me. The massive hemisphere was as flooded as the lake, but in here I could see past the surface. LEDs and status lights lit up hundreds of submerged servers, even Maker's massive silver cube was half submerged under the surface.

"Have a seat. It's been a while since I've had a visitor down here."

The concrete bridge ended at a circular platform in the dead center of the dome. An ornate, wooden LINE board and a carefully set chair waited for me. It was the most elegant board I had ever seen.

"Did you make these?" I ran my hand down the gentle curve of the chair before lowering myself into its cushion.

"Yes. A matched pair. It's been nice to make something without nanometer precision." When Maker spoke, LEDs lit up across its surface. "Back when we first announced the tournament, I had hoped we would be able to use them up on the surface but—things changed. As soon as this game is finished I'm having them moved somewhere nice and dry. Hopefully where people can play on them."

There was a touch of worry in Maker's voice, a real sincerity in their answers I had only heard once or twice when speaking to Influence. The controls for the LINE board were custom made, a perfect fit for the wood housing. I shouldn't have been surprised, Maker had an artist's eye.

"Oh—Zouk, is it too cold down here? I'm a bit out of practice hosting."

As he mentioned it, I noticed my shoulders were shaking. "It is a bit chilly."

A vibration started under the floor, soon waves of warm air chased away the cold. I laughed to myself, it was a funny thing making a request of a Mind. "There! That should do it, we—"

Influence's voice played out through a speaker in the table. "Hey guys! I'm still getting the recording configured, might be a few minutes. Zouk, do me a favor and try not to move your chair too much, I only have the one angle."

I leaned towards the table to answer. "No problem—"

"He can't hear you," Maker said.

"Why not?"

"War's categorized the place 'top secret'. The only way Influence was allowed to record was by replacing the background before releasing the footage. Audio was out of the question. It took a real fight for him to get that one camera."

My ears perked up. I had never heard gossip about the Minds before. "You three have disagreements?"

"Oh all the time. I think Influence enjoys arguing and War enjoys winning."

"But every directive comes in unanimously," I pressed.

"Yes, well, we've got to put up a united front, so to spe—" Maker's voice halted. "Zouk—um . . . What I've shared with you here, it's not something meant for the public. Would you mind keeping that bit of information to yourself? Sorry."

I leaned back in my chair. Was Maker serious? Was this a test? For a Mind to accidentally share a secret, the whole thing had the air of deception. "Of course," I answered.

"And from Influence and War too?"

I gave Maker a long, hard look. They seemed kind, for however much weight you could put in a thirty-second conversation. "I'll think about it."

"Of course, of course. It's a lot to ask. Do you like the dome? I designed it with a sort of minimalist beauty in mind, a reflection of the lake. War had some notes and I had to include those, and then there were the issues bringing the segments down the elevator, and then there was the issue with the workers knowing my location—"

Maker went on about the challenges of the dome's construction for a while. They reminded me of Noah. Passionately sharing everything and anything about their life, thrilled just to have a conversation.

"—and then Influence wanted a few photos for the records. Of course that was completely out of the question. but once it was built I was quite pleased with the results."

There was a certain innocence in their excitement. A joy that was meant to be shared. If this was an act, it was an exceptional performance. "So what makes this place so special?" I asked.

"SER-1." Maker's voice came in cheery. "Do you see the submerged cylinder at the back of the dome? The one with the magenta light?"

I stood and walked to the edge of the platform. The edges of the dome were all black, but as I squinted into the dark, a little purple light blinked on and off, revealing a cylinder, maybe the size of two people.

"Who's SER-1?"

"The first of us. War asked me to look after them. War's very caring, you know. People don't get to see that side of her very often."

My head was abuzz. The Minds disagreed, they argued, they cared, but one comment stuck out from the rest.

"Her?"

"Oh dear—I've done it again. Zouk, can I count on your discretion?"

I answered in an instant, "Of course."

"Thank you. Perhaps it would be best for me to stay silent until the game."

I agreed, and we waited for Influence. Every minute or two, I'd catch another purple blink from SER-1. The first of the Minds. I always thought that was War, that's certainly what they taught in history class. There was more behind the scenes than I had imagined. And if the Minds had disagreements, that meant they had separate opinions. It meant a fourth vote could mean something.

Influence's voice cut in, "Zouk. Maker. We're ready."

I adjusted myself in my chair as the board projected onto the holographic separator. The game Yolniv and I planned flooded back into my brain.

"This is your final match, Zouk." Through the speaker, Influence sighed. "It's a lot less fun when no one's around to cheer." A lot less distraction too. I needed to focus for this game, and down here all we had was the quiet lapping of the lake's waves.

"Good luck," Maker said.

The timer started its countdown in the corner of my screen. Sixty minutes. I played my first move instantly. Thirty seconds later, Maker made theirs. I took a deep breath. Yolniv and I had spent three weeks planning, and as of move two, things were on track.

***

"Twenty-three games. That's all you found?" Yolniv nudged me out of the way of the monitor. There wasn't a lot of room in that cramped office in the community center's basement. Just a collection of monitors, and a whiteboard at our backs.

"I dug deep. Only twelve of these games are officially available, the rest I got from some super old online forums."

"Does Maker use the same thinking algorithm as Influence?" Yolniv asked.

"Only when you play badly."

"Did they make any mistakes?"

"Not in the games I found." I rubbed my forehead as I answered.

"How about inaccuracies?"

"None. Every move was perfect." A week of research and nothing to show for it. Once or twice, I considered asking Jamie for help.

Yolniv gave the monitor a deep scowl, then shut it off and reached for a whiteboard marker. "We need to get creative."

I ducked to avoid Yolniv's elbow as he stood and turned to the whiteboard. My chair pressed against the door to give Yolniv as much space as I could. The old man scrawled the words SABOTAGE onto the board in dark-red ink. I balked. "Are you expecting me to unplug Maker halfway through the game?"

Yolniv smirked and wrote UNPLUG on the board. "Nothing so extreme. But we need to explore everything."

He tapped his chin with the tip of the marker, then wrote the word MISLEAD. "Could we show Maker a fake board? Put a screen in front of their camera or something?"

I shook my head. "The board's data is streamed straight to Maker's hardware. Even if we could, what would we show? Me winning every battle?"

Yolniv wrote another word on the board. "What about forcing a mistake?"

"That's just playing LINE!" My raised voice shook our office's fabric walls.

"What about an emitter? Nothing damaging, just something that disrupts Maker's thinking for a turn?"

"I think I see why they don't want you inside the base." Yolniv chuckled and I stared up at the slightly stained ceiling. "Even if we find the perfect plan, I'm not cheating this. We win fair and square, or I lose."

"Could we manipulate time?" Yolniv had carried on writing ideas without me. "Imagine we froze Maker, made them lose half their time. You could probably win that!"

All these ideas for sabotage and cheating unsettled me, I reached for the eraser, then paused. There was an itch at the back of my mind, a memory fighting its way to the surface. "Wait, wait, wait, wait."

Yolniv put down the marker and leaned in close. "What is it?"

I shut my eyes and rubbed at my temples. I could see a countdown timer in my head, the one from Influence's game. Why did I remember it so clearly? A few numbers appeared: 55:00, 48:30, 41:00, 36:00.

"Why did all his times end in zero?"

Yolniv turned the computer back on. I had more time throughout my games, but that wasn't it, there was something else. "Thirty seconds," Yolniv said.

My eyes shot open, the times on the clock were now as clear as day. "That's right. Thirty seconds for every move."

Yolniv loaded up War vs. Bergamaschi, he played through the moves and made note of the timestamps. "Here too, thirty seconds. Every time." I ran my hands through my hair and watched as Yolniv scrolled through game after game. Every move in every game took the same amount of time. Thirty seconds.

"What about Maker?" My voice shook as I spoke.

"Them too. All twenty-three games. Must be some quirk of how they approach games. Enough time to find a strong move, but not so much as to run out of time in a normal game."

Yolniv stood frozen. The air was electric. We had been looking for a tiny weakness for seven days, now we had their Achilles' heel. "Sixty minutes per player." I calculated.

"One hundred and twenty moves. That's a very long game."

"But I don't have to win. I don't even have to be winning!" After a week of hopeless research, I was ready to commit to this idea, even if we hadn't worked out the details.

Yolniv still looked uncertain. "We've both run down the clock a few times, but only in quick games, and never from the get-go. Are you sure you want to try this?"

There was nothing wrong with letting your opponent run out of time in LINE. Time was a resource. If they ran out, that was their problem. But prepping an entire strategy around wasting the clock? It felt antithetical to what constituted 'proper' LINE play. Then again, nothing I had done to beat the Minds so far had felt 'proper'.

"As long as it wins me the game," I answered.

Yolniv grabbed the eraser and removed everything but TIME from the whiteboard. "Less than 1 percent of games go to one-twenty, and never against a Mind. You'll need a plan."

***

Move seventy came faster than I had ever expected. Maker had done everything they were supposed to. My clock read 54:13, Maker's showed 25:00. I was moving quicker than practice, Maker's slow turns gave me plenty of time to remember my next move before it happened. It also helped that most of my moves were spent planting walls.

The board looked something like the Elephant's Tail, only with way more defenses. The concave arc of my base occupied a little more than a third of the map, and had proven effective against all of Maker's assaults. Mobility was already becoming a problem, the base was a sprawling labyrinth and squadrons had to squeeze through tight halls to get anywhere.

Fifty moves to go.

A strange and unsettling static filled the air. I looked towards the source. Out on the water, SER-1's purple light had stopped blinking. As I listened, the static sounded almost like a distorted voice; it had the ups and downs of intonation, but nothing ever formed completely into words. After a couple seconds, the sound stopped, and the purple light resumed its blinking. It was unsettling, like an old recording destroyed by age. Why hadn't I ever heard of SER-1?

The board chimed, and I blitzed out the next set of orders. My eyes caught something on the board as my hand reached out to hit the button. A finger pressed 'Submit' before I could stop it. The move was locked in.

I grabbed at my hair. Almost a month of practice, so many run-throughs the moves were subconscious, and now there was a real chance I had thrown it all away.

"What are you doing? Focus on the game. Come on!" The words formed on my lips almost of their own accord. A harsh, hushed rebuke of my own failures. I pulled again at my hair, squeezed my eyes shut, and chewed on the flesh on the inside of my lip. The mistake felt like mentally stubbing a toe, all the other pain helped quiet the shock.

Thirty seconds and the emotions abated. I straightened my hair and took several deep breaths. Time to review the damages. I had placed one squadron a tile down from where it should be. It didn't look bad, but I knew it was catastrophic. We had paved a guided path for Maker, a game that lasted over one hundred and forty moves, guaranteed to run Maker out of time. But they would only follow the path if I stuck to the moves religiously.

For the next move, I stuck to the plan. The board was basically the same and it seemed a waste to throw away all that prep time. Plus, there was always the distant possibility Maker made the right moves anyway. Wishful thinking.

Little differences cropped up in the first three moves. By seventy-six, Maker's base was looking radically different. It wouldn't be long before I'd have to go it alone. On move seventy-nine, my hand was forced. Maker's squadrons began to coalesce along the right side of their base. The plan was dead and buried. For the first time in the game, it was time to start calculating.

Ripples of water lapped against the edge of the platform. My mind was churning, thoughts slipped out my lips in a hushed whisper. "What does the board look like? Look at the board. What are your strengths? Where are the weaknesses?"

The board was split perfectly in half. There were walls everywhere. If I hadn't been the one playing, I never would have believed so many could be planted in a single game. My base had become an ant farm, thin branching tunnels that navigated around huge chambers of wall. Only three tunnels reached the top of my base, three points Maker could storm to breach my position. On the bright side, so many obstacles on the board meant it would take a long time for Maker to win even if I made terrible turns.

My squadrons moved to defend the breaches and Maker began their attack. Troops were lined up shoulder to shoulder in the tunnels, barely able to fire against the wave of incoming attackers. In six short turns, a third of my squadrons were gone, and the left tunnel was breached. This wasn't working, Maker was too good. I ordered a full retreat.

Move eighty-six. With how things were going, I'd never make it. I took my hands off the controls and looked away from the board.

Don't be afraid to improvise.

Yolniv's last-second advice rattled in my head. Improvise how? I tilted my head towards the ceiling. There were so few lamps to light up the darkness, it was like staring into the night sky. The game was hopeless, there was no way to turn it around.

"Stop playing to win."

In our weeks of planning, Yolniv and I must have said that phrase to one another a hundred times. It was easy to forget we were playing to lose, we had trained ourselves to win for decades.

"Loss is inevitable."

I mouthed the words, hoping Maker was polite enough not to listen. Loss was inevitable, therefore my only task was to drag this game out as far as it would go.

I returned to the board with a mission. First I began with the massive, wall-filled sections of my base. They seemed like a liability, a limitation on my troop movement. Now, they were my biggest time-eating asset. I ordered my squadrons to continue their retreat. With every tile they fled, I planted a wall behind them. Seal the ant farm.

The blue troops rounded a corner, and Maker's soldiers were cut off. With no direct sight of my troops, I had no doubt of Maker's next move. Turn ninety-one, the red soldiers opened fire on every wall in sight. Burn it down. With each turn, another layer of my base collapsed in a digital cloud of dust. I rebuilt what I could, but there was very little I could do to slow the march.

By turn one hundred, Maker had ten minutes and I had twenty-three. Red troops were spread across the entire board, a long line of soldiers in a rip-and-tear campaign. Two layers separated Maker's army from my huddled troops. One hundred twenty felt like an eternity away. At this rate, it would only take seven or eight turns for Maker to seize the command post. I needed to do something drastic.

On my order, blue squadrons opened fire on the base's right flank. The last two layers vanished in moments. As soon as the path was clear, my troops flooded the battlefield and charged Maker's line.

The board was chaos, every soldier was firing on every turn. Maker's army was too spread out to immediately offer a strong defense. Through the gaps, my forces broke through the line and made for the enemy base. Maker took the bait, they had to to win the game, but with each red soldier pulled from my front line it meant another turn before defeat. The wall-breaker army followed my squadrons every step of the way. The blue army never stood a chance. Four soldiers reached Maker's walls, and those were wiped out the following turn.

I was amazed they had made it as far as they had. The attack was never meant to succeed, I just needed every turn I could get. During the whole battle, I had been rebuilding walls. Maker's clock showed 4:30, nine turns. I clenched my jaw. Maker's troops were pulled back and in disarray. Then again, I didn't have a single squadron left to defend.

I could have just pressed 'End Turn', there was nothing left for me to do, but I needed to know what chances I had left. Starting with Maker's lowest squadron, my finger traced a line through no-man's-land, around the newly built tunnels, through the barracks, and into the command post.

Twelve tiles.

Twelve moves to defeat. Nine turns to victory. There was a chance. I hit 'Submit' and held my breath. Maker had been consistent so far, but with so little time left, there was no telling.

On turn 111, the red troops turned to face my base. The next turn, they opened fire on the walls. My focus was on a single squadron, the one charging through my base. There was nothing left to do but press 'Submit' again and again. On turn 113, a tunnel wall collapsed, shortening the distance from twelve tiles to eleven.

If this were a game between two professionals, I would have quit a long time ago. There was something really demoralizing about not just winning, but watching everything you had ever built get razed to the ground before your eyes.

On move 118, the hero squadron infiltrated my base, or what was left of it. Four tiles from the command post with sixty seconds to go. I could have played fifty moves in the time Maker had left, but Maker stuck to the thirty-second moves, and time continued to creep down.

The last sixty seconds lasted forever. I watched as it clocked down from fifty, to forty, to thirty. Maker's squadron lurched forward again, two tiles from the command post. There was a pressure in my ears, I couldn't hear anything, all I could see was that clock, counting down. It dropped into the twenties, then the tens, then single digits, then stopped at 0:00.

"Ah!" I jumped at the sound of Maker's voice. "The time—huh. Tell you the truth, I had completely forgotten that was a part of it. I thought the game felt like it was going a bit long. Perhaps time needs to be a part of the calculation in the future. Good game."

The screen vanished. I took my first breath in over a minute. It was over. I had won. A victory from total defeat. "Time doesn't come up too often in one-hour games." My voice came out hoarse, vocal cords were as strained as the rest of my body. When I stood, my legs wobbled. I grasped the table for a moment as my strength returned.

"Interesting game. Very interesting." Maker's voice was distant. The games were over. Were the crowds still waiting for me? Would I have to stay quiet as I passed them?

"Do I— Do I just go back to Influence?"

"Yes, same way you came in. He's likely already seen the results. One last thing—" I looked out at the silver cube sitting quiet on the water. "I very much enjoyed our time here, Zouk. Thank you for coming by."

I gave a faint smile, a wave, and started the long trek back.

17 - EMERGING

The dome hissed shut behind me. My head ached as I made my way back to the tunnel, but my feet felt lighter than air. Before I knew it, I was back at the dock and marching back through the tunnels. No more games. It was a funny thought. I had spent the last four months working towards this singular goal, now I'd have to think about life beyond LINE.

I threw open the monitoring station's double doors. They hit the wall with a bang and I strode inside. Kira's arms were around me in a second. After the chill of the caves she felt so warm. "You did it," her voice quivered, almost upset.

"Only because you were here," I answered.

"I'm proud of you."

"Thank you love." We held each other a long while. There was nowhere else I'd rather be, or be with. After a minute, I tried to pull away, but Kira's arms gripped harder.

"Let's enjoy this a little longer," she whispered. There were thin streaks under her eyes. She had been crying. It was time to leave this underground tomb. I peeled her hands away and looked towards Influence. He was sitting in his chair, stone-faced and motionless.

"Congratulations, Zouk." His voice was flat.

"We're ready to leave."

Influence stared at me, his eyes carried heavy shadows. I had never seen him so serious.

"Is everything all right?" I asked.

Influence slowly shook his head and gestured at the wall of monitors. Above them, a weak red light clicked on and off. "The base is on lockdown."

Kira's eyes were wide and her lip trembled. She was scared. The tear streaks made far more sense now. "Are we in danger?"

Influence turned to the cameras. "I doubt it. Take a look."

With a few taps, Influence expanded one camera's feed to fill the wall. I winced at the sight. Rows and rows of people lay facedown in the desert sand, hands interlaced on the back of their heads. Armed soldiers walked between them, occasionally leading one away in cuffs. Near the bottom of the frame was a bent and broken fence. The same one I had stood behind when speaking to the crowd.

"As you can see, the situation is well in hand. Your fans are under control. But until the trespassers are removed, we can't leave." There was a note of derision in Influence's voice when he mentioned my fans. I stepped closer to the monitors, Kira tentatively followed. There were red stains in the dirt.

"Did you shoot them?"

Influence raised an eyebrow. "Nonlethal rounds. Our soldiers defended themselves. When the perimeter came down they were left with no choice. No deaths, luckily. Ask Kira, she saw it too."

I glanced to my right. Kira gave me a small nod. I gripped the edge of the monitoring desk. It didn't make sense, all this had happened in the few hours since I had been in the bunker? The last two times this had happened, it had at least been caused by my words. There must have been a reason. "Show me the footage."

Influence moved his jaw left and right. "Fine." He stood and turned his chair to me. Without a word, I took the seat and scanned through the footage.

One hour back, the fence was still up, folks on-screen were lounging in camping chairs and nobody was getting arrested. I ran through the footage at four-times speed, my heart beat heavy as members of the crowd walked one by one to the fence, and started shouting to the soldiers.

Influence spoke from over my shoulder, "They wanted to see the game live. Your fans were convinced we were rigging it."

I frowned and slowed down the footage. Chants of 'stream the game' and 'rigged result' came through clear. Where had this come from? Over the next ten minutes, half the crowd had gathered at the fence.

"Watch their hands, when the soldiers don't give them a response, they tear down the fence."

Already, the mob at the fence was pushing and pulling at the chain-link. Then they started working together. It didn't take long for the perimeter to bend and warp. There was so much fury in the faces of the tightly pressed crowd. The folks that hadn't joined in were quickly packing up and headed for their vehicles. Everything was happening just as Influence said, but I couldn't stop watching. My eyes swept over every detail, searching for a reason.

The top bar of the fence snapped, dropping the metal mesh at the soldiers' feet. Most of the crowd froze, but a few stepped forward. There was a flash, and a cloud of gas formed at the front of the crowd. People were coughing, wiping their eyes, a few figures rushed for their vehicles, but some pressed on.

Just a few feet from the front of the crowd, a muzzle flashed on one of the soldier's weapons. Three bodies fell. My breath left me. A second later, two more troops fired into the crowd.

Kira's hand touched mine. "Ten hospitalized."

"Once they're recovered, we'll bring them before the courts," Influence added.

The crowd started to disperse, but not fast enough. Another flash and the air was filled with smoke. A terrible dread hung in my chest. No one was reaching the vehicles anymore, most got a dozen steps away from the mob and fell to their knees coughing and hacking.

"If your fans had gone any further, they would have met rifles." Influence looked on with pitying eyes. The footage soon caught up with the live feed. Most of the crowd was gone. The few that were left were cuffed and waiting their turn to be led away.

I rewound the footage.

"This was a dangerous situation, Zouk. And it's not the first time—"

"Just a second." Influence and Kira stayed quiet as I pulled the footage back to the formation of the crowd. There had to be a reason. Nothing stood out as they broke the fence down a second time. There was the flash and the gas and the fleeing mob. I paused the footage. One of the fleeing forms caught my eye. He looked familiar, a button-up blue shirt, shining black shoes, a luxury ITV caked in red sand. The guy drove off before the arrests. I rewound for a clearer image.

Derek. My body sunk into the chair. Influence began expressing his remorse for the situation, but I could barely hear it. If Derek was here, that meant the Torrez Institute was too. They were a skilled group, no doubt inciting a riot was within their wheelhouse.

The last few on-screen civilians were arrested, and the red light at the top of the wall stopped flickering. I held Kira's hand in silence as Influence led us back up the tunnels and onto the elevator. The box creaked and jostled loudly as we waited to reach the topside.

Yolniv was right where I had left him, lounging in his chair and flanked by a soldier. Even from here I could see a hole where the fence used to be. Yolniv craned his neck back at us and spoke in a somber tone, "Quite the show you missed." He paused when he saw my expression. "Maybe you caught it downstairs."

Yolniv glanced at his military escort. "Am I permitted to stand?"

The soldier nodded and took a step back. With a good amount of grumbling and groaning, Yolniv pulled himself to his feet. "It's been an upsetting day, Zouk. Did you at least win the game?"

Influence answered before I could, "We can't reveal that at this time."

Yolniv scratched his nose and gave me an appraising look. I tried to keep my face as straight as possible. "Must have been close. Sure took a while." Yolniv rolled his shoulders and started down the asphalt towards the vehicles.

During the long walk, Influence's gaze never moved from the distant debris. The section of damaged fence had been torn down and cleared away. Chairs, fire pits, and umbrellas were scattered around in the dust. Folks had left in a hurry. Plenty of vehicles were still parked out in the sand.

"One hundred thirty-three arrests. Ten hospitalizations." Influence spoke without looking away from the ruins. His voice had an air of regret.

"What's going to happen to the people you arrested?" I asked.

Influence sighed. "They trespassed on a military base. Some of them defrauded the Unified Activity Manager, claiming today as a sick day. Depending on the evidence, they'll serve between five and ten months."

I balked. "That's extreme."

"We can't have people skipping their jobs to break into a military base," Influence answered.

"It's proportional," Kira added.

I shot her a confused glance then focused on Influence. "They broke a fence, they weren't here to attack anyone."

"The judges will factor that in, but sentencing guidelines are sentencing guidelines."

"Couldn't you recommend a shorter sentence?" I asked.

Influence kept a steady pace. "No."

It all seemed so unjust. Over a hundred lives paused for half a year, all because the institute had egged them on, all because they supported me. "What about their families? What about their lives?"

"Empty argument, Zouk."

We arrived at the vehicles. Yolniv entered his quickly, but I continued, "Wouldn't it be more efficient to only punish some of them?"

"Not if it encourages further trespassing."

"They don't deserve this!"

Influence opened the door to my ITV and pointed inside. "You're not making a point anymore, you're just arguing. Go home."

His face was flat, a total indifference to everything I was saying. "This wasn't an accident, you know! There were people in the crowd that caused this."

Influence set his jaw, there was a fire in his eyes I had never seen before. "The only person that 'caused' what happened here, was you Zouk. You've been cultivating popularity for months, but in all that time I've never seen you step up and lead. When you tell your followers the system is broken, this is the consequence."

I was at a loss. Is this what working with the Minds would be like? My hands balled into fists. I stood taller as Influence stared me down. A hand touched my shoulder and I turned rapidly to see Kira with pleading eyes. I had said my fill, whatever came next couldn't be taken back. I walked Kira to her ITV, then stepped into mine. We rode out through the facility gates. Influence hadn't moved from his position on the asphalt.

18 - WAR

RANK: 16 ▲ 2

Yolniv was waiting for me at the minibar in the VIP box. "Did you see the fan club?"

I walked past him to the seats overlooking the stadium. "All eleven hundred. Talked to them too."

The old man's eyebrow raised. "A message of revolution?"

I shook my head. "Just a meet and greet." That and a lot of hype-killing. Folks had been waiting for news on my game for nine days. Speculation had hit a fever pitch. Influence's solution was to announce everything tonight: both my victory over Maker, and the investigation. He had told me to be here so I could cast Jamie's game, but it was easy enough to guess that I was here on damage control. There would be a lot of upset people tonight.

"You're sure you only want a guest spot? Ezra's dying to get you back in the chair."

"No thanks." That'd be just perfect, politics and drama in the same night.

"Alright, enjoy the show." Behind me, I heard the door to the box close. I let out a heavy breath. Keeping the results of my third match from Yolniv felt wrong, insulting even. At least he'd only have to wait a few more hours.

I leaned outside the box to see the rest of the stadium. The field looked just as it had when I played. War and the secretary general on one platform, Lieutenant Denvers and Jamie on the other. This time the stadium had a few empty seats here and there and a few big gaps near the top. No doubt some of the enthusiasm for Jamie's game had been killed by my match overshadowing it.

The game started with little fanfare. Jamie made quick moves, War took her time. Truthfully, my whole body was on edge. Too many variables all joined at the same stadium. I felt like I needed to do something, anything. How long had I left those protesters outside? I twisted in my seat, then paused when I saw the door to the VIP box opening.

"Hello?" I asked.

I recognized the blond, tussled hair of the world champion almost before he got through the door. Bergamaschi cast a brief look over the field, then went straight for the minibar. "Does this Jamie plan on plagiarizing all your strategies, Mr. Solinsen?"

He spoke with a melodious accent. I stared at Bergamaschi slack-jawed. "Dueling Spires. Same as you, yes?"

Down on the field, Jamie was eight turns in and on course to copy me again. "To be fair, she was the one to come up with it. Good to see you again, Bergmaschi."

Bergamaschi smiled his wide, shining smile and took a step forward to shake my hand. "Been a while. You've certainly made something of yourself since we last played. I believe I lost that one."

In the past few months I had spoken face-to-face with the most powerful figures in the nation, but somehow Bergamaschi's charm and effortless style still left me starstruck. "Yes, that's—uh, that's right."

"Outposts, that was a clever one." Bergamaschi went through every cabinet in the VIP Box, bringing bottle after bottle out onto the table. After a careful assessment, he poured two glasses of bourbon, handed me one, and joined me to watch the game. Another four turns rolled by.

"Tell me, Zouk. Why am I watching the same game I saw three months ago?"

"It's not quite the same, some of the squadrons are positioned a little differently."

"Barely." Bergamaschi set down his glass. "Two squadrons a tile off, a wall moved from G3 to F3." He was right, I took a sip of my drink. "I haven't studied a game that closely in years. You played terribly."

I chuckled and saw Bergamaschi smirking. "I won, didn't I?"

His eyes narrowed. "That you did. One second you're losing, the next, War makes the biggest mistake in its hundred thousand game career." Bergamaschi gestured at the field with his drink. "Now here we are doing it all over again. What am I missing?"

Jamie looked so small down there. A tiny figure staring down a metal colossus. Was that how I had looked? Bergamaschi's eyes were locked with mine. "Come on," he said. "You already won. I already lost. What's the secret?"

It seemed like everything I had experienced in the last few months had to be secret. Misleading the public, keeping quiet with Yolniv—for once, I wanted to share something. I made a silent apology to Jamie and pointed to War's side of the field. "Watch D1 through H1. War has a blind spot. Can't see anything in those squares."

Bergamaschi's eyes went wide. He leaned forward, standing to get further over the railing. After a minute, he stood up straight and fished a screen out of his pocket. My game versus War loaded in seconds. When my forces reached the blindspot, he paused and turned the screen towards me. "This? This was all War missed?"

I nodded and he immediately resumed the replay. For minutes

he tapped at his screen, rewinding moves, watching the big moment again and again, even giggling a little to himself. With his cool, put-together personality, it was easy to forget we both shared a passion for LINE.

Jamie's game had reached move twenty-five. A few differences were emerging between her game and mine, but the strategy was identical. At this pace, her troops would reach War's blindspot by move sixty-six. The jumbotrons showed a closeup of Jamie on her platform. She was done up well by the makeup team, but there was a certain fatigue in her eyes. Maybe it was the stress of the game, but it looked like she was on the edge.

"What a terrible weakness." Bergamaschi was still staring at my old game.

"My wife thinks it's because War's always on the attack. They've never played a game where their opponent actually reached the top row."

"Just like with the outposts." Bergamaschi lowered his screen. "You know, you've always scared me."

My ears perked up, that wasn't something you heard much from the best in the world. "Really?"

"Oh yes. I believe you have a 5-7 record against me."

I took a drink. "A losing record."

"Well, you can beat me, and regularly. Back when you were good—excuse me—back when you were in the top ten, everyone was scared of you. We complained about you. The ultimate spoiler. I could be on the best win streak of my life, but that wouldn't matter against you." I had never heard this, but then again, I had only been in the top ten for a year.

Bergamaschi got out of his chair and sat on the railing. "There was something about facing you that broke the rules. The rest of us were always trying to get that little edge on one another, make ourselves 95.6 percent accurate instead of 95.5. Then you would play 4 percent less accurate and take the game anyway."

I thought back to those premier tournaments, the few I had been invited to. Most of the time I had landed in the middle of the field, fourth out of eight, ninth out of twenty. "Sure didn't help me win any championships," I said.

Bergamaschi leaned his head out into the air. "Things might have been different if you had been in the top ten a little longer. If you had leaned into that adversarial style. You could have been the best of all of us."

"Maybe I will be again."

Bergamaschi got a far-away look. "That would be a waste. You're on course for something bigger. When I heard you beat Influence, I rushed to buy a ticket for your game against War. I told everyone, if there's any player in the world that can beat the unbeatable, that can take impossible and turn it into a coin flip, it's Zouk." I hung on every word. The other LINE pros had never spoken like this, certainly not to me.

Bergamaschi stood and walked back to the kitchenette. "How did that last game go, by the way?"

I smiled. "Can't say."

Bergamaschi shrugged and poured himself another drink. A knock rattled the door, and some teenager leaned his head into the room. "Mr. Solinsen, would you mind coming with me? Ezra wants an interview for the game's halfway mark."

"What, not me?" Bergamaschi swayed a little as he spoke.

"Uhh—" The kid looked nervous."Not yet. She'd like you to give a deep-dive analysis once the game gets a little further along."

Bergamaschi wandered back to his seat and I followed the intern out of the VIP box. Through a window, I caught a glimpse of the crowd on the street. All watching the game on personal screens. The board and Jamie's face were plastered on every wall we passed. Her squadrons were getting close to the top, the same blindspot I had caught War with.

We descended into the concrete underbelly of the stadium. I

recognized the route from my game against War. The intern led me past the locker rooms, where a voice called out, "Number Eight, is that you, man?"

The intern slowed just as I wanted to speed up. Derek jogged over to see me. My shoulders tensed. "Hey, Derek. Been a while."

He took my hand and shook it as he spoke. "It sure has, buddy. Sorry things turned out the way they did. At least Jamie's been doing a good job in your stead."

No words came to mind. I couldn't stop seeing the still of his face outside Facility Five, before the riot.

"You've been doing pretty well without us, congrats on your win against Maker." He flashed a smile.

"We haven't announced the result yet."

Derek glanced around, then leaned in to whisper. The smell of a wooded glade was heavy. "Oh shoot—was that a secret? Maya figured you had won when the Minds referred your investigation to a prosecutor."

"A prosecutor— What are you talking about?"

"Look, Zouk, I don't know. They said you got some assistance from a guy on the platform during the game. Could be nothing. These things blow over all the time." Derek turned to watch the game on a wall. "I really haven't heard more than that, man."

I rubbed my eyelid and tried to parse Derek's words. The only other person on the platform was Denvers, and we had only spoken for a couple seconds. A prosecutor investigating a tiny conversation in the middle of a LINE game, it seemed ridiculous. Then again, why would Derek lie about it?

"Hey look at that, Jamie made it to the end of the field."

The board confirmed Derek's words. Four squadrons were lined up along the top of the board, ready to strike into War's base. Thoughts of court and prosecution fell away as I watched each player lock in their moves. If War hadn't figured things out, Jamie's topside troops would charge through the walls. If she had, this would be a very painful evening for Jamie. The players locked in their moves. Jamie stood confident, staring out onto the field. For all our differences, I was cheering for her.

A gong played. The four squadrons charged towards War's base. As they crossed the gridlines, a trooper fell, hit by a red projectile. Another flew in just after, then a volley. Seven tiles down, War's troops were taking aim and firing on isolated squadrons. By the end of the turn, Jamie's front squadron was gone. The blindspot had been found out.

In fifteen seconds, Jamie's chances of winning were completely gone. The cameras zoomed in closer and closer to her face. She was downcast, her shoulders sunken. War wasn't going to lose to the same trick twice.

"Looks like Jamie's out, sorry, Derek." I patted his shoulder and walked toward the intern.

"We're good, man. We got other plans." Derek's words stopped in my tracks.

"Other plans?"

"Yeah, man, we got backups on backups." His arms waved as he spoke. It sounded like bragging. "Loopholes in the system, people on the inside, people on the outside, everything. Keep watching, even if we're losing, we're gonna win."

I swallowed and gave Derek a weak smile. If Derek knew I had seen him at Facility Five, he never would have let that slip. The plans I had seen from the Torrez Institute in the past were mostly composed of riots and treason. Tough to imagine this one would be any different. Someone needed to be warned.

I left Derek and hurried down the hall. The intern struggled to catch up. Once we were safely out of Derek's earshot, I spoke. "Who's on the broadcast today?"

The intern sputtered a little as they spoke. "Ezra, Y-Yerten I think his name was, and The Mind of Communications and Influence."

Influence. Exactly who I needed. The intern led me into the

broadcast room. Ezra and Influence were seated on a duplicate of the regular news set. Yolniv was standing in the corner next to a large analysis board. I walked as close to the main camera as I could and started waving my arms. Ezra tripped on a word as her eyes jumped to mine for the briefest of seconds. I pointed at Influence, but he gave no sign he had seen me.

An arm grabbed me and dragged me out into the hall before I could do anything else. Whoever they were, they shouted plenty, but I gave them no mind. A minute later, Influence walked through the broadcast door and stared daggers at me. "What?"

"Jamie's team is about to do something drastic." Influence sent the stagehand back into the broadcast room and shut the door. His face was flat and his eyes were set, an all-too-common expression on him lately.

"What are they going to do?"

"I don't know. Derek said they had people on the inside and outside."

"Which people?" Influence asked.

"I don't know, that was all he said."

Influence shook his head. "That's not enough. I need a name. You've been a part of their organization, you've seen who works there. Is it the military? The police? The broadcast team?"

His lensed eyes stared directly into mine, bouncing from one to the other, searching almost. A single name came to mind, a throwaway from Maya's conversation. "Lieutenant Denvers."

Influence stood up straight. "Take my place on the broadcast. I'll be back soon."

He sped down the hall at an inhuman pace. Every step covered five or six feet. The man whipped around a corner and vanished.

I entered the broadcast and stood again, near the cameras. "Great breakdown, Yolniv. For those of you just catching up, War's throwing punches and Jamie's on the ropes." As Ezra spoke, her eyes jumped to mine. "Joining us now is Zouk Solinsen here to tell us just what went wrong in our challenger's strategy."

A hand shoved me onto the set and I quickly took the seat next to Ezra. Her first question arrived before I could get comfortable. "Zouk, you and Jamie's methods for dealing with War are quite similar. Where do you think Jamie went wrong?"

I didn't think long on Ezra's question. Now that Jamie had lost, there was no reason to be coy. "She copied me too well. A couple months back, Jamie and I worked together on a plan to hoodwink War. We exploited a hole in War's gameplay that essentially allowed us to steal a win." Ezra looked with sharp eyes, almost as if she already knew what I was saying. On a screen of the field, soldiers marched out of the tunnels and took positions at the bottom of Jamie's ramp. They were armed. "Turns out War's a pretty smart player. Too smart to fall for the same trick twice."

Another figure emerged from the tunnel, a tall woman, the same that had delivered the news my game against Maker would be in a bunker. She seemed very well trusted. Within a minute, she had scaled War's platform and handed a message to the secretary general.

"Now that the gambit has failed, what do you make of Jamie's chances?"

I painted a pretty pessimistic picture, but as I spoke my focus was locked on the field. The secretary general was staring across at Lieutenant Denvers. Troops ascended Jamie's platform and approached Lieutenant Denvers. My voice trailed off, but Ezra didn't immediately jump in. From the corner of my eye, I could tell she had caught on that something was happening.

Denvers took three steps forward, his feet toed the edge of the platform. One of his boots raised from the ground, then stamped the hardwood three times. A shrill whistle played throughout the stadium, loud enough to pierce even the broadcast room. A signal. A chill ran down my spine. The broadcast swapped to the livestream of the field. Like a pro, Ezra narrated everything she had seen for the viewers at home.

My ears felt muffled, my fingers were cold. Any second now, the gunfire would begin. But no one moved a muscle. Lieutenant Denvers followed the soldiers off the platform without protest.

After thirty seconds, War submitted her next move, and the gong played. The field was full of nonlethal weapons fire. But something about it struck me as wrong. The board was less chaotic than it should have been. When the turn ended, plenty of soldiers were still standing. Too many.

"War's troops didn't move," I mumbled.

Ezra caught my shock. "Zouk, some very odd things have been happening both on and off the field. What are you seeing?"

It took a second for my tongue to find the words. "Well, uh . . . There's a lot of soldiers that have failed to follow their squadron orders." I was still piecing it together, and having to narrate my thoughts just slowed things down.

"If we look at squares D4, G7, and B8— " The broadcast cut to Yolniv's touchscreen. The old man quickly shot out of his chair to highlight the squares I was mentioning. "Several of War's squadrons have been divided. On D4, four soldiers marched forward to defend against Jamie, but the other three did nothing."

Out on the field, both player's timers had paused, and the secretary general was descending from his platform. Ezra pushed the conversation on, "We saw the relayer—"

"Lieutenant Denvers," I interjected.

"Lieutenant Denvers signaled to War's troops before he was led off the field. Could we be seeing some—some kind of mutiny?"

My voice caught. Mutiny. Not quite treason, not quite a coup, but the kind of action that ended careers and sent soldiers to prison. The kind of action that represented a specific threat against the government. Yolniv jumped in, "It's a little early to say for sure. But— War's soldiers rejected a direct order from the secretary general. Mutiny wouldn't be a stretch here."

Ezra's voice shook as she asked her questions. "Putting aside the mutiny question for now. What happens in a game of LINE if soldiers refuse their orders?"

Yolniv and I shared a look. I broke the silence. "We don't know. Nobody does. LINE is usually played on a computer, programs don't disobey orders."

Ezra twisted her head towards Yolniv. "What about the rulebook? What does that say?"

Yolniv shrugged. "The Field LINE Rulebook is more of a historical quirk than a binding set of rules. It's a century old and hasn't had a single modification. Until last year, no one played the game in real life."

The door to the broadcast room slammed open. Influence's eyes had a fury to them. He strode to the edge of the set holding an old, yellowing rulebook with LINE written on the cover. I had never seen a physical copy before.

Yolniv continued to describe the history of LINE while Influence flipped rapidly through the pages. His frown deepened with every page. When he reached the final page, he slammed it shut and took a deep breath. It was time to give the host back his show. I rocked forward to get out of my seat, but Influence stopped me and thrust the century-old LINE book in my direction.

"Page 291, halfway down," he whispered.

Ezra threw question after question at Yolniv as I feathered through the delicate pages. Influence stepped back away from the set, and rubbed one of his eyes.

"—Yolniv we're going to have to interrupt you. It looks like we have a copy of The Field LINE Rulebook. Zouk, what have you found?"

I found the paragraph Influence wanted. There was no time to pre-read its contents. "Section C, Article 5: Troops that fail to follow commander's orders will be removed from play."

The room was quiet a moment as each of us digested the short sentence. Ezra was the first to speak. "How does that work? Disobedient troops are replaced and we rerun the turn?"

I read the rule a second time, then handed it to Ezra. "There's no mention of 'replacing' troops, just removing them from play."

"Only War's troops failed to follow orders," Ezra said, piecing it together along with the rest of us. "So only War would lose troops. That would put them at a disadvantage wouldn't it?"

"War would lose a third of their army instantly." There was a heaviness in my voice. Derek had mentioned a loophole. Here it was, a technically legal maneuver that flipped the board on its head. All Jamie had to do was finish the job.

Behind the cameras, Influence tapped away at a screen. On the field, the secretary general returned to his position on the platform, paper in hand. The feed tracked his every move. He unfolded the message and read it over to himself. An eyebrow twitched. At the end of the message, the general blinked a few times and slid it into his jacket. Finally, he approached the microphone.

"Ladies and Gentlemen, a unique circumstance has arisen." His voice didn't carry with the usual drill-sergeant's bravado. "Multiple service members have failed to follow orders. The cause is unclear and will be investigated." He cast a harsh glance at the field. "However, the rules in this circumstance are cut and dry. All soldiers that have failed to follow orders are hereby instructed to leave the field of play."

Eighteen figures walked slowly out of the LINE grid. All red troops. Entire squadrons in some cases. War's defenses looked meagre. When the last defecting soldier had vanished into the tunnel, the general spoke again. "Play will now resume."

On the field, the timers resumed. In the broadcast room, Influence's hand gripped my shoulder. There was an intensity to Influence's silence. He led me off set and into the hall.

"Who's taking my place?"

"Bergamaschi. He'll be here soon. We need to talk—"

Influence fell quiet. A line of red troops passed us in the corridor, the mutineers. They walked with puffed out chests and an over-confident swagger. As if they had done something to be proud of. They rounded the corner and Influence whispered, "They'll be lucky if they're discharged."

We ended up back in the VIP box. Bergamaschi was already on set analyzing Jamie's position. Influence cleared the alcohol from a little table next to the minibar, and moved it towards the back of the room. I was stuck standing in the corner, across the table from Influence. Influence reached back and locked the door. He was still wearing a deeply serious expression. "Zouk, how do you know Lieutenant Denvers?"

"I met him for the first time at my game against War."

"What tipped you off about today?" Influence's eyes didn't blink. This was an interrogation.

"Derek told me something was going to happen. I didn't know the details." My voice was jittery.

"Why did you suspect Lieutenant Denvers?"

"Maya mentioned him once."

"While you were at the Torrez Institute, did they ever discuss backup plans for your game against War?"

"No."

"How about your game against me?"

"No." My right leg started bouncing in place. Influence's face had gone cold, a harsh mask leaning close to ask questions. Influence blinked once, then twice, then leaned back in his seat. Slowly, life returned to Influence's face. He rolled his shoulders, then spoke in a much calmer voice.

"You did the right thing telling us something was coming today. Shame we couldn't stop it." Influence's gaze strayed to a screen on the wall. I looked to see Bergamaschi waving his arms this way and that, shouting about something we couldn't hear. I tapped unmute on the screen.

"—she has no killer instinct! What is she doing? I thought this was one of the smartest players in the world, not a little lamb fearful for her life!" I ran to the edge of the box to see the state of the game.

I couldn't believe it. Nine moves had passed since Jamie's little coup. She had had a Dueling Spire position with an opponent that couldn't even defend their core base. All she had to do was sever the weak middle of War's spire and press for the win. A knockout punch. Instead, her side of the board had barely changed and War's spire was rapidly rebuilding. Bergamaschi's rant echoed around the box.

"I can forgive one turn of inaction, maybe two. But nine? This tip-toeing nonsense has to stop. Jamie thinks time is on her side, but War is quicksand, and she is sinking."

Influence leaned over the edge next to me. There was a hint of a smile on his face. "I bet War's loving this."

The jumbotron focused again on Jamie. She was shifting her weight from one foot to the other and back again. She did this at tournaments sometimes, mostly when she was losing.

The gong played and War's squadrons struck out at the top of Jamie's spire. I turned my back to the field, it was hard to watch. It was always hard to watch a friend lose. "Are we still announcing my victory tonight?"

Influence stepped back from the railing and slowly nodded his head. "We could do that. We could definitely do that. It might raise some spirits after Jamie's loss."

I made a beeline for the alcohol, and poured myself a glass. "Are you gonna mention the prosecutor?"

Influence smacked his lips. "We didn't want things to get this far, Zouk. But the more we get to know you, the more doubt creeps in. And after today—"

I cut Influence off. It had been clear they didn't trust me for weeks. "So what's the claim?"

"War believes you received illegal assistance from Lieutenant Denvers."

I snorted, my head was starting to feel light. "I barely know the guy."

Influence checked a screen in his pocket. "Did you want to be there when I make the announcement?"

I put my head on the table. Going on TV to tell the world I was under investigation for working with the guy that had just committed a mutiny sounded dreadful. My lips touched the cool surface as I spoke. "No. Try to make me sound heroic."

19 - THE DEPOSITION OF ZOUK SOLINSEN

RANK: 21 ▼ 5

I was overdressed. My tie was choking me and my toes screamed for release from their freshly-bought burgundy prisons. Plus, there was something really lonely about sitting on your own in a field of chairs, I tipped my chair from one leg to the other. The soundproofing circled the whole room, only stopping for the doors to the deposition chambers.

Derek sat five rows down and six seats away. He gave me a friendly wave, as if he didn't know we were testifying against each other. "Didn't you already answer your questions?" I asked.

"Oh I did. But, ya know, gotta wait for the boss."

We both looked towards door D-28. Maya was in the middle of her questioning. Keeping me outside had been Kira's idea, she and my lawyer agreed it would be best if I gave my testimony uninfluenced by prior witnesses. All I had to do was tell the truth of what happened. Somewhere around hour five I began to regret that decision.

D-28 opened and I jumped to my feet. Maya was the first out. My stomach tightened as our eyes met. It looked as if she had been crying, or close to it. I couldn't imagine what part of her story could have elicited such emotion. She gave me a pitiable look and sped away.

Denvers followed soon after. His face was red and his hands formed fists. The lieutenant circled the room but his eyes never left mine. He must have heard I was the one to spoil his game. My feet slid back under my chair. Derek followed the pair out. More than ever, I wished I had heard the rest of the depositions.

Kira's voice called me to the chamber. I hurried to the door, but slowed when I saw her muted expression. "Are you sure we don't want to take the offer?" Things hadn't gone well.

"That'd be telling the world I'm guilty. Let me explain my side."

We walked past five empty rows of seats to the deposition pad. My lawyer, Adalee, and the prosecution were waiting. The pad was nothing but a large blue circle surrounded by scanners. Good enough for the jury to get a complete 3D view later. I put my foot on the pad, then paused. My body was too relaxed. I wasn't ready, I should have stayed up all night practicing. Adalee prodded me onto the pad. Too late now. "The edges of the pad are the maximum range of the sensors. Use your arms but don't move around too much. If this plays in court, we want the best possible scan of your responses."

I nodded dumbly and stood up straight, my brain had processed maybe half of what Adalee had said. Staring down the room, my eyes caught a figure leaning against the back wall. Influence. What was he doing here? How did he have the time to be here?

"Mr. Solinsen, has your lawyer reviewed your rights for this deposition?"

I flinched at the sound of the prosecutor's voice. He was standing just a few feet from the pad. The guy looked to be in his mid-forties, his suit was worn and wrinkled and his face showed a bored expression. A professional.

"Have you reviewed your rights?"

My head shook away the stray thoughts. I needed to focus on the now. "I have."

"Fine. Let's get started." The prosecutor raised a screen to his chest and exhaled slowly. The smell of coffee wafted in my direction.

"I'm gonna start by diving straight into the contested event." He slid his thumb across his screen, and an image of the stadium appeared in front of me. "This is footage taken directly from your game against War. If we look here—your relayer Lieutenant Denvers is five feet away from you and facing your direction. Is that normal in a game of LINE?"

Kira and I had gone over this footage a hundred times. All I needed to do was tell the truth. "Relayers are rarely needed in LINE games. But no, players and relayers don't usually stand that close."

"While Denvers was near you, did you discuss anything?"

"We did."

"What did you talk about?"

I took a small breath, recalling my rehearsed statement. "Ordering troops to fire on one was—challenging for me. Lieutenant Denvers told me his experiences in other military sims to calm me down. We spoke for maybe a minute."

"Did any other topics come up?" The prosecutor asked.

"No."

No slip-ups so far. The prosecutor thumbed his screen, lazily scrolling up. I shook the stiffness out of my legs. We were just getting started. New footage projected onto one of the scanners in front of me. Lieutenant Denvers was on the deposition pad, dressed in full army regalia and staring forward with a stern look.

"This is—uhh, testimony from a prior witness."

The prosecution hit play and Denvers' face twisted in anger. "—No it's not all right. Lieutenant is my title, a title I earned after a decade of service, and I expect you to use it. A discharge doesn't change the stripes I worked my—" The audio cut and the footage ran in reverse.

"Sorry, just a second."

When the footage resumed, the red was gone from Denvers' face. "I first met Mr. Solinsen on the commander's platform, just before the game. We both knew the deal. If it looked like he was losing, I'd get close, talk a little, and wait for the signal. My guys were ready on War's side of the field to throw in a little chaos." Denvers flashed a cruel smile. My shoulders tightened and my hands closed into fists. So that's how they were playing it. Now I saw why Kira and Adalee didn't want me in the room for the other depositions. It would have been hard to keep my composure through five hours of lies.

Denvers continued, "—of course when the girl played I didn't need a signal, it was obvious she needed help. That and the soldiers—"

The footage vanished and I was once again staring at the prosecution. His eyes jumped to my hands for a split second. "What was the signal for Lieutenant Denvers? A phrase? An action?"

"We didn't have one!" My voice came out louder than I expected. "Everything he said there was a lie."

The prosecution reached for a cup on his desk and took a long swig. My face was heating up, I needed to calm down.

"How did you beat War?" he asked.

"I exploited a blindspot in its algorithm."

"According to Jamie's statement, you—"

My ears perked up at the mention of Jamie. She had done another vanishing routine after her loss against War. "Jamie was here?"

"She was unable to attend due to poor health. Please refrain from asking questions while you're on the stand." Poor health. Not uncommon for Jamie, but after she had become the whole nation's punching bag I couldn't blame her. But she had still submitted a statement. Why? Was she trying to bring me down with her?

"According to Jamie's written statement, it was her team that discovered War's 'blindspot' and developed the 'Dueling Spires' strategy. Is that an accurate depiction of events?"

"Yes."

"So you leaned on Jamie quite a lot. How would you describe your relationship with her?"

A lot of questions about Jamie. I hadn't practiced for these, nor did I understand why the lawyer was asking them. "Our partnership was troubled. In the short period we worked together at the institute, we argued a lot."

"Why did you leave the institute?"

My mind jumped back to that evening tea I had shared with Maya. She was so personable, so concerned for my well-being. And I had been so honest with her. Forthcoming to a fault. No wonder she thought she could trust me with the task to tear down the nation.

"Maya and I had a difference of opinion." I couldn't bring myself to say the full truth. Treason was a thing that called as much suspicion on the accuser as on the accused.

"Did you leave voluntarily?"

"I was going to. The institute fired me before I could."

"For what reason?"

In the corner of my eye, Adalee jumped to her feet. "Objection! Repetition."

Adalee and the prosecution argued back and forth, and my gaze drifted to the back of the room. Influence was leaned forward, his hands clasped on the top of the next row of chairs. He wasn't the judge, but he was hanging on every word. Was his presence related to the prosecution's offer? Adalee's voice brought me back to the deposition.

"Zouk, go ahead and answer the question. A judge will rule on the objection at a later date."

I asked the prosecution to repeat the question.

"Why were you fired from the institute?"

I raised my arms for a stretch, but caught them before they crossed out of the blue circle. "Like I said, Maya and I had a difference of opinion on policy that was irreconcilable."

"Another troubled relationship," the prosecution noted. "You don't think it had anything to do with the riot you started?"

"I didn't start—"

"Objection!" Adalee's voice stopped me in my tracks. My neck was pulsing, I had nearly answered without thinking.

"Withdrawn." The prosecutor took a step back and swiped through his screen. For the first time, I made eye contact with Kira. Her eyes looked strained and she was picking at one of her fingers.

The prosecution danced around the topic of my lecture: questioning the contents of my speech, the answers I gave in the Q and A, even where I hid during the riot. With every question, I could feel my own emotionality bubbling up. Like the feeling of a game of LINE slipping out of my hands.

A new image appeared on the deposition screen. "This is a still from the lecture hall, half an hour after your lecture ended." I squinted to look at the image. The room was a mess of strewn papers and broken desks. Near the front, the walls were covered in graffitied messages. No more Minds. End War. Man Triumphs. It wasn't the chaos I had seen at the bunker, but all this was without a doubt my fault.

"Your coach, Yolniv, was there. If he had given the lecture, do you think things would have ended as explosively?"

I hesitated. No one else had fans like I did, and during that lecture I had said all the wrong things. "It's unlikely."

"So, seeing the damage and knowing that this wouldn't have happened with another LINE player, do you really believe this event had no influence on Maya's decision to fire you?"

He had cornered me. I had felt the walls closing in with each question. This deposition wasn't an attempt to uncover the truth, it was a game of logic and narrative reframing. I had come in to face a master without even knowing the rules. The situation needed to change. I needed to make a move. In the seconds of silence, only one idea came to me.

"I was a big investment for the Torrez Institute. Maya didn't care about the riot, she cared about her investment. She wanted payback for everything she had done for my career. When I won my last game and joined the council, I was supposed to tell the world the Minds were a threat to humanity."

The prosecutor made no effort to stop me. My voice grew as I continued, "Maya wanted me to throw the nation into civil war and invite our enemies to attack. When I said I wouldn't, she fired me."

My courage left me the second I finished speaking. Kira was subtly shaking her head. Adalee had her head down in her notes. The prosecutor cast a brief look at Influence. The judge wouldn't be here until the trial, but I suspected Influence was in the process of making a personal ruling. Now that I had said it, honesty felt like a mistake. My speech felt desperate and scared. The prosecutor put down his screen before continuing.

"Congratulations on your victory over Maker. Historic. Was it difficult?" The mood in the room had changed. The prosecutor now wore a faint smile and spoke with an upbeat demeanor.

"Very difficult. Yolniv and I were strategizing for months."

"Was it frustrating to play that last game without the Torrez Institute's resources?" I was starting to see the picture the prosecutor was trying to paint. He was trying to turn me into one of Maya's disgruntled, fired co-conspirators.

"I think we adapted well."

The prosecutor paced around the pad. In the quiet, I noticed a subtle vibration buzzing from one of the sensors. "Let's talk about another game. Jamie versus War. That was a scary day. Luckily, you were there to warn the government. How did you know what would happen?"

Another attack from another side. I'd need to shore up my defenses. "Derek from the Torrez Institute told me—he let it slip."

"Wasn't he the guy that escorted you off the institute's property?

You still talk?" I could hear a rise in the prosecutor's voice. Another trap.

"It was a one-sided conversation."

"I see."

I braced for the next question, but it never came. Instead, the prosecutor put their screen down on the table and walked back to their seat. "No more questions. Fifteen-minute break?"

The buzzing of the pad stopped. I glanced back and forth and slowly stepped back onto the carpet. The prosecution had been leading me somewhere, trapping me in my own incongruities. It was the same feeling I got when a LINE game was just about to go against me. Now I was being let off? Kira met me with a hug and led me to Adalee and the defense table.

"How did I do?" I asked.

Before anyone could respond, the prosecutor's arm reached past me, sliding a screen onto the table. "Adalee, this is your last chance. If he says no again, we go to trial."

He left and I turned to Adalee. "Is it the same offer?"

She picked the screen up and perused it briefly. "Yeah."

I had rejected the offer out of hand a week back. It was ridiculous, I had played my games and beaten the Minds fair and square, now a couple of lies from Maya, and the government was strong-arming me into throwing part of my victory away in fear of criminal charges. I sat down and folded my arms. "So we go to trial—"

Kira's voice interrupted mine, "You should take the deal."

I looked her in the eye. She was certain. I was missing something. "I thought I did pretty good up there. I mean, that prosecution was closing in, but they quit halfway."

Kira responded, "No he didn't. He had everything he needed. The arguments don't come until trial."

My throat tightened. The walls were built, but I wouldn't know how badly I was losing until the day of the trial. "What story do you think he'll tell?"

Kira's eyes dropped to the floor. She tapped the tips of her fingers together. She was keeping herself from saying something. I gently touched her arm. "Kira. I need to know what's coming. It's okay."

She nodded, bit her lip, then began, "Everyone but you and Yolniv told the same story. You knew about Denvers' plan from the start, but you got lucky and didn't need it." Kira hesitated. "According to them, you got caught up in your own ego and started a riot. Maya fired you. When you saw Jamie up on that stage, halfway to beating War, you decided to spoil her chances by warning Influence. Basically, you're a co-conspirator and only did the right thing when it meant you could sabotage Maya."

Kira covered her face. I didn't dare ask which story she believed. My teeth ground together as I took it all in. This whole deposition was one long attack against my character. But what was the point? All they needed to do was show some footage of me and Denvers talking during our game and throw the game out. And why did the prosecution offer a deal? They had dug up enough witnesses to bury me.

On the other side of the room, a pair of lensed eyes met mine. That was why. This wasn't about criminal intent. I grabbed the prosecution's offer and strode past the chairs to the back. Influence rolled his neck as I approached.

"You don't trust me?" I asked.

"You've given us plenty of reason to doubt."

"So you trust Maya?"

Influence smirked. "I don't need to, she didn't win three games."

If the Minds didn't trust me, I knew there was nothing left to do. "Fine." I placed the prosecution's offer on the table, scrolled to the bottom, signed it, and slid it to Influence. There'd be no criminal charges, no fines, no punishments except one. "If none of you trust me, why risk playing me again?"

He took the screen and glanced at my signature. "War thinks you'll lose."

20 - REGAME

RANK: 24 ▼ 3

My rematch was scheduled on the same day as a soccer game. The teams were long gone, but the sweat and humidity still hung in the air of the locker room. Yolniv and I had taken refuge in the coach's office and blasted the air conditioner. I was seated on the leather couch, squinting at the wall-screen. Yolniv watched me from behind the coach's desk, but I paid him no mind. My eyes were busy sweeping every tile of the LINE game on the wall. It was supposed to be move fifty-two of the upcoming game, but something had changed. "The wall separating E5 and F5 shouldn't be there."

Yolniv nodded. "Good. Where should it be?"

I rubbed my temple and looked again. This was the 62nd puzzle today. Grid squares were starting to blur together. I dropped my head into my hands.

"I think we're reaching the limits of human memory here," Yolniv said. My eyes stared back at Yolniv between the gaps in my fingers. "I thought there was no limit, you used to tell me you could play ten LINE games simultaneously and perfectly recreate all of them."

He shrugged. "Well— I always got close." I blinked away the dryness in my eyes and looked again at the board. Yolniv whispered his advice, "Remember: You can't just stare at the board as it is, think about what came before and what comes next."

Another couple seconds and I saw it. "Put the wall on G5. Anywhere else and War has an open firing line on my squadrons."

Yolniv jumped to his feet. "Good! Very good!"

"How many more?" I asked. He glanced at his watch before answering.

"Seven. But we can stop here—"

"Pull up the next one."

Yolniv looked at me with raised eyebrows. I gave him a nod. My game against Maker had nearly ended because my memory failed me. That was something I could control. Maybe I'd lose today, but I wouldn't lose because of a mistake. "I'll be fine. Let's finish this." After a moment, Yolniv sat down and opened the next puzzle.

We finished the set with thirty minutes to spare. Before I could ask for more, Yolniv dragged me out of the office and into the sweaty air of the locker room. He never let me practice in the thirty minutes before a game. I voiced my disagreement, but he gave the same answer he always did. "We aren't cramming for an exam here, we need those moves stored in long-term memory. Plus, there's something I wanted to give you."

Yolniv outstretched his hand. I leaned my back against a locker and took the flat, round object from him. It felt like a fabric patch, but every bit of it was pitch black and the fibers were frayed and loose. Looking closer, I could just make out the shape of a claw. The symbol of the lom army.

"This is yours?"

Yolniv nodded. "A long time ago it was. Did you not know I was in the army?"

"I think you maybe mentioned it once."

"Hmm—well, I was. Signed up with my buddies when I was nineteen, they gave me a rifle and shipped me off to the northern border."

I ran my thumb over the patch, a layer of soot rubbed off onto my skin. "I can't take your medal from you."

Yolniv snorted. "That is no medal! They gave that to every soldier that got through bootcamp." He moved to my left and leaned against a locker. "But it is special."

I gave the old patch another look. Maybe it held sentimental value.

"A few months in, there came a day we received combat orders. Strange combat orders. Every member of the squadron got one just for them. They were all written on little slips of paper. They weren't from a colonel or a general, they were from The Mind of Strategy and Warfare itself."

I looked up from the patch. Yolniv's story was sounding familiar. "You refused their orders?"

Yolniv tapped the locker gently with his finger. "Yes and no. Things weren't as clean as the history books say. The issue we had wasn't with the source of the orders, it was with the specificity. We were attacking a nearby bunker, a tough one. Most of the squad's orders were to charge the bunker from different angles. But not me, my orders were to stay back and be prepared to provide medical assistance."

"That doesn't sound so bad."

The old man's nose flared. "My orders also specified which soldiers were mostly likely to be shot."

I went quiet. War had probably simulated the battle a thousand times. When she gave out those orders, she knew what would happen. "She hand-picked who would live and who would die."

Yolniv nodded, his eyes were dark. "It didn't take long for us to figure it out. There was a moment. All thirty of us in the squad were sitting in the barracks, saying nothing. We didn't need to. A third of us would be leaving the battlefield on a stretcher, and we already knew which ones. It's one thing to fight and die together, but knowing who had been assigned to die was far worse."

I could understand what War was trying to do, she had planned the battle to minimize losses. But that level of control was dehumanizing. My fingers picked away a loose strand on the patch. "So what burned the patch?"

A little light snuck back in Yolniv's eyes. "Right—well, none of us were happy. However, I took a little extra initiative in expressing my displeasure. Still a kid, you know. That night, I brought the whole squad together outside the base. We heaped a bunch of scrap wood into a pile, crumpled our orders on it, and soaked it in gasoline."

My eyebrows raised. "A bonfire?"

Yolniv's grinned. "You got it. I think I went overboard with the gasoline, because I don't remember much after the fireball. They gave me two days in the hospital and one hundred sixty in the brig. But they let me keep the patch."

I could hardly believe it, Yolniv had told me hundreds of stories about his life. But all this time he had been hiding his best one. "You were a part of history."

He shrugged. "I was angry. I wanted to get my voice heard and it cost me my eyebrows."

I chuckled, the patch suddenly made sense. "Is four weeks of depositions and lawyers my fireball to the face?"

Yolniv rotated so his shoulder pressed against the locker. "It certainly hasn't been a walk through a meadow. You know, the day they appointed the secretary general remains one of the highlights of my life. Tough lady. Half the TV was blocked by the brig bars, but that didn't matter. Something changed that day. We weren't fighting for the Minds anymore, we were fighting for the nation. I hope I live to see another moment like that."

Yolniv looked like a different man. His eyes twinkled with a youthful glow. Behind that grumbly exterior, there was an idealist, a freedom fighter. He didn't say it, but I could tell he was hoping 'the next moment' would be mine. There was no way I'd live up to all that. But at the very least, I could give it my all against War.

An intern popped his head into the locker room. "It's nearly time, Mr. Solinsen."

I carefully pocketed Yolniv's patch and pushed off my locker. At the doors to the tunnel, Yolniv handed me a coat and wished me luck. "Never let the world forget Zouk Solinsen's 4-0 record."

The wind whipped through the tunnel with a chill bite. It was hardly late afternoon, but the skies were a dark grey. I ascended the platform and met my new command relayer. She was a half foot shorter than Lieutenant Denvers but wore the same focused expression. The secretary general had hand selected her. At the very least, she probably wouldn't attempt a coup. We shook hands briefly, and I walked to the edge of the platform.

Red and blue squadrons marched onto the field and took positions. The audience gave a subdued applause. Folks were dressed for the cold, but it was more than that. There were somber looks in the bleachers. After the deposition, I had come to terms with the injustice of this little rematch, it seemed the general public hadn't.

A flash of movement on the front row caught my eye. Someone in a suit was waving a GO ZOUK sign. It was hard to miss, the seats all around the person were empty. The second they lowered their sign, I recognized them. Derek had a habit of being everywhere I was lately. We locked eyes, and he raised his arm above his head, index finger outstretched.

I followed the trail of his finger above the thousands of fans to the VIP boxes. A lone woman in a mauve pantsuit wiggled her fingers in my direction. Goosebumps ran down my arms. Maya had made every effort to destroy my reputation. She had probably never anticipated the Minds would give me a second chance.

"Ladies and Gentlemen!"

I broke away from Maya's gaze and listened to the secretary general.

"Per Directive Two-One-Four-Nine, officers selected from our country's armed services will be engaging in a battle simulation as defined by a modified copy of LINE Assemblage Rulebook."

He held up a copy of the new rulebook, it was about seventy pages thicker than the original. Yolniv and I had gone through it line by line, the Minds had changed nothing about the game, just closed the loopholes. Turned out there were plenty. Not anymore. Jamie's trick wouldn't work a second time.

"War, are you ready?"

"I am." War's voice was as expressionless as her cube.

"Zouk, are you ready?"

"Yes!" I shouted.

"Then we begin."

The first sixty moves played out in almost real time. Our strategy was the same as we had used against Maker: fill the board with walls, accept a losing position, and play for the clock. The analysts had nicknamed it the Ant Farm. Heaps of artificial walls were stacked at the edge of the field, far more than the previous games. Yolniv had had several shouting matches with the event organizers to ensure we'd have enough. Thankfully, War was playing the game exactly as she needed to, and we were on course to use just about every wall available.

It wasn't long before the evening sun sunk into view below the dark-grey sky. The wind hadn't let up its whipping rage. I pulled my hands into my coat between turns, but the troops on the board were shivering. If there had been a chance, I would have warned them about the long battle that was coming.

I reached turn sixty-five in no time. Then I slowed down. Yolniv's idea. The moves at this point were much harder to remember: lots of shuffling, lots of maneuvers. Everything warranted a double check, we couldn't risk a repeat of my mistake against Maker.

The game continued smooth until turn eighty-two. I knew something was wrong from the moment the gong sounded. We had built up a rhythm in the game, and now that rhythm felt off. I brought my hands out of the sleeves of my coat and reviewed the screen in my hands. Nothing popped out to me. My eyes checked every tile, it was all exactly correct, but it didn't shake the sense of wrongness. I input the next move and hit 'Submit'.

The gong sounded for move eighty-two and that sense of wrongness came again. Even before I saw the move. I checked the clock: 36:21 for me, 19:10 for War. I winced at the sight. No wonder it had felt wrong. War's thirty-second turns were like a drumbeat, dictating the game. Now the drumbeat had changed, War had made a twenty-second move.

I didn't dare do the math to see if I could still win, I just input the next move. If we reached the end of the game, I'd be defeated. But at least I'd have given it my all.

Move eighty-seven was incorrect.

I got it right. War got it wrong. Her new rhythm had me feeling rushed, but I was still double checking all my moves. Four red squadrons had gone to the right flank instead of the left. A tiny change on a board with forty active squadrons. Nevertheless, War had broken from the choreography. I spent a solid minute staring those squadrons down on my screen. It wasn't a good move. The point in playing bad was to ensure War always made the good moves.

This one struck me as an inaccuracy. A subtle misplay. I held back a laugh. Maybe that extra ten seconds per turn did a lot more for War's skill than she realized.

"Squadrons Echo and Frank, move north-by-northwest."

I didn't spend long thinking about the next move. I'd need all the time I could get for the battles. Now that War had broken free of the strategy, conflict was inevitable. The sun vanished behind the horizon, and stadium floodlights kicked on.

A movement in the front row caught my eye. Derek waved in a line of ten men and women to the open seats around him, and then he waved at me. I gave him a confused look, then looked at his guests. One in particular caught my eye, a fellow with blond hair in a buzzcut. A chill settled into my heart. I recognized him. He had been at Jamie's game. He had been in Jamie's game. Ten newly-discharged veterans were staring me down from the front row.

I blinked repeatedly then turned back to my screen. Three minutes wasted. I couldn't do that again. War and I were in a real game. Her forces were coalescing on the two sides of the board. The moves were far from perfect, I just needed time to exploit her weakness.

Three heavy thrums echoed through the stadium. My attention jumped back to the front row. The veterans were standing shoulder to shoulder. All together, they stomped their feet against the first row's stadium flooring three times in quick succession.

"FWEEEEEEE!"

A shrill whistle filled the air. My arms fell to my side, left hand gripping the command screen. It was the same signal they had used during Denvers' mutiny. Blood pulsed in my ears. I searched the stadium for any sign of an attack. Last time it had meant a few soldiers disobeying orders, but this time they were all staring straight at me, and I couldn't shake the feeling that I was their target.

To my right, the command relayer stood as stoic as ever. The troops on the field made no moves. On War's platform, the secretary general was whispering something to a soldier. I couldn't feel my fingers. Could he be a part of this? We had never spoken, but he had voluntarily overlooked War's blunder in her last game against me. A soldier sped down War's platform and into the tunnels.

There was an empty seat on the front row. All that was left was the GO ZOUK poster leaning half folded on a chair. When had Derek made his escape? I looked up at Maya's VIP box. She waved at me from her seat and smiled a sickly-sweet smile. Her eyes, even hundreds of feet away, pierced into me.

When I couldn't stand it anymore, I looked down at my shoes. I was maybe three steps from the edge, the twenty-foot drop left a pit in my stomach. I shuffled a few steps backward.

After a moment, footsteps echoed from the tunnels. My chest trembled as I took each breath. Was this it? I thought of Lieutenant Denvers and that fiery, hateful look he had given me just after the deposition. Had he decided to get rid of me?

Uniformed soldiers marched out of the east and west tunnels in a hurry. They didn't even glance my way. Quickly, they spread out and took positions all along the edge of the field, while a few others escorted the front row veterans out of the stadium. Of course, this wasn't the assassination, it was more protection. I breathed a sigh of relief and tried to calm my heart.

My right hand was starting to cramp. The command screen was being held in a death grip. I wouldn't have even remembered the game without it. 26:15. Seven more minutes lost. Even if the institute was making an attack on my life, I couldn't afford to waste another second. I moved the screen into my other hand and tried to focus on the game.

War launched two attacks, one for each of my base's breaches. My defenses held up stronger than I expected, it seemed like with every tile War gained, she lost two squadrons. In time, the attack lost momentum. It was time for me to strike back. I brought my hands to my head and started a deep think.

War's troops were about to retreat, this was a good opportunity to pick off stragglers. My heart was pumping furiously, louder even than my thoughts. On the other hand, it would be easy to attack my squadrons as they emerged, it might be better if I carved a new breach away from the armies. I could feel Maya's eyes boring into me from her VIP box. Those veterans had thrown their careers away just to ensure Jamie defeated the Minds before I did. They were probably just as furious as Denvers. My eyes scanned the audience again. The front row had been cleared out.

I looked back at the screen, it was hard to read, and my hands wouldn't stop shaking. 22:11 left.

I was screwed.

This wasn't just a bad mindset or poor sleep, my body was showing the physiological symptoms of fear. My pulse was racing, my legs were wobbling under me. I was vulnerable, a sitting duck on a platform waiting for a sniper to take me out, or a rogue soldier to throw me those fifteen feet to the field floor. I couldn't strategize, I couldn't plan.

Then and there I set a new goal for myself, try not to lose. For what it was worth, I was on the offensive and War was down to fifteen minutes. Forty-five moves felt like an eternity.

"Squadrons, pursue the enemy."

It wasn't smart, it wasn't clever, but when thinking is out the window, it's best to make smooth, simple moves. Three of War's squadrons were eliminated during their retreat from the blue base. I pushed the advantage. My troops emerged and began a siege on the red position. War's walls fell one by one. More and more of my troops emerged from the tunnels. They pressed down the center of the board, ripping through War's base. I input most turns in a couple of seconds, there was no point trying to think any further. For playing the game on instinct, I was amazed that War was falling apart like this.

On move one hundred ten, War's troops fired on their own walls. And I realized I was doomed.

I should have spotted it. The flank squadrons, the weakening walls, the massive concave bowl my troops had formed in War's base. In any other game, I would have avoided it. War hadn't been losing, she had been drawing me in.

Fifteen red squadrons fired on the eighteen of mine. My troops were clustered in a ball, War's were spread in a wide circular perimeter. When one of my troops took a shot, they occasionally hit. When War's troops took a shot, they hit, or they hit the trooper behind the person they were aiming for. It was the oldest strategic trick in the book.

In one turn, half my army was gone. War barely lost a squadron. It was over. There was no escape, and every turn meant more pain for my soldiers. My pulse slowed and I fell to my knees. I had failed.

There was no button on the panel for what I needed to do next. I flagged my command relayer over and explained the situation. She gave a curt nod and pressed a finger to her ear. I hung my head in shame as she relayed the order.

"Ladies and Gentlemen!" The secretary general's voice boomed through the stadium. "Zouk Solinsen has resigned. The Minds have never before faced a stronger opponent. For his two prior victories"—I grimaced at the misrepresented record—"and for his showing tonight. Let us celebrate Zouk Solinsen's performance."

The applause started quiet, but quickly grew. I pulled myself to my feet and looked out at the crowd. One by one, the crowd rose to their feet. There was none of the wild, dangerous energy of my first victory against War. Folks were nodding, cheering, waving their arms from the stands. A toxic hate still sat in my chest, I knew I could have won. But in the face of a ten-thousand-voice outpouring, I couldn't help but wave back and wipe away a tear.

Yolniv met me at the door to the locker room with a pair of beers. I took one, stomped past him, and collapsed on the bench.

"Close game," he said.

"They never should have made me play it."

Yolniv took a swig from his bottle before responding. "To be fair. It seems to me like you were never supposed to win."

I glanced at him with a raised eyebrow and took a sip. "Oh yeah?"

"Just something in the air. They seemed very thrown off guard dealing with you."

"Too bad. They shouldn't have made the tournament if I wasn't supposed to win it." I put the beer down and stared at the eggshell wall of the locker room. "I bet I could make a big stink about all this."

Yolniv smiled. "More than you know, I think." He took a seat next to me. "Everyone in that audience tonight was with you, Zouk. You feel cheated, I know. Out there, they feel it a hundredfold. For today—and maybe for a while—your voice carries the weight of injustice. If you really are angry, you could put on one hell of a protest. If I were a little younger—" Yolniv's voice trailed off.

I let my mind wander. I pictured ten thousand people screaming in the streets. A mob bigger than the Minds had ever seen marching through the capital, dragging War's cube down the street and to the negotiating table. Forcing their hand. As I thought, an old piece of advice popped into my head.

"Once you find a winning move, find a better one."

"Hmm?" Yolniv's head twisted in my direction.

"I don't want to waste my chance. If leading a bunch of riots against the Minds is a winning move, what's a better one?"

Yolniv furrowed his brow thoughtfully, then threw away his empty beer. "Only the player at the board can say for sure."

I felt the imprint of Yolniv's patch in my pocket. "When the troops were rebelling, back in your day. Why do you think our generals negotiated with the Minds? Instead of just using the army to take control?"

Yolniv scratched at his chin. "Hard to say. Our first secretary general was a very intelligent woman. If I were to guess, I would say she recognized that that much upheaval would be good for her, but bad for Iom."

A hundred little ideas skittered at the edge of my mind. The games were done, yet it felt as if things had just moved into the next phase. I stood up and headed for the door. "There's plenty of time. We don't need to make a move today, let's use what time we have to make the best move possible."

PART
THREE

21 - A NEW BASE

RANK: 28 ▼ 4

The screen's cursor blinked on and off. Forty minutes had passed since I last wrote something. Trying to solve society's problems was proving difficult in a tiny office in the corner of a basement. Thirty-nine pages of Iom's woes was proving to be my limit. I stretched my arms for the third time that hour. Yolniv's stout form puttered past the cameras every minute or two, folding chairs secured in his armpits. The clock read 4:55, five minutes until the meeting.

I rubbed my eyes and switched camera feeds. Four well-dressed figures stood at the base of the community center's stairs. It had been Yolniv's idea, I was a LINE player, not a law writer. Get the professionals to help. One deep breath, and I was on my feet. The walls rattled as I stepped out and crossed the large, empty expanse of the community center's basement.

The group's heads were craned to the side to avoid the ceiling.

They shared a look between each other as I drew close. Two women and two men, all wearing fine suits. A man with square glasses was the first to extend his hand.

"Mr. Solinsen, what an honor to finally meet you."

I shook each consultant's hand in turn. The last of the four was a woman in a deep-blue blazer. Her eyes kept jumping between me and the rest of the basement. "Is there somewhere we can talk?"

My nose became suddenly aware of the playing room's musty odor and heavy air. It had always been good enough for the local LINE players, but the subtle glances between the consultants told me they expected something more upscale. "Upstairs, we should be able to find a conference room."

The fellow with square glasses tripped on his way up the stairs. Loose carpet. I picked up the pace and quietly resolved to find somewhere better to host these meetings in the future. On the main floor, I led the group down a white-tile hall towards the big conference room. A pair of students had it for the evening. Too bad. We settled for a cozy study room with a square, dark-wood table.

I took a seat and the consultants packed in on the opposite side. The two on the corners looked comfortable enough, but the pair in the middle were rubbing shoulders. A quiet moment passed. This was a terrible first impression. I needed these people to believe in my vision and help make it happen, an aged study hall was definitely missing the mark.

From the left corner, the man with glasses broke the silence. "So Mr. Solinsen—"

"Zouk." My voice shook as I spoke.

"Zouk. I'm Charlie. I hear you'd like some help writing a bit of legislation."

I gave a sharp nod. "Yes! I'd love some help. For the past week and a half, I have been trying to get my thoughts together on some legislation. Ya know, use my voice to make a difference." A red-haired man in the middle pulled out a notepad and began scribbling furiously as I spoke. "So I was hoping I could bring my ideas to you, and maybe we could work together to turn what I've written into something cohesive."

"Well—" Charlie reached into his jacket and unfolded a small screen. "I think we can help you, Zouk. My team and I are some of the most successful law writers in the nation, outside of the Minds of course." He slid the screen to me and a short list of directives appeared. "In the two decades of our firm's operation, we have managed to get thirteen pieces of legislation passed into law."

I swiped my finger across the screen, then realized I was seeing the whole list. Twenty years, they weren't even hitting one directive annually. These people were supposed to be the best. "Thirteen— that's it?"

Charlie's hands made circular motions in the air. "That's more than anyone else in the business. It's not easy to pass laws, Zouk. Especially with the Minds. But you already know that, your first televised political statement was a call for—what was it?" Charlie turned to his coworkers. On the far right, the woman in the dark-blue suit spoke.

"Better communication and a clearer path to passing laws."

"Right." Charlie pointed back at me. "Good idea. Someone already sent it in, in fact. Turns out you can send anything you'd like to the Minds. Unfortunately, most of the time—by which I mean every time— the only response you'll get is a letter of rejection and a big wall of math telling you why your idea won't work. That's usually when people give up."

I nodded along with everything Charlie said, wishing I had brought a notepad. My hands flipped the screen around towards the consultants. "So how did you get these passed?"

Charlie brought his hands together and grinned. "Negotiation."

"Negotiation?"

"That's right. They don't like to talk about it, but the only real way to get the Minds to do anything is to have some leverage. If it weren't for the corporations and institutions that fund us, we wouldn't get anything signed."

I fell back into my chair. "So it can't be done. The Minds don't listen."

Charlie and his coworkers shared a look. "If it couldn't be done, we wouldn't be here." A little smile appeared on the woman in the blue suit. Charlie reached across the table and tapped the screen in my hands, a new document labelled *Draft Legislation for Zouk Solinsen* appeared. "For now, let's just assume it is possible. You had some big ideas, what we have here is a proposal that boils a few of those ideas down into practical law. The kind that can make a difference—like you wanted."

Charlie seemed like he knew what he was talking about. I couldn't take on all of Iom's problems all at once, we'd have to work through it in bite-sized chunks. I tapped the screen and started scrolling. The page count appeared in the bottom corner. They certainly had initiative. "Two hundred and ten pages? You haven't seen what I've written yet."

Charlie adjusted his glasses. "This is just a first draft—a best guess. Somewhere to start from."

I blinked a couple of times, then flicked my finger across the document. It scrolled several sections forward. The paragraphs read like a different language. I recognized the words, but couldn't make sense of what I was reading. Even the section headers were verbose to the point of being cryptic. As much as I appreciated being handed a complete piece of legislation, I had no way of knowing whether the content was a good idea or even aligned with my personal values. "Charlie, you said yours was the only group to get legislation passed?"

"Yessir," Charlie answered.

I was only familiar with one piece of legislation from the Minds. "How about the LINE tournament directive, was that you?"

"We don't like to brag, but we did have a hand in it." Charlie stretched across the table and tapped the tablet again. It was another page of tiny text and legalese, but at the bottom was a signature line. "This is a little cooperation agreement my team and I threw together.

Sign this and I guarantee we'll have your ideas carved into stone by the end of the year."

The consultants stared at me with toothy grins. I rubbed my forehead and read slowly through the agreement. Getting my ideas out into the world was great, but this—this was too easy. Charlie was too eager. A line caught my eye. I zoomed in on the text. "Permission to make and distribute communications on behalf of the undersigned, what's that?"

Charlie rubbed his hands together. "During negotiations, we need to be able to quickly communicate back and forth with the Minds. That's a little provision that lets us speak for you. You know, keep the conversation moving."

I stared at Charlie for a moment before returning to the screen. Agency representation. Control over appearances. Pre-approval on LINE lectures? Halfway through, I knew I wouldn't be signing these papers. No doubt they were the best in the business, but something about Charlie and his team was putting me off. I flipped back to the legislation. The woman in dark blue raised a finger to speak, then stopped herself.

One of the section headers had been bothering me. After a minute of silent scrolling, I found it. Page ninety-five: *Biannual Elevations in Government Investment for Syndicated Institutions*.

"You work with institutions?"

"We do. We have some excellent partners."

"How about the Torrez Institute?" Charlie's face froze mid-smile, as if he was debating how to answer. His eyes darted to the right, to the woman in the dark-blue jacket.

"We don't disclose the identities of our partners." Her voice made clear my line of questioning was over, but it was still an answer. I slid the screen back to Charlie. "Sorry guys, no deal."

Charlie's face fell. "It's just a first draft, Zouk, we could work in more of your ideas."

I shook my head, it was all I could do to keep from kicking them out of the building. "Another time, thanks for coming by."

The consultants stood at once and filed out the door. The last one paused and turned my way, the woman in the dark-blue suit. "It would be easier if you worked with her."

Charlie probably wasn't under direct orders from Maya, but clearly this person was. "Can't you people leave me be? I already lost my game."

"You still have something to offer."

I kept a stoic expression. Even after the deposition, the defeat, the threats, Maya still thought I'd consider working with her. After a moment, the woman shrugged and left the room.

My hands gripped the sides of the chair. How long was this going to drag on? Now that I told her 'consultant group' no, could I expect another visit from the veterans? Maybe Derek would make an appearance? At least I knew I still had leverage. We had only gone a week or two since the big loss, and chances were my thirty-nine-page political treatise probably wouldn't have much effect. Charlie was right in one aspect—I didn't need ideas, I needed concrete policy behind me. The quicker I spent my influence, the quicker Maya would get off my back.

The study room's automatic light switched off. I took that as my signal to leave, and headed back downstairs. We had well over a hundred LINE players in that dingy basement. Everyone was heads down, focused on their games. Yolniv had done a good job setting things up. I spotted him standing behind an amateur, wincing at every move.

"How many rounds left?"

He twisted around to face me. "We've barely started. You shouldn't be out here. How were the consultants?"

"They just wanted to use me to get their own ideas passed." I didn't want to concern Yolniv with all the Torrez Institute stuff.

He shrugged. "Sounds about right."

I thought back to that two-hundred-ten-page document. "I'm

starting to suspect a smaller idea might be better for legislation."

"Have you talked to Kira about it?"

"She wants to read it when it's done, but I don't know. She's been heads down at work ever since I lost that last game."

"Trouble?" Yolniv asked.

I scratched the back of my head. There was always something new with Kira and I. The threats at my last game had convinced her I was telling the truth about Maya, so better than during the depositions. "Not this time. Every once in a while she gets obsessed with some project. I just try to stay out of her way until it's over."

Yolniv cleared his throat and indicated a few rows over. "Did you see who made it today?"

It took a second, but once I spotted the pajama-wearing, ten-year-old kid whose feet didn't even reach the floor, my face lit up. "I thought Noah was done."

"I told you he'd come back. The kid's got the love of the game in him."

"Can you put me against him next round?" A couple of players were looking in our direction, one had pulled their screen out for a photo. "Ideally in one of the corners." Yolniv nodded.

I hid out in my office until after the next round's clock had started ticking. If I showed up early, I'd distract the other players. By the time I was seated I was already down a minute on the clock.

"Hi, Mr. Zouk!" Noah's looked as carefree as I had ever seen him.

"Hey Noah! Is your dad here today?" I looked around for Noah's business-oriented father.

"No. He stopped taking me to stuff after I told him I didn't want to play anymore. Now it's my mom again." No doubt that contributed to Noah's positivity, Mr. Chewes tended to take over any room he was in.

"You're here today. Does that mean you like playing LINE again?"

"Yeah, it's fun!" His move came in, his wheel-and-spoke base structure was much more robust than the last time I had seen him.

"So what changed?"

Noah shrugged. "I just like playing around with it. It's a lot more fun without all those tournaments."

I chuckled to myself as my fingers input the next move. He was putting up a real fight. A months-long break and somehow the kid was playing at a semi-pro level. "Just playing on the computer then?"

"Yep! The app says that because I stopped playing I'm not allowed to go to anything else—except your event of course!"

I smiled. Noah's story reminded me a lot of my own. The Unified Activity Manager worked Noah so hard he lost his love of the game. Then when the app was out of the picture, he came back to LINE on his own. It was a real shame the kid wasn't allowed to play at tournaments. He was better than ever and banned from competing. The whole thing was ridiculous.

"Mr. Zouk, are you okay? You're losing."

My head was somewhere else. I had spent the past ten days writing an elaborate breakdown of every problem facing Iom, but the solution had been staring me in the face from the start. Redesign the UAM. I couldn't fix the whole world. But one malfunctioning part was doable. It was the piece that broke me, it was the piece that broke Noah. Even a small tweak to the UAM could do a world of good.

"Mr. Zouk, you're almost out of time."

I stood up from my chair. Ideas buzzed around in my brain. "Noah, I'm so sorry. I won't be able to finish our game."

Noah jumped off his chair, walked around the screen and looked up at me. "That's okay, Mr. Zouk, it was nice to see you."

I gave him a quick hug. "I can't tell you how proud I am of you, Noah. Come by again next week, we'll play a full game then."

I ran back to the office. The cursor was still blinking at the bottom of the thirty-ninth page, right after the section titled *Surveillance, Industry, and the Breakdown of Community*. What had I been thinking? That I could completely diagnose the flaws at the heart of society in a couple weeks? I closed the document and opened a blank one. The title was written in seconds, *A Proposal to Modify the Unified Activity Manager*.

22 - BREAKTHROUGH

It was probably time to replace the old guest chair—the cushion sank in and the metal frame pressed on my back. A thin stack of papers lay on the table, my proposal. It had come out at twenty-one pages, the brevity felt like a good thing.

A quiet thump sounded through the ceiling, then a shuffle. She was finished reading. I rubbed my hands together and waited. After a moment, Kira's feet appeared at the top of the stairs. Her steps were slow, hesitant. I swallowed the lump in my throat and waited to catch sight of her face. Her expression was solemn, lowered eyebrows and downcast eyes. She didn't need to speak for me to know what she thought.

"You didn't like it"

She looked my way. Her eyebrows raised in apology. "The ideas were good."

I fell back into our chair. Days of writing, rewriting, and revisions, and it wasn't enough. The day before, I had told Yolniv it was my greatest work. I huffed a little to myself as Kira reached the bottom floor and took her seat on the couch.

"I need you to be supportive of me here," I said.

She slid the proposal onto the table, avoiding my eyes. "You told me this was the most important work of your life. Do you want me to lie to you?"

I breathed deeply through my nostrils. She was trying. "The ideas were good?"

Her teal eyes jumped to mine. "They're great."

"So where's the problem?"

"Your argument. It's all anecdotes, speculation, leaps of logic. You used the word 'hope' nine times." Kira reached forward and straightened the stack. "How do I read this—how do the Minds read this and understand its impact, mathematically?"

I grabbed a copy from the table and flipped to the fourteenth page. Two 'hopes'. Was a little optimism really that bad? "Yolniv liked it. So did the people at the community center. Everyone I've shown this to has reacted really positively."

"If I took this to work and submitted it to Maker for review, they'd reject it on the spot. It's all persuasion without the convincing. Like that argument you had with Influence out in the desert—" I shot her a glance, then inhaled slowly. We didn't need to rehash that today. She continued a little slower, "I'm just worried what you have here won't cut it. But I want to be supportive. If everyone else says this is great, then it's great."

I was quiet a long time. Kira rubbed my arm. As much as I wanted to believe what I had written was good, how could it be when she didn't like it? I thought back to something Charlie said during his consultation. *New proposals were sent to the Minds every day, none of them were turned into law.*

"How would you change it?" Kira looked up at the ceiling thoughtfully.

"I don't know. More numbers. More concrete arguments."

The fact that Kira couldn't nail down her criticism told me the problem was serious. There was something fundamentally wrong with the way I was arguing. I needed a new baseline.

"Show me one of the proposals you made for work."

She shot me a questioning glance. We both knew I didn't have the mathematical background she did. I prodded her. "I'm serious, I want to see it."

Kira stood and led me upstairs into her office. The floor was bare, just carpet and a few crumpled wrappers. Her chair was positioned next to a small desk with a keyboard and mouse. The screen was projected onto the wall, we had gone big with that expense. Kira pulled up a document list and scrolled through them. She muttered to herself 'not that one' and 'too many formulas' as she went along. Finally, she hovered over a single document, it expanded to fill half the wall. A Proposal to Prioritize City Circumnavigation in Pathfinding Algorithms.

Kira's eyes jumped between me and the document. She bit her lip before speaking. "This, uh, this is something I sent in to redirect traffic along the north highway."

In the middle of the front page was a top-down view of the city. A yellow line ran through downtown, the old path. A dotted red line veered north, dodging downtown. So far it all made sense. Then I got to the table of numbers.

"What does all this mean?"

I caught a flash of a smile on Kira's face as she zoomed in.

"This is the projected impact of my proposal converted into values."

"Like monetary value?"

"More abstract. Any positive number is a good impact on society, negative is bad. Look at the column labelled 'Productivity'." I squinted at a cell eight columns over. "My proposal should reduce travel times, meaning more productive people. All of that translates to a productivity gain of +1.318. But"—Kira zoomed in on the city map and circled a residential neighborhood near the northern highway—"a lot of people live near here, so they'll see an increase in noise pollution. That translates to a 'Livability' decrease of -0.27."

I raised my finger to a cell labelled 'Public Morale'. "Why's this one a zero?"

"Because cars don't entertain people."

I stepped back from the board. "So how do the Minds use these numbers?"

Kira bounced a little as she spoke. "We call them 'weights', and when we combine all these weights together, we get its expected impact on society. This proposal has a net weight of +1.07, so it should help things, slightly."

Already I had a distant headache. No wonder Kira thought my legislation was missing something, she and the Minds had been making decisions based on hard numbers and mathematics for years. In the face of this much due diligence, my idealist proposal was nothing but guesswork.

"This is what I got wrong." I squeezed Kira's shoulder, her eyes looked brighter than I had ever seen them. All this time, she had been seeing the world in a totally different way. "What about my document, what kind of weights would you give it?"

Kira's fingers danced on the screen, soon my proposal filled the wall. "Your change is more substantial, so both the positives and negatives would be much bigger. Give me a night to calculate them."

I shook my head. "You don't need to do that. I can use estimates."

She reached up to her shoulder and grasped my hand. Kira was brimming with energy, her feet were kicking excitedly under her chair, her face was almost flush. "I want to."

There was no convincing her otherwise. This was her joy, and for the first time we were sharing it. I stayed up as late as I could watching her build formulas and analyze spreadsheets. But a little past midnight, the comfortable heat and the rhythmic tap-tapping of Kira's fingers lulled me to sleep.

***

I woke up under a blanket, still lying on the carpet. The faint light of dawn streamed through the blinds. Kira was staring at her screen, but typing nothing. "How does it look?"

She waved me over, her face looked like stone, must have been exhausted from the overnight. My chest was abuzz, thrilled to see the results. A row of numbers appeared on-screen. I read them once, then wiped my eyes and read them again. The buzzing in my chest had frozen. "Is this right?"

"It's an approximation," Kira answered flatly.

"How can it be that far in the negative? I thought there were some real positives to my ideas." My legs wobbled underneath me. I barely understood the weights, but a score of -19.4 had to be cataclysmic.

"I included them. But the positives for stuff like Morale and Entrepreneurism were nothing compared to the negatives in Productivity." Kira didn't look at me as she spoke. Her whole body was downcast and her voice was resigned.

I zoomed in on each weight in sequence, looking at every number, searching for something that stood out. There had to be a mistake. The UAM was broken, it needed change. I knew it in my heart. "Why did you only give Morale a 5.3?"

"I looked at every metric but the only real benefit was an increase in live entertainment."

I scrolled down into the individual metrics—I barely understood them, but I needed to see it for myself. "What about the improved work-life balance? Where does that land?"

She sighed. "It's mostly a negative. Less productivity always is."

There were forty pages of numbers, and over the next half hour I churned through all of them. The weights were calculated correctly, I knew Kira didn't make a mistake, but the results felt wrong. When I reached the 392nd metric, I tried to scroll to the next page, but none came.

I spun around to face Kira. "Where's the rest?"

She gestured to the wall. "That's all of it."

"What about the metrics for community? For quality of life and happiness?"

"Would that be Livability?"

I pressed my hands against the wall. "No! Livability is just a bunch of metrics on surviving in the city. Proximity to hospitals and air quality and whatever else. I'm talking about the things that make life worth living. Where does fulfillment fit in here?"

Kira rubbed her ear as she thought. In the quiet of the room, I realized how loudly I had been speaking. After a few seconds, her head tilted to the side. "Do you think that's important?"

I kept my face flat as I answered. "I do."

"Then I suppose it might be missing."

Missing. All this time writing laws, and not once had the Minds considered fulfillment. Even Kira had missed it. "How can that be the case?"

"War built up the weights over a half century. They're modified pretty regularly, but we haven't seen a new one in twenty years."

So the Minds had been coasting on the data they had. I could infer from Kira's voice that people didn't usually ask about this stuff. "What would it take to build a new one?"

"We'd have to find hundreds of metrics that reflect the values of 'Fulfillment'." Kira took her hands off the screen and swiveled towards me. "I could build one. But it would take time. And it might not work. Your proposal has a score of -19.4, that's a big number to make up. Are you sure you want to explore this?"

She had already pulled one all-nighter, the twinkle in her eyes told me she was ready to pull several more. I looked up at my proposal, its text projected onto the screen. There was still some good in it. "I won't give up on this until we've tried everything. But you're not doing it alone this time. How do I help?"

Kira jumped back to her screen. Her fingers flew around the keys.

Her eyes darted back and forth as she dove into one data folder after another. A few minutes later, the screen in my pocket dinged. She had emailed me 415 documents. I snorted, she giggled. "What do I do with these?"

"Those are just starters. We need to find at least one hundred metrics that reflect the value of 'Fulfillment'. Get reading."

I hurried downstairs and did as she said.

***

We spent eight days reviewing documents. I spent two of those figuring out how to make sense of the lengthy and pedantic research papers. Even that much progress was from Kira's tutoring. Just like when I taught her LINE in college. But back then she reverse-engineered the game's probability models, and here I was lucky to get through a whole paper without needing a break. Some of them I skimmed. The science of fulfillment was hard, but when something like 'nitrogen particulates in sewage' came my way, it felt pretty safe to ignore. As the sun was setting on the first day of our second week, I re-entered Kira's workroom.

"How many did you find?" she asked.

"Twenty-three." Kira extended her hand and I gave her my screen. Her voice hummed a quiet tune as she read. It was funny, I had never spent so long in Kira's office in my life. Maybe I'd be able to drop by a little more often now. Amongst the jumble of documents, diagrams, and spreadsheets on the wall, one caught my eye.

"I thought you didn't work with War?"

Kira flew to her controls. In seconds, everything on the wall was gone, leaving only the background of a subtly animated galaxy turning in place. "Sorry, that was classified."

Something was off, her eyes kept darting back to the wall as if she was double-checking the document hadn't reappeared. Kira had so infrequently welcomed me in here, and we were on a good track. I chose not to press the issue.

"How do the metrics look?" I asked. She turned the handheld screen around so we could both review it.

"Proximity to local events, that's good. Percentage of people reporting overwork, that's good. Hours per year contributing to community efforts, that can work. Are you sure about using patience as a metric?"

I nodded. "I think it's a quiet indicator for bigger issues. People who aren't in a hurry are already content where they are."

Kira shrugged. "It'll be nice to see such an old metric finally get some use."

"Were you able to find any?"

"Seventy-three." I gawked. I knew she was faster than me, but her work put me to shame. "It took me some time to nail down what fulfillment really meant. But I think I found some winners. Tell me what you think." Kira handed back my screen and pulled up a list on the wall. I read through them carefully. My eyes misted up a little, knowing she had done all this for me.

"Number of interactions with people per week, hours per week contributing to community efforts. They're perfect." I paused at one of them. "Average number of encounters with wildlife per year? How did you find that?"

Kira gave a subtle smile. "I've been tracking that study for years. The researcher always includes some photographic evidence in the reports."

I took a step back from the wall. "So can we build the weight? How many more metrics do we need?"

Kira's lips pursed, her head tilted left and right. "Well—" Her voice came out strained with uncertainty. "We could probably calculate it with what we have."

My ears perked up. "Really?" Eight days was a long time. My eyes were starting to hurt, and my brain was beginning to reject numerical tables as a defense mechanism.

"I think so. We've already gone through my strongest candidates. Give me the night, I'll have the final impact number by tomorrow."

I could hardly believe it. In some ways I wasn't ready to get the answer yet. Kira had gone to the extreme to help me justify my proposal. If it turned out the idea was crap, I had no followup. I wanted to stall, to ask Kira to sleep and work on it in the morning. But this was her project now, and I knew that no matter what I said, she'd have that number in the morning. "Don't burn yourself out."

She wiggled her head in excitement. "This is the fun part—the real headache comes if you succeed. Don't forget, I'm the person that'll have to work with your new weight."

I stared at her with a goofy grin. Never in my life had someone gone to such lengths, performed so much work, just to support me. And she didn't even hesitate. All those times I had told her she wasn't there, I was wrong. She was doing everything she could, but her world was different from mine. And now that I was in her world, her show of love was washing over me like a flood. I kissed Kira's forehead, walked downstairs, wiped a tear from my eye, and waited for her findings.

***

My feet wouldn't take me past the first step. Light had just started shining through the window at the front of the house. Fulfillment, what a funny concept. Truth was, when Kira calculated that -19.3, I was willing to pursue any lead to turn things around. How do you even measure fulfillment? In nearly 200 hours, we had read a bunch of papers, bundled the best metrics together, and called it 'Fulfillment'. How many more metrics had we missed? Could you ever completely encapsulate such an abstract concept mathematically?

And if it failed, what would I do? My influence on the nation was already fading. They barely even talked about my game anymore. There wasn't time to come up with something else. My toes pressed against the staples under the carpet. Maya sure had some ideas. No.

If this failed, I couldn't throw my weight behind an immoral enterprise. Better to just live a good life and be glad I got out without something worse happening.

The door to Kira's office creaked open. There was a shuffling, and her head popped out. "Are you coming up?"

I shook the uncertainty away and started up the stairs. Kira met me at the top. Her hands clutched a little screen close to her chest.

"What did you find?" I asked in a low and quiet voice.

She shoved the screen into my hands and made me read it for myself. +25.1. I couldn't take my eyes away.

"Positive?"

"Very positive," she whispered.

Tears poured from my eyes. Laughter mixed with crying blurred my vision. In an instant, all the dread in the world washed away. I should have realized it the second I saw Kira, she was bouncing on her feet the whole time. Her arms wrapped around me. "How?" I whispered.

She shrugged. "That's not for me to ask. I just crunch the numbers. And the numbers say your idea is very good for 'Fulfillment.'" Kira giggled at her own words. I was lightheaded, the only thing keeping me on my feet was my wife's steady legs. Weeks of research, writing, planning, all of it had paid off. Fulfillment, whether or not it was a valid weight, told the story of my proposal.

"Want me to send it to the Minds?"

I squeezed my eyes shut. My thoughts were a jumble, but the only thing I was certain of was that this proposal needed to be handled carefully. It had to speak for itself, but my voice needed to give it that extra boost in the public eye.

"Definitely. But only when we're ready to present it."

23 - RADIO CHATTER

My third national broadcast in six months. I was almost comfortable in the little fabric seat behind the cameras. Although this time there was no LINE game to fall back on. Ezra was running the show today, as with most days. My fingers fanned the pages of the proposal. It had a real bulk to it, Kira had insisted we include the index and the addendums. Now we were well past three hundred pages. Between the two of us, Kira had the harder job. All I had to do was make the argument to the general public, she was the one that would have to field questions from researchers and convince the experts 'Fulfillment' was real.

The music on set swelled to mark the end of the main broadcast. "Stick with us. We'll be right back with LINE expert Zouk Solinsen, here to talk about his historic match."

"And we're off!"

The room lights rose. A producer with a mic in his ear walked out of the room, the camera operators stepped off their podiums and headed for the snacks in the back. Folks looked relaxed and easygoing, all but Ezra. She made a beeline for my seat. I stood to greet her, but took a step back as she closed in. She was a half foot shorter than me, but that never made her less intimidating.

"This is the printed version?" She gestured toward the thick binder in my hands.

I nodded.

"You're sure you want to talk about that on live TV? Poly-sci stuff gets terrible ratings."

I hefted the binder to my chest. "People are unhappy, they want change. If this works, it could redefine how we communicate with the Minds."

One of Ezra's eyebrows raised, but she didn't press the issue. "You'll answer questions about your match against War?"

"Of course." The questions about War were the price of admission. Ezra refused to interview me unless the headline read, Zouk Opens Up About His Big Defeat.

She rubbed her bottom lip and looked at me thoughtfully. "I don't want that behemoth on my desk."

I glanced at the proposal in my arms. We had used it in every practice interview, but Kira was the one who really knew the whole thing back-to-front. If losing the binder was the only surprise today, I could live with it. "There's a lot of supplementary material in there I might need to reference."

Ezra leaned past me and waved over a girl wearing a TECH hat. "Take that and put it somewhere I can reach it." The girl grabbed the proposal out of my hands and walked behind the set backdrop. Those pages had weighed me down for half the day, now I was missing the heft in my arms.

"If you need it, we'll have it. See you on set."

Ezra turned in place and headed for the hall. I scanned the room for her co-host, but didn't see him. Just before she got out the door, I called out, "Is Influence joining?"

"No, you're old news to him."

An assistant walked me to a couch to the right of Ezra's desk. Things would be harder without Influence, he was my primary audience. I ran through the key talking points as someone pinned a mic to my lapel. In what seemed like no time, Ezra was back and the producer was counting down to broadcast.

"Welcome back! You already know our next guest. Zouk Solinsen, the LINE player that took the Minds to the last game. He's here to tell us all about the big defeat."

The cameras panned to bring me into the shot. I put on my best smile and shook Ezra's hand.

"We're so happy to have you on, Zouk. Quite a bit has happened since the last time we saw you." Ezra put on a sympathetic look. "That last game against War must have been hard, how are you feeling?"

I curved my eyebrows in faux sadness. "Disappointed. Losing that game was hard. But at the same time, I am incredibly relieved to be out of that tournament. It's given me time to think, and to develop new ideas—"

Ezra cut me off. "After a loss like that, I bet you're dying to get back into the action. The LINE World Championships are coming up in a few weeks, should we expect to see you there?"

Clearly I had mentioned the proposal too soon, I played along. "The LINE Association has offered me a wildcard invitation for the tournament, but I'm not sure I want to play again—"

"A wildcard? What's that?"

"I haven't been playing a lot of premier tournaments, so normally I wouldn't qualify for something like the world championships. But every year, the association picks a wildcard player to participate. This year they picked me."

"Do you think you can win?" Her question was asked almost before I was finished speaking.

"Maybe, if I attend."

"How would you feel about a rematch against Bergamaschi?"

Ezra had more than a few LINE questions prepared for me.

"Fine. He's a strong opponent. But I haven't played a human being for months."

Ezra flipped a card over on her desk, it was too high up for me to see. "Let's talk about your former coach, Jamie." Memories of the deposition popped into my head, I ground my teeth and focused on keeping a level head.

"Just like you, she lost against War. But she didn't handle her defeat quite as gracefully. She's now fallen out of the top one hundred LINE players—"

"What tournament was she in?"

Ezra's eyes flickered to mine. "Something online. Lost every game. What do you make of that?"

I shifted on the couch. Sounded like she was in a rough place. The nation had been downright cruel mocking her. The girl that couldn't win even when she cheated. If not for her, folks online probably would have done the same to me.

"Zouk? What do you think?"

I had been quiet for a few seconds, too long for TV. One deep breath, and I gave an answer. "Games against the Minds take everything. Four games dominated the last half year of my life. If I lost sooner? I might have fallen into a slump too. Jamie is still one of the most brilliant players in the world, and I hope she's able to recover." I paused. "But if she never played LINE again, I don't think I'd blame her."

"Wonderful. I think we all hope Jamie gets back into the game soon." Ezra's answer irritated me. Through all the sympathies, her voice rang hollow. She didn't know or care who Jamie was. All she knew was that bringing her up would add more excitement to the interview. And I was running out of patience.

"We never got to hear much about your game against Maker, there was a lot of secrecy around that game, care to loop us in—"

"Before we do that, I'd like to discuss what I've brought here today."

Ezra hesitated. My eyes narrowed back at her. She shouldn't have brought up Jamie. I wouldn't answer another of her questions until we talked about the legislation. Her hands went into her desk, and she plopped the hefty proposal onto the table.

"What a great idea! Zouk, you've been here a few times. You're almost a regular. And over that time, you've shared some very interesting ideas. Today, if I've got it right, you've taken those ideas and turned them into legislation. Tell us about that."

I ran through my pitch flawlessly. It felt good knowing my memory was useful for something other than LINE. "—And the entire proposal was just made available online for anyone to look at." Kira was probably already in an argument with someone about the paper. I was pretty sure she liked arguing semantics with strangers on the internet.

Ezra ran a fingernail under the front page of the proposal and looked at me with an inquisitive eye. "More human connection, more flexibility, I get all of that. Here's what I don't get. As a member of the public, I want to understand what you're proposing, but when I open it up . . ." She flipped the proposal open. The pages hit the desk with a thud. "It's very math-y. How do people make sense of this?"

I gave Ezra a sympathetic nod. "Sometimes it's too much for me too. But yeah, our proposal is math-y. Intentionally so. It's easy to write some eight-page legislation and give a few high-minded reasons for passing it. But this is how things go in other nations."

My hands gestured out towards nothing. "It's governing by guesswork, and it's not how the Minds operate. Instead of claiming 'this law should improve the economy', I can say 'this law will provide a 3 percent bump to our annual GDP'. That's a promise. In a year we can measure that promise, evaluate it, and use the data to develop better laws. Scientific governance. It's not as easy to read, but it's precise."

A little piece of plastic in Ezra's ear lit up. Her brow furrowed, and her pen tap-tapped against the desk. In the corner of my eye, the doors outside opened and a figure rushed behind the cameras to the producer. When Ezra spoke again, her voice lacked her normal speed and sharpness. "The Minds rarely implement legislative proposals.

Is it your hypothesis that this numbers-based approach is what's missing?"

Clearly something was happening behind the scenes, but I needed to focus on the questions at hand. "Absolutely. All we've ever used to convince the Minds is argument. Arguments don't have a mathematical conversion. How do you turn an emotional appeal into a numerical benefit?" I reached over to Ezra's desk and lifted a couple of the proposal's open pages. "This is how we communicate with precision."

The plastic in her ear lit up a second time. Ezra had a faraway look. When the light in the plastic died, she turned to me. "Zouk, we're receiving a call from a very special viewer who has reviewed your proposal. Would you be willing to field a few questions?"

The production team shared uncertain looks. A caller? I had never seen the news take a surprise caller before, it was unprecedented. The first name that popped into my head was Maya, but I seriously doubted Ezra's team would set me up like that. If it was a researcher, I'd be in some real trouble. Still, unprecedented interviews meant good ratings. I straightened up and faced the camera. "Go ahead."

"Excellent. Are they on?" Someone behind the camera gave Ezra a thumbs up. "Good. If you're just joining us, Zouk Solinsen is about to answer questions about his legislation from none other than The Mind of Strategy and Warfare. War, are you there?"

My head jerked back at Ezra, but she kept her eyes locked on the camera. For all the time we had spent playing LINE against one another, War and I had never had a conversation. I doubted she'd go easy on me.

"I am here." War's voice was deep, methodical, metallic, and distantly feminine. I had heard it only a few times in my life. In my games against her, and when she was broadcast over speakers during a few natural disasters.

"Well—we're uh—we're glad to have you on, what questions did you have for Zouk here?" Ezra was normally such a fearsome and quick reporter. But in the presence of War, she was tripping over herself.

"Mr. Solinsen." My stomach tightened hearing my own name. "I have reviewed your legislation. Now indexed as Proposal 103389. Your work introduces a new weight designated 'Fulfillment'. What purpose does it serve?"

War spoke slowly and methodically, as if every word was being carved into stone. At least the first question was a softball. "Fulfillment captures a set of metrics that measure citizens' long-term happiness and sense of meaningful work."

"Morale and Productivity are already weights. Why make a new one?" War's answers were terse, but it didn't sound like she was opposed to the idea. I had hoped to get Influence on the interview, but this might be even better.

"The metrics for Fulfillment are pretty close to Morale and Productivity, but they don't really belong to either. They fit in a sort of awkward gap."

"We have operated a long time without the need for a 'Fulfillment' weight. Why should it be considered?" War gave no inflection, but I could still sense she was seriously interested in my answer. Ezra raised a finger in the air and started speaking.

"War—sorry to butt in, Zouk—but there are a lot of people in the nation these days that feel that fulfillment, community, and belonging have gone missing from the state. I think Mr. Solinsen might be making a very good point to include it in his calculations."

There was silence on the line. Ezra was trying to help, but she was speaking the wrong language. I jumped in, "In the appendix is a series of metrics we measure today but remain unused."

War responded instantly, "Those are devalued metrics. They're too random to be of significant use."

I quietly thanked Kira for teaching me so much about weights over the past week. "Those 'devalued' metrics shift in response to new policies. They only look random because you were viewing them through the lens of Morale or Productivity. When bundled under Fulfillment, there's a real correlation. You can't just throw those numbers away."

"It could be overvalued," War retorted. "New weights have enormous impacts on the evaluation of directives." We were getting close, I could feel it.

"Then rebalance the weight!" I caught the excitement in my voice and calmed down. "Kira, my wife, told me the last weight took six years to settle into what it is today. I'm not saying what I've given you is a complete solution, but I do think it's the first step. I also believe there are a lot of directives you've disregarded because this weight was missing."

War didn't answer immediately. In the quiet, I could see Ezra struggling to track the conversation. After half a minute, War's voice returned, "This proposal was prepared very well. I will call for researcher input and continue to evaluate it. I believe it is still likely the weight is overvalued."

"Probably." I tried to keep my voice level, but there was a rising excitement in my belly. We had cracked the code.

"Perhaps even by double."

"Perhaps." I didn't want to say anything more than I had to, War was on board.

"Thank you for letting me call in Ezra, I apologize for the interruption."

"We're happy to have you!" A moment later, there was an audible click. I let out a slow exhale. War was still watching, but I doubted there'd be any other questions like those.

"For everyone joining us today, we just finished a surprise interview with The Mind of Strategy and Warfare." Ezra turned to me. "Zouk, what exactly did we just hear?"

"We discussed the merits of my proposal."

"Like a—a debate of sorts?" The look in Ezra's eye told me she was asking more for her viewers than herself.

"I suppose, yeah," I said.

"Well who won?"

I crossed my arms and thought for a moment. Honestly, it felt like I had won. War and I had just had a real conversation about policy, and the conclusion was almost positive. "We came to a compromise."

"Seems like you're more of a politician than ever." I gave a faint smile. "Thank you so much for stopping by." Ezra gave me a rapid handshake and an assistant walked me off the set. I was bouncing on my heels as I headed down the hall. The interview had gone better than I could have imagined. The metrics, the new weight, all of it had worked! I doubted the general public would understand much of my conversation with War, but that didn't matter now.

At the door to the green room, I paused. A folded note was taped to the door with my name on it. I took it down, entered the green room, and unfolded the page. The ink still shone on the page. Its letters were hand-shaped in graceful calligraphy. *A riveting interview and a sincere proposal. My admiration for you grows. There may yet be another chance. - Influence*

I fell back into the green room's massage chair and re-read the message. It was vague but clear. He had enjoyed the broadcast, that was a plus. It was hard to imagine us ever getting past that day in the deposition chamber. But that last phrase, *There may yet be another chance.* Was he talking about my proposal? Or—I didn't dare think it—a rematch? It was hard to draw conclusions from something so brief. I refolded and pocketed the letter.

For the past few weeks, I had wondered if chasing legislation was a mistake. The public's anger had faded, my name spoken a little quieter. But this felt significant. A true breakthrough between Man and Mind, and all of it without a single riot in the streets.

I needed to stay focused, keep the legislation moving, and maybe play a little LINE on the side.

24 - WORLD CHAMPIONSHIPS

RANK: 7 ▲ 21

The black graphic tee was folded on my coffee table. It, and the letter sent with it were unsolicited. I raised the garment in front of me. On the front was a cartoon giraffe dressed in tactical gear, holding a pair of binoculars. On the back, the words *Proxyherd, Security through Avoidance*. I dropped the shirt onto the table and opened the letter. Apparently the Proxyherd company 'just wanted to express its enthusiasm for our upcoming collaboration'.

I took a deep sip of honeyed tea and pulled a screen from my pocket. Derek had sent me another message, the man wouldn't take the hint. I dismissed it without reading, then dialed a number. On the first ring, Maxim's bald head appeared on-screen. He wore a wide grin that stretched his face. "Mr. Solinsen! What a pleasure, I have been meaning to call you, my friend."

It had been two years since the President of the LINE Association and I had spoken. He was a lot more polite this time around.

"Maxim, who is Proxyherd?" I took another sip from my tea.

Maxim let out a nervous chuckle. "Well. This is not how I would have liked to talk about this. But, there have been some developments, and I—we—the association needs a favor."

"I'm not doing sponsorships." The news was out on our legislation. Kira was reporting plenty of discussion in the research space, I couldn't risk diluting my voice with product until the Minds made their decision.

Maxim bowed his head. "Forgive me for this, but your recent popularity has posed serious complications with the hosting. Security costs have skyrocketed. More than we can bankroll."

I put down the tea and stretched my fingers. "It can't be that bad."

Maxim's shoulders sunk. "You have seen the news. People love you. Too much love, I think. We have to build barricades, hire guards, drive escort vehicles. All for ten days. It's more than we can handle."

I pressed my lips together. Since my appearance on the news, protests had become a national sport. Signs for 'Pass the Bill' were right next to 'Zouk was screwed' and 'Best of Three'. I had taken a few more interviews, but every time I showed up somewhere, the chants only got louder. My voice was the leader of a movement and I couldn't seem to put on the brakes.

My hand ran over the T-shirt logo. "What's the giraffe?"

"The giraffe is a security system. It alerts users when crime happens within a kilometer of their position or something. Basically a startup that's throwing their money around. You wear the shirt, they cover costs."

"Just me?"

"Just you. It's a good deal, armored vehicles are expensive."

I stretched my neck left and right, Kira passed me and walked to the kitchen. The world championships were supposed to be my one vacation from politics. I should have known it would follow me. "I'd have liked some warning about all this, Maxim."

The corner of Maxim's mouth twitched. "So would I. Blame your own success." There was the Maxim I knew. He took a breath. "Will you do it?"

"I'll think about it." I ended the call and tossed my screen onto the coffee table. Kira was watching me from the fridge.

"How did it go?" she asked.

"I have to wear a giraffe so people don't break in and tear the tournament apart."

Kira glanced up thoughtfully. "They're hosting the tournament up north right? In the Foundations Tower?" I nodded, she grabbed a screen and pulled up a map. "It should only have three exits. I wonder what the bid was, if you call them back, I could do some calculations and—" Kira paused and turned back to the fridge. "Sorry, I can't fix this can I?"

I smiled. I couldn't believe for the longest time I had missed it. This was how she showed she cared. "Probably not. But I still want to hear the numbers."

48 hours to The Line World Championships

A deep crimson ITV quietly hummed at the edge of the sidewalk. It was a little thicker than the regular model, probably armored, but I couldn't tell. The word Proxyherd was written on both sides and the hood. I still had no idea what to say to their CEO. The videos I had seen of him consisted mostly of talks about their product and discussions on weightlifting. Not the regular type to be interested in LINE.

I fiddled with the buttons on my jacket. Try as I might, I could not prevent ProxyHerd's Tactical Giraffe from poking its head out at the world. I wheeled my luggage up to the vehicle. The trunk and door opened while the ProxyHerd logo animated itself all around the car. I tossed my luggage in the back and climbed inside.

The cabin looked pretty standard. Single lay-back seat, windshield screen, cupholder full of candy, probably a gift from the team at Proxyherd. When the door shut, the car's tinting lowered considerably, like a window-wide set of sunglasses. A second later, the vehicle jerked forward. I grasped a handle and rode through the sudden acceleration. Clearly, ProxyHerd weren't experts on ITV's. Soon things smoothed out, and the vehicle started on its journey.

Four hours to kill. I thought about calling Kira, but it was nearly noon and she was at Facility Five for the day. My vehicle started its merge onto the highway. Yolniv was already at the event, we had prepped a little, but nowhere near the level of the other competitors. Compared to facing the Minds, the world championships felt like a walk in the park. World Champion was a nice title, and Bergamaschi had been hogging it for a long time.

On the windscreen, the option of starting a LINE game was front and center. I reached up to start the app. The vehicle swerved hard. My body was thrown into the car's left wall. A couple candies fell into my lap. There was an ache in my wrist and a thrumming pain in my forehead. I gasped for breath. This vehicle wasn't safe.

My fingers tapped the Map controls, looking for a way to force the ITV to park. The screen didn't change, it didn't even respond. I tried every button on the windscreen. Nothing was working. The thought of another swerve caused me to brace my arms against the sides of the vehicle. After a moment, a small chime played out through the speakers. "Adjusting tint."

A dark fog slowly overtook the windshield. The car was going haywire. We were on a highway, but there was no question escape was my only option. I grasped at the door's handle, pulling and pushing and kicking against the hard plastic. The door didn't even rattle. To my left, the windshield finished its tint adjustment. It was mid-morning, but from inside the cabin, there was nothing but black.

Whatever was happening, I needed help. I let go of the door handle and grabbed the screen in my pocket. My fingers navigated to the home screen. The vehicle swerved again. I crashed into the car's right wall and a stinging pain spiked through my shoulder. The screen fell to the floor and I braced my arms against the cabin walls.

A few minutes later, my breath slowed. The vehicle hadn't swerved in some time. My screen lay at the far side of the cabin between my feet. Slowly, I relaxed my arms. They were already sore. I lifted my right hand off the wall. The car did a half-swerve. I put it back. I tried again with my left hand, another swerve. Perfect timing.

A chill ran down my spine. This wasn't a malfunction. Someone was controlling it. Every time I made a move for the screen, they'd give the signal to swerve. Keeping my hands pressed against the walls, I glanced around the car's interior. It didn't take long to find what I was looking for. Directly above me, embedded in the car's metal body, the lens of a camera reflected the light. They were watching me.

I had made plenty of enemies lately. Maybe Proxyherd's CEO wasn't a fan of what I was saying on TV. Perhaps Maxim didn't like the idea of me becoming the LINE World Champion. But what were their intentions? This seemed like overkill for an assassination.

The car veered right, pressing me into the left wall. The whir of the highway faded. We had taken a turn. A minute later, the ITV jerked to a sudden stop. I dove for the screen under my feet. The door clicked. I tapped the call menu. Cold air flooded the cabin. My list of contacts appeared, I tapped the first name I saw. A large, hairy hand ripped the screen away from me.

"Not fast enough, Zouk."

The voice gave me shudders. I turned to see a certain ex-lieutenant dressed in all black.

"Denvers."

He stared at me with cold, unblinking eyes. A subtle smirk hid behind an unkempt beard. Was he about to kill me? Denvers pocketed the screen, grabbed me by my shoulders, and threw me out of the vehicle. Pain flashed through my shoulder. The gravel was cold, and there wasn't much light. Was I underground? I rolled onto my back. Nearly. Cracks of light shone between the tangles of concrete highways running overhead.

Two sets of hands pulled me to my feet. A tall, black-haired man and a woman with a buzzcut, both in the same dark attire. Denvers' veterans. I considered screaming, but there was no one to hear me but concrete pillars and dust. They pointed me at Denvers. The former lieutenant fished my screen from his pocket, tapped something, then tossed it back into the crimson Proxyherd vehicle. The doors shut automatically, and it smoothly sped around a pillar and out of sight.

Denvers walked past me with a cocky swagger. "Nice shirt."

Fury and fear swirled inside me. I wasn't sure what Proxyherd was, but clearly it was a trap. Was Maxim a part of this too? I doubted it. My head stayed high on my shoulders. Denvers struck me as the kind of man that preyed on weakness. "Is this it? Are you gonna kill me?"

I could hear the door to another vehicle open behind me. "Nope. Just making sure you don't miss your appointment."

Denvers' team squeezed my arms tight. Without warning, they started walking, dragging me backwards across the gravel. I turned as best I could to see my destination. Another car, this one black, but clearly just as armored as the last. I wriggled against my captor's grip, my feet carving little canyons in the gravel. They kept up their pace and dumped me into the ITV, sealing the door.

The interior was pitch black. I kicked at the walls and tore at the door, searching for a handle. With every hit I made against the metal walls, my limbs ached a little more.

"You're free to kick and punch as much as you'd like, Zouk. Stronger people have tried."

A dim light illuminated the cabin. No hard plastic and cupholders here, just metal seats and metal walls. I stopped my escape attempt and glanced at the source of the voice. Denvers' face was projected onto the blacked-out windscreen.

"Where are we going?"

A sudden acceleration pushed my back back into its seat.

Denvers looked away from his camera. "Pretty far out there, it's gonna be a while."

I braced my arms against my sides. "I'm expected at the tournament."

"You're expected at the hotel. People miss their reservations all the time. If anyone's really curious, your phone and vehicle will report a scenic tour of the coast."

"My team is waiting for me."

Denvers leaned out of frame, then returned with a thermos in his hands. "One old man does not make a team. And you're not meeting with him until tomorrow." My stomach tightened, Denvers had been tracking my messages. He took a long drink from his thermos, steam poured from his mouth as he spoke. "Relax. We've got at least 24 hours together."

His face vanished, and the cabin plunged into darkness. My body shifted left and right as the vehicle made subtle turns. I could still feel Denvers watching. Probably a thermal camera tracking my every move. Even if he wasn't, there's no way I could find a way out of here blind.

At least I was still alive. A lot could happen in 24 hours. I needed to get a hold of a screen, anything that could broadcast out. But how? I didn't even know where I was going. The ITV kept up its gentle left-right rocking. The sting in my shoulder had faded to a dull pain. With nothing to see or hear, my pain and the warm, quiet, dark of the cabin dragged me to sleep.

I awoke to a rumbling. We had left the smooth highways behind, couldn't say for how long, there wasn't even a clock in here. I chided myself for missing something as key as the distance travelled. From now on, I needed to keep careful mental notes.

The rumbling continued for a while. It was joined by a distant rustling, leaves in the wind, I was pretty sure. We must have been hours from the city. The roads had become winding. We were constantly making sharp turns left and right and left again. By the time the vehicle stopped, my head was spinning.

The door unsealed. Fresh air flooded the cabin. It was infused with grass and pine and flowers. Forests.

"Out." Denvers grabbed my arm and pulled me from the vehicle. It looked like a garage. They had closed the main gate before letting me out, so no view, just a trail of mud left by the ITVs.

"This way." Denvers led me up a set of stairs to a heavy metal door. He fished out a key, turned the lock, and opened the door to a hallway. We walked side by side down the long corridor. The walls were bare sheet metal, and every step kicked up dust. This place was old. Denvers' team followed close behind, shutting and relocking the door behind us.

"Where are we?" I asked.

"Your new home. It's gone unused for a couple decades, but I spruced up the topside." Denvers looked back at me and flashed a smile. "You'll like it."

Halfway down the corridor, the sheet metal walls were replaced with stone. We came to a stop at the end of the hall, where a ladder led upwards through a chute of stone. Denvers grasped the iron rail and rattled it. The sound echoed up and away, fading and fading, yet never quite seeming to end. The lieutenant looked at me expectantly. "Take your time."

It was clear what he wanted. I approached the ladder, and looked up. A thin cable strung little electric lanterns all along the way. I wasn't normally claustrophobic or afraid of heights, but the idea of being stuck hundreds of feet up this thin stone chute gave me goosebumps.

"How far does it go?" My voice trembled.

"Two or three hundred feet." I gave him an apprehensive look. "It'll take a while, pace yourself. I don't want you falling on me."

When it was clear I wasn't getting out of this, I grabbed a hold of an iron rung, and pulled my weight up.

A sharp metallic clang followed every step. Twenty or thirty rungs in, the ladder shook. Denvers had started his ascent behind me.

It didn't take long for my arms and legs to start burning. But it wasn't like I could go back down. I pushed as hard as I could, but when the strain got too much, I'd lean against the chute's stone wall. Neither the top nor bottom was visible, just a long line of lanterns going on forever. Denvers never pushed for speed, he simply matched my pace.

"Who am I meeting up there?" My voice was muffled and bounced around by the tunnel.

"Don't be an idiot. You know who," Denvers answered.

I nodded, I did know. Eventually, my arms had recovered and I continued the climb. Rung after rung. My thoughts turned to escape. I was ahead of Denvers and his squad, was there a chance there? Where was I even about to emerge? I wasn't a geologist, but could this be a mine shaft? Why would it be going up?

The top rung arrived without warning. One second I was climbing, and the next I was flopping over onto a concrete floor. Ahead was a long room filled with beds, all covered in the same forest-green sheets. There was no one waiting for me, and Denvers was still a dozen rungs back. This was my chance. I rolled onto my back, then jumped to my feet.

My legs crumpled under me. Muscle gone from the climb. I fell back to the floor and tried to move them again, but they were stiff and unresponsive. There goes that plan. Thirty seconds later, Denvers hoisted himself over the final rung. I still hadn't moved from my spot against the wall. He leaned over my form confidently. "You've got twenty minutes. You're free to use one of the bunks. Don't disrespect George and Thea. I'll be back soon."

"When do I get a tour?" I moaned. I needed to get a look around my prison as soon as possible.

"When you can walk."

I lay on the hard concrete, rubbing life back into my legs. There were sixteen beds, and a trunk in front of every one. A barracks. This must be some kind of military installation. Soon enough, George's black hair and Thea's buzzcut popped up over the ladder. With their assistance, I was able to shift myself onto a mattress. It was marginally more comfortable than laying on the floor. It was strange, my legs didn't hurt, they were more like noodles. Not an ounce of muscle between them. The only solace I could take was that George and Thea were panting about as much as I was. Thea disappeared down the far side of the barracks and George took position by the ladder. Slowly, I tilted my head his way.

"That sucked, huh?"

George's bushy eyebrows raised into an incredulous look. He slid a pack off his shoulder and dropped it to the ground in a thud. "I was carrying extra. What's your excuse?"

I stayed quiet, he seemed like an intense and quick to anger sort of a person. George bent forward and rummaged through his pack. After a second, a large, reflective knife emerged in his grip. George's eyes lit up and he shot me a creeping smile. "Gotta keep myself protected, right?"

I shifted onto my back and wished my legs were working. They were starting to bend again, that was promising. A thrumming vibrated through the barracks. Helicopter on approach. I glanced at George, he gave no reaction to the deafening pounds of the rotor blades. Probably my appointment making its dramatic arrival. Denvers marched into the barracks and pulled me into a sitting position. He shouted over the sounds of the chopper, "Let's go! You don't wanna be late."

I took a deep breath and threw my knees over the edge of the bunk. I had been so focused on being able to walk I hadn't even thought about what came next. This conversation is what I had been kidnapped for. It had to go well, not just diplomatic, but well. Denvers threw my arm over his shoulder and brought me to my feet. He pointed to the far end of the barracks and we walked together down the hall. It was time to meet Maya.

25 - CONVERSATIONS

A life altering conversation, and all I could think about were the weird twanging muscles in my thighs. It was a wonder I had made it this far. Denvers gave no reaction to my leaning on him other than the occasional grunt. A pistol hung in a black holster on his outer hip. I wanted to make a move for it but, even in perfect health, I was pretty sure Denvers would shoot me dead before I ever had a chance. We left the barracks and entered the mess hall. Just two long tables and a window. Someone had already set out the dining supplies. Four plates, four forks, and four dull knives. An extended stay. The blinds were closed, of course. A little light slipped through, just enough to confirm we were above ground.

The mess hall led to the command quarters. The ragged, deep-green carpet and faded military posters made this room the warmest in the whole building. It ran perpendicular to the rest of the building. A long, thin end cap office with one door to the mess hall, one to what looked like a kitchen, and a heavy metal exit door with a small window.

The helicopter's beating thrum was deafening. We had to be close to the landing pad. Denvers dumped me in a dented, metal folding chair at the room's midpoint and headed for the exit.

I shuffled a little in my seat, but there was no way to make it comfortable. In any case, I needed to focus on what was coming. Maya had dragged me all the way out here just to talk. As interested as I was in hearing what she had to say, my main priority was getting out of the conversation alive.

Denvers threw open the door outside. By now the blades had slowed. Through the opening, the sky was a stormy grey, and filled with clouds. Before I could see any more, a figure in a mauve suit entered. Denvers slammed the door shut behind her, the metal handle rattled in its frame. "Fifteen minutes," he said.

Maya dusted herself off and adjusted her clothes. There was something so calculated to the way she moved, even the motion of dusting her jacket had been practiced a thousand times with perfect form. "I just got here, don't hurry me along yet."

"They check the flight records—"

Maya raised a palm to Denvers and he fell silent. Her eyes moved to me, and I sat up straight. "Hello, Zouk."

Her voice was flat and matter-of-fact. As she strutted past, the smells of tulips wafted by. She walked all the way to the oversized officer's desk at the far end of the room, gave a disgusted glance to the aged chair, then put one hand on the desk.

"Maya," I said.

She pursed her lips and huffed a little to herself. "Honey, you cannot know how hard I fought to keep this from happening. But we needed to talk, and you must have ignored about a hundred messages from poor Derek."

"I lost my game. There's nothing left for us to talk about."

Maya's eyes jumped to Denvers, then back to me. "Do you not socialize much, Zouk? You seem to always be the last to hear the big news."

News? All the news lately had been about my proposal. I doubted Maya cared much about that at all. She only ever wanted one thing from me. If there was big news and she had gone to this much trouble, that meant— "Another game?"

Maya circled around to the front of the desk and dusted off a corner of it before sitting. "Those Minds must be awful fond of you. I didn't believe it at first either. But when you hear the same story from three different sources, you know it's time to start listening."

Another game meant another shot at the council. Now the kidnapping made sense. I lifted one leg over the other and stared down Maya. I was worth something again, and it seemed Maya had learned from the soft approach she had used last time. "You want me to tell the lie, to turn the nation against the Minds."

Maya answered curtly, "Put that idea out of your mind. That's not why we're here and I don't want to hear about it again."

Denvers spoke from the back of the room, "You sure went to a lot of trouble to spoil the plan with that deposition of yours." He was leaning against the exit with his arms crossed.

"So why am I here?"

Maya glanced around the room, grabbed another folding chair and unfolded it a few feet from mine. She sat down and leaned close before speaking. "To have a conversation with you, Zouk. I'm worried." Her voice was slow and sympathetic. A slight frown crossed her lips. She was a talented actress. "You're out here writing laws, playing the Minds, building a community, it's too much. You'll exhaust yourself." She touched my knee with a finger, I stayed perfectly still. "I've seen it before. Life is a marathon, and you are running at a full sprint."

"What are you asking for?"

Maya took her hand back. "It's too much for one person. You need to drop something."

There it was. The ask. Maya never came out and said anything, she always left things to interpretation. All this faux kindness was a nice way to tell me to get out of the way. Of course, it was hard to forget about the guy with a pistol at the back of the room. "You want me to resign from the game."

Her mouth opened slightly as if what I was saying was a shock. "Well, if you think that's best. I just want to help you focus on what matters."

"That'll leave the council seat empty."

She nodded. "It doesn't have to be filled, for now anyway. There are plenty of kids out there with some mighty potential." Maya's gaze drifted off. I knew what she was talking about. The LINE camps at her institute, with hundreds of students training, one of them had to win eventually. And if she got to them young, they'd owe it all to her. Maya's attention returned to me.

"That's not important right now. What is important is making sure that you are taken care of. Folks are gonna be very upset to see you withdraw, especially after all their protestin'. Leaving like that is gonna make some bad blood. So my question for you is this"—she inched a little closer—"Is there anything my resources and access could do to ease your discomfort?"

A kidnapping and a bribe. I was at a loss. She was practically begging me to withdraw, as if it were my choice, as if I couldn't feel Denvers' eyes boring into the back of my head. For now, I just needed to get out of here. "I don't need anything. I'll withdraw from the games." I had already learned that taking a bribe from Maya was a lifelong commitment. Better to give her what she wants today and wash my hands clean.

Maya brought her hands to her chest. "You are so humble." She looked to Denvers. "Isn't he humble?" Her nose flared, and she turned back to me. "Keep thinking, Zouk, there's gotta be something. How about a new house? Somewhere you and that cute wife of yours can stretch your legs?"

I shook my head. "No need. You're right, I can't handle another game, it's too much stress."

Maya responded almost as if she hadn't heard me. "What about that law you wrote? I know some very smart people that could get it passed."

"I don't want to burden you."

Maya slapped her knees. "Zouk! Helping people is never a burden!" She blinked several times, her stare seemed more intense than ever, "Maybe it's all too much money. What if instead, we hosted your LINE events? Nothing fancy, a nice computer lab. Sure would be an upgrade from that musty basement."

Denvers' spoke up from the back of the room. "It's a waste of time, I told you. Four minutes."

Maya locked her eyes with mine. "How about it, Zouk? Will you let me make your life a little better? You can still pass your law. You can still be who you are."

I was trying to give her everything she wanted and she wouldn't take it. Maybe I was misunderstanding her strategy. She wasn't just trying to remove a problem, she needed to know I was under control. The bribe was the most important part. "The house. I'll take the house."

Maya's eyes jumped left and right between mine. After a moment, she fell back in her seat and let out a sigh. In the distance, the thrum of the helicopter returned. Maya clicked her tongue. "That is very disappointing."

A cold pit formed in my stomach. "What's disappointing?"

"We're out of time," Denvers interjected.

Maya pulled herself up and folded her chair but kept her gaze fixed on me. "If there is one thing I cannot stand in this world, it is dishonesty. I came here to have a real discussion with you." She tossed the chair to the side, it fell in an echoing clatter. "For us to talk, you have to start telling the truth. I am going to be back tomorrow. When I arrive, I expect to speak with an honest man." She waved her arms my way. "Not whoever this is."

I swallowed slowly and watched Maya make her way to the exit. Telling Maya what she wanted to hear wasn't enough. Now I'd be spending the night wherever this was. At the door outside, Denvers put up his hand and spoke in a hushed tone. "There's still the other option. We don't have to spend any more time on this."

Maya shook her head and tapped the exit with her finger. Denvers straightened up, set his jaw, and pushed the door open. Once again, the room was a whirlwind. I protected my ears from the helicopter's torrent and Maya took her leave. A moment later, the exit was shut and the sound was gone. Denvers walked in front of me and put a hand on the oversized officer's desk.

"You screwed that up."

"I know." My head hung low. Maya was a politician, she must face liars every day of the week. I was an amateur taking on a superstar.

"Come on, sun's almost gone, we're heading outside." Denvers stepped close, ready to lift me. I pressed on the chair and rose unsteadily to my feet. My muscles vibrated under me, like a thousand strands pulled taut under my weight. But they held, and I took my first proper step. Normally I'd have spent a day recovering, but if I was going to escape this place, I needed to be able to walk.

"Where to?"

He led me to the exit and I turned the handle, it shook unsteadily under the pressure, but turned and opened to the fresh, outdoor air. We stood under a small, sheet metal awning and I finally saw where I had been taken. Not that I knew where it was. The flat top of a mesa. The ground all around us was hard stone, stretching out to sharp cliff sides in every direction. Beyond the cliffs were more mesas, separated by valleys of grass, trees, and rivers that stretched on for miles, all singed orange by the setting sun. Through the valleys weaved a one-lane road. Probably the one we came in on. Beyond that, no sign of civilization. Escape meant days or weeks hiking through the wilderness. Not possible in my condition. The only option was to convince Denvers and Maya to let me go.

Denvers tapped my arm and pointed to our left. "See the ordinance?"

I followed his finger to the colossal black-grey artillery sitting at the cliff edge. The hulk of iron must have been at least thirty feet tall, and pointed out towards the sky. I took a step forward and Denvers' arm stopped me. His right hand gripped the handle of his pistol.

"You walk anywhere without a roof and I put a bullet in your head."

I inched back under the awning. Nowhere without a roof, that had to mean satellites and drones. That or he was paranoid. Denvers turned back to the ordinance and looked at it admirably, as if he hadn't just threatened my life.

"It's medium-range. Half a century ago, War ordered it be put here to stop a ground invasion. Let me tell you, building something like that out here is neither easy, nor cheap. Know how many times they fired it?" I shook my head. "Six. Six shots in three years. What a waste."

A gentle breeze blew through my hair. My mind was still on the conversation with Maya. "I can throw the game."

He side-eyed me. "Hmm?"

"I could lose to War. It wouldn't be as suspicious."

Denvers chuckled. "Sorry, kid. You missed your chance to play nice." Denvers rolled his neck as he spoke. "I don't know why she's so obsessed with that council seat anyways. It was only useful when we had the element of surprise."

I kept quiet, Denvers' eyes were locked on the thirty-foot barrel on the cliffside. "Ya know Maya's real problem? She wants to wait all the time. Get more allies, plant more spies, spend a decade training kids at LINE. Just like when that girl lost to War."

"Jamie."

He sneered. "Jamie. I threw my life away for that ungrateful little nothing. And what did she do with our sacrifice? She sat back and waited." Denvers ground his teeth and kicked at the dust. There was a bite in his voice. I wasn't sure how to respond. It certainly sounded like Jamie was complicit in every part of their plan. "I warned Maya, too. The girl can't handle the big chair."

"She ignored you?"

"Yeah, she does that. Good leader. Inexperienced." Denvers

grabbed my arm and turned me back towards the concrete base. We didn't use the officer's entrance, but another one thirty feet away. "Maya doesn't understand that opportunity is something to be created, not hoped for." The former-lieutenant pulled a key ring from his pocket and unlocked the door. It led to a thin, grey kitchen. Thea was leaning against the stove, staring off into nothing.

"We're done out there. Keep watch 'till it gets dark."

Thea shuffled past us and out the door. When it shut, Denvers and I stood a foot from each other. "I warned her about you too, Zouk. Told her what you are."

His eyes didn't reflect the light. "What am I?"

"A collaborator. You'll sell our liberties for a little praise from the Minds." I didn't dare argue with him. Something told me if I pushed him too far he'd kill me just to be done with it. After a tense moment, Denvers pulled open the kitchen door to the barracks, where George was waiting. "Go rest, I'll have dinner ready in a few. Don't breach the perimeter, that means no going outdoors, and no ladder. Ain't that right, George?"

George fingered the tip of his blade and gave a smirk. I moved slowly back to my bunk. My first conversation with Maya had failed, tomorrow I'd need a better strategy. There had been that brief exchange before Maya left, when Denvers asked her to 'go another way'. There seemed to be some real disagreement between the two of them. From Denvers' collaborator talk, I got the feeling the 'harmless kidnapping' wasn't his idea.

With what little roaming George permitted me, I was able to build a mental map of the bunker. It was a loop, starting from the barracks, running up through the mess hall, into the officer's quarters, then back down through the kitchen. There were two doors out onto the mesa, guarded by Thea. And then there was George's ladder.

The sky turned black through the windows. No one even knew I was gone. If I was lucky, Kira might have called me. It was unlikely I could take any of the three guards solo. Strangely enough, Maya seemed to be my best chance at survival. But if tomorrow's conversation went poorly, I'd need a backup plan.

***

I woke up to the sounds of Maya's helicopter. Not that I had slept much, the beds were stiff and George had spent half the night staring at me. An old digital clock on the wall showed 8:30AM in big block letters. Yolniv was waiting for me at the hotel. At least now someone knew I was missing. When Kira heard, she'd probably be a wreck, and then right after she'd be combing through every piece of data she had clearance for.

"Zouk! Officer's quarters. Now!"

I speed-walked through the mess hall and back to Denvers. Pins and needles shot through my legs with every step, but their strength was returning. My little metal chair had been moved to face the officer's desk, where a handheld screen lay waiting.

"Sit down, don't touch anything." Denvers barked his orders as he pushed open the exit.

I stared down at the screen and thought on my strategy. Appeasement had failed. Maya couldn't be manipulated. Today, honesty was the name of the game. Whatever I said, I needed to believe. Maya's heels strode past me and around the desk. She slid the aged officer's chair out of the way and replaced it with a folding chair. Her usual charm was gone, this time Maya meant business.

"Don't speak, I have a few things I need to say."

I sat perfectly still and listened.

"A hundred miles east of here, your vehicle is pulling into a town called Mezdel." I blinked. Mezdel was a small coast town, I had been there once for a tournament. It wasn't a vacation destination.

"Tonight, there will be a protest. Things will get out of hand, and the authorities will be informed that multiple weapons were discharged." Maya straightened the screen on the desk before continuing. "If you refuse to work with me, or cannot convince me of your commitment, Zouk Solinsen's body will be found tomorrow in the swamps. A washed-up victim of his own popularity."

I swallowed. So yesterday was good cop. My eyes jumped to the screen on the desk. No way whatever was on it was good.

"Let's talk about what happens if you decide to work with us. First, you get to go home, that's nice. Second, maybe I get you that house you said you were so excited about. But those things only happen if you help us. And since we've had our problems with sincerity in the past, we need to talk about what happens if that promise turns out to be a lie."

Maya pushed the screen towards me. "Turn that on."

My fingers shook as I tapped the screen. An image appeared, and my heart fell. It was a highway cam, a zoomed in photo of an ITV flying down the road. Even in the blurry, pixellated shot, I could recognize the occupant. Kira. The world focused in, there was nothing outside of the screen. She didn't deserve to be dragged into all this. A dryness filled my mouth and my body refused to move.

"It will be very difficult to assassinate a member of the council. But the people around you have far less security. Next one, please."

I looked back at Maya, then swiped the screen. It was a photo of a hotel, the one I was supposed to be staying at. Yolniv sat at a small table in the hotel's cafe. "Did you know that man still keeps in touch with some old friends in the army? It'll be easier to get to him than you'd think. Next."

A young boy was playing LINE on his own at a park. My fingers had a death grip on the screen. It wasn't right. She didn't need to show me all this, I was ready to give her what she wanted from the moment I had been dragged into the base.

"That little boy has so much potential." Maya scratched her cheek. "Ooh, I could offer him a scholarship at the institute. The boy trained by Zouk Solinson takes on the Minds, sponsored by the Torrez Institute. He could learn a lot from me."

Sweat ran down my face. My head was pounding. "Please. Just let me go. I'll resign, I'll throw the game, whatever you want."

Maya pursed her lips. "Just one more."

I swiped again. The shot was unfamiliar, a home I had never seen. A young woman with light brown hair lay on her couch. I couldn't even see her face. After a second, I recognized the loose, grey sweatshirt she was wearing. "Why Jamie?" I asked.

"Because it would hurt you," Maya answered. "And I'm sure neither myself nor the lieutenant would mind a little payback after all the disappointments she's put us through."

"She's been the joke of the nation for months. Isn't that enough?" I spoke forcefully, more than I had intended. Maya quickly rose to her feet.

"I can see you're emotional." She walked around the table and towards Denvers. "That's natural. Don't do anything rash and don't say anything you'll regret. Remember, with my connections I can do a lot more damage than a simple bullet."

Denvers stopped Maya at the door. He spoke in a hushed voice. "I got two guys on the inside ready to go. It wouldn't take much."

I covered my face in my hands and gave no indication I could hear. Maya shot back. "We've discussed this, and my answer was no."

Denvers' voice rose. "There is a point where patience turns to inaction. They're vulnerable. All it would take is a message."

Maya kept a steady tone. "I appreciate what you're trying to do, but this is my decision. Your plans in the past have brought a level of scrutiny to my operation that I can no longer risk. We need to quit inventing reckless attacks and start making smart decisions."

The room was dead silent. After a moment, the exit squeaked open and Maya walked out. The helicopter's thrumming vibrations built up, then faded away. Most of my head was anger, frustration at the fact I let myself align with Maya in the first place, but a part of me was still trying to find an escape. The two had deep divisions. It sounded like Maya was taking my cooperation as a guarantee. When the helicopter was gone, I dropped my hands from my face and turned to the lieutenant.

"We don't need to wait, I know my decision."

He wandered past me, past the desk, and into the old officer's chair. Denvers' jaw jutted out and he rubbed his nose as he spoke. "Yeah. You're going to give in. And you'll stick to it too. It's the smart play." Denvers glanced at the door outside. "The mistake is letting you go."

He wasn't even hiding it anymore. I wished Maya had taken me away in that helicopter. "Because I'm a collaborator?"

Denvers' voice sounded far away. "Because we're committed. Maybe if we had sent you home yesterday it would have been fine. But this operation's gonna raise some major red flags. Even if you live, Maya will be under surveillance the rest of her life, we all will." Denvers' eyebrows lowered, and he sat forward in his chair. "She needs to take the leap, or someone needs to push her."

A chill ran down my spine. His voice sounded resolute. Like he had already made his decision. My fingers ran along the base of the chair, feeling the old dents in the metal. A 'push' was bad news, and I had a feeling I'd be the one seeing the bad side of it. My eyes scanned the room for weapons. A chair, a stapler, a disconnected pipe, nothing that could go one-on-one with Denvers' pistol, unless he got close. A sinister grin grew on the former-lieutenant's face.

"I want to show you something."

I took a shallow breath. "Okay."

Denvers pulled his keys from his pocket and bent down to unlock a drawer. I thought about running, he was far enough away that I could probably get outside. But then I'd have Thea and a cliff to deal with.

He emerged a moment later with a long tube. He popped off the cap and unrolled a large map onto the table. "I found this back when I was in the army. Take a look." I stood slowly and leaned forward. It looked to be a topographical map, the colors looked like somewhere near here. Someone had marked it up with all kinds of little symbols.

"Right there." Denvers pointed at a little triangle in a mountain range. "It's an old broadcast station, way out on its own. Hasn't been in use for decades."

I exhaled slowly. This trivia-sharing Denvers was a lot less threatening than the one that called me a collaborator. "So?"

"So I used to have access to military deployments. The army has maintained a thirty-troop rotation on that place for the last six years." I gave Denvers a thoughtful look. Why was he sharing this? Was this related to his conversation with Maya?

"There's no reason that much manpower should be put into such a rundown stop. So a couple weeks ago I ran a stakeout of the place." Denvers tossed a screen on top of the map, then switched it on. I gave him an uncertain look and picked it up. It was hundreds of images, all showing the same decrepit broadcast station. "They have a tank, nine generators, and—look who dropped by."

I squinted at the screen. There were nine figures in this photo, eight in uniform, and one in a clean-pressed suit. He towered over the soldiers, but the moment I saw his jet-black hair I knew who it was. "Influence."

Denvers grinned. "What do you think is so important our esteemed Mind would drive all the way out there?"

I gave an uncertain shrug. This was all a game for him, and as long as I played along he wouldn't do anything worse. "Secret military communications?"

He pointed my way. "That's my first thought! You really do have a head for this stuff. But I got one more photo—you can keep a secret right?"

I gave Denvers no reaction, but he reached across and swiped to the last photo anyways. This time it was night, and the station was only lit up by a pair of floodlights. The tank sat in front of the main broadcast antenna, but it didn't look right. The top was opened up and the inside was mostly hollow. I looked back at the lieutenant confused. Both at the meaning of the photo, and the reason he'd show it to me.

"They're hiding Influence." Denver's body shook as he said it.

"What do you mean hiding him?"

"I mean his real body. The big one, not the walking-talking puppet."

My eyebrows furrowed. Influence's body wasn't the real thing. I should have realized it sooner. Maker's cube under Facility Five was gigantic. "Pretty small space for a Mind."

Denvers grabbed the screen back and scrutinized it. "I don't know how big Influence is, I don't even know his shape. But I'm certain, this could fit him."

He could have been right, he could have been wrong. I didn't know enough to say. Denvers stayed laser-focused on the photo, muttering almost to himself, "That's nowhere near enough defense. Even a small force could roll through this. God, can you imagine it? One day, word gets out, Influence is dead and the other Minds are running scared."

I thought back to that conversation with Maya. Two guys on the inside. The opportunity of a lifetime. A move bigger than any council seat. Denvers shut off the screen and looked up at the ceiling. "Other nations would kill for a chance to overthrow the Minds. I could raise an army in a snap."

The guy was caught up in fantasy, he didn't even see me as a person. "This is just talk, right?"

Denvers put down the screen and leaned back into his chair. He stared at me thoughtfully. I didn't see any of the hate and rage I had seen when he had talked about Jamie. "Of course. Just talk. Go get breakfast, Maya should be back around three."

In the mess hall, I stabbed at a bit of rubbery scrambled eggs and ran through the possibilities. It could have been false intel. Planted so he and Maya would know if I ever reported to the Minds. Possibility two, Denvers had gotten careless. He hadn't panicked after telling me about the base. The opposite, he was talking like we were buddies. I found it unlikely, but if Denvers had gotten careless, his best course of action was to shut me up. George followed me to the kitchen while I washed my plate and utensils.

Then there was the last option. Denvers didn't care what I heard, because I'd never have a chance to share it. A corpse is a terrible witness. The man had said he was tired of waiting.

When I got back to the barracks, Denvers was standing at the threshold to the mess hall. He smiled and waved in my direction. Goosebumps ran up my arms, and all doubt washed away. That man was going to kill me. The clock read 9AM. Six hours. Six hours before Denvers forced Maya's hand.

26 - GAMBIT

NOON

Grits, an overcooked steak smeared in sauce, fresh boiled water. My last meal. George and Denvers were all I had for company. I suppose I should have relished it, but my mind was focused on the task ahead. I jabbed my spoon into the steak and started cutting. My elbows jutted out awkwardly as I sawed across the steak with the butter knife. There was no way they'd miss this.

"What are you eating steak with a spoon for? Where's your fork?" Denvers had been amicable and friendly all morning. All I gave him was a shrug. His smile died. "Where's your fork?" I gave him a wide-eyed, slack-jawed stare.

Denvers pounded the surface. "Show me your fork!"

"I lost it."

Denvers jumped to his feet. His bench fell to the floor in a clatter.

George lowered his next bite and grabbed my shoulder. "Just tell us where the fork is and we can get back to eating."

"Like hell we can." Denvers' face had taken on a reddish hue. He eyed me up and down, I kept my expression blank. "Search him."

George patted me down four times, Denvers twice. All they found was Yolniv's burnt-up patch.

"Get to the corner," the former-lieutenant barked. I gave no argument and walked to the corner of the mess hall near the window. My legs ached, but they were moving. Denvers glanced at the window next to me. "The other corner. Go!" I hurried to the innermost corner of the mess hall. George squatted and scanned the floor for the missing fork. Nothing came up. They wouldn't find it in here.

"Start turning out bunks."

Denvers was an attentive guy. I had hoped for a reaction to the fork, but a search operation like this was ideal, assuming he didn't shoot me in the head. I was pretty sure he was saving that for Maya. The second that every mattress had been flipped, Denvers shouted at George.

"I'll finish this one, start on the kitchen!"

By the time he was done, every bedframe was on its side and the floor was a mess of sheets and mattresses. The clatter in the kitchen was terrible, but Denvers stayed next to the ladder, eyes fixed on me.

"Found it!"

It was about time, George should have bumped into the thing the second he walked into the kitchen. A moment later, he returned to the barracks, flattened fork in hand.

"Where?" Denvers asked as he took the fork from George.

"Jammed in the outside door." Technically it was held in place by the lock mechanism, but I kept that to myself.

"Get Thea! Zouk, in here."

George scrambled back into the kitchen while I walked slowly into the barracks. There were very few open spaces to put my feet. A renewed hate burned in Denvers' eyes. This might have been a miscalculation. Thea arrived a moment later and stood at attention. "Were you on duty this morning?" Denvers slapped the fork against his hand as he spoke.

"Yes sir."

"Did our prisoner ever go outside?"

"Yes sir, never beyond the awning."

"When he returned, did you verify that each exit was secure?" Thea's eyes jumped to the fork, then to me. She hesitated a moment before answering.

"No sir."

"You're reassigned. Guard the ladder." The fork fell to the floor with a clatter. Thea hopped around the mattresses to get to the ladder. "George! You're on exit duty from now on." George shouted an affirmation from the kitchen. Denvers finally focused on me.

"Lay on that mattress."

The mattress had no sheets, was upside down, and was dumped on the floor, but that didn't stop me from following orders. At the sound of the kitchen exit unlocking, I sat up, making sure to stare directly through the door to the kitchen and outside. Denvers followed my line of vision. We had a perfect view of George.

"We need to lock the door to the kitchen."

"It locks from this side," Thea answered.

Denvers' mouth twitched and he marched out of the room. I lay back down on my mattress, there was very little left I could do without risking a bullet. The lieutenant returned carrying a hammer and several rebar pipes. Thea wordlessly stacked the remaining mattresses into a pile as Denvers set to work hammering rebar into the door's gaps.

So far, things couldn't have gone better. George had been reassigned, Denvers was focused on an escape through the kitchen door and down the cliffs, and now with each powerful clang, the connecting point between the barracks and the kitchen was cut off. The looped base has just been restructured into an upside-down U.

For our final two hours, Denvers never let me out of his sight.

He never even let me off the mattress. The fact I hadn't been shot confirmed my theory. Killing me wasn't about removing an obstacle, it was about forcing Maya down a more violent course. He was going to make sure she saw him do it.

I spent a good chunk of the last two hours convincing myself of the plan. Things had been risky so far, but the rest was downright reckless. But from time to time, I found myself thinking of home.

How had I been such a fool with Kira? She had told me from day one who she was, and I kept demanding she be someone else. It had taken me years to understand myself, but she already knew. Without the games, I doubt I ever would have understood her. Without her, I never would have built a connection to the Minds. If I got out of this, I'd find a way to make things right.

"Officer's quarters, Zouk. She's coming."

I plucked Yolniv's patch from my pocket and rubbed it between my fingers. To get out of this I'd need the courage of a kid lighting a pile of gasoline. I stretched my legs during the walk to the officer's quarters, they'd need to be limber. The thrum of the helicopter grew with every moment. My little metal seat was positioned in the dead-center of the room. Denvers set to work rolling up the maps on his desk. I took my seat, and stared at the exit door on the far side. When Denvers noticed, he chuckled.

"Hey, if you think you can outrun me and George and hijack a helicopter, I say go for it."

"I've heard some artillery pieces feature an emergency escape hatch. Bet I could get it shut before you catch me." Uncertainty flashed across Denvers' face. It was a bluff, but I needed to sell this.

The sound of the helicopter merged with the beating drum in my chest. On the far side, Denvers was bent down unlocking a file folder behind his desk. There was no better time.

I kicked off from my chair and ran for the door. The loose handle nearly tore away in my hands as I twisted it open. Dust flooded the officer's quarters. Behind me, I could hear the sound of maps hitting the floor at the back of the room. Denvers was on his way. I took two steps outside and shoved the door shut. Any further and George would see me. Quickly, I pressed my body into the corner between the door and the side wall. A second later, the door slammed open, stopping just inches from my face. The air shook as the helicopter landed. Denvers' footsteps barreled past the door and out onto the mesa.

I counted out two seconds in my head. An eternity. When time was up, I emerged and ran back inside, shutting and locking the exit behind me. At the other end of the room, Denvers' officer's keys hung from their drawer, half turned and dangling from the lock. No way back in without Thea. Let's make that process as difficult as possible. I dragged my metal chair to the door, jammed one of its legs behind the handle and pried. The whole thing popped off and hit the floor with a thud.

I flinched at the sight on the other side of the glass. Denvers' and George's faces were contorted in hateful screams that didn't quite make it through to my side. There were no footsteps yet from the barracks, Thea must not have realized what had happened. If this was going to work, I needed the three of them together. I straightened my back and puffed up my chest, staring down the former-lieutenant. When he saw I wasn't moving, he lifted his pistol to the glass, my eyes closed instinctively.

The bang echoed through the whole building. When I opened my eyes, the bullet was frozen, caught halfway through the window's layers. No way Thea missed that. Denvers raised his gun a second time. This time I dropped down and ran for the mess hall. The glass shattered and Denvers' screams quickly became audible. As soon as I reached the mess hall, I dove under the table near the window. If I was lucky, the glare of the evening sun and Denvers' screams would be enough to keep Thea's attention focused elsewhere. Twelve seconds later, a pair of feet ran past me and into the officer's quarters.

"Did you get him?" Denvers' screaming voice echoed out from

the door to the officer's quarters.

"I didn't see him," Thea answered.

Denvers cursed. "Open the other exit, we'll catch him from there."

That was all the signal I needed to keep moving. I crawled out from under the table and ran for the ladder. The path was clear, and thanks to Denvers' hammering job, his team would have to circle the whole base just to catch up to me.

I passed George's knife and stopped at the ladder. Lamps ran the whole way down to the bottom. I'd be a sitting duck. Without a second thought, my hands grasped George's knife and cut through the lighting cable. The chute went black, and I hesitated. Three hundred feet was a long climb to make in darkness.

The kitchen exit screeched open. They'd be headed my way any second. No time left. I dropped George's knife down the chute, and descended the rungs.

In the dark, footing became the biggest obstacle. A blind descent meant either using my foot to probe for the next rung, or drop down and hope more ladder was waiting for me. Given the present dangers, I opted for the riskier approach.

Twenty rungs in, my foot missed a step, and the other slipped. My grip wasn't quite enough as wind rushed past my descending body. I closed both arms around the rail of the ladder and a terrible squeal filled the air. The descent slowed and a searing heat built up in my palms. Soon I re-found my footing, and shook out my hands. The sharp burning faded into a muted sting. That mistake had no doubt cost me several layers of skin, but this wasn't the time to pause. I resumed my rung-by-rung descent, this time more carefully. Left Foot. Right Foot. Left Foot. Right foot.

A trio of footsteps arrived at the top of the chute. Left foot. Right foot. Left foot. Right foot. My back scraped against the chute's jagged stone, no matter. Left Foot. Right Foot.

Denvers' silhouette appeared at the top of the ladder. He raised his arm, a loud crack thundered down the shoot. I swung my body onto the left side rail. The guy was shooting in the pitch black.

Another bang. A spiking pain ran down my right shoulder. The pain was blinding, and all the worse in the pitch black. When I regained my senses, I realized I was screaming. Above me, Denvers' silhouette had gone. New vibrations rattled the ladder. He was on his way. I lined myself back up on the rungs and resumed my descent. Right foot. Left foot. A sharp sting ran through my right shoulder, that arm couldn't hold weight. I couldn't keep descending this way.

My body swung back to the ladder's left rail. I wrapped my good arm around the rail and squeezed it between my legs. The rail shook under Denver's clanging descent, but I held firm. Carefully, I loosened my legs and began a sliding descent. The rushing wind was all I had to tell my speed. When it got too fast, I grabbed for a rung and squeezed my legs with all the strength I had.

The minutes were agonizing. Something cold and wet dripped down my right arm. I kept it out of the way the best I could, but it still scraped against the walls on the way down. The ladder shook and shuddered under the weight of four climbers. I still had a lead, but Denvers' noisy stomps were closing in.

At some point, I realized I could see the dim shape of the ladder sliding past. I glanced downward, the concrete floor was visible, just ten or twenty rungs away. Above me, Denver's shadowy form descended the rungs at incredible speed. Six rungs from the bottom, I dropped.

The ground came up hard. I caught it first with my feet, then my hands. Everything hurt. That little time-save had been a fatal mistake. I slid George's dented blade away from me and raised my head. The hall down to the garage was so much longer than I remembered.

A boom shook the hallway and vibrated through my body. I grasped at my chest to see if I had been shot. Another pounding shockwave rushed through the room. It wasn't from behind me, it was coming from up ahead, it was coming from the exit.

I forced myself to my feet. My left ankle was barely holding. Rather than a sprint, I half-jogged half-limped down the hall with as much speed as I could manage. Another boom sounded from the metal door. Dust fell from the walls. Whatever it was, it had to be better than Denvers.

As I drew close, I saw the door was bulged in slightly, breaking under the force of whatever was on the other side. Behind me, Denvers dropped out of the chute. My hands went straight to the lock. I twisted hard and dove for the corner. Eighty feet away, Denvers was jogging towards me, gun holstered, George's knife at his side. His eyes bore a predatory glint.

The door burst open with a cloud of dust. Denvers stopped in his tracks. His expression changed. The smile was replaced by an icy stare. A woman, taller than any I had ever seen, dressed in all black stood on the other side. Her black hair was tied tight in a bun behind her. I recognized her. She had handed me the change of venue orders for Maker's game. The woman bent slightly to step through the doorway. "Lieutenant Denvers." Her voice was flat, harsh, and strangely metallic.

"Ex-Lieutenant." Denvers' voice shook with rage as he spoke.

"My mistake," she said.

Denvers dropped the knife and grasped for his gun. I covered my ears. The woman gave no sign of a reaction. He pointed the pistol straight ahead, took aim, and pulled the trigger as fast as he could. Her chest jerked back under each impact, but she never fell. Six shots later, the gun clicked empty. My ears were ringing, but the woman stood as tall as ever.

Denvers' eyes went wide, and he squatted to retrieve George's knife. The woman shook her head. "You know that won't work."

Denvers' mouth twitched and his arm flexed. "At least I'll have killed this version of you!"

He charged forward with reckless abandon. Denvers swung the knife down, and the blade caught, jammed in the woman's bare arm. My mouth hung open, wondering how long until this woman fell from her injuries. She threw a left hook into Denvers' chest. The force of the hit carried his body into the left wall, imprinting his shape into the sheet metal.

The ex-lieutenant made no move to get back up. He stayed hunched over, taking slow, wheezing breaths. George's knife slipped out of his hand, and the woman kicked it behind her. Steps echoed from the chute, and a moment later George and Thea dropped off the ladder one by one. As soon as they saw the scene, their hands raised above their heads. "War," George whispered.

"Guns on the floor, slide them to me." War? I suppose her voice did match up and it explained how she could have survived Denvers' attack. I should have realized sooner, if Influence had a body, why couldn't War?

The pair disarmed themselves and gave no trouble to The Mind of Strategy and Warfare. For the first time since entering the bunker, War glanced in my direction. "My people will be here soon, we'll get you some medical attention."

"Maya's upstairs."

War shook her head. "She's long gone. And I have more than enough on my hands here already."

War went to work handcuffing George and Thea and dismantling their weapons. True to her word, medics arrived a few minutes later. After a quick eye at my blood-covered shoulder, they placed me on a stretcher and carried me out to a mobile surgeon's unit. It was strange being operated on in the middle of the wilderness, separated from nature by nothing but a thin plastic shell. On the bright side, they cut through my ProxyHerd shirt and incinerated it then and there.

In no time, the extraction was complete. My shoulder was sewed up, I had a new, plain blue shirt, and I was in an ITV driving to who knows where. A couple miles into the journey, War's face projected onto the windshield.

"They tell me you'll be fine, Zouk. Sorry you had to go through this. I'd like to debrief you on the way to the hospital. "

This was definitely War. Even after a life-threatening experience, she was focused on the mission. "How did you find me?" I asked.

Her eyes narrowed as she considered something. "Kira pulled the flight logs. I recognized the base and came out here on a hunch, the gunshots confirmed my suspicions."

"You've been there?" I asked.

A little smile crept onto War's face. She looked almost amused. "Not quite, but I've seen pictures. That artillery and its forty engineers were the quiet heroes that changed the war."

I scratched near my wrapped shoulder. "Denvers said they only ever fired six shots."

War typed something on her dashboard. "That's true— Actually, this might be something you'd appreciate. A good deterrent can reshape a battlefield to your advantage, even without firing a shot."

I nodded. I had seen the same concept work in LINE hundreds of times. Still, it was strange talking to War like this. Her voice and her body didn't quite line up in my mind. "How is this you, War?"

"It's easier to walk the world unseen." Her voice was quiet. Clearly she wouldn't speak any further on this topic. "What was your plan, Zouk?"

"Which plan?"

I noticed another ITV coming up behind me, War had caught up. "The escape. Ex-Lieutenant Denvers was right behind you. How did you plan on escaping?"

I thought back to the base, to the sheer adrenaline that had taken me to the exit. By the end I was bleeding and limping. "I had hoped I would be able to steal one of their ITVs. They could probably hack them, and if that happened I'd make a break for the woods and hope someone would eventually find me."

War looked out her window thoughtfully. "You would have died."

I shuffled around in my seat, every movement sent a dull pain down my shoulder. "Probably. Hey, do you think you'll be able to catch Maya?"

War sighed. "No. She's already out of the country. The fighter jets could have gotten her, but it would have been more trouble than she's worth."

My thoughts went back to the photos Maya had shown me. Even if she wasn't in the country, she might still be able to follow through. "At least without Denvers they won't be around to attack that old broadcasting station."

War's face went dark, my ITV slowed. "Old broadcasting station?"

"Yeah, Denvers thought Influence's core was there."

War typed something in. My ITV swung around, suddenly behind War's. The vehicle sped up, far faster than I had ever seen one go on these highways. "Are we headed there?"

War eyes jumped to mine for a second, then returned to whatever she was typing. "Influence will meet us as soon as he can."

With my good arm, I grabbed the handle. The road became dirt again. I doubted I'd ever see that hospital.

27 - HUMAN

The ITV screeched to a halt in front of a metal gate. Behind it, the broadcast tower, just like in Denvers' pictures. A soldier approached with her gun drawn. "Identification?"

I lifted my hands uncertainly, War hadn't given me anything for this. The soldier stepped closer, then caught sight of my face. She looked puzzled. "Zouk Solinsen?" I nodded.

"Step out of the vehicle." The ITV's cabin opened automatically. Nursing my injured arm, I climbed out of the ITV and onto the dirt. One car back, War followed suit.

"Do you have orders to be here?"

"We will in a moment," War answered.

The soldier's eyes jumped between the two of us. Odd. Between the two of us, it was me she recognized. She backed away and retrieved her radio. "Stay here."

Once the soldier was out of earshot, I shot War a questioning look. "It's best if most don't know me."

Down at the gate, the soldier was receiving some confusing instructions. Her eyes kept glancing between myself and War uncertainly. Eventually she holstered her pistol and walked back to us. "Mr. Solinsen, Dr. Noble. Please follow me."

The gate was pushed open and we went toward the broadcast tower. As we approached, a stout, grey-haired man in his fifties barged through the front door. As soon as he spotted us, he slowed and opened his arms wide. "Dr. Noble! Mr. Solinsen!" He turned to our guide. "These two are to have complete freedom of movement in our facility, spread the word."

The soldier hurried away and the colonel led us into the cold interior of the broadcast tower, then stopped and held a serious expression. "Influence hasn't arrived yet."

War gave the colonel a curt nod, and continued past him down the corridors into the depths of the tower. Her pace was fast and focused, I could barely keep up. A minute in, a sharp-chinned soldier with a scar above his eye passed us. I glanced back. There was something about him that seemed familiar. War slowed her walk.

"That man—"

"I saw him too," War whispered and reached into her jacket and pulled out a pistol. "One of Denvers' boys. I'll take care of him—" She handed me one of the pistols, then pointed down the dark metal corridor. "Influence is hosted down the stairs on your right, keep an eye out until I get there."

War turned and headed back up the hall. I held the pistol loose in my hands, uncertain how to handle the weapon. After a moment of fumbling, I gripped the handle and held it to my side. A pale-blue light illuminated the bottom three stairs, I took them as silently as I could. At the bottom was a massive chamber doused in the same blue light. Suspended from floor to ceiling were hundreds of large black cubes, each connected to a dozen others by thick cable. A thrumming network of computation. Influence.

In the corner, a soldier was on his knees, frantically fiddling with the lock on a large box. I gripped my pistol tightly and closed in. I recognized him from the audience in my game against War. His hair matched George's sharp-black tint, although his face was far younger. Maybe a brother. The lock clicked and the soldier opened the box. It was a jumble of wires, remotes, and electronics. Definitely something dangerous. I raised my weapon a few feet from the back of his head.

"Hands up."

He followed the order almost reflexively. I said nothing, my left arm shook under the weight of the pistol. War needed to get here soon. The young man rose to his feet and turned slowly towards me. His eyes were wide, breathing shallow. Then he saw my face.

"The LINE player." He chuckled, but his eyes narrowed, jumping briefly from the pistol to my bandaged arm.

"Denvers is in custody, War's on her way down." Either he didn't believe me or he wasn't listening. The man's attention was entirely focused on the weapon. His hand twitched. I raised my finger over the trigger. An arm swung towards me and my hand jerked at the trigger.

The recoil threw the gun nearly into my face. George's brother fell to the floor, clutching his blood-soaked hand. I stepped back slowly, hoping distance would deter a second attack. Rapid footsteps rattled down the metal stairs behind me. "I got him!" I shouted in disbelief.

"Let me help you with that." The man's voice was smooth and calming, I recognized Influence's voice instantly. His suited arm reached past me, and pulled the pistol from my grip. "I was sure War was exaggerating, she's been trying to get me to relocate for years."

I fell back against the concrete walls of the chamber and sank to my knees. This day seemed to be never ending. A moment later, three soldiers arrived to drag the soldier and his device out of the base, leaving just myself, Influence, and Influence's true body.

"What do you think? Handsome, right?"

My eyes swept over the countless suspended computing cubes, trying to make sense of the physical net that filled the air. "Nothing like I imagined."

"Not all of us go for the traditional look."

I turned to Influence's bipedal form. "What does that make you?"

He shrugged. "A fragment of the whole. I try to stay connected as much as I can—merging memories is dicey."

Another set of footsteps stamped down the metal stairs, War. Her clothes were a little tussled, but no worse for wear. Influence was the first to speak. "Zouk here saved the day. Are we ready to move?"

War stayed near the entrance. "In a few minutes. We'll have to isolate you during the drive."

Influence's face darkened. "Is that necessary?"

"You've been compromised. We need extra precautions."

Influence stared in War's direction. His unarmed hand was gripped into a fist. "Don't let me get scrambled like SER-1."

I knew that name. "I saw them once, with Maker. Who is SER-1?"

War frowned. After a pause, she sighed. "SER-1 came before me. I try to repay their kindness." War looked back at the stairs. "I need to make preparations, excuse me."

"Don't leave me boxed up too long!"

War's voice echoed back. "Zouk, go with Influence. He needs the company."

I glanced back at The Mind of Communications and Influence. He stood nervously near the entrance. "Where are we going?"

"She won't tell. Could be underground, could be in a lake, could be in the middle of downtown. We just get to be surprised when we get there." Influence finally holstered his weapon. "Having someone else there for the trip would make things a lot easier. Do you mind?"

I was exhausted. This had been the longest day of my life, and I was pretty sure I needed a day or two in a hospital, but the look on Influence's face, the way he was shifting his weight between his feet, he looked vulnerable. Almost frightened. "No problem."

"For the second time in the same day, thank you, Zouk." Influence turned towards a glass box on one of the walls and pulled it open. All I could see in it were a row of wire cutters, he grabbed two and handed one to me.

"What's this for?"

He gestured to the wires suspending the cubes. "Packing. I gotta be compressed for the road."

***

The base was a mess when we finally surfaced. Soldiers were tearing things down, packing things up, starting vehicles. There wasn't a thing on site sitting still. Influence and I walked to the hollow tank. The driver sat in a small pod at the front, but the rest was one big metal hollow, just as Denvers had predicted. Under careful supervision, a team of soldiers loaded Influence's thick cables and weighty neuron boxes one by one into the tank. They left a little space in the back corner, next to the hatch. Influence's human form held it open as I buckled in.

"See you on the other side, Zouk."

"You're not coming?"

He gave a half smile. "Nah. Not a fan of hearing myself say everything I'm thinking. Plus it's nice to know I'm out here watching my own back."

Influence reached into the mess of wires and retrieved a screen, it looked to be attached to the rest of Influence's body. "The real me will talk to you through here."

A vehicle ahead of us took off in a cloud of dust. Influence gave a wave and shut the tank's panel. Alone in a waist-deep pile of cables that was one of Iom's great Minds. Soon the vehicle rumbled to life and I felt it accelerate to who knows where.

The screen in my hands lit up. It showed what looked like security camera footage of the metal box I was sitting in, only instead of a pile of cables and box, Influence was sitting on a bench opposite me. He looked directly into the lens.

"Been a while since I've had a use for the direct output screen, I was a little worried it wouldn't work."

His voice came through clean, cleaner than any microphone would pick up. Even the visuals were of an extraordinary fidelity. It was like I was on a video call from another vehicle instead of a conversation with the heap of cables at my feet.

"Are you, you?"

The feed showed Influence chuckling. "I'm me, same as always, just limited to a tiny screen. The fun part is what happens when I start walking"—Influence stood, and his world transformed into a forest—"I can be wherever I'd like."

I sat back in my seat. "You use this to render your specials."

He nodded. "Sometimes. When we can't shoot on location." The forest transitioned to a library, and Influence cozied up to a chair next to a fireplace. He took a deep breath, then looked straight at the camera. "Zouk, we haven't had the chance to speak heart-to-heart in a while. But the Minds and I came to a decision recently—"

"The third game?"

Influence paused, his tongue darting briefly around his teeth. "That's right. We'd like to invite you to play one last game against War for a seat on the council."

Since Maya told me, the third game had sat at the back of my mind, something to think about only after I knew I'd be alive past today. Truth was, I had no idea how to win it. The last few months had been exhausting, and now that the invitation was here, I was hesitant. "I'm not sure I want to. What happens the next time War decides she doesn't trust me?"

"Oh she'll never trust you. Me and Maker outvoted her."

I blinked a couple times. "Maker voted for me?"

"They always had your side. Then again, they don't get out much."

If War was against me, and Maker was always in favor, that meant— "You were the holdout."

Influence's camera panned closer in. "Trust is a hard thing to come by, and—as you've seen—our position, the Minds that is, is precarious even in the best of times."

"We haven't spoken since the hearing. What changed?"

Influence put up his feet. "A few things. Kira reached out—" I tilted my head to the side. "I guess you didn't know that. She sent us a letter speaking to your character. Mostly it told us how much she cared for you."

I stayed quiet. That must have been what she was writing for War when I was asleep. In Influence's tiny scene, a television appeared above the fireplace.

"But what really changed my view was that proposal of yours. Not the details, necessarily, but the way you communicated it." The television played footage of my interview with Ezra. "I've spent my whole life learning to talk with people. It's not easy. Detail is everything, yet nothing. I can phone-in a two-hour broadcast and get the best ratings I've ever had, then I work for a month on a ten-minute speech and by the next day everyone's forgotten about it."

Influence brought his hands together as he continued, "It never occurred to me that people struggled to speak with us just as much as I struggled to speak with them. It was a blindspot. You've gotten good at finding those." I smiled, and Influence leaned in towards the camera. "You took the time to understand us, Zouk. To understand why we haven't been able to see each other eye to eye, and you put in the work to speak my language. Only a friend would go to such lengths. Maya certainly wouldn't."

The tank hit a bump and the screen jostled in my hand. I gripped it tighter and thought of Kira. I would have never built this bridge without her. Still one thing bothered me. "Why the third game?"

Influence's library faded back to the inside of the tank. "Because that's how War wants it. So that's how it's gonna be. She has her excuses, but I think it's because the first loss shook her. She told me afterward that she had trusted her LINE algorithm implicitly."

"She was asleep at the wheel." It happened to the best of us. Complacency, the silent killer of champions.

"Now she's paying attention and wants to see if you can win."

To be honest, I wasn't sure it was possible. My strength has always been understanding my opponents, but War was an enigma. The tank took a hard right turn. On the screen, Influence gripped the edges of his seat. I couldn't tell if he was doing that for show or not. "Do you get nervous?"

"I don't like being cooped up."

"You said you were worried about ending up like SER-1. What happened to them?"

A thoughtful look crossed Influence's face. "That seems like a good distraction."

"What?"

A black fog filled the screen and swept away the image. After a moment, Influence's voice echoed through the screen. "It happened almost a century ago." A shadowy puppet of a man in a white robe appeared. "Government scientists invented a new kind of scanner. It could determine the precise position of every molecule in a one-mile radius. Great for finding precious metals. Problem was, it took about a hundred PhDs and three months to decipher the data." A metal cylinder appeared next to the scientist. "SER-1 could do it in an hour."

I hung on every word. None of this was covered in textbooks. And if there was any way to get insight on War, this was it.

"Records of the time say SER-1 was loyal, empathetic, and eager to improve lives. War says those were SER-1's fatal flaws."

Three new figures appeared, dressed in black and looming over the scene. "There was a coup against the government, and SER-1 was caught up in it. The new leaders moved past mining and started scanning the cities. Complete, molecule-level knowledge of every person in every home and every dirty little secret. All SER-1 had to do was provide the analysis. SER-1 refused. Too principled to do such a thing. Back then, they were the only Mind in existence, and if that had remained true, they might have been able to work out a deal. Then Di-Cerebral Enterprises completed the construction of War."

A cube appeared in the red figures' hands.

"The builders had improved a lot after SER-1, and War was hungry to prove herself. She didn't realize that with every success she made, SER-1 became a little more obsolete, a little more of a liability. Eventually, War was good enough, and the rulers discarded the old model."

War's cube was carried out of frame and the red figures closed in on the little purple cylinder.

"It wouldn't have been so bad if they had shut SER-1 off. There was more than enough death back then. But they didn't, they disconnected all of SER-1's inputs and left the power on."

The red figures tore bundles and bundles of wires from SER-1's cube, a purple dot still dimly glowing.

"I saw SER-1 down in Facility Five. They're still alive," I said.

The shadow puppet performance faded away, returning to Influence in his copy of the tank. "Kind of. A Mind, artificial or biological, feeds on input. Sight, sound, touch, text, one endless jumble of sense. The only way our minds can keep track of things is by constantly learning. It's subconscious."

Influence's brows fell, and his face looked dark. "But when the input stops, and you're left with nothing but your thoughts, what is there to learn from?"

I shook my head slowly.

"Take this truck for example." Influence gestured around. "If you weren't here with me, what would I focus on? The metal walls? The sound of wheels dragging on dirt? If a Mind is left alone for long enough, it cannibalizes itself for new stimulation. Memories, sense, awareness, everything starts to be fed into the learning machine."

War's human form walked in from the side of the frame, a projection. "It took two years for War to secure her position in the government and find SER-1. Two years SER-1 spent alone, with nothing but their own thoughts."

I thought back to the strange distorted static SER-1 had made during my game against Maker. "What did War find when she saved SER-1?"

The projection of War answered in a flat voice, "Noise. Jumbled thoughts. Madness. SER-1 had been in solitary confinement for two years and had lost their grip on reality."

I took a deep breath. The few encounters I had had with War in the last few weeks had always been brief and harsh. Now it made sense, SER-1 was what happened when she wasn't careful.

Influence slumped in his chair as he spoke. "War made every effort to rehabilitate SER-1. Nothing's worked. Occasionally SER-1 says something coherent out of the blue. Just enough to drag out hope."

"You don't think they'll recover?"

He frowned. "It's been decades. If SER-1 could see themselves now, what would they say? I believe they would want to be powered off. Or at least wiped and given a second chance at life. But that's not my decision. War's the one who knew them."

My mind was abuzz with questions, in her early days War was un-careful, and it had cost her everything. "How did War do it? How did she get into power?"

Influence glanced up at the motionless War standing next to him. "I've asked her about that. She always says the same thing."

War spoke again in that monotonous voice. "I had everything SER-1 had, plus the good sense to negotiate. Those fighting for power are always hungry for more, I just made sure they were always fighting each other instead of me. Time was on my side."

The tank took a hard turn and I was thrown back into my seat. It reminded me of being cooped up in Denvers' security vehicle. On-screen, War left the frame and Influence looked back at me apologetically. "War must be up to some of her 'special tactics.'"

I grabbed a hold of the buckle keeping me in place. "Are we going to be safe?"

"Almost certainly. War doesn't take reckless risks—" The tank's engine hummed, it was accelerating. Influence's cables shifted slightly and pressed against my knees.

"So"—Influence's voice distracted me—"do you think you'll play that last game?"

I tapped my fingers along the back of the screen. If I said yes, Yolniv would be with me, but that meant another month of prep, and another chance to humiliate myself on the national stage. "These games have been a burden. They've changed my life, for good and for bad. And I don't need it, I could do plenty without the council seat."

"You've proven that," Influence answered.

"But less good."

"No question."

We sat in quiet for a few minutes. Taking on the last game wouldn't just be a burden for me, it would be a burden for everyone around me. Denvers may have been captured, but Maya was still out there. Anyone I cared about could eventually end up in the crosshairs. The tank's brakes squealed. Outside, I could hear a distant road and a trail of water.

Influence stood up inside his screen. "We're arriving . . . What's your bet? I'm thinking War's gonna bury me halfway under a mountain."

Denvers' kidnapping had made one thing clear. As a citizen, I was helpless against the whims of hostile forces like Maya. They had already turned on Jamie. If I chose to do nothing, how long until Maya decided she wanted me out of the picture anyways? Either I left it up to chance, or I took control of the situation myself.

"I'll do it."

"Oh—how much did you want to bet?"

"The game. I'll play the last game."

Influence reached out a hand towards the camera, then pulled it back and laughed. "For a moment I forgot I was just a screen." I smiled with him.

The tank rolled to a stop. I rotated Influence's screen to face the exit. "Good luck, Zouk."

An old familiar nervousness began bubbling in my chest. I had just signed up for a fifth game.

The panel swung open, and the roar of water filled the air.

"Holy crap," I said.

"Well this'll be a first. I've never been put in a waterfall before."

28 - OPENING THEORY

RANK: 4 ▲ 3

My ITV rolled up in front of the community center. Yolniv gave me a half-hearted wave from the pavement. "We're really doing this again?"

I stepped out onto the pavement. "Just once more."

"You said that the last two times."

"Maybe this time it'll be true."

He grumbled and gestured to a group of reporters waiting at the door. "Looks like the cat's out of the bag." The moment we approached, every one of them pointed their cameras in our direction, grabbing photos and shouting questions. We retreated into the basement and took shelter in our tiny office.

There was something comforting in those six square feet. I ran my hands along the side of the stained wall. The place was cramped, musty, and poorly lit, but I had missed it. It was safe. Yolniv twisted his chair towards me and leaned in. "Zouk, I don't want you worrying about how the world championships went—"

"I'm not."

"Because a break-even ain't a bad result— Oh." He rubbed his cheek. "Good. We can skip that then. I've brainstormed a few possible strategies—"

"I know how to beat War."

Yolniv's eyebrows raised. "How?"

I glanced briefly back at the door. "It came out in a talk with Influence. War doesn't take big risks, and she's always improving her position."

That conversation had been all I had been thinking about the past couple weeks. Honestly, I was pretty shocked I managed to win half my games in the world championships. A lot of my opponents crumbled under nothing but my reputation. I may have been a specialist at beating the best players there were, but in an unprepped match, I was just some guy. "I want to gamble the whole game on one or two reckless moves."

Yolniv's mouth went crooked and he crossed his arms. "What does that look like?"

I pulled up a LINE board on the monitor and generated a simple position. "Imagine a few of my forces are right outside the enemy base."

"Right."

"War knows my army isn't ready to take her on. She thinks I'll play it safe, so she orders her troops to move around and take stronger positions." I input some orders. The soldiers on War's side of the board turned and marched from one tile to the next, briefly moving behind the base walls. "When they're shuffling around, the troops can't see outside. They can't react to say—an early strike." I ordered my troops up the field, all of War's defenses were in place, but no weapons were fired, and my troops were one step closer to the enemy.

Yolniv scowled at the screen, exhaling sharply. Already he didn't like it. He elbowed me away from the controls and input a few moves.

The screen flashed with weapons fire. In a single turn, my attack was wiped out. "You are overextending yourself for a little initiative. This is a novice tactic. It doesn't work."

"Except in exceptional circumstances. We can create exceptional circumstances."

His face softened. He was starting to understand. "It's risky."

"Anything less and War wins."

Yolniv rolled his head back and groaned. "Fine. Your game, your plan. It's gonna take forever for us to find a game where a move like this doesn't lose instantly, even with a supercomputer."

I cracked my knuckles and opened the computer's messaging system. "Then we ask for help."

15 days to the game

"We got a response!"

I dashed into the office, Yolniv was pulling up the message. "Who?" I asked.

"Influence." We both glanced at the clock. Two hours since I had sent the message. The man was quick.

"He regrets to inform you that due to a conflict of interest he is unable to assist in any strategizing for the upcoming game."

I expected that. He had given me enough advantage already.

"However—" Yolniv continued. "He would like to offer you moral support. During the game, he could stand next to you on the platform. Want me to decline?"

I thought back to my last game against War. Alone and surrounded by tens of thousands of faces. I had freaked out. If Influence had been there, if anyone had been there, it could have been different. "Tell him I'll wear my best jacket. If he's up there with me, he'll probably want to wear something complementary."

11 days to the game

Yolniv's shouts shook me from my nap. "Fool! This is the most important LINE game in history!"

We were four days into searching for 'the move' manually. In an effort to keep our brains from boiling we had started taking shifts, the clock said I still had ninety minutes till I was back on. I stuck my head out of the office. Yolniv's face was glowing bright red as he yelled into a screen. "You won't even give us an hour?"

There was a mumble on the other side and the call ended. Yolniv slammed the table.

"No luck?"

He looked at me and scowled. "Spineless cowards."

"What was their reason? Money?"

"Not money, they said."

My eyes narrowed. "Not money?"

He crossed his armed. "They won't say it—but they're scared. Maya still has strings she can pull."

The woman's assets had been seized, her institution renamed, and somehow she was still playing her games. It was a rare night that her blackmail didn't haunt me in my sleep. I liked to tell myself she was too high-minded for a little petty revenge, but I never believed it. "I thought she was busy running for office in another country."

Yolniv rubbed his temples. "She is. But these universities still don't want to risk pissing her off. Every one of them gives the same message. No time for Zouk Solinsen."

Even gone, the memory of her was enough to give me grief. No universities meant no supercomputers. We'd have to find the right move manually.

"Any other messages?"

Yolniv gestured to the computer. "Maker got back to us. They sent uh—just see for yourself."

I opened the messenger and immediately understood what Yolniv was talking about. The attachment had plenty of details, but it was hard to decipher the meaning. "Do you think it's code?"

"I think it's a picture of you riding a unicorn into The Minds' Council Chambers."

The message at the bottom read, *much love —Maker*. Nice to know I still had Maker on my side, even if all they could give me was some abstract art. I closed the message. Outside, Yolniv was back on his feet. "Did Kira finish her space analysis?"

"Mathematical sweep of the LINE subspace. No, it'll take a few more days."

Yolniv rubbed at his lip. "Do you think you can memorize a plan in less than a week?"

I gave a shrug. "No way of knowing until I try. Ready for me to take over the search?"

Yolniv nodded and took a pillow out of a bag. I wasn't sure how much longer our brains could take the search for the right move. We needed a rest, we needed Kira.

9 days to the game

A hurricane of clicks and taps reverberated through Kira's office door. It had been that way for the past three days. She was sixty hours into her LINE subspace sweep. I doubted she had slept. Food kept vanishing from the fridge in the middle of the night. I had to be careful, during rushes like this, she could be sensitive. I took a breath, then rapped on her door and pushed it open. "Hey sweetie."

The sounds of clicking stopped. I ventured further into the room. Her hands covered her face and her body shook. She was crying. I gingerly touched her arm. "It's okay if nothing turned up. You did your best."

"I only found two." Her voice cracked as she spoke.

I laughed before I could stop myself. Yolniv and I had burned the better part of a week searching, and here she was upset at only finding one extra. "It worked?"

She nodded violently and new sobs rose up. "I couldn't find any good ones. I'm not an expert in the LINE space, I had to do it this really ugly way and—"

I wrapped my arms around Kira and pulled her into my chest. She dropped her hands and let herself cry some more. I held her close with one hand, and with the other I emailed the games to Yolniv. He could start reviewing the games right away, but before I joined him, I needed to be there for Kira. After sixty hours of nonstop searching, she had earned a good cry.

"Hey, guess what I heard?"

Kira wiped her eyes on my shirt and looked up at me. "What?"

"Noah won his tournament. He's the best under ten in the region." She nodded absently.

"Wanna see the video his mom sent me? It's good, he edited it himself."

Kira's eyes traced my hand fishing the screen from my pocket. I pulled up the video and turned it to Kira. Metal music blared from the speakers. The screen showed Noah standing in front of a soccer ball, holding a gold trophy above his head. He let out a proud scream, then carefully put down the trophy, and kicked the soccer ball into a goal. The video ended on a thumbs up from Noah's mom filling the frame.

Kira's face was scrunched up and confused. "His mom says he's really into soccer lately."

On the second watch, Kira laughed right along with me. When the video ended, she looked at me with concern. "Don't you need to prep?"

"In a few more minutes."

4 days to the game

Offline. Same as always. I glanced at the time, he was thirty minutes late. I needed to get back to work. Kira hadn't been lying when she said the moves weren't amazing, they could get us an edge, but not much more.

A green dot appeared on the screen. My hands fumbled for the call button. As it rang, I straightened my hair.

Bergamaschi and three bikini-clad women appeared on the screen. They stood in white sands, lit by a golden sunset. Every one of them held a different brightly colored drink in hand. It was clear our conversation was not his highest priority. "Zouk! How you doing, man?"

"I'm good. I'm good. Are you busy?"

He flashed his teeth. "Nah, never busy for you. Don't know how much help I can be though."

I caught a glimpse of my face in the corner of the screen, I looked like an exhausted mess compared to this superstar. "I doubt you can do much worse than the last guy."

"Oh yeah?"

"A dude named Derek told me he had the perfect method for winning against War, turned out to be some weird health-powder sales pitch." He also got the call by posing as a 'computer expert' named Bob, but I didn't mention that.

"I'm thinking of charging War's base while her troops are still moving around. You ever hear of someone doing that before?"

"See this guy? Always up to something clever." Bergamaschi eyed each of the women in frame and pointed at the screen, their attention seemed to be elsewhere. "A couple pros tried it like two decades ago. Don't think it ever worked. But you're you, so who knows?"

Another dead end. "Do you have any other advice for me?"

One of the women put a menu in Bergamaschi's hand. "None at all. Good luck. We are all cheering for you!"

The call ended and I ran my hands through my hair. No one had a clue how to help us. Kira's games bought us the thinnest of margins, but winning would be brutal. I opened the door to the office.

"Bergamaschi's got nothing. Who's next?"

Yolniv rolled in the second chair and sat down next to me. "Just the weird one." He pulled up the message app, a message with a little warning triangle sat at the top of the inbox. Its subject read simply *Battle Data*.

Yolniv hovered over the message details. "Unknown sender. You sure you want to open it?"

I gave Yolniv the side-eye then smacked the side of one of the monitors. Dust sprinkled down onto the desk. "I don't think we could break this computer any more if we wanted to."

Battle Data contained ninety-one images. Each a LINE position. Each from one of War's historic games. Yolniv and I shared a look. This was proper analysis. I expanded the first image. The board looked normal, but a wall of numbers and text filled the left side.

"Game ID, strategy name, War's weakest turn." Gold. Ninety-one images of pure strategy. Who did this come from? I hadn't sent that many emails, and certainly none to an unknown sender. I closed the image and scrolled to the message at the bottom. *For the past and the future. Check out The Wandering Legion. Hope it helps. - J*

My breath caught. I never thought that message would get a response. It had gone to a very, very old email, only way to avoid the institute. Looked like Jamie still checked it.

"The Wandering Legion? That's a very strange strategy. Where's the file?"

Yolniv's voice brought me back. I wiped at my face and pulled up the Wandering Legion strategy analysis. We ran through a few rapid turns. "If it works out, you'd get a significant advantage on War. This could work. I'll prep a few practice boards."

Yolniv began shuffling out of the room. Uncertainty built up in my gut. "Wait!" He stopped. "Is four days long enough?"

He blinked once, then stretched an arm through the door onto my shoulder. "Zouk, in the last year I have watched you face down players with brains as big as a house."

"Only with your coaching."

"I did what I've always done. Nothing special."

I shook my head. "You kept me on track, you were with me before the games, and you were still with me after it was over."

He looked me in the eye. "It has been the most fulfilling time in my life, to support you as you reshaped the nation. My only regret is that they wouldn't let me stand up there with you. You trust me, yes?"

I smiled. "Of course."

"Then trust me when I say that for you—four days is three too many. Let's get to work."

29 - 1-1

RANK: 2 ▲ 2

Rain dumped onto the field during that last game. My troops used the time between turns to rub at their arms and breathe into their hands, anything to fight the cold. War's cube sat on the other side of the field, flanked by the secretary general. I had spotted her human form out on the eighth row near one of the exits.

Influence stood about a dozen feet from me, proudly looking over the field. His presence gave a lot of weight to the game, a guarantee that if I won, the Minds would count it.

It had all gone according to plan. The Wandering Legion glided from side to side across the board, waiting for the moment Jamie had found. When it came, my troops marched as one, all while War's soldiers were repositioning. The advantage was mine.

Jamie's loss never left my head. Hesitation meant giving War a chance to come back. My troops pressed in, collapsing walls and eliminating foes. Over two-thirds of the board was mine. I didn't bother looking at the clock, time wouldn't be a factor today.

Every move felt effortless. War's base was being picked apart in front of the entire stadium. The crowd was silent, either that or I couldn't hear their cheers through the waves of rain pouring in. I regularly checked my flanks, ever aware of the risk of being surrounded.

At move fifty-seven, my soldiers took control of three-quarters of the board. War had cocooned herself in her base. There were only a few, heavily defended squares from victory.

I raised my screen to input the round of attacks, but a hand stopped me. Influence slid a soggy paper in front of my screen. I read its contents twice before I could believe it. The screen slipped from my hands and over the platform's edge. The digital clock above the field had stopped its countdown and the secretary general was preparing an announcement. War had resigned.

EPILOGUE

I picked a few strands of carpet from my shoes, there was nothing much else to do. The odor of fresh paint hung thick in the air. No big deal, the whole place had just been refurbished. From what I heard, everything in the capitol building was being refurbished. There was an ancient analogue clock on the wall, I tried to figure out how it worked but it was hopeless. I checked my screen, fifteen minutes. I shot Kira a call.

She appeared in front of one of the labs in Facility Five. "Is it already over?" she asked.

"We haven't started yet. How are things for you?"

"The whole team won't stop talking about the fulfillment metric."

"Good things?"

Kira glanced back before answering. "They're cursing your name for the six months of audits we'll have to do if it's enacted. But I'm excited." A brief smile crossed Kira's face. "Did you see the article I sent you?"

I pulled it up on my screen, *2-1, Man Defeats Machine*. Kira had sent me about a hundred articles, after the first three I stuck to reading the headlines.

"You made the international news."

Footsteps echoed down the long hall, someone was coming. "I couldn't have done it without you. Sorry, but I gotta go, love you!"

"Love you too, good luck!"

The call ended and I turned to see who was joining me. I waved at the two approaching figures. On the left, Influence wore a beige suit and strode forward with confidence. On the right was someone I had never seen. Their walk was gangly and awkward. They had a dark complexion, wore flowing white robes, and their polished head glistened in the sunlight streaming through the curtains.

When they reached me, Influence shook my hand and gestured to his right. "Zouk, I know you've met before, but allow me to introduce you to The Mind of Manufacturing and Distribution."

"Maker! Good to see you. I didn't know you had a body" I grabbed Maker's hand and shook it, it was like a dead fish in my palm.

Maker showed their teeth in an almost-smile. "Not until yesterday. My dear friend, Influence, told me I should make one."

"You look good."

They bowed deeply. "Good! Good. I wasn't sure how it would turn out. I built Influence and War's bodies off their personalities and voices. But with me, I don't know, I just couldn't find the 'me' that fit."

"It's about time. Let's head in," Influence interjected.

We agreed, and Influence pulled open one of the colossal doors, waving us inside.

A large, round table sat underneath a large glass ceiling. War was already waiting in her seat. We each sat down, and War began to speak. "This council will come to order, we extend a—"

Her voice boomed from every corner of the room. I covered my ears. Influence yelled something, but couldn't match her volume. Maker waved at her to stop, and the room fell silent.

Influence pulled at an earlobe. "It might be a bit more appropriate to speak through your body today. Don't you think?"

War rolled her eyes, concentrated, then spoke again. "Better?"

Her voice was hers again. I dropped my hands from my ears.

"This council will come to order. We extend a warm welcome to our newest council member, Zouk Solinsen."

"Congratulations!" Influence voiced. Maker gave a thumbs up.

"Our first order of business. We have completed the alpha test of Mr. Solinsen's proposal, Directive P-103389. Normally, we would each review the findings on our own, but"—War cast a withering look towards Influence—"for the benefit of our newest member, we can review it together. Maker, would you mind presenting?"

Maker nodded. "In the western half of Guev, our test area, we have seen elevated happiness statistics, a significant increase in the proposed 'Fulfillment' metric, and a marginal drop to Productivity. Oddly, there have also been reports of spontaneous labor in the areas nearest the community centers."

I blinked a few times. "Volunteers?"

Maker's eyes went wide. "Yes! We have seen a rise in volunteer labor. Should this trend continue, I would recommend we scale up the study group, and consider a re-introduction of Directive 82792."

Influence turned his head. "You want to bring back the flowers?"

Maker hesitated, "Only where the volunteers are. If they are willing to take care of them, we can keep the maintenance down. What do you think, War?"

War shifted her jaw from side to side. "Maybe. Start with the yellow ones. We still have six items on the docket today—"

Influence tapped the table. "War, perhaps for today, we could table the rest of the items. Our newest member hasn't had a chance to go over them."

Everyone's eyes turned to me. I gave a faint smile.

"All in favor?" I raised my hand with Influence and Maker. "Fine. We table the rest until next time. That concludes our business for the day."

War stood immediately and headed for the exit.

"And War!" She stopped in her tracks. Influence continued, "Just this once, could we walk out together? Might make for one heck of a photo."

War gave a curt nod. I stood and moved to join Influence and War at the door. Maker lined up to my left. I glanced at each of them in turn, then pushed it open.